Praise for Robert

City for Ransom

"Walker's masterful prose cuts like a garrote, transporting us with panache and style into an historical thriller with teeth. Ransom's the best new hero in period fiction. Action on page one holds till the shocking finale. Enough twists and scares for a dozen books." –J.A. Konrath, author *Whiskey Sour & Bloody Mary*.

"Walker's taken on Caleb Carr's territory, upgrading it to a dark dirge of demonic grace with a superb haunted protagonist with a graveyard on his back...alongside the most eccentric character to shadow the halls of noir in a long time. It's the best pairing of two damaged souls since Lucifer chose an ally...while nailing Chicago to the depths of its odd, maimed glory. Ransom your soul for this one; it's that mesmerizing." –Ken Bruen, Macavity Award Winner for *The Killing of the Tinkers*

"Gut-wrenchingly suspenseful, luridly atmospheric, and utterly plausible, Walker's creation is a brilliant mix of Conan Doyle, Erik Larson, and Wes Craven. You'll be shocked, stunned, beaten to hell, and riveted to the peerless quality of this page-turner." –Jay Boninsinga, author of *Frozen & The Sinking of the Eastland*

"City is crime noir at its finest." –David Ellis, Edgar Award Winner, author *In the Company of Liars*

"Chicago World's Fair pageantry juxtaposed by outrageously colorful characters... evoking the city's mystical past as neither gala nor carefree. Inspector Alastair Ransom's Chicago is brutal and violent, cloaking mysteries and intrigues in a facade of propriety as spectral and illusory as the grand and gleaming buildings of the vanished "White City." –Richard Lindberg, author *Chicago by Gastlight: a History of Chicago's Netherworld, 1880-1920*."

Other Books by Robert W. Walker

Alistair Ransom
City Series

City of the Absent (*2008*)
Shadows in the White City (*2007*)
City for Ransom

Jessica Coran
Instinct Series

Absolute Instinct
Grave Instinct
Unnatural Instinct
Bitter Instinct
Blind Instinct
Extreme Instinct
Darkest Instinct
Pure Instinct
Primal Instinct
Fatal Instinct
Killer Instinct

Lucas Stonecoat
Edge Series

Final Edge
Cold Edge
Double Edge
Cutting Edge

Sequel -
Deja Blue

For Pat + 5 12 07

PSI

Psychic Sensory Investigation

Blue

Happy Mother's Day !

By

Robert W. Walker

I hope you Love my Book

Robert W. Walker

Echelon Press

Publishing

PSI: Blue

A Psychic Sensory Investigation Thriller

Book One

An Echelon Press Book

First Echelon Press paperback printing / December 2006

Art Design © Stephen Walker

Titling Design © Nathalie Moore

2004 Ariana "Best in Category" Award winner

Echelon Press

9735 Country Meadows Lane 1-D

Laurel, MD 20723

www.echelonpress.com

ISBN 978-1-59080-508-4

1-59080-508-9

Library of Congress Control Number: 2006931527

PRINTED IN THE UNITED STATES OF AMERICA

10 9 8 7 6 5 4 3 2 1

Affectionately dedicated to
Miranda Phillips Walker
whose support and love are prized above all.

Acknowledgements:

The author would like to thank son Stephen R. Walker for the beautiful and detailed cover art and for suggesting the idea for the street children and their street religion. The author also wishes to thank Lyn Polkabla for her insights and helpful suggestions on the novel's paranormal aspects in particular. Finally, great thanks to publisher and editor Karen Syed of Echelon for her incisive cuts, good nature, and wit. No editors were harmed in the writing of this book.

Prologue

"You be good," said Carnivore Man as he slapped on the last of the paint, covering Toby's hair and head and the last unpainted portion of his face–even as the squealing old merry-go-round took Toby off again for another revolution.

"You be good, boy, and maybe I'll let you live," Carnivore man said just before Toby spit in his eye.

Toby Slayter, on his thirteenth birthday, had awakened to a kaleidoscope of color and the sound of Calliope music filling his mind; so loud in fact, it seemed to smother him, and yet no one came rushing to his rescue in this strange back-of-the-yards area of the carnival. No one wanted to challenge Satan.

The villainous man, in paint-streaked, rainbow-colored red pants and shirt, dribbled orange, yellow, green, and blue from his palette, but mostly he slapped the child with a paintbrush dripping with blood-orange Kilz; Sears' cheapest oil-base bulk buy–an exterior deck coating. He was nearly finished with his masterpiece. Just had to do the close-in work of the recesses about the nostrils, the coil of the ears, and the eyelids. Usually the hardest part to deal with. Kids fought like hell during the finishing touches, but soon after, the skin, unable to breathe, they'd quit flailing.

Toby would join two other 'works of human art' in the spook house. One, an eye-popping chartreuse, the other a neon moon-glow yellow, so a blood-orange kid would set the others off perfectly. Some of Satan's victims didn't get that honor or ease of passing; others–for no reason the handyman-turned-murderer could fathom–somehow invited a weeklong torture session. It was satanic of him, he knew, but it was the only way he could feel anything; only through the pain and suffering of a child, could he arrive at any sort of heightened sexual gratification. He understood the needs of the infamous child killers labeled as sociopaths, like the Red Demon of Russia in the film *Citizen X*. Some would call him a monster. Some scientific types, like those who trained under Dr. Mitchell Graham and FBI agents who understood the inner workings of DNA imprinting, or just plain old ancestral wiring in the brain, might call him a throwback to the early European Kurgans, blood-thirsty savages, survivors of the last of the ice age glaciers. Kurgans today can be found on every street corner. Such men would likely gawk and drivel and spit tobacco wads at his art, while the scientists might call his artwork the expression of the long-dormant, recessive genes of pagan ancestors. Might even call his art an expression of primal urges.

He consoled himself that all art must first pleasure the artist, perhaps more in the *doing* than in the final product, and he was an artist after all, in love with process. However macabre the content. The children on the street and those who found their way to the carnival, and especially those who found their way to his side of the curtain, just called him Satan. They knew intuitively in their little hearts and minds and spleens that Satan always assumes, on this plane, a pleasing human form. "The Devil made me do it," has everything to do with the supernatural taking on a natural shape. In this case, that of a humble man doing a simple, necessary job that brought a smile to the lips of a child.

It's been proven by authorities and demonstrated on Oprah's TV show that children don't heed warnings, and whose fault was that?

Certainly not his, and not even Satan's. Kids gotta learn; in a sense, he dispensed a public service here. His victims brought it on themselves. All he did was put out the lure. If these damned kids weren't evolved enough to avoid his simple lures, what kind of future did they have in the first place? And if not painted and put on display here, what else lay ahead for them? They invited him across a certain threshold when they accepted him, when they eased back on their natural instincts and their God-given gift of fear, getting comfy around him. He then took complete and swift advantage like a long-tongued frog that strikes a fly at an impossible distance. Not the frog's fault, frog is just following its frog nature.

Quantico, Virginia northeast woods

Children at play in the shadow of a wrecking ball that beats a rhythm with jackhammer screams, all amid squalor and trash and discarded bottles, broken pyramids of brick in dusky red and gray yards like a red bone factory. It's a dream. Just a recurring dream, part of Aurelia's brain tells her, but the other part sees the images. Discards mixed with dull brown adobe crumbling to dirt...all visited by and bathed in a blinding blue light that transforms the brickyard of destroyed buildings into a lush green-carpeted park filled with stylized, rigid trees in a land where no wind blows, where even the leaves resist change, and sadly, no birds flirt among the unbending branches.

Within this eerie stillness, a verdant Gauguin-like green hue is cast overall, replacing all that is dirty red brick and dull with a warm, glowing still life. In this painting, children are now angels in stiff-winged pose, lifting up on tiptoe to embrace one another, some floating in the thralls of their embrace like Chagall lovers. However, the overall effect lacks beauty and flowing life, as the angels, like the trees, rigidly pose like cutouts placed against a canvas not wanting them, or painted with hesitation, perhaps trepidation. Fear of a wrong rendering? A separate backdrop overall in this oil on canvass world comes now again–a pair of curious childlike eyes framed in a rectangle opening in the sky, looking on in curious wonder.

Eyes looking on. The eyes of God? Those of an angel, a cherub? No, Aurelia recognizes the questioning orbs as her own, at perhaps age five or six. Yes, they are her innocent eyes. She is like the artist Dali, who painted himself into his own canvass, depicting himself as a child dressed in a sailor suit, holding a balloon and observing the strange life created from his own mind, curiously wondering at its existence, purpose, and meaning–and wondering if perhaps it came via some supernatural filter or challenge or channel.

Like Dali, Aurelia often felt the same way while looking on at her own visions. What did it mean, and why the dark horn-rimmed edges of a frame around her eyes, like seeing herself in a rearview mirror? Only the bridge of her nose showed with her symmetrical black eyebrows. A penetrating, searching black Asian eye on the left, and a cerulean blue eye on the right. One eye stamped her Japanese, the other indelibly her mother's Irish child.

It was as if she looked in from out of a box, some kind of trap. Caged perhaps. Only able to see from a tiny barred window in the corner of the universe the size of a wheelbarrow...relegated to the point of view of a single restraining portion of a canvass too vast to contemplate at once.

Painting, art–it was at the heart of this mystery: To all who enter this garden of children beware. Beware its lull, its lure, its peace, as mere illusion within illusion; some powerful message, some thematic counterpart, some echo of whispers, some inherent warning as when Aurelia's mother so often said, "A curse can be wrapped in a compliment."

Some warnings go up like red flags, but the moment was shattered again by the strange mantra of metallic noise: *Ba-Kerrrack! Ba-kerrrack! Ba-kerrrack!*

The new environment is a dream within a dream, from some far away place on a distant dimension; Aurelia's Irish Wiccan mother might decipher it in her unique way, her Buddhist father quite another. She could hear her mother's reassuring voice now: *Dear one, it's just a dream. Dreams can't hurt you.*

How wrong could a mother be?

Aurelia's deceased mother kindly lied. *You can put your mind at ease; find pleasing sleep, if you put effort into it.*

"But Mother, shouldn't pleasing sleep come effortlessly?" she'd asked at age four.

"The darkness within that tells you to embrace your fears can make you strong in a dangerous world," had been her mother's reply.

Now this 'harmless' adult dream had come repeatedly, had evolved as a series of screenings now for over a month. The children had not at first had angel wings; now they did, and they kissed one another in less rigid manner with each visit. Loosening up. They held hands and hugged and chased butterflies and sparrows streaming now through the greenery, when in the early versions there were no birds. Now even, the stylized trees and leaves had begun to show signs of life, taking on the sheen of full-blown chlorophyll-filled life.

And there was the oddly angelic blue light bathing the scene.

The angel children played lovely music. They splashed in the fountain, giving vent to gaiety and mirth, when suddenly a sinister darkness obliterated the blues and greens, until an inky blackness covered all. Then a red glow filled the sky like an angry single Cyclops' eye, blotting out even her window on the scene for a flashing, blinding, explosive second.

The devastated landscape returned with added horror, bodies now buried in the rubble that had been the brickyard.

Then the brickyard became fluid, the red bricks dissolving into clay, then mud, and next morphing into a red ocean. In this flaming ocean lay, naked and helpless, the angels joined by humans, male, female, child and adult alike. Now in a writhing river of one another's bodies, the features and limbs of the child angels all coalesced, as if mixing colors in a jar–bodies spiraling fluidly–blood dropped into water.

They all hung below the surface of the red ocean current that had engulfed and obliterated the greenery and the blue light. They lay caught in a tangle of coral wreath that cut and bled them. Like a dancer with graceful moves, straddling the children as a giant, a Lucifer creature with a dragon's tale like an external backbone thrashed as he stood dominating the helpless, writhing masses below him.

Nothing of kindness or caring, nothing but horror and mutilation filled the mind of the Hellion as he stabbed children with his scorpion's tail, paralyzing each with its stinger. Then the red demon in the red sea devoured each helplessly paralyzed blood-orange-red child with a glee beyond joy. Repeatedly, the small angelic life of each prisoner in this strange coral nest disappeared into the demon as if swallowed whole.

Aurelia Murphy Hiyakawa awoke in her night slip, nestled in her bed, her wide Oriental eye jade black, her Celtic eye blue in the darkness–both searching the room even as her brain searched the horrible dream for useful clues, images, symbols that might make sense. But nothing of the sort readily leapt to fill in the blanks of what this extraordinarily powerful vision might portend.

"Does it ever?" she audibly reminded herself.

She realized now that shivers shot through her. The images had been so cartoonish–surreal; yet real beyond mere dream to what Jung called the Big Dream–the life-altering dream. On the order of the one that'd sent her to a divorce lawyer to alter her real life accordingly, else live in a perpetual state of suffocation.

Aurelia's best friend, Etta, scoffed once, "Aurelia Murphy Hiyakawa, you are the only person I know who ever divorced a man on the say-so of a little bad dream."

"It was no *little* dream; it was a *big-assed* nightmare! A whopping compensatory one at that, and Carl Jung would've run screaming from that marriage long before I did."

Now *this* dream. So real. So much so that she prophetically guessed it related to one of her cases at FBI headquarters, but which one and how? So large, this dream, that her thin frame had shaken and perspired from the heat of Satan's coral reef! A fiery bubbling cauldron amid a reef that burned with far-reaching fingers below the unnatural waters of Satan's domain until you looked closer and realized the bloody reef was made up of bloody bodies.

"Silly," she told herself and the silent room. "I don't even believe in freakin' Satan or a place called Hell." Aside from learning self-protection in the form of Jujitsu from her Buddhist father, Aurelia had learned that Hell was the negative life some people chose.

Her kindly father had told her once that in a sense, planet Earth was the asylum for the universe and that's why mankind was placed here. That the human race was a child, and in need of much therapy. And that heaven and hell existed only in the mind. "We control the controls in perception. Perceiving the world and ourselves positively is up to us." He would smile and add, "One day science will catch up to mysticism and prove it right."

In any event, Hell was not a physical location where demons and devils and agents of Satan sat about contemplating attacks on mankind. Much as the egocentric child called mankind wanted to believe–but such symbolism floated about in the minds and genetic wiring of countless generations of Christians and other religious followers. So the symbolism and the sum of all such fears could certainly be counted on to have meaningful resonance.

But what were these recurrent images and sounds and that stifling, choking air filled with odors of earth and vermin and metal and decay and sweetness like the mix of flowers left too long at a gravesite mingling with oils and canvass and blood?

Why did such things assail her now with these odd night sweats? Something wicked just over her horizon–coming at her with such force as to have sound and odor? And from what mysterious source?

Who had repeatedly sent these signals that held her telepathic mind in such rapt embrace? No answer came.

Who seemed bent on her receiving such horrid snapshots from the ether of an astral plane as busy and as populated with thoughts as conscious life populated with the babble of tongues? No ready reply.

Who created the PSI world that set sub-atomic nano-images adrift on a psychic wind, which bombarded every sentient creature on the planet? A wind invisible to, and ignored by, all save a few? Still no answer.

Who were the angels...the children? What time frame was it? Past, present, future? Where might the greenest ever park bathed in bluest ever sky be? Was it a real place or a figurative one? A billboard sign on I-95 or a rural Georgia road, or along a road that was the actual metaphor? What did these colors signify beyond hope and courage and honor and honesty? And what of the giant watery Satan and his coral hell so filled with vibrant, living fires of every shade of red? Was it an event long over or one approaching? Or was it ongoing...in the now?

She stared across at her image in the mirror. She saw a beautiful woman with a mix of Asian and Caucasian features in a blue chemise nightgown alone in bed, seemingly destined to be alone for the rest of her life.

"Perhaps the horror of the bad recurrent dream is beginning to take its toll," she told her image and brushed back her long-flowing black hair with both hands.

The dream had begun soon after the divorce. Perhaps it was as Lyn Polkabla, her shrink, said: "It merely reflects your inner turmoil, Aurelia–the angel in you being overwhelmed by Tomi Yoshikani's venomous and self-centered need to punish you."

"Punish me? For what? He's the one that broke our marriage vows, and became abusive!"

"All the more reason for him to hate you for divorcing him. The arrogant Japanese-American mogul some call the Japanese Donald Trump? And you sue him for divorce and child support? Get real."

Aurelia knew she'd never see a dime of child support or alimony from the cheating bastard and consummate liar. He had an army of lawyers arrayed against her.

Sure, the dream was compensatory, reflecting her current life and its overwhelming problems. An idyllic comfortable lifestyle gone, replaced by an uncertain future.

This satanic takeover of the green garden–certainly it could all pertain to the war going on within her deepest psyche, the war that had sent the demon in her life, Tomi, on the path to destroy her. The very person he once proclaimed his one true, undying love–along with Nia, their daughter.

She desperately tried to piece the dream and the reality together, starting with the question of how Tomi had first become estranged, then verbally abusive, and mentally cruel to only graduate to open physical abuse that began with breaking and throwing things, and evolved into wanting to break or throw her. Painfully, she had not seen it coming. And she had not predicted his having gotten involved with other women. Yet she called herself a clairvoyant, a seer, a medium.

Her marriage ended one night in a spat of fighting and with her sending Tomi packing at the point of her Smith and Wesson FBI .38 special.

Sure, the children with angel wings must represent her and her daughter Nia. Like the angels, Nia's brightly painted world had become utterly desolate and grim, thanks to a faceless, nameless force that had taken up residence in her father. Tomi, who'd once been a loving, caring, tender man.

Yes, this made sense now. Her dream was exactly what Dr. Polkabla said: "A dream that compensates for what's going on in your waking life, Rae. Your unconscious attempting to deal with your conscious decisions and choices—good, bad and misguided."

One of the children dying alongside her and the other children in the dream park kept pointing an accusing finger. Nia, she imagined. Her once loving daughter, so filled with an unconditional love before now...now blamed Aurelia for the loss of her father. The poor child had witnessed the ugly final fight, and she'd seen the gun her mother had wielded at dear old Dad.

Aurelia accepted what her mind told her about the images now in relentless pursuit of her. "It has to be what Dr. Polkabla says," she whispered to her image just to hear herself again.

Then she heard a noise in the house that had its share of things that went bump in the night. But this...this was something new. She'd bought the old place in a rash moment of "smart" investing with the nod of her financial advisor as a write off and a future for Nia—under the mistaken belief that payments would coincide with alimony installments. It was to've become a cash cow for Nia when she was old enough to take it over. At the back of the plan, also, lie the fear. A recurrent fear that one day Nia would be left alone, that Aurelia would die in the line of duty.

"In my line of work," she'd told Nia on more than one occasion, "anything can happen."

But the old bed and breakfast, her 'cash cow' had already become the ugly 'heffer'–a complete money pit! It was an exceptional day when the old place didn't demand attention and repair or announce another problem in the form of a groan or a squeal.

Rae slid from beneath the sheets and out of bed, and silently found her bedside weapon of choice, a heavy Glock 9 millimeter.

She inched toward the door, down the corridor, looking in on a sleeping Nia for a moment. Knowing there were no guests in the old bed and breakfast house until tomorrow, knowing too that her live-in maid Enriquiana had the weekend off to visit her mother in Costa Rica, Aurelia feared the worst. Intruder? Tomi? She wondered which she preferred.

She held the huge firearm ahead of her, prepared to fire, capable of it, trained to it. Again, more noise. The source, the kitchen. Someone coming through the sliding glass doors in there.

She tentatively reached out for the light switch, an image of the satanic beast of her dreams coming through her back door, and she hesitated turning the light on. What if she were confronted with the very demon of her nightmare–Tomi Yoshikani doing some sort of O.J. number, coming at her like a Ninja in the night?

At the instant she turned on the light, a toaster fell to the floor with a rattle, and she shouted, "Freeze or I shoot!"

The dark shadow screamed in the same instant, "Geez, Ma! Don't shoot! It's me, Nia!"

Aurelia stared at her fully clothed daughter sneaking back into the house from a night of partying with God knows who and God knows where. Meanwhile, Nia shook, obviously terrified that in the next nanosecond a bullet would rip through her insides like they'd seen so many times on TV and in the movies.

"I can't believe you were going to kill me!"

Aurelia looked at the gun in her hand and put it on the kitchen island beside the knives, pots, and pans. "Damn it, Nia, I might've killed you! Are you crazy? I went by your room. Who's in your bed?"

"Pillows McGee."

A stuffed toy the size of a Bengal tiger beneath the sheets.

"Geez Zeus! Where in the name of heaven've you been? And how long've you been sneaking out this way?"

"I wouldn't have to sneak out if you'd just let me be." Nia, still shaken, pushed past her mother, going for her room.

"Stop," Aurelia ordered.

"I just wanna go to bed. Can't we discuss this tomorrow?"

"After one thing."

"What?"

Aurelia stepped up to her daughter and threw her arms around her, tears freely flowing now from both. The long, heartfelt, quaking continued along with more tears welling-up. Mother and child hug lasted an entire minute. It'd been a long time since they'd been so intimate, and it felt good. Too bad it had taken a just-averted tragedy to come to this embrace.

"Sorrry…I'm so sorry," Aurelia repeatedly said.

Nia took up the mantra. "Me, too. Sorry… sorry…sorry."

"I thought you were a burglar."

"And you've got to stop going for that damn gun every time you hear a board groan in this old house."

Once more, they found refuge in the word sorry, which erupted repeatedly from each, filled as it were with meaning far greater than this incident.

Tearfully, Aurelia said, "Nia…what's become of us?"

"Whataya mean, Ma?"

"This sneaking in and out like a stranger. The lying."

"Lying? I never–"

"Nia, a stuffed toy beneath the sheets as your decoy? Come on…. I might well have killed you!"

"Maaaaaa, it's all right! Nobody was killed. You're a trained marksman."

"All right? It's hardly all right! I could've killed you," Rae repeated.

"Sit down, Mom. You want something for your nerves?"

"Nerves? I ought to have my head examined. Should've sent you to that camp we talked about!"

"I'm screwed up enough, Ma. I don't need Shrink Camp! It'd only make things worse, and you can tell your shrink Polky or whatever her name is the same!"

Aurelia gritted her teeth and found a seat. Her knees did feel weak. "All right, I want to know exactly where you've been and with whom?"

"I was just out with Trudy and some friends is all."

"How long've you been sneaking out this way?"

"I wouldn't have to sneak out if you'd treat me like an adult!"

"Do you call this adult behavior?" Rae fired back.

Nia pulled away and rushed for her room, Aurelia in pursuit, but Nia was quicker on the stair, and she slammed and locked her door before her mother could put a foot in it. A person's room was sacrosanct in this household, a place of refuge, and a closed door stood...respected...as hard as that was at such a time.

She stared at the door as if her eyes might penetrate it, and she imagined Nia inside softly crying, leaning against the door. They had grown so far apart, and for that brief moment in the kitchen when they held onto one another, it was like Nia had reverted to a good place, as when younger and accepting of her own vulnerability and needs. Now this.

"She slams a door in her mother's face, going back to the offense-defense strategy taken for almost a year now. Damn it," Rae said. Her words and her groan could be heard through the door, but she got nothing in return from the other side. But from the other-other side–Aurelia's Gaelic mother's voice wafted through her mind as if her ghost meant to continue helping raise Nia, but Mother's advice proved useless: "She needs a good talking to from your father. Ten minutes with him'll set anyone straight."

"You think so, Mother? Too bad he's no longer with us any more than you are."

"Hey," replied the ghostly voice from within, "life has a way of working out...and remember 'When one door closes, another one–"

"Opens, I know...cute, Mother. We did put it on your tombstone like you asked."

"Who are you talking to?" It was Nia, curious. She'd pulled the door open as Rae started back toward the kitchen to retrieve her forgotten Glock and go back to bed.

"Ahhh just to myself, Nia. Just talking to myself."

"You're so strange, Mother. No way I can ever have a normal mom is there?" Nia slammed the door closed again.

Rae dropped her head. "No, sweetheart," she shouted at the door. "The Greenbrier High PTA refused my application! Sorry!"

Phoenix, Arizona same time

The child, helpless, tied, felt life slipping away, yet he furiously fought his bonds on the merry-go-round. Still without result, and now Toby felt dizzy from being tied to the merry-go-round with the wooden seahorses, tortoises, dolphins, and other water animals. And he'd tired of hearing the demon ask, "Are you havin' fun yet?" and then slapping on more paint. Each time he went whirring by on the machine, the madman just cackled like a delighted old hag.

In a single turn of mind, the demon had taught him to hate the once loved joyous sounds of the carnival, as this particular 'fun-land' had become wicked, creating a poisonous disgust that spread like jet black ink over the boy's mind–a murderous hatred for his jailer.

This spreading poison of anger, horror, and hatred seared his young brain as if it lay on a hot Arizona pavement. The dizzying mix of music, movement, and terror, of bondage–the cold hard reality of handcuffs–along with the stench of paint filled his nostrils and mind. The monster slapped his face so many times now with the fluorescent oil paint that it'd turned the dark-skinned boy into a glowing creature. Beneath the layers of paint, the trapped boy wondered, when does my hatred become real, alive? A living creature itself that'll swallow my killer and save me? What would it take?

What'd it take in the movies and in video games? Brainpower. The mind over matter. Maybe his hatred could bring on a stroke in his killer. A heart attack. Why not? Something big enough and strong enough and powerful enough to kill this madman–a Spiderman or a Superman.

Toby Slayter felt angry at himself, too; he'd been led here

by the nose, been made a fool, and amid the pretty sights and sounds of a carnival backlot, he'd not realized that his body and soul were being bartered over–that he'd stood idle while being traded off like a slave to the madman.

Instead, Toby'd been standing before a huge mural on one wall, staring, fixed on the strange details. Children in a park.

Toby'd soon discovered that the mural ran along all the walls of the circular room, at the center of which stood the old merry-go-round. Somehow the massive mural had grown as if organically from a peaceful and lovely depiction of angels in a park holding onto one another and kissing to Satan's arrival. This scene stood at the center on two sides. But the carnival man–who called himself Carnivore Man–now busily and obsessively created a deplorable, grim red and orange hellish world in which Satan straddled all of the lost souls of Hades– lost souls who lay not beneath the usual dark subterranean cauldron normally depicted, but rather bodies in a row below a sea of fire.

All of the art was being painted over scenes portraying turn of the century cityscapes with busy stevedores working to unload packed oceangoing vessels docked at the end of a busy market street, people milling about smoking, shouting, haggling over scales and prices.

Carnivore Man was having trouble getting the sea of fire and foam to rise off the wall, to 'sing' as it were, to look as real as he wanted. At one instant, he pretended to want young Toby's thoughts, and how Toby might improve the depiction of Satan's sea if he were the artist.

"What can we do with it? What should we add...what should we take out? What do you think, Toby?" When all the while, he really didn't give a rat's ass about what Toby thought, and all the same while, Toby suggested a white to gray foam here, a lilac blush there, but it'd all been a charade down to the maniac's sly use of the pronoun we.

Sometime earlier, during the course of the evening, he'd been drugged and staked here–tied to a hard, cold brass post that spiked through the backside and out the stomach of a carved walrus. A surreal sort of crucifixion for the unfeeling walrus, but an even unhappier circumstance for Toby. As the boy found himself restrained here on the outer edge of insanity and the wood platform, his ankles dangling over the side, his shoes and clothes replaced with thick oil-based paint, Toby knew he'd been consigned to Carnivore Man's Hell. He'd been placed on the outer ring of 'the ocean' with no sign of the saving grace of the Blue Lady except as he saw her go by amid the painted figures on a myriad of murals in this place–murals presumably painted by his conqueror. But Toby knew that the murals stood still, that it was he and the damn walrus that were moving.

Toby knew immediately and instinctively how vulnerable he was, and that he lay sprawled naked, his body almost entirely lathered in the lurid red-orange paint. The paint odor, thick and pinching, choked off his breathing with an overwhelming metallic odor.

"Just a bit more...just a bit more," chanted the brush-wielding madman.

Only little dabs of Toby's head, hair, and face remained to be painted now as his restrained body moved with the dizzying merry-go-round.

FBI Headquarters, Quantico, VA the following day

Special Agent Aurelia Murphy Hiyakawa sat clothed in a virgin white terry robe, in the lotus position, electrodes attached and grounded to the open-air copper pipe pyramid which she'd designed to enhance her psychic projections and astral journeys. A small sterile white mat lie before her and on the mat lay six items she'd been asked to "read." The objects held a strange communion with her. Rae fingered each item in turn, tossing several out of the pyramid; true to form, she only cast out "control" items the others had provided. Within the confines of her pyramidal world, she must have only 'hot' items–such as a high school graduation photo of the missing Ms. Van Holder, heiress to a fortune who'd caught the eye of her abductor or abductors.

The photo levitated a few inches off the mat with her fingertips hovering just above it. In the photo, a lovely faint blush of red along the girl's throat suggested a pinkish hue of life beneath the skin. Also now—in the photo of the missing woman—life throbbed. The image of the young woman pulsated with life beneath Aurelia's fingertip as the single right hand digit lilted now between this world and another, on the verge of discovery…her mind's eye putting all energy into this moment. Her fingers palpitated now, still not quite touching the image of the girl, yet feeling the emanations from the beating heart of the seventeen-year-old life the image represented.

"She's alive…just barely…faintly…stifled… gasping for breath…but alive…in a pitch black room…confined space that feels like a…a box. Locked away. Air supply dwindling. But she is alive."

Aurelia's voice and a myriad of images flowing into one another came on the plasma screen outside the isolation booth. Her voice boomed, her image filling the screen at one moment, replaced by alternating cryptograms—the secret code language of the brain—symbols it could deal with, ciphers of simile and metaphor of what she saw, felt, intuited, smelled, tasted, and heard. Sometimes the images proved, in retrospect, the very images teleported to Aurelia from a victim's terror. All such important images competed, however, with images from Aurelia's "normal" life—such as a gloomy Nia sulking while hugging her stuffed tiger.

Today the victim's name was Muriel Van Holder, and the images were three parts feelings and imagery straight from Van Holder's five senses, one part confused items out of Aurelia's own expressive mind. Items screaming for her personal attention—all playing out on the screen overhead, a blowup, in a sense, of Aurelia's "third eye." All projected onto the plasma screen via the computer software created by a genius.

Whenever Aurelia viewed the taped psychic images translating her mental sleight-of-hand or 'sight', the technology so impressed her. It represented both the ultimate invasion of privacy–her thoughts–and the ultimate in ciphering the symbolic language of those who psychically project, send, and receive PSI messages. Put together by a boy genius of twelve, whose twin sister had been born a vegetable, the program proved remarkable. The boy's sister had been unable to do the least thing for herself, and remained confined to a crib and a chair all her life. It was indeed an amazing technological feat of agile programming done by young Edwin Arlington Coffin.

Coffin had found a way to communicate with his sister through thought imagery–images and thoughts emanating from her brain waves and translated through young Coffin's program. It'd been the driving force in the young genius's life until the FBI recruited him to utilize his genius in law enforcement. Police science had taken an enormous leap due to Coffin's inventive mind. Ever vigilant, The FBI, getting wind of this remarkable young man, had recruited him at age fourteen to develop his software for the express purpose of criminal warfare and crime detection. Meanwhile, his ill sister had died, sending out her final images to Edwin who interpreted her final request, that they be left alone and their parents leave the room. No one ever knew what Sybil Coffin's final image-talk said to Edwin.

Aurelia had met Edwin two years before, when he'd first begun research and development of his amazing Cerebral Remote Viewing and Language Stratagems or CRVLS as it was called by everyone who saw it 'crawl' inside Aurelia's head.

Young Coffin's controlling parents had been wise enough to turn him into a corporation. After all, their kid was worth more now than Bill Gates, his 'mind-crawler' gaining entry into a number of new medical venues, including image capturing and translation from comatose patients, not to mention as a new toy installed on every computer sold since its development. One fellow had already turned the tool to a criminal use by attempting to read the thoughts of young children for the express purpose of pedophilia.

"Damn, sixteen? Only fucking sixteen?" Etta Page–

Aurelia's best friend–had complained on learning about Coffin's earnings, abilities, and age. "If he were of marrying age, shit Aurelia, you'd have it made."

"He's a great kid who needs a mother and father, not a wife."

"Anyone to replace those robots he calls parents."

"Keepers, he calls 'em, and Etta, God help anyone who marries that screwed up kid."

"Parents–what was it Carl Jung said about parents?" asked Etta.

"Kids are doomed to struggle against the unfulfilled lives of their parents?"

"Yeah, something like that. They push their kids into their own neurosis. Shit, look at me."

"I just wish that Edwin's parents would quit treating him like a market share."

Etta had laughed at this, but Aurelia found nothing funny in it. "God, breaks my heart how he's been brought up, so I might adopt him, but no, I have no plans to marry him."

"Despite his crush and his crush of money?"

"Despite, yes!"

That'd been her last word on the subject to Etta, and it had also been the last time she and Etta had talked before the major falling out between them–which had come as a result of Etta's boyfriend.

Now even as Aurelia worked, her concern for young Edwin must be embarrassing him, because the one thing the boy genius had not figured out was how the 'crawl' could filter out the back-scatter of personal consciousness, private concerns, and the imagery of emotion. And at the moment, part of her brain was going that way as her thought telegraphed the fears she held for young Edwin.

Aurelia's mix of Asian-Irish features–a reddish hew to her black hair, one eye blue, one black–now pinched at the thought of Coffin's parents.

These thoughts found their mental counterparts in hideous caricature-icons of the two holding pitchforks and standing before Fort Knox. Bloated huge on the large plasma screen for all to see; how the parents might be interpreted by those monitoring her at the moment was anyone's guess, but all who worked in this secret FBI facility knew she enjoyed a special relationship with Edwin.

Her feelings for the boy genius had increased along their maternal path over the two years she'd known him. What a sweet son he could've been and should be, and she'd never had a son.

She'd met the genius's parents who had created this machine named for the somewhat obscure poet Edward Arlington Robinson, one of whose poems had become a Beatles song–Richard Corey. A ballad of a wealthy man who commits suicide. At the same time that Aurelia had first met E.A or Eddy as she variously called him, she had shaken hands with his proud parents. She had since learned that Eddy's parents were more proud of themselves than they ever would be of their son, proud for having "spawned" him.

The elder Coffins hovered over the kid as if their lives depended on an invisible cord attaching the three of them–and certainly, financially, this was too true.

"Genius seldom precludes dysfunction," Aurelia reasoned and instantly realized her mind was wandering from the case as it was want to do, and now her brain decided this line would make a great bumper sticker–Genius seldom precludes dysfunction. Then she recalled where she'd first heard it–from her Buddhist father.

She was unaware that a license plate appeared on the screen over the observation area now and on it the words: Genius seldom precludes dysfunction. Keep 'em reading over and over that one, she was thinking at the same instant. Damn but Pappa would be proud; better jot that down and put it up for a day when I need it.

Now, on the wall plasma screen which she could monitor, a ghostly image of her dead father appeared in traditional Japanese attire, at his back her Celtic Wiccan mother in Celtic garb, but the images were quickly replaced as if made of smoke. A reminder her parents had done a number on her without even trying. At least she could laugh about it; at least she had a sense of humor about her parentage, a traditional Japanese Buddhist falling in love with a flame-haired Irish lass who had a Celtic-Wiccan mix for a religion.

She had to maintain a sense of balance and humor; she needed every ounce of wittiness each time she encountered the brilliant young Edwin Arlington Coffin. The boy had once confided that he was upset with his parents for their having named him after some silly poet rather than their secondary choices: Albert Einstein or Galileo, or Copernicus. He further confided that when he came of age, he would officially make the name change himself. He talked a lot about going counter to his parents and their wishes in small ways, but he never faced the big problem, that of their entire relationship.

She would broach the subject with him from time to time, but Eddy would only laugh at her and remind her of her own poorly shored up relationships, and then he'd simply return to the unhappiness with his christening. "Even Newton would be better, or Pascal, or Locke, or...but Copernicus, man! That...that'd've been way cool."

"Have you had this talk with your parents?"

"Countless times, yes."

"I see...and their reaction?"

"They tell me that when I come of age, I may change my name to whatever suits me, but in the meantime, I'll answer to Edwin Arlington, and they do not particularly like it that you call me E.A. or Eddy. Fact, it rankles them that you have paid no heed to their repeated wish that you refrain your motherly impulses."

"Really?" she teased.

"They ask that you refer to me in the manner they intended."

"Ahhh...but in nature and in the science of chaos," she countered, "the unintended response is how nature has got along for eons. Take T-cells in humans for instance. A direct result of–or rather response to–parasites, and you take the discovery of penni–"

"Now you are sounding Asian again."

"Thank you."

"As for the unintended isn't that a definition for your middle name? Murphy? As in Murphy's law?"

"Touché!"

"And it is Edward in front of mommy and daddy… dearest, unless you follow Murphy's Law."

They had laughed at the end of the exchange. They made each other laugh a good deal, a thing E.A. did not do around his parents unless he fired off a zinger at them.

E.A.'s gift of brilliance came at what Aurelia believed a horrible price–the loss of a childhood. It was one thing to lose the innocence of childhood someplace along the winding road to adulthood, but to have had no childhood to begin with? Unbearable, Aurelia thought, like a child in the middle of a war, but this war was a war of wills between parents and son. It was akin to the old saw that 'it is best to have loved and lost than never to have loved at all'. It was best to have had a state of graceful innocence than to have never graced that state. Hmmm…not so good an axiom there. Buddha would not be proud. Pappa would laugh at it. Don't think I will jot that one down. Oh, yes, she finally told herself, best concentrate on the case at hand.

An uncomfortable side effect of CRAWL–an unreasonable feeling that a legion of phantom creepy crawlies had free reign in your head–distracted her even from her own thoughts. Aurelia inadvertently thought now of the alias army of invisible nano-sects invading her brain. This caused unusual Hieronymus Bosch-like, metallic-looking creatures to show up on the plasma screen. She hated it when that happened. And so did Edwin.

Not that I can control such mental monsters, rants, or raves, she reminded herself.

But while resolved to be 'on' for the show, for the gathered dignitaries here to see Edwin demonstrate his "CRAWL" through Aurelia's mind, and to marvel at her gift of sight, her concerns for young Edwin seemed even more persistent and resistant and disobedient this morning than the nano-sects with their tickly hairy nano-legs. The boy's brilliance came at her as a blinding light, and like a gift of sight, this unusual power proved Edwin's most outstanding quality and his downfall, even his curse. But in that sense, she reminded herself, she was in the same boat.

The two of them had a great deal in common–being FBI 'freak opps', although no one said so aloud. Both in his and her own way had proven many times over to be that rarity among FBI family, the truly indispensable. No one on the planet could rightly replace either of them, and it took a certain level of maturity to deal with such notoriety within one's own head, much less within the public arena. As for any semblance of a genuinely private life–one in which they were not on call 24/7– forget about it…impossible.

In fact, each had been assigned secret servicemen until Rae drew a line in the sand, insisting this end, so she might have a life outside the bureau without revolving strangers wandering her peripheral vision. For a time, Edwin reveled in the idea of having his own shadowy bodyguard at every turn, until his man followed him into a men's room where he watched Edwin pee. As Edwin stood at the urinal, a stranger holding up a Canon digital and assuming him to be Leonardo DiCaprio, asked for an autograph and a photo 'with Leonardo'.

That was the end of it for Edwin; it was no longer fun. Posing beside the urinal as Leonardo, struck by the absurd and surreal nature of the situation struck him. He oft repeated the story and loudly spread it around that 'Leonardo' would never again give out an autograph. "I felt so cornered–so used."

"Urinally violated," Rae had jokingly replied.

Aurelia flashed on a shopping incident involving one of her entourage in New York City. A conscientious Macy's department store female 'dick' tried to arrest a secret service officer assigned to Aurelia. Seems her agent had become bored and actually shoplifted a deck of Edgar Cayce Tarot cards. Later, Robert Hershey the agent, said, "They weren't for me.

They were for my wife."

Rae sensed it a lie. She'd moments before been fingering the cards, trying to decide on them as a gift for herself. She knew that Hershey nurtured a crush on her, and seeing her finger the cards, he'd planned on gifting them, stolen, to her!

Low profile indeed!

A running joke at Quantico headquarters claimed Aurelia and Edwin Arlington Coffin were more valuable to national security than President David Montgomery–'Monty' himself! Or the director of the FBI, or the CIA, or the Cabinet for that matter. Still, the two of them felt a right to their personal lives and neither of them had the kind of notoriety or familiar faces that required a constant protection program.

Nude beneath the terry cloth robe at the center of the isolation room, connected by electrodes to Eddy's computer, Aurelia came back to the moment.

No one on the other side of the observation glass had to tell Aurelia Murphy Hiyakawa what was now on their collective minds–and it wasn't her lovely, untouched-for-too-long cleavage. The assembled agents, senators, congresswoman, and president's lackey watched Aurelia literally transfer images from her mind to the plasma screen.

Although nothing new now, the process never failed to amaze the uninitiated. She managed this magic feat by merely handling the photo and other items linked to the victim– beamed directly from Aurelia's brain to a plasma monitor wall outside the glass even as she remained conscious.

In the plasma monitor all of Aurelia's impressions raced dynamo-fashion with the quicksilver speed of her mind. And while free-flowing parade images of a busted shoplifting secret serviceman, and Edwin's urinal encounter, and Aurelia's deceased parents, and her friend Etta Pace's features, and those of her shrink, Lyn Polkabla, and her daughter Nia, and her dog Geoffrey–and more recently a stray black cat Nia had given a home to, Tim O'Shay! So much chaff to be separated out so that experts–a whole room full of experts–would eventually mull over the tapes created from Aurelia's mind to form an uninterrupted film of images pertaining to abduction and possible murder.

Now came a new and most ominous dark image, one that settled over all the brighter mental pictures on the screen. A large eye, perhaps her third eye, hovered over an emerging new shower of images struggling to the forefront. This firmer set of dire images of headstones won out. Each headstone read differently: freezer free Mesopotamia, mastodons have more fun, molasses over moles, mold grows on decaying veins–not vines–veins, blood veins. Images of funeral accoutrements came through, along with a coffin being carried to a hearse, only the coffin was bulged out cartoon-fashion, noises, screams, and kicking emanating from within. The pallbearers came into focus as zombies without faces, all with birdlike beaks and huge wide shoulders; white slate countenances without eyes or nose, and so without any emotion.

The hearse turned into a black box. Onyx and mirrored, reflecting images of children staring all in a row as the procession passed. The black coffin then coalesced into a stiff body, a black silhouette now carried off in the disappearing procession.

Later, the unit investigating the Van Holder disappearance would scrutinize such images. So each frame must be examined closely for clues to be zoomed in on and enhanced. Certainly, Aurelia thought as she saw this fleeting image reflected in the onyx coffin, this would be a key hit–the image of the man who had stolen a life.

Then came a shadowy image of a female form suffocating inside a box. Some of FBI Director Raule Apreostini's guests had already turned away, bored perhaps, watching another image flash by; at her side, Aurelia's monitoring assistant, Gene Kiley, began taking steps to bring Aurelia safely back to this reality when it became apparent that Aurelia herself was suffering the pangs of a physical suffocation in absolute empathy with the victim.

Kiley carefully began removing the electrodes and Gene, a tender soul, spoke warmly into her ear a welcoming whisper, bringing her out of it, bringing her down. Choking, coughing, smelling the nearness of death as damp earth weighing heavily on all sides, Aurelia not only knew where the victim was–in a buried box beneath the earth–but she knew now the terror and fear of being buried alive. So real.

Gene Kiley found her shivering almost imperceptibly but shivering nonetheless. He placed his arms around her and worked to warm her hands. He next placed his large bear paws on each of her cheeks and made her look into his eyes. "Concentrate on me, Rea, right here, my baby greens. Get lost in 'em...fall in love with me, marry me. Whataya say?"

"I say I have issues," she muttered, part of her mind going over one of these issues: "If I am not careful, my weight will skyrocket. Did I say that out loud?"

"You did."

Unable to see what was left of the spectators who'd come to talk about Raule's funding, she felt the eyes boring into her nonetheless. She felt like what her lovely little Nia had as a four-year-old mistakenly called a "raaab lat" with everyone looking on, anxious to see if she would thrive or die as a result of the experiment or latest toxin introduced into her system. But the toxins here took the form of horrid psychic images, and the system she referred to was in fact her mental apparatus–the soul even. Not that she didn't have a rough time of it physically as well. One of the reasons she must work out daily and remain in top physical condition for a girl her size and weight, 5'9 at a hundred and eleven pounds.

Aside from having two distinctly different colored eyes, Aurelia had her father's black hair with her mother's auburn highlights. "Too bad someone so beautiful is so weird," was not an unusual summation she'd catch from fellow agents of both genders.

Aurelia filtered out all the noise and buzz of all so-called 'normal' agents and authorities interested in the current case: the disappearance of the heiress to the Van Holder estate. A small army of them looked on at her shivering form at the center of the safe confines of the pyramid, she did her readings and made her "quadruple triple blue cop sense" turn a white heat into successful "hits"–correct psychic assessments. Each image, if analyzed and seriously turned over, up ended, come at from all angles–below, beside, beneath, around, and through– just might provide one, perhaps two clues so telling they could not be ignored. When this happened, what appeared to some as the miraculous happened...hits happened.

To others, Aurelia's gift or prescience, her preternatural abilities to 'read' the language of symbols, especially images of criminal and cruel behavior, and to interpret these seemingly random clips, appeared a sideshow, a carnival of light and shadow and smoke and mirrors with no substance. To the true non-believers, Rae had no answers, and she had long ago decided she need not answer their skepticism, and that in trying to do so, she only sounded more the charlatan than they have already built up in their minds. As a result, she no longer gave credence to those who questioned her motives or her gift of sight. She thought of the gift as having come from afar. A place with a strange sounding name...a name she herself could not pin down or produce on paper. A place also far away in time, perhaps another entire dimension, visited upon her by some restless spirit that in life could not fulfill a need to save others from harm, but in death felt compelled to do so.

"Ghosts?" asked the congresswoman before Gene could get her past the guests, who Raule had invited to ask questions of her.

"You're telling us that ghosts visit you and interpret the icons and symbols you see in your trance state?" asked the president's man.

"Spirits of good," she countered. "Not your typical, run of the mill, white-shrouded cemetery or haunted house ghosts, but yes, benevolent spirits. And technically speaking, it's not actually a trance only a trancelike state that–"

"Ancestors?"

"You're Asian right?"

"Asians are big on ancestors, right?" came the explosion of questions, none of which applied.

"So are my Irish relatives," she countered. "I'm part Asian, part Irish. Murphy on my mother's side, but I don't believe in elves or fairies if that's what you're getting at."

"What *do* you believe in?"

"My gut...my intuition...my basic and primal instincts."

"They speak to you, your instincts?" asked the congresswoman.

"That and my benevolent spirits."

"But you're the only one who can hear them?"

"They select a conduit. I'm their conduit."

"Do these benevolent spirits have, you know, features?" asked the president's man. "Do you give them names?"

It was a conversation Aurelia often faced, and she expected to soon be put in a sideshow called a Congressional Review. I oughta make a tape, a DVD, she told herself now. Raule desperately wanted to educate all FBI agents to what his mysterious PSI Unit did. What they were capable of, as most of the cases brought to them came far too late to affect a good outcome.

It might well be too late for the Van Holder kid.

Although hardly a secret any longer, the Psychic Sensory Investigation (PSI) Unit of the FBI's Behavioral Sciences Division (BSD) remained the butt of jokes. The majority of law enforcement called PSI the "Spook Files" and referred to Aurelia as Scully, referencing some TV program that Rae knew nothing about. Others came to them in a last ditch effort with a flaming red ball case like the Van Holder deal–one in which the victim proved an 'important' person.

Often the subject of her unusual work for the FBI came up at home with her daughter Nia, in conversation with her hair stylist, Madge, her bookie, Stu, her bartender, Joannie, her best friend Etta, and her shrink, Dr. Lyn Polkabla, or some perfect stranger like a cabbie. Else it was her mirror image. And sometimes ghosts, as with her father and mother.

Sometimes she made up answers just to appease people and put them at ease. If they knew the truth, the whole truth about where her gift came from, she might be put behind a padded cell. She'd never dated or even met a man of interest to her romantically who could take the truth, as it was too bizarre, and Nia simply shut down on her if she tried to confide her deepest secrets.

So now the collective "They" from the normal divisions of the FBI had deemed to allow her in on their case, to sully it with the taint of mysticism and voodoo that only *she do*! They had finally come to her with the case of the missing heiress. She had already made some conclusions about the circumstances of the case, conclusions culled from experience and ceaseless TV, radio, and newsprint accounts. But this morning, she'd wiped her mind clean and had begun like a blank slate, and the revelations proved startling, even to her. Handed an envelope filled with items belonging to the young heiress and the photo of a vibrant, smiling, happy young woman on horseback in the outdoors in one photo, at her graduation in another, at the piano, a radiant glow coming through, a woman obviously at peace and most likely in love.

Love kills...love is murder.

So many headstones in so many cemeteries across the globe could well be chiseled with those words. And so it was with Ms. Van Holder. She was not only the victim of her own love— someone she had trusted, someone she had given her entire heart and soul over to, but she'd also sadly been betrayed by young love, perhaps first love. Now she lay buried under disillusion, regret, and earth. Buried by love. As Shakespeare put it, 'Love doth make fools of us all'.

"She's buried out there somewhere alive. We haven't much time. We've got to locate freshly turned earth somewhere along the path of her day-to-day existence."

One agent from Florida said, "Whoever she was seeing."

"Yes, the grave he created for her will be close to his day to day. Think paths, the patterns of his existence must be found and now, and these patterns will lead you to her."

"Is she...you know, still breathing?" he asked.

"I believe so, yes, but she's in a locked box...quite possibly beneath the earth or in some sort of shaft.

"A boyfriend?" asked the chief investigator on the case.

"A new love...someone who worked with his hands...possibly works with earth and animals. I could smell it."

"Hold on," said the congresswoman. "You get smells as well as images?"

"All five of my senses can be under assault, yes. Look, just read the headstones."

"The headstones hold the answer?" asked the agent.

"Yes, read the damn headstones."

Rae walked through them and out of the isolation chamber, her robe flying open, but she caught the tie and re-did it. She went to the controls and hit replay on the plasma screen and backed it to where she'd projected the series of headstones. She read them aloud, playing with the sound of the words, listening to the sound of the bell they rang.

"Freezer free Mesopotamia, mastodons have more fun, molasses over moles, mold grows on decaying veins..."

"Meaningless mess of mish-mosh," said Senator Raymond Benson, who'd remained ominously silent throughout.

"Not necessarily," cautioned the working agent close to the case, one who knew the Florida map. "There is a place off old Highway 75, old Tamiami Trail. There's a restaurant called Messa...Messa Bohemia. It's not far from a race track."

"What's a race track got to do with it?" asked Senator Benson, an old friend of the Van Holder family.

"Tampa cuisine–Tampa Tex's Race Track," said the Florida agent to his partner, who shot back, "Horses. Horse track. Stables. Barns. She rode horses. Suppose..."

"Suppose she is buried somewhere out at this stable?"

"The girl had her own stables on her father's estate," said Benson.

Rae asked, "Was she seeing anyone who worked out there?"

"If she was, she'd obviously have to keep it a secret," replied one agent.

"Her father hated her dating the hired help," added the other.

"I think we have our focus," replied Rae.

"But just try to get a search warrant in a Florida courtroom on the basis of a vision–FBI agent or no. No offense."

"Then we'll get a federal warrant," countered Director Raule Apreostini in his booming Italian bass.

The CRAWL device did not catch all the images that sped through her mind; it did leave some fleeting images it considered trivial by the wayside. She wondered if CRAWL did or did not consider an affair with her boss trivial.

She stood among the spectators now, a hand up for silence. She studied the images as Crawl re-ran them. "Stop right there," she ordered and the images froze on the young woman, helpless yet able to see her lover from where she lay in the blackness all round her. Rae concentrated on the image and through her psychic empathic connection, laced with a gauzy, hazy distance, she saw the silhouette of the man who placed the Van Holder girl here.

She rattled off his possible height and weight.

"Do you mean to say you see him?" asked the slack-jawed congresswoman.

"Yes, I am looking at him. Nice features maybe to go along with his size and build maybe, but all I see is in shadow. Smugness or assurance in his handsome swagger."

"How can you see that if you can't see his features?" asked Benson.

"I don't exactly see it; it is how he moves. How he makes me feel about him."

"If you can tell us anything at all about him, please go ahead," said the FBI lead agent out of Tampa.

"He looks tall, rugged, a real cowboy and a player, but way out of his depth here."

"Meaning?" pursued her chief, Raule.

"Meaning...he empathizes with his victim, which means he is no sociopath but rather has a heart. So there may well be an accomplice, someone doing his thinking for him."

"Really?" asked Benson, rubbing his bristled chin.

"But I definitely feel this fellow knows something about her disappearance. Met with her, fooled her into thinking he loved her, and she's inside a cold dark box, while he's sweating being caught. His usual calm gone."

"Sounds like Blevins, the one we grilled out at the family stables."

"We'll need to dig there, too."

"If you rattle his cage one more time," said Rae, "you may not need a warrant. He'll confess."

"I have an FBI Beech Craft standing by, gentlemen," said Raule. "I suggest you use it, now!"

"What about the mastodons?" Gene Kiley asked in Aurelia's ear. "Rea?"

"Mastodons were the shaggy ancestors of elephants, cave men hunted them, lived off them for generations," she attempted a light joke. "I don't know from mastodons. How do I know?"

Gene was immediately sorry he'd pointed this out because now Benson asked, "And what about molasses over mold, and…and moldy veins?"

Rae began making it up: "Molasses is sweet and clingy, just like the girl, and she's soon going to be mold down to her veins."

She really had no idea what the connection might be.

"Hold on," said one of the agents on the case. "There's a film theater for kids at that race track–to keep rug rats busy–"

"And right now, they're playing that Disney movie, Mastodons," said the second agent from Florida. "I know…I got kids and a habit."

"How do you do it, Rae?" Gene asked, his thick wide features smiling.

"If I told you, I'd have to kill you."

"I thought you trusted me?"

"I do, Gene, but what I know frightens friends and relatives. Not sure I want to weird you out so far that it'd jeopardize our friendship."

"Nuttin'd ever do that, Rea."

"You don't know that."

She felt a wave of exhilaration filling her every cell and pore, and Gene, a quite empathic and sensitive person himself, saw this energy waft over her like ocean surf. "I feel like I could run a marathon," she confided in Gene.

"I can see that, but don't tell the director or he'll have you on cases all night. Glaze over in a show of weakness, and let me get you out of here."

"That is what they expect, isn't it? You're my savior."

"All part of the show."

Gene knew that a psychic exploration left her filled with an intense emotion, a sense of power, and a need for activity. While most people believed the use of psychic energy draining, it was in fact just the opposite, leaving her energized.

Gene ushered her off to the recovery room, a quiet, peaceful place filled with the strings of classical music, soft light, aromatic candles, knowing this to help quell her inner tornado. Rather than lay down, she paced the floor here, not listening to him as he advised she relax. She simply shooed him off, but Gene went reluctantly, like a friend who did not wish to leave the keys with an inebriated woman. Finally convinced she was okay, he left her in peace.

Alone at last, she felt the true pangs of ugly hatred, anger, and violent desire that had also wafted through her being during the reading; feelings that the young heiress and equestrienne directed at her once and short-lived lover, Joe...or a name like Joe or Grow or was it Glow...yes, she called him her 'moon-glow lover'. She met him by moonlight. All very romantic. All very adolescent dream, which he so easily took advantage of. He held her, kissed her with such passion, stealing her breath away while all the along working a scam to steal from her family. Rae felt the Van Holder girl's depth of loneliness fill her entire being as she'd given in to Joe Moonglow. Anything he wished for, anything he asked, down to climbing into the very coffin he wanted her inside of. She'd complied with all his wishes, including his wish to extort money from her estate. Photos were necessary, Joe told her. Only at the last moment, before the lid came down over her, did she see the other woman.

Aurelia immediately got on the phone to Raule and passed this additional information forward for the Tampa agents. Raule would take care of it and would not be surprised that new thoughts and feelings–like aftershocks–hit her now.

Aurelia only prayed they'd find the young foolish heiress alive. No one should have to die of love, whether it is true or false, she told herself. Unfortunately, it happened all too often.

"For now," she told the empty room as she prepared to leave Quantico headquarters for her car, "I need a drink."

Phoenix, Arizona–same time

His close-in detail work in the eyelids of Toby Slayter was

complete now. He felt confident no one had heard the boy's cries over the music. It proved either no one cared or that the Calliope created a perfect cover for the carnival handyman and billboard poster artist.

Enough coatings and no one would recognize the child as anything but a neon sculpture hanging in the fun house, his body just another beacon in the darkness.

At his feet, Carnivore Man noticed the activity of fire ants that'd discovered the sticky spill from when Toby had dropped his free Coca-Cola when the roofie had hit him.

"Damn bloody ants," he muttered, stopping long enough to grab a canister of Raid. He fired off the toxic spray too close to the tiny creatures, sending them in a cascade of blown air in all directions. He cursed as the new chemical odor mingled with the paint stench. His nose twitched madly now, uncontrollably, and he feared his throat would clog as it hit him. The odors made Carnivore Man feel both nauseous and light-headed.

He left his art and the boy for the moment, found his cot in the back room, and lay down to regain his bearings. It had been another all-nighter.

Charles Street Tavern, City of Quantico, VA

Two hours twenty minutes into her bar tab, Aurelia controlled the conversation at the bar.

"My father practiced–no, lived–as a Buddhist, quite devoted and humble, a clay pot dish-turner as they called him in the old Japanese section of LA where he lost his life. While mother lived quite happily as a witch–"

Someone nearby repeated the word witch in a startled manner.

"Okay, not a full-blown witch out of Bulgaria or Romania. She lived as a Wicca, actually–not quite the same thing 'cause true Wiccans will tell anyone willing to listen that they do not practice black arts but white only, you know, the healing sort of witchcraft."

She had everyone's attention now. She liked attention.

"At any rate, when distraught friends carried my father's body from the scene of the crime and into our small apartment, they did so with the mistaken belief that her Wiccan remedies could heal the man we all loved. Instead, Mother died that night as well–figuratively speaking.

"Pour me another whiskey sour, will you? Do so, and I'll go on...."

Joannie, the bartender, poured the drink from a pre-made batch. She always mixes me a small pitcher of Jack Daniels whiskey sours. She knows my schedule, and I usually stick to it. Joannie is a doll, a redhead with bright green eyes that make you feel like the only one in the room when she's listening to your woes. She thinks I drink too much. I reply with a sing-song bluesy Tom Waits song that sounds like a dead cat raked over a washing board: "I got-ta bad liv-er...an' a bro-ken heart....but I don't have a drink-in' prob-lem..." Okay, perhaps I do drink a bit too much...or perhaps not enough.

"Damn tough," says Joannie the bartender. "You were just a kid, right?"

I lost them both that day; lost them to the great realm of the Eternal Father, a phrase they had both come to agree on, he from his Buddhist teachings, and she from her Wiccan ways. She was a Gaelic beauty, tall and fair-skinned, auburn-haired. It's where I get my highlights.

I wiggle on the barstool and fuss with my tired backside, and my otherwise black hair with its reddish highlights, mostly to point out the fact that down to my cuticles, I am a true genetic mutt, Murphy and Hiyakawa's daughter. Not a little challenged.

"Yeah...I've seen your ma's photograph," replies Joannie, who now has to see to other customers. For a bartender, she is surprisingly kind, generous, and polite. Young yet, she hasn't been at it long enough to be jaded. I only trust jaded people, but for some reason I cut Joannie slack.

"Oh, yeah...right. I did show you her picture. I remember now." I call this out with Joannie's back to me. "But I don't remember doing so, not really."

"Fit right in alongside John Wayne as the Irish heroine." Even as she mixes drinks for others, Joannie continues the conversation with me. A good friend, as she has heard most of it before, but she pretends otherwise.

I nod and toast to Joannie's last remark. "Indeed, yes, to...to...to rival Maureen O'Hara, and she could have."

"Could have what?" asks someone else at the bar.

"Could have kicked John Wayne's ass."

A general laughter erupts, but it is short-lived as no one at the bar is having a particularly good time of it. And I'm just buzzed enough that all that I say is muffled as if I am wearing earmuffs.

The conversation shrinks back to Joannie and me when Joannie says, "Yeah but you, kiddo, you got all Asian features."

"Mother…my mom…sheeze, she didn't know how to be the actress, not really. You could read her like a book. Anyone could. She held nothing back. No secrets. No lies, no pretenses, and certainly no excuses. Not like me. Not like my life. 'Fraid my life is a series of excuses."

"Oh, now come on kiddo, you're just being way too hard on yourself now."

"I know that I need to hear such reassurances, words that counter what my own nasty mind tells me. I pretend to ignore Joannie's kind words.

Mother was a hellion where her religion and her New Age shop goods were concerned. She ran a place she called Phoenix & Dragon. Her dress and her shop raised eyebrows. Raised eyebrows, I can tell you. Her with her return to Earth Mother routine, and being born the same place Scarlet O'Hara came from, the red earth country of Georgia. I gotta laugh out of that, how far she'd come, eons past Scarlet, she was. Her and her abiding belief in the goodness and richness of all things provided by God, even if she did call Her an uncaring bitch in those waning days, the days before Mother's overdose.

"Yeah…right…and Father was a Buddhist, but he didn't die for his beliefs or because of them, or anything quite so dramatic. No, he died as a result of being hit by a drunken driver, one wearing a priest's collar. Newspaper headlines played that one up big: Buddhist killed by DUI priest. It was in a literal sense how Christianity overran Buddhism in LA. The fundamentalists ate it up, and those calling for the Rapture saw it as a yet another sign. The story got its fifteen minutes in the Times and on CNN, Fox, all of 'em. Was hardly…hardly a fifteen-minute thing for me."

"Easy on that stuff, kiddo."

People at the bar began to disappear around me. Ghosts. Corporeal ghosts for the most part. Real people. But the man now shaking his head at Joannie and me…the one sitting at the opposite end of the bar is a true spectral hologram. A real ghost, my father.

"Why because…because…because I had foretold its

happening–his death," I tell Joannie now.

"And while my parents laughed, just like he's smiling now–" I stop to point out the ghost at the other end of the room, "I…I cried at their ridicule, him and my mother's. Then it came to pass, and for years…years afterward, I blamed myself for both their deaths. Right, old man?" A toast to the spectral shape at the dark end of the bar.

For as long as I've known Joannie Childs, I had never seen her standing aghast with nothing to say. She kept looking from my eyes to the ghost's eyes and back again. She knew my secret in that moment, and it frightened her. That I sometimes saw and spoke to Pappa's ghost.

Still…no one ever knew if Mother's overdose on valium was intentional or accidental, and me, the great fortune-teller and born gypsy, had not seen that one coming anymore than I had acted on the prediction of my father's end.

"You really ought to explore this with that high-priced shrink of yours–just how you and your mother might've handled things better between you, Aurelia?" Joannie's concern, even as she wipes down the bar, is genuine. It doesn't just seem genuine; it is genuine. She has not one equivocating bone in her body. But that moment of knowing and fearing me for knowing, that will never go away, not entirely.

I call out my own name aloud, "Aurelia Murphy Hiyakawa," I say to Joannie as we are now completely alone–me slurring my words…alone with the best bartender in DC.

Joannie downs a Scotch and water she'd been nursing.

I continue with a question. "How fucked up is that, Joannie? Murphy-Hiyakawa? Even in my name I'm fucked up. Murphy-Hiyakawa. Think about it. What in the name of Buddha and the Earth Mother were the two of them thinking of when they–"

"Love, baby bee. They were thinking love, and you're the walking, talking result of love. What can possibly be wrong with that?" asks Joannie, a dyed-in-the-wool romantic, her shoulder-length red hair aflame in the strobe lights of The Charles Street Tavern on the Green, a kicking nightclub on weekends when the bands come in, but right now just another bar winding down for the night. It's just off the highway as you enter downtown Quantico.

"So I am a love child. That really makes me feel better about myself, Joannie," I tell her.

"How's your kid doing in the new school? What is that, third one this year she's had to move to?"

"Don't want to talk about Nia."

"Such a pretty girl."

"I was once a pretty girl. Now what am I? Mother to a pretty girl who hates me."

"Bullshit, she loves you, and you ought to go home to her and hold her and hug her to you and kiss the daylights outta–"

"Nia doesn't do hugs and kisses anymore, unless I hold a gun on her."

Joannie laughs at this.

"I tell you, Joannie, we fight non-stop. We need freaking Oprah help or counseling or something. She's more messed up at her age than I ever was, and I had to deal with two dead parents at her age. She says she's got issues, and that I am her major issue–calls me an issue! I'll give her issues."

"How often you throw that line up at her?"

I could not respond to this.

"How old is she now, thirteen?"'

"Oh, cripes…a lot of sympathy here. I expected I'd get some empathy from you, Joannie, of all–"

"You reap what you sow, sweet'ums, and you know that better'n any of us."

"I'm out of here." I plunk down Joannie's sizable tip along with the bar tab.

"You work too hard," Joannie shouts after me.

"Right 'bout that!"

"Your girl needs more time with you, and you need–"

I wheel on her. I shout, "I've got a shrink, Joannie! I don't need your advice on raising my kid. And as for that man at the end of the bar, pour him one on me!" Said while closing the door on her as she tosses her bar rag and gives my fading image a blank stare.

I stagger to my car in an empty lot.

Only an hour before, Aurelia had learned that the FBI field office had taken a man into custody in the heiress case in Tampa. "I do good in the world," she told herself, knowing she did excellent work for the Psychic Sensory Investigation unit. That much even the booze could not take from her, she reasoned now as she made her way out of the circle of what felt like a campfire. Orange light–the glow of lamps around the Charles Street Tavern's parking lot.

Aurelia made it to her car and continued talking to herself now. *Called it amazing and excellent work, Raule did, so why doesn't he return my damn phone calls? Calls me a gift...calls my gift a gift. Some gift...the "gift of fear" and that works for me, because I do fear my own "gift" as it is as much curse as gift.*

The drive home from the bar near Quantico was uneventful except when her dead father showed up in the seat beside her. Twice in one night was a bit much.

Another issue: Pappa's constant vigilance is unnerving, and he can be so critical.

He sat shaking his head, a finger pointing accusingly at her. For the longest time, he said nothing. Then he opened up with his first salvo. "This is not how I raise you to deal with problems. Get hold of this drinking problem before it destroys you, Rae."

His voice came out as if he were alive. She knew it to be exactly, word for word, what he'd say under the circumstances. She blinked and found him gone.

Killed he was by a drunken priest on his third probation, driving without a license. Killed outside his Los Angeles religious temple, not six blocks from where another Japanese man had been brutally attacked and killed with an ice pick rammed through his brain by a teenager high on drugs and a dare. The other Japanese gentleman had been a college professor at UCLA, had written several books on the history of Japanese-Americans relations, and a book on the underpinnings of Buddhism, and how like Christian secular thought, philosophy and belief it is. A so-called Christian killed Professor Sheito Yoshita for the twenty-nine dollars in his wallet.

Her own father, Hiro, loved life. He loved his children and his grandchildren, all nineteen of them, including Aurelia's daughter, Nia Kim Hiyakawa. Her father loved his birds, as he kept songbirds. He loved the sound of things, just the lilting rhythms of the street, the same LA streets that'd bred the drunken driver who'd killed him.

"This is why I took the job here, Pappa," she spoke aloud to his departed soul. "Why I uprooted my baby, who has not been my 'baby' since we came here in search of a new life." Rae blinked at trees going past in the darkness like escaped ghosts.

"Embrace your inner self, and be kind to the child within you, my daughter," Hiro said from a world away.

She nervously laughed and reached out a hand that went to the seat where his image had been beside her. "When ever did Marshal Dillon, or Annie Oakley, or Calamity Jane ever embrace the child within? Law enforcement officers don't do such things, Father. All due respect, but *you* are out of touch."

"Embrace your psychic self as well."

"God you are so annoying. Go away."

"The only safe place for you is in knowing yourself thoroughly."

Another Asian platitude. Try being direct once, and would it kill you to simply say, Rae, dear, I love you, too? And why couldn't you have heeded my word when I was a thirteen-year-old. If you had…"

"Then you would have no problems in your life?" he asked, his image slowly coalescing again. She saw that slow grin that ended in smiling eyes.

"It's no longer a secret, Pappa, that you and mom made me an overachiever, an alpha wolfette. Not since *Time* and *Newsweek* did their stories on me."

"You may've cut your own throat granting interviews!"

"Might've put my career in the proverbial toilet. And I think

Raule'd got in trouble over it."

"Sure he would…with the 'Company'. Didn't he shut down afterward?"

"All the publicity. Gee, even Playboy was after me to do a spread–"

"I don't wanna hear about a spread."

"Psychic Asian Babe on FBI Payroll Catches Crooks with Her Mind Not Gun…. All that."

"My goodness, Rae."

"Created a month's worth of prattle and gaggling among the male agents both at the cooler and in the locker room, I can tell you. But I didn't do the Playboy spread."

"Excellent move."

"Though I could've used the kind of money they were throwing at me."

"So what was your reservation?"

"I didn't want to bring any bad publicity down on our unit. That certainly was not my aim. Point of fact, I wanted to shed a bright light on what we do. We're good at it, and we are proud of our record, our amazing hits, although truth be told, we lose a lot of cases to the bad guys and the system, if you want the truth. Then there was Director Raule Apreostini's reaction to my "over exposure" as he called it."

"He's a married man, Rae. What were you thinking?"

"Called me into his office, Pappa. On the carpet…literally. I mean it didn't start out that way, but once he got over the rant. It went a little like this, if I can recall:

"You've embarrassed the FBI family, and it could become a problem."

"It's only a problem if I believe my own hype," I had begun to assure him when, suddenly I realized what I was seeing in his eyes. Damn it, he wanted me. He stood there and took me in his arms and passionately kissed me. I was caught off guard to say the least. Me. A psychic, but then again, I had never been any good at seeing–truly foreseeing anything in my personal life except the ending of a relationship before it even began, and it took no psychic power to foretell where this sudden infatuation was going. Although, Raule claimed it was hardly sudden and no simple infatuation, but I guess he lied."

"You of all people should know bullshit when you hear it," Pappa said, a little shake of the head showing how transparent he actually was.

"Raule's so handsome and so passionate about his work, the unit. We have that in common. And I began to burn inside with a need for him I really didn't take time to analyze."

"On the carpet you mean..." her father's voice came again in her ear.

"Yeah...on the carpet..." She began laughing. "Literally called to it, that big white Alpaca one in his office."

Aurelia tiptoed past her daughter's bedroom, the live-in housekeeper having dozed off downstairs in the living room, as was her habit. She had always told her daughter that Enriquiana was just that, a housekeeper, never daring to use the term baby sitter. Nia would have a fit if she knew the middle-aged Spanish housekeeper was also being paid to keep an eye on her. Enriquiana had orders to immediately call Aurelia in the event she should see, hear, or smell anything unusual coming from Nia's room. Enri, as they called her, was to call no matter where on the continent or the world Aurelia might be at that moment.

Enriquiana represented a kind of insurance policy against Nia's unpredictable nature and newfound rebellion, what Dr. Pokabla called every girl's natural teen angst. "Girls just wanna have fun," the doctor had broken out in song, playing her favorite instrument badly–an accordion–before regaining composure on seeing Aurelia's surprise. The doctor used the accordion as a weapon of sorts in her practice, that and ping-pong balls. She threatened the accordion if her patients stopped relating, and she sometimes hurled ping-pong balls as warning shots whenever the patient became hesitant to open up or she felt a person was playing games or lying.

"I will not brook a lie," the doctor would say and "toss."

Aurelia had found a poem that Nia had written and folded into a secret cubbyhole in her room, and fearful that her daughter might be suicidal, she'd taken down the poem, line by line, but she'd been unable to truly interpret the words. So she had shown the poem to Dr. Polkabla, whose opinion must surely be worth her fee. Lyn Polkabla stared at the words and read the poem with great interest. It had read:

* * *

PSI: Blue

States of Being
In that place we call the borderland,
that neither this nor that state,
lives reality.

It's where what might be already exists.
It's where the one or the other
has yet to be...yet created.

It's where being and non-being
play and dance with one another.
It's is a fecund,
a source place of all things that are,
and were, and yet shall be.

I do not wish to live where things are;
I choose instead life in that no man's land
between breaths,
where all is possibility
in iridescent color.

It is a female place of mystery,
a part of all our secret rites.
It is living outside–or maybe, inside–
the boundaries,
perhaps, within the edges
of the boundary itself.

This state is a slender, high tightrope
that I dance upon.
Below, crowds look up to watch.
Some pray while others chant,
hoping I'll slip and fall:

Fall into illusion, fall into maya,
lose my life, lose reality,
to live as Soul-less as they–

They who've forgotten
how to reach that state again.
And yet...

And yet I recall cooling water
to 29° and it stayed liquid,
denying crystalline imprisonment.

"So what in God's name does it mean, Dr. Polkabla? Is my kid depressed, suicidal, nuts?"

"Oh please! She is merely exploring the boundary between this and that...night and day, dream and reality, safe and comfy versus the uncharted lands labeled 'here be dragons', and as for you, Rae! You need to cool your jets!"

"But suppose there's something really bothering her? She's my little girl, and since we hardly talk..."

"Nia is a lovely, healthy, well-rounded child you should be enjoying and not suspicious of. She's just looking at herself–body and soul–and like any young teen, asking questions and seeking answers."

That had only been a week and a half ago.

Aurelia caught a glimpse now of herself in the full-length mirror in the hallway on a swivel frame outside her door. Stupid place for a mirror. Stupid of her for placing it here. Purely ornamental. Purchased for its antique frame. Beautiful and in near flawless condition. Not meant for anything more than to fill and lighten this ugly, empty section of hallway in the old bed and breakfast. But here it sat suddenly judging her, insinuating itself on her as clearly as her father's ghost, providing her with the horror of the moment–her reflection.

For a nanosecond, she checked out the thin, shapely, athletic body, the shoulder-length black hair with its shining auburn highlights, her demure Asian features, her weary eyes, and soft nose. Still cool...looking as if in her twenties when in fact she was five years away from the dreaded forty–a horrid thought, as she had gone through a real emotional upheaval at turning twenty and again at thirty. Consequently, she feared forty less as a number than as a psychological earthquake. At twenty she'd disowned her psychic self and vowed never to use psychic powers ever again. Action taken in the name of love, in order to be a devoted wife and mother. Action that asked I deny who I am, she thought.

This resolve having failed and miserably so, by thirty, she found herself unceremoniously dumped–cut off at the knees by her own faith, tolerance, and an unsuspecting heart. A good heart used against her. In fact, her best qualities had been cruelly twisted to somehow become faults and personality defects. This, more than all of Tomi Yoshikani's cheating and lying, had wounded her.

Divorce had dropped her like a charging rhinoceros struck by an elephant round. After which she found her feet again, found her strengths scattered about the debris field of her shattered life, and she dusted her hurt away and concentrated on Nia and Nia's needs and future, putting her own on hold until that day she watched the world being shattered on 9/11. After that, Aurelia Murphy Hiyakawa went on a personal crusade to answer a higher calling, one put out by the government. Contacting the CIA and the FBI, they asked if she could read, write, or speak Arabic. She had to say no to all three, but she added the caveat that she spoke another language, the language of extra sensory perception and psychic sensory perception, ESP and PSI. The CIA hung up on her.

Their loss.

She had not settled on the FBI so much as the FBI pounced on her, especially once she had gone through a battery of tests for them, tests ordered by Chief Raule Apreostini. This on seeing a demonstration of her unique and unsettling abilities.

Now Aurelia wondered what forty might bring…what the heralding of a new decade in her personal journey would do to her, or if she had learned enough to beat back any disquieting hurly-burly visiting on her fortieth birthday, looming five years hence. Certainly, she would be braced for it this time. Just as certainly, she could make no predictions, not when it came to her own life and love and fortune. Her special brand of fortune telling could never be used for personal gain or benefit, it would appear. She had never picked a winning lottery number or racehorse, and most certainly not a winning man.

Still staring at her image, she thought of Wade Benton, tall, handsome, masculine, stupid, and good in bed but lousy at caring a rat's ass about her needs. She'd thrown him over only days before and had dodged all his calls. She had seen the end to their relationship before it'd begun, as always, and she had been unable to change the course of it as it raced with precision-like inexorableness to its bad end, perhaps its only possible end. Not a prediction but a knowing, an instinctive knowing that any woman with any intuition at all could as well make.

Sadly, she could see an end, but she could not see the why of a relationship going south and sour. Part of her held onto the belief that she could change the future's end to a relationship before she got to that point in time—if only she worked harder at it. This voice of hope—'hope has a place in a lover's heart'—proved wrong so far, one hundred percent wrong. Maybe even evil. For hopelessness had characterized every relationship Rae'd had the nerve to pursue since the divorce.

But the looking glass had captured her in the here and now of the darkened hallway where she stood. The mirror told no lies, had no reason to; as a camera lens, a photo, what you saw was what you were, she reasoned—on the verge of losing everything, teetering here on the precipice of failure in all but her professional life. As she took a step closer, Rae reached out to her mirror image, a sadness coming over her, and she knocked over a small table. The knick-knack littered little table clattered and reverberated down the silent hallway here on the second floor.

"Shit...shit...shit."

"Why don't you sit yourself down and get it together, mom!"

She thought it her own voice in her own head but there was the accusatory reflection of Nia in the mirror with her now, the perspective weaving with her exhaustion and the drink.

"Nia...sweetheart...I thought you were...asleep."

"I haven't been asleep since I was twelve, mom."

"What's that supposed to mean?" she asked, wheeling to face the real Nia, and to determine if she were really standing here in the hallway outside their adjoining rooms.

Nia stood, eyes accusing, hand stroking a black Tomcat, a stray she'd begged to keep. She carried Tim-O'Shay about like her second self nowadays, ignoring her lovely terrier, Geoffrey.

Issue: I hate cats, thought Aurelia.

Nia had no use for cats either; she had only taken to the stray when it had come begging at the back door to the old Victorian bed and breakfast. She'd taken the animal in for one reason only–to test and peeve her mother. Downstairs and up, at any given time, strangers lived in the house with them. It did little to help with the guests when Nia would burst out in her most perfect innocent voice with, "Tim-O'Shay cuts down on mice!" Nor did this help when the realtor brought the infrequent interested buyer responding to the Cook-Hamilton Realty *For Sale* sign out front.

"When are we going to unload this stupid house and get a normal place?" Nia had been arguing this for a year now, pushing photos and ads of new development homes in Clover Hill, and places named for arboretums and sun-filled gardens. Places like Silver Lakes, Interlocken Estates, Shining Leaf Isles (isles flanked on all sides by I-95, the Beltway, and other super highways, thus the word isles). Her latest love affair appeared to be the sheik and elegant Mount Carmel by the Lake. It sounded to Aurelia like parfait treats on a dessert tray. Nia said she needed a lake, that she was a water person, born under a water sign.

"You were born in the year of the rat," Aurelia had joked in response once, only to make Nia run from the room in tears. "That's only on the Chinese calendar! You are not Chinese!" She tried to correct her words, but the teen preferred tears all the same.

Nia now seethed inwardly, and she stamped her still developing right foot, twirled on her left, and slammed her door on her mother, her final look one of disgust. Had she gotten a whiff of the Jack Daniels?

It represented a harsh and sudden return to this reality–one often laughable, sometimes truly funny, but at such moments sad.

When had Nia become such a brat? She knew that people studying the mind equated the confusion and red flares in the brain of a psychopath with those of a teenager, but it felt as if

Nia's body had been taken over, possessed by another personality altogether. So where was her daughter's real character being held hostage? Character... something she'd so wanted to build and mold and shape and have a hand in as her parents had done with her. But Nia would have none of it. Nia hated all things her mother stood for, and Nia misunderstood Aurelia, her motives, her psychic gift, her work, her goals, and somehow managed always to see only the twisted interpretation that a teen filled with angst could possibly make. She wondered if the two of them would ever be capable of finding the kind of love they'd shared before Nia had reached puberty, before the divorce.

The whiskey sours had worn off, and she knew the crash was coming...had come in fact already with Nia's image in the mirror beside her. Now the tall, freestanding swivel looking glass reflected back a frightful, disarrayed sight. Yet it wasn't so long ago that Aurelia'd been complimented by her reflection. Not anymore...first honest sight I see tonight, she thought. She saw, across from her, the featureless outline of herself back at headquarters sitting in her "lucky" robe, electrodes in place, hooked to a machine, upright and stiff in the lotus position below her brass-pipe pyramid, looking like part of the machinery around her. The shadowy reflection grinned evil back at her as a glint of anger flit through her brain–anger of the self, for the self, by the self. It wanted to strip back layers of her eclipsed other self, the one that gave in to pain and tears–now just a silhouette–to reveal the loss and ache kept hidden from all others. Even from Nia.

How could she share with Nia the horror and the glory of her job?

How could she complain about the life she had chosen? What was it father had so often said? As if on cue, Hiro appeared in the looking glass, saying, "Success is obtaining what you want."

"I know...I know what you are going to–"

"But happiness is wanting what you get."

"–to say. Please, Pappa. I thought I'd seen the last of you

tonight."

"As you wish." Then he was gone.

"I don't need more bumper-sticker slogans." Aurelia stumbled into her room, wanting no more conversation with the looking glass. "What bloody choice have I had in being who I am...what I've become?"

She had helped bring horribly evil people to justice, had saved countless lives in such cases as Atlanta's Child Snatcher case, and Seattle's Collector case. But what of my identity? Is it life's creation, or is it my creation?

In her darkened bedroom a shadow moved with her, a circling giant black bat wing as large as a blanket, filling the space overhead. Hiding its gruesome features like some Phantom of the Opera, beating wings in a frantic attempt to disappear altogether, fearful of the light, fearful of her stare, and then it-or he-as it had a definite maleness about it–was gone, as if spiraling through the chimney of another dimension.

She rushed for her bed, shutting out the darkness that came from within, a darkness she'd always from childhood felt, a darkness that could under the right circumstances do real damage to someone, if she gave it full vent, if she gave it the word.

Aurelia fearfully sought out the pencil and her professional notebook kept bedside at all times, hoping against hope to recall everything as it had happened, in its entirety, telling her diary what she must recall for her psychiatrist when next she visited–this weekend. She paid dearly for weekend visits to Dr. Lyn Polkabla, but given her workload, it couldn't be helped.

She heard the old Victorian house, erected in 1849, groan a pre-Civil War sound around her as if disappointed along with Nia. What kind of woman needs everyone's blessing, everyone's liking her, everyone's telling her she is okay, wonderful even. On a deeper level, she understood perfectly why Nia so condemned her and the job that took so much of Rae's time; a job that sent her spiraling through space and time. A job during which she lost track of time. If she must see Dr. Polkabla this weekend, where did that leave Nia's soccer game?

Could she squeeze in both and have no telephone call sending her back to headquarters? A fifty-fifty proposition.

Rae stripped away her business suit down to her underwear. She turned on the shower and let the spray heat up, returned to her bedside, and stared at the blinking red light on her answering machine. "Let it blink till morning," she sternly told herself. "Anyone needs me now can go to hell."

She dropped her bra and panties at her feet and returned to the shower, climbing into the refreshing hot spray. She washed off the day, wondering if the poor girl in the coffin had been found alive or dead. Perhaps Raule Apreostini had gotten word by now, perhaps there was closure on the case, and perhaps she should check her messages after all, so that she could sleep in the warm glow of knowledge she'd helped save another life...not her own

Another part of her fatigued brain cautioned and counseled to go nowhere near the answering machine. Certainly not to answer it. If there were anything critical or final on the case, Raule would've buzzed her via cell phone.

Anything else can wait on sleep. Nude, she stretched out against the cool sheets and soft pillows. What she most needed now.

She had always preferred sleeping in the nude. "Go to bed. Rest your mind. Be at ease, child," her father said, his hand on her brow as she dozed off in her pillows.

In her mind's eye, she saw her mother beside him, each wrapped about one another. She had never found that kind of happiness in this life, certainly not with Nia's father, another issue, and a pulsating sore point between Nia and Aurelia. Nia blamed her for the breakup. Nia had been seven, going on eight, sharp as a razor, nothing whatever getting past her. How many years now had she remained angry at Aurelia for something out of her control? Nia would soon be sixteen.

Above her a dark wind hovered just the other side of her eyelids. Aware of this entity and the sound of a wrecking ball and Calliope music all mixed, this force, this visitor–as curious as he or she or it might be, it could not drag her now from the arms of Morpheus. Sleep perchance to dream...perchance to make perfect that which resisted perfection–her life.

Again Cy hit replay on the iDVD film on his G-4 Mac laptop, the film of the final unrelenting torture and death screams of Freddie Quan, the boy sacrificed before Toby Slayter. Cy played the horrid DVD so that Toby could hear the screams reverberate off the garishly painted walls here in the underbelly of the amusement park. The boy's screams, real as they were, came soft out of the limited speaker on the Mac, but no less horrific for it.

In the background, Toby could hear the continual play of the Merry-go-round he remained tied to here, and the Ferris wheel music outside in the safer world of public thoroughfare.

"The final screams I get out of you, Toby, boy! They're gonna be freakin' better'n that fat little China doll. The one who came before you. Friend of yours?" Cy asked the emaciated Toby as he untied him and carried him into the deep recesses of this horrid haunted house. An animal harness like those to hold a horse or a cow in one place awaited Toby.

Toby fought with what little energy remained in him. But Cy proved a powerful enemy, one he could not shake off. In a moment, Cy had Toby helplessly inside the animal harness from which he dangled. It felt like being in a fish net.

Toby now hung suspended above the wooden boards of this place in the dark. His every exposed limb shining with the glowing paint that kept hardening and tightening about the epidermal layers of his body.

Cy realized Toby was dying and doing so in silence. A last ditch effort to get something on camera, to tape his pain, to make him scream was in order. Cy had set up his iPod here in the dark and again played the Quan tape. He did so and then pressed his burning cigar through the painted boy's colored skin, searing paint and skin. Toby ruthlessly and stubbornly held his silence, even now.

"Shit....you suck, kid. When do you give in?"

Cy tried repeating the cigar burns all about Toby's body,

leaving ugly green melt spots on the painted body, marks that made the Toby exhibit appear the victim of some sort of virus or parasite, like an Ebola victim. Kids coming through the haunted house would love this, he thought.

He continued to run the Freddie Quan scream-fest snuff film on the Mac as further inducement to bring Toby to some kind of audible reaction that he could tape.

Nothing.

Silence.

Cy sucked on his cigar, tasting the oil-based paint mixed with his tobacco.

An old woman in ratty clothes and lying asleep nearby roused from a drunken stupor, a rye bottle rolling out from under her as she struggled, grunting and panting to her feet. The taped screams awakened her and had somewhat disturbed her. "How the hell'm I 'spose to get any sleep 'round here?" She did not expect an answer. Sunlight filtered through the creaky old shelter, a kind of roundhouse for repairs at the amusement park connected to the haunted house. The door between the two structures stood wide, morning light slithering in like a tentative cautious snake from the outer building.

"Morning, Ma," Cy greeted with a sinister smirk. "Sorry...but you're so much like the trash in this place, I forget sometimes the fact you're here."

"How many times I say don't call me your ma! Huh? I get ya what ya want, you get me what I need, but you're letting me down, Cy! I'm fresh outta rye and gin."

She waddled forward, leaned over, and lifted the empty rye bottle and tossed it across at him here in the semi-darkness. She'd become accustomed to darkness; her eyes preferred the dark.

Toby somehow managed to lift his head at the sound of the woman's voice, and seeing it was her, his eyelids stiff with paint, fought to go wider. "Mother Mary, full of Grace, help me! You once was an angel, Jesus' mother! For God's sake, help me!"

Cy gleefully clapped at Toby's pleas, getting them on tape,

the iPod running.

The old woman cackled like a mad bird and exposed her breasts–pendulous giant sacks straining nearly to her knees.

Cy said to Toby, "Here's your Mother of God. Don't ever count on an addict and an old whore...sweetie."

The old woman gave Cy a dirty gesture and felt her blood curdle, hearing the Quan boy's screams playing over again. The sound of horrific fear in the voice in the video image sent an electrifying current of disgust through the old woman.

The same sound and image sent pure sexual delight and ecstasy through Cy's thick, lumbering yet paradoxically fluid and agile body.

Cy rushed at his captive, Toby, and spit-shouted into his bruised, battered orange glow painted face, "Why don't you scream like that, like Freddie Quan? That fat little China boy screamed like a stuffed pig, huh? What in hell are you made of, boy? You think you're tough, that you can beat me with this silence! Damn your silence!"

Even the old woman knew that without the screaming, the boy was ineffectual rubbish to Cy. It made her laugh and say, "He's useless to you, Cy–as useless for your erection as...well as I am!" She cackled as if it were the funniest joke ever told. "Useless, so why don't you just end it? Give up the ghost."

Cy still believed he could squeeze out the prize he sought. He just needed to break the kid. Toby was different. He represented an enormous challenge that Cy could not step away from. An hour before, a debate raged in Cy's brain over the life and death of this recalcitrant child who refused to scream out, and who refused to plea, and who refused to answer. Somehow this child had innately learned that his only weapon against Cy was this infernal silence.

Until now. He'd gotten a plea out of him; or rather old Grace had.

But Toby Slayter had simply shut down as if not even here. He had gone someplace deep within himself, someplace all but ethereal, as if he were out of body on some sort of extended astral journey.

Cy stepped away.

Paced the darkness.

Ignored the old woman whose sounds were those of badly fitting false teeth, the sucking on the empty rye bottle, belching, grumbling under her breath some unintelligible nonsense. Meanwhile, Cy felt a pair of eyes boring into the back of his neck again–eyes out of the void, like those of an angel or a devil, or God himself. Eyes that oddly enough were mismatched–one blue, one black. Eyes that had been visiting like some spectral snoop ever since Bloody Mary Grace and the kid had brought Toby to Cy's secret place below the rides at the park.

Cy paid old Grace–her real name–good money to play act the role of the fallen angel of Christ's mother, La Llorana Fantasia–The Weeping Spirit, Bloody Mary; he paid her to keep an eye on the children, and to pick out the ones she thought Cy would like. She and Cy had thrown such a fright into one of these midgets that they'd converted him to their bidding to procure others for Carnivore Man's funhouse. Else the little pimp would suffer the tortures of the harness once again himself.

But what were these feelings Cy had begun to experience since Julian had come to him? Julian who lay in wait. Julian who remained handcuffed to Cy's water pipe even deeper in the bowels of this place.

Why did Cy feel that something different was going on, that a corner had been turned, that things were not as before, and that Julian was fundamentally at the heart of what had caused this boy, Toby, to be so damnably different? Julian and Toby had spent some time locked away together before Cy'd chosen Toby to experiment on. Had Julian Redondo said or did something to make Toby this way?

If so, how tough was this Julian kid?

Cy had fought this notion. He could break Toby as he had broken every kid before him. He could rip out a spirit, leave only a husk, the material body before he killed Toby outright– or allow the paint to do this for him. This part of the processing of the children he tortured–this sense that he'd plucked out the element of the soul itself in his bid for power over the life he held in his grasp, this proved more important than any other benefit derived, including sexual gratification.

With all the others, each day's torture saw less and less of the soul in the eyes. But not with Toby, Julian's good buddy. The fire remained. The hatred remained. The belief in revenge intact, irascible, petulant, and in place.

He slapped Toby with the back of a hand, and bone cracked like a gunshot, sending the boy into unconsciousness. "Damn you!" Cy stomped about the room, pushing the ratty furniture over, kicking out at a trashcan, sending its contents flying at Grace, trash raining about her. Cy continued his shouting and throwing of small items.

"Another happy day in the fun house with Cy," she muttered and showed her few remaining broken back teeth, their sharp ends looking vampiric. "Just give it up, Cy. Get onto the next boy. He'll likely be just what you want."

"And if he doesn't cooperate?"

"The streets are full of 'em. I'll get ya what ya need."

"You do that! You get me another boy."

"Why not a girl? That one who's so mean, throws stones at me?"

"Boys...I like boys!"

"She knows too much that one. You know she followed me here last night."

"Did she see you come down?"

"No...never."

"Then she's no threat?"

"But she will see me one day come here, and her being her, she'd go to someone... maybe the police."

"If it comes to that, I'll take care of her."

"Sure...sure you will, my boy."

They were not related, but she often called him *son* and my *boy*, just as he often called her mother.

Cy could not stand his real mother when she was alive, and Grace had not seen her real son for twenty-eight years.

The old woman, tattered clothes dragging behind like the rags of a mummy, waddled out of the underground room and found the maze of tunnels that ran below the amusement park, going for her secret exit.

She left to the sound of screaming and pleading and crying, but it was all the Mac DVD. She heard not a peep from Toby. She gave a brief thought to Julian, who had decided to tag along at the last minute. Grace had not seen Julian since.

She found the light at the end of the tunnel and went toward it. At the moment of stepping into the sun, her large dark glasses perched over her eyes, the old woman breathed in the morning air. It had rained just lightly enough to wet down the heat from the desert city of Phoenix, but in fifteen minutes, given the sun and time of year, no trace of the wet coolness of this morning would be left. It will have vanished, even the deepest roadside puddle of it. Not unlike Toby and Julian and Freddie before them.

Back inside the underground of the park, Cy felt the eyes again upon him. So sure was he that someone was watching him that he wheeled and scanned the room. He imagined the eyes not of Toby but perhaps those of the nearby Julian, as they looked more feminine, like those of a woman, and Julian had feminine features, so maybe….maybe…or maybe just perhaps the girl the old hag had spoken of. Definitely someone with magical powers, with the eyes of a seer…eyes of two colors.

The eyes were felt more than seen, but what he felt bearing down on him seemed framed in a definite outlined box of some sort, like some kind of ethereal rearview mirror.

Were the eyes reflected in a mirror or pool? Cy, a gaunt, angular awkward man tried to shake all thoughts of this pair of free-floating disembodied eyes looking in on his world as if from another dimension.

Quantico, Virginia, the following morning

Rae woke up worrying about Nia. She wondered what had been said between them the night before. She recalled a day when she'd become excited in the belief she could regain a good footing with her daughter. It'd come about alongside the publicity she'd brought down on the FBI's PSI unit. It was supposed to be a good thing. No longer was the PSI unit a well-kept secret. Surprisingly, the public mind embraced the idea of psychic alternatives and solutions paid for by tax dollars. This recent reassessment of such stark events going on behind the closed doors of the FBI did make it far easier for those working in the field. The cloak of secrecy about what they did only extended now to the details of an ongoing case. It took a great deal of stress off a person, and for Aurelia, it meant the first time she could explain to Nia exactly what she did, how she used her gift, and why it was so important.

Rae had thought it'd be an eye-opener for Nia, and that the truth would, as they say, set them free–free of the misunderstandings and wrangling. However, it'd had the opposite effect with Nia. She only went deeper into herself. She had gotten up and walked away from her mother on learning just what she did for the FBI. As if she had known all along and learned nothing new....

"Damn it, mom. It was bad enough to have an FBI agent for a mother," she had shouted in a later argument, "but to have an FBI X-File agent mother who deals in spooky shit all day long...occult stuff, witchcraft! That's going to look real good on mother-daughter day at Jefferson High!"

Aurelia now climbed from bed, getting dressed for the day. She threw water into her eyes and face to clear her head, and after toweling off, she stopped to stare. Framed in the mirror were here black Japanese eye and her cerulean Irish eye. She sized up herself in close-up. She felt pleased for the most part, unlike the night before. Her eyes clear, she saw glistening skin, taut and yet soft at once, her black hair and auburn highlights framing a thin face.

She worked out daily, unless the job demanded her give up her workout, or unless the old Victorian house demanded her attention due to some pipe, conduit, or wire, or worse crisis in the walls–such as a dead mouse rapidly decaying; or unless Nia had another emergency at school.

School officials knew Aurelia by Rae, she was there so often, either in the principal's office or in the infirmary. Nia had taken to girl fights, and she was damned good at it, and Aurelia feared she secretly liked the physicality of it, wanted it like a drug lately. Warnings and groundings had had little effect.

What is the girl after? What does she want? Why choose to make her mother's complicated life more complicated? Aurelia talked to her shrink about Nia all the time, and for a few sessions, she had actually gotten Nia to come along with her, but it hadn't helped their relations in the least, and perhaps had had the effect of chilling interactions even further–if that were possible.

Of course it is possible, she silently admonished herself at this. A relationship in Aurelia's mind was the single most difficult thing on the planet to care for and nurture and keep whole and healthy. A relationship died on the vine so wantonly, so anxiously, so readily should you put off watering and nurturing it, should you convince yourself that it can go one more day without attention. It was easier to keep a bonsai tree or a German shepherd happy than someone you loved if it felt like a chore, and if the two parties made it feel like a chore–generally due to a strange admixture of chemistry and circumstance beyond either individual's control–and then it simply failed.

She feared her dearest love, her Nia, ready to fail her, and she to fail Nia, and she wondered what she could do to salvage the most important connection she held to another human being.

Rae went to her nightstand and lifted the handful of brochures she'd picked up last Sunday at the travel bureau. She so wanted to just take Nia, and the two of them to travel, to see some of the country together. She wanted to book that train trip to the Grand Canyon or that other one through the Canadian Rockies. She had always wanted to see the Grand Canyon, and she believed it would heal them, or at least help to heal them…something they must do themselves. But a catalyst like the Grand Canyon, some called a religious experience, why not? It must get them talking like they once talked, caring like they once cared.

Aurelia could no longer hold back tears. In a room next door lay a brooding child that she loved, her child, the one she had lived with so closely for nine months and given birth to and raised to pre-adulthood. Yet now, Rae felt so horribly separated from Nia, so horribly far apart. She knew something must be done, and quickly, before Nia did something absolutely adolescent.

Phoenix, Arizona same time

Toby was gone; alive yet, but absolutely unfeeling and gone–eyes glazed over, skin choking beneath the paint, silent as a bronze statue… almost as if he'd willed himself toward death rather than allow Cy to have his soul for another moment. It was almost as if the kid had fallen into something akin to a coma–

And in Cy's ear all the whispers.

Phantom voices vying to be heard.

Phantoms inside his head wanting his attention.

A parade of them, climbing over one another.

The sounds of people in all the rooms inside his head, all talking at once, none making any sense, but so close on him as to be in his ears and in the deep recesses and winding coils of his mind. His brain. Yet nothing really coming through, nothing intelligible, nothing useful, nothing like a clear order or directive, and certainly not the voice of a god or gods or demons. Just crap…idle, useless tearoom chatter amounting to a buzzing waste of words and noise and time and energy and worry and confusion. Just meaningless formless gibberish.

And it filled his ears…constantly.

He needed screams and pleading–words that had inherent purpose. Words of contrition and begging. These had power to whip Cy into a wonderful state of sexual excitement and lovely cessation once he released all the pent up rage that was *everything* left in him. All that mattered in his life–his own sexual gratification, as he was living proof on earth that nothing existed beyond what man could feel at the singular moment of release.

All else was shadow, smoke, cemetery fog, foxfire, reflection, mirrors on mirrors, and the soul died with the flesh. So that in a sense those lives he shortened were saved.

Saved from flea infestations, parasites, viruses, lice, and the flesh. Saved from lacerations, head injuries, curses, road rage, heat rashes, HIV, cancer, polyps, hernias, hemorrhages, kidney failure, locusts, serpents, Ebola, and all of the nastiness the gods of a parasitic world loved to rain down on mankind. Saved from heartaches, broken dreams, broken promises, and shattered emotions.

If Cy believed in souls, which he did not, then he was sending souls to a better greener lusher world–if he believed in such things. And if he did believe in such things, he could certainly believe that someone or some thing was at this moment watching him, listening in, actually hearing his thoughts, and the gibberish in the bargain.

Impossible.

No such thing. No such entity. No such reality. Not in this dimension. But what of the phantom parade of voices like a ballroom full of whisperers in his head? And what of the damned bloody eyes that seemed bent on watching him? Could it be an entity from another dimension?

Or some worm parasite eating its way through his brain, hence the whispers that were not whispers at all but the sound of a moving slug boring out its random slug trail inside his head? He had read somewhere that parasitologists theorized that the human brain had increased to its current size and ability in response to the constant ongoing war with the *parasite rex*–the parasites that made mankind their feeding and reproducing ground.

Cy did not doubt this awful truth in the least. It only proved his belief in having no belief beyond what a man could see, taste, touch, smell, and hear.

Yet he felt this creeping fear coming through his pores and his hair follicles; felt the dead certainty that someone or some thing was coming for him, a hungry thin dark-eyed creature like a cat. It felt as if someone invisible stood over his shoulder, seeing him, knowing what he was doing. Creepy spirits? Impossible.

If he did believe in such things, Cy might be even more inclined to worry. He momentarily wondered if somehow Toby was told by some sort of wandering spirit to fight Cy with this damnably mature, clever sword of silence; he might believe that if he were superstitious, a believer as they say. But he was no believer.

Nonsense. All nonsense.

So far as Cy believed, nothing went on in this world that had anything whatsoever to do with spirits, ghosts, or astral forays. "Stop it. This is all ridiculous, such ideas," he told himself. The voices were as wind in the tunnel of his mind. Just a touch of normal brain paranoia in the medulla oblongata. One of those strange loops they talked about maybe...like memories of a childhood he'd blacked out, or *déjà vu*. Just enough to annoy.

He tried to shake it off as such. Still he felt the warmth of a steely gaze on the back of his neck.

Damn, he thought, now the very hair on the back of my neck is feeling this paranoia. Why did he feel as if he were being watched? There had to be a physical, logical, corporeal answer.

But suppose it were the eyes of God upon me? So what! After all, God has led me to this time, this place, this hunger, this need...so if anyone is to blame, it is God himself for creating me...after all.

One night, the sense that someone was watching had become so real to him, so overwhelming, that he began searching through the maze of tunnels here.

The boy Toby remained past feeling now, passed out in that seeming coma. Cy decided to go down into the tunnels again, to be sure that girl that Mary Grace had spoken of had not in fact followed the old hag down here to his lair. To this end, he grabbed his huge flash and flooded the tunnel maze with light.

He went on what was becoming a daily search.

Suppose someone was coming for him?

Suppose that someone was already here?

He heard the pile drivers, the concrete eaters, the drills, and the wrecking ball churning into life again. The workmen had taken a break, or there had been a shift change, and now the incessant sound of de-construction and tearing down continued unabated overhead. Deafening if one got too close, but now—always in his head–this sound of the workmen set loose on the oldest ride in the park, the FLESH-REAPER. This wood-scaffold coaster built in '79, had gone out of use and presented a safety hazard, several code violations, as well as an eyesore, a space problem, and more recently a fire hazard, according to the city hack they sent out to make such assessments. Thus the wrecking ball was eating it away from its center out, and the jackhammers chewed at its foundation. The sad old wooden structure was coming down piece by piece. It made him nervous to hear it come down in fragmented sections. How like his brain the thing had become.

As Cy checked out the tunnels and got nearer the surface, his fears eased; of course, the noise of voices in his head whispering must be the reverb from the jackhammers and the wrecking ball as it traveled through the pavement overhead. Still, as he made his way back through the tunnel labyrinth, Cy's head felt a twinge of eerie uncertainty. It felt as if something big was going to happen.

Someone is coming for me, someone who means to take me on. Someone dangerous. "Gotta get that damned kid to scream out, get off, and get him on his way…outta here, I think….way outta here," he sternly told himself to the cadence of the wrecking ball and jackhammer in their weird harmony.

"And–and–and they'd requested any backup experts on serial killers available, and Aurelia, they specifically asked for you, me, and CRAWL–for our special input as they call it. Aurelia. You there?"

It was Eddy E.A. Coffin on the phone, filling her in on the case of a serial killer on the tear in Phoenix, Arizona. "Phoenix is quite close to the Grand Canyon, isn't it, Galileo? That might well be a case I want to take if I can get a trip to the canyon out of it."

"That's perfect 'cause they want you on site, uh, in Phoenix, Aurelia."

"So glad you're finally calling me Aurelia. Tired of Dr. Hiyakawa from you, Edwin."

"Well it has been a few years we've worked together, and you don't seem so much like a doctor anymore."

"Likely as close to a compliment as I can expect from you."

The boy genius sometimes displayed no finesse or social grace whatsoever. He did however display a crush on her, and she'd dealt with this aberration with as much sensitivity as she could muster, knowing his emotional state teeter-tottered between his self-awareness as a prodigal, and his desperate need for approval and love. How alike they were, and if he were not a young boy? Would she react differently toward his awkward advances? She doubted it. She feared that as a man, Edwin would have so many complexes and syndromes bouncing around in his wounded psyche and brain that there'd be zero chance for real love to flourish.

Too bad, really. He had such a good heart.

"So shall I tell them we're there?" His eagerness intrigued her. She didn't wonder at his excitement; after all, this was something they had both lobbied for, an opportunity to work in the field and test out CRAWL in its portable form, a little item that Edwin had invented–a handheld, pocket-sized, palm-pilot version of his CRAWL.

"I want my daughter with me."

"What? Not Nia."

"I only have one daughter, and no telling how long we might be camped out in Phoenix."

"But Rae!"

"Tell the boss I'll do it only if Nia and Enriquiana are with me."

"Your housekeeper and your kid? Are you trying to kill any chance we have?"

"I can't see Nia any less than I already do."

"And the housekeeper?"

"Raule knows she's more than a housekeeper. Just put it to him and sell it, Edwin!"

"All right…see what I can do…but no promises."

"Tell Apreostini that this stipulation is boiler plate…a deal breaker."

"It's going to be costly, transporting me, my computer, you and your entire household…"

"How badly do they want to crack this case?"

"We can't make guarantees."

"How badly," she persisted.

"Extremely, dreadfully, exceedingly."

"Do you always have to be a walking thesaurus, Eddy?"

"Sorry it annoys you. All right, see you in Phoenix."

"You sound positively happy, Edwin. What gives?"

"Are you kidding? Rae, this is our chance to prove the system works in the field!"

"Yeah…but there's something else, isn't there?"

"No, just awfully interested in going to Phoenix, Rae."

"I'm sensing an ulterior motive. Why is that?"

"Ask me no questions, I'll tell you no lies." He hung up.

It was supposed to be her day off, but that had changed with Edwin's call. If she was going to Arizona and taking Nia with her, she'd best get underway. This meant she must pull Nia out of school, but as it represented a chance to get nearer the Grand Canyon with her daughter in tow, then so be it. Holiday! Not that it was a work-free trip, not in the least. It had never been the cost keeping her from enjoying time with her daughter, but time. That most precious of all commodities–time chosen to spend with loved ones, family, friends. It marked a person as having a normal life, and as worthy of love and caring. Rae knew this was at bottom of Nia's problem with her, and she could not blame the teen.

Their trip to the great *Grande Canyon* could be fitted in around the job, she reasoned, and if all went well, she and Nia would have this trip to share forever. Their shared experience at the canyon would solidify their relationship. It must. It simply must.

Besides, the case in question could help her reputation, and the PSI unit. It looked just the sort of case the PSI team could and should sink its collective teeth into. And for a change, they hadn't gotten the case in thirteenth-hour fashion.

In Phoenix, the press had begun calling a serial killer there the Phoenix Phantom.

The case already involved local, state, and federal authorities working through normal channels. Now FBI officials in Phoenix had turned to the paranormal, seeking answers to questions about the nature of this particular evil directed at homeless shelter children in Phoenix's poorest ghettos.

Hearing Nia on her way down to the kitchen, knowing she'd be out the door for school, Rae called out. "Nia! I have a surprise for you!"

Nia shouted something unintelligible and kept going, stomping down the stairs. No doubt whatever she was wearing would cause a fight between them, and so she chose not to come to Aurelia's room, not even for a surprise.

In her terrycloth robe, Aurelia stormed after Nia. She caught up with her in the kitchen, where Enriquiana was plying Nia with an array of Pop Tarts, and Nia had one foot out the door in a skirt far, far too short for school.

The cook-slash-housekeeper was also preparing meals for several adults who'd straggled into the kitchen.

Aurelia had to stop and start her discussion with Nia by acknowledging the new guests who'd arrived the night before, two families who had planned this trip to the nation's capitol to see the sights. "Nia, we have an opportunity to go to Phoenix, Arizona."

"Phoenix," she whined. "Isn't that where old people go to die?"

"I'm taking you out of school so we can–"

"When?"

"–rent a car and drive to the Grand Canyon to see this wonder–"

"When?"

"Today…now…you'll fly out tomorrow."

"No, I won't go! I can't," Nia protested.

Aurelia was shocked, her eyes wide. "What? Why the–why not?"

"I've plans! And you're talking about a month or more! I can't miss that much school."

"Since when did school become a priority with you?"

"Mother, school is of utmost importance, and I love school."

The houseguests began to rubberneck the conversation, listening to the give and take like a tennis match.

"New boyfriend, right?" asked Rae.

Nia's body language said yes. "That's none of your business."

"Make up your mind to it, Nia. I've gotta be in Arizona. I have no choice and–"

"I can't miss that much time off the soccer squad."

"–and I am not leaving you behind to be…to get into trouble while I'm gone. Besides, when will we ever get another chance to see the Grand Canyon as a family?"

"But I've got too many commitments here–unlike some people."

The wiser guests grabbed their coffee and rolls and ran.

Aurelia softly added, "It'll be fun!"

"Oh?"

"Like that time we took scuba lessons when you were thirteen."

"I'm not a kid anymore, mom."

"But it meant so much, taking our first dive together in the Keys. We could take the donkey ride into the canyon."

"Check your geography, mom. The Grand Canyon is not outside Phoenix."

"It isn't?"

"You're confusing it with Flagstaff or someplace else."

"Well even so, people from Phoenix visit the canyon. It can't be that far. We can rent a car and do a Thelma and Louise number."

Nia just laughed at her. "I can just see us sailing out over the side in a Civic Honda."

"Just be sure to tell your counselor or whoever needs to be told you are not going to be at Jefferson for at least two weeks."

"Oh yeah, just like that, come barge into my life and snatch me out of it. I have a life, which is more than I can say for you."

Nia stormed from the room and out the door, her book bag causing the front door to send back a thunderous report as if the door were precariously weighing the merits of shattering or not. In the end, it only cracked, but this would cost big time, as the cracked glass in the door window was stained glass, irreplaceable...there since 1914 when a new door was put onto the old Victorian in what then was a rural town west of DC.

"Shit," muttered Aurelia.

"You want some pancakes, Ms. Hiyakawa?" asked Enriquiana, punctuating with her ladle.

"No, I want you to pack for Phoenix."

"Pack the child's things, you mean?"

"Yes and your things as well."

"Me?"

"You have family in Phoenix, don't you?"

"Well, yes, I do."

"You're going with us."

"What about our guests?" she indicated the strangers here for a week.

"This is a B&B. People who come to B&B's are resourceful, intelligent, monied. They can fend for themselves. You have to get Nia all packed and in Arizona in twenty-four hours. Hold all receipts for reimbursement by the FBI."

"Twenty-four hours, *aiy dios mio!*"

"You're lucky! I have to be there this evening!"

She dropped at the table and nibbled at the hot cakes and drank Enriquiana's strong Mexican brewed coffee. It helped clear her head, but she detested the stares of the strangers and the condescending smiles. They had no idea the horror her personal life had become since purchasing the old Victorian. All in an attempt to fulfill a lifelong dream and simultaneously create a tax shelter. How long had she planned to one day have a beautiful old bed and breakfast? To, with Nia's enthusiastic help, furnish and decorate it. Together, to make it their own, but she'd wound up doing it all alone, as it was not Nia's dream, and after several half-hearted attempts at a mother-daughter fun time of it, she'd had to give it up.

This disappointment proved greater than the leaking roof, a section of which had begun to sag from rot, and it was greater than the discovery of mice, or the lead content in the water, or the Radon rising from the earth beneath the house, or the failing pipes and questionable wiring.

She could sue the previous owners. She could sue the realtor. She could sue the assholes supposedly looking out for her interests, her own realtor and his appraiser, but again time proved the problem. Time frightened her into inaction. Still, a part of her, along with her father's adamant opinion on the subject whenever it crossed his spectral brow, kept nagging at her to sue the hell out of them all. But who had time?

"I think getting Nia on that plane will not be so easy," said Enriquiana, always the master of understatement.

"You just tell Nia this for me," countered Rae. "If she doesn't cooperate and get on the plane, she'll see that bank account of hers and that credit card of hers disappear, along with her cell phone."

"Really?"

"It'll be like David Blaine had hold of her wallet."

"David who?" asked Enriquiana.

"The street magician...never mind, just tell her it's either come to Phoenix or lose her spending privileges and her phone again."

"Ahhh...that always works with Nia."

The two locked eyes, and for a moment all was silent, and then they burst into laughter. "Money talks," Aurelia said between laughs.

Enriquiana added, "No money, no talk."

Cy worked the graveyard shift at the carnival midway, his job encompassing anything and everything. It was a living. But most of what he did was garbage detail. They wanted the Midway sparkling and every byway, nook and cranny cleared of gum and candy wrappers, blowing popcorn, smashed cups, discarded cans and bottles, cigarette butts and lost or thrown away jackets, sweaters, hats, socks, shoes, and the occasional pair of panties, not to mention the array of condoms accumulating under various bleachers. Kids and bleachers and sex went hand and hand, he thought, no pun intended. He laughed at his own crude joke.

They had provided him with a gunnysack and a stick with an ice pick length of nail at the end for efficient stabbing and discarding of blowing trash and runaway tubs. Garbage detail was in addition to his handiwork, his mechanic's work, his painting of signs and murals.

Someone was behind him... someone on cat feet, silently had come right up to him. He could feel this presence directly behind him, yet he or she had not made the least sound.

He smelled something.

He sensed it there.

Hanging in the air just behind him.

Whoever it might be, this person was reaching out toward

him here where he stood on trash detail.

Whoever it might be, he...or she...was about a second away from touching him.

Going to tap on his shoulder.

Ask for a light.

Likely Joe or Stan, one of the other guys working the kiosks at the midway.

He wheeled to see who it might be.

He stared into empty night, into cloudless air, nothing.

No one there.

But someone is here now in his personal space. He feels it so strongly that he backs off to preserve his personal space. But whatever it is, whoever it is, he, she, or it remains invisible. Invisible and menacing. Like some sort of astral spirit haunting him; like maybe the kids he'd murdered amassing their combined auras against him.

It had wanted to reach out to him; had wanted to touch him for its own reasons. He stood alone yet not alone here on the midway, and he began to wonder if Joe or Stan and some of the others hadn't banded together to make it their life's work to *gaslight* him.

Sure...sure that made sense.

That'd be real...a tangible.

No chaos or spirit shit here, no way, man.

Get behind this truth: a human hand was somehow, some way involved.

Whoever it was, he was good. Far superior to Joe or Stan, even if they'd put their heads together.

And the ringing in his ears? The soft voices scratching at his eardrums like something scratching at a door? What of that. Something slipped into his drink? How the hell would Stan Tyler and Joe Kleindennan have pulled that off?

Then he felt a touch like a whisper on his shoulder, and he wheeled expecting to see who was fucking with him, to see the one who liked to watch and sometimes even to help torture the children. The other. The one who liked to bite them so much. At times he wondered if the other existed outside his head–for real–or if he were just another projection of himself.

But it wasn't the notebook carrying, palm reader-carrying associate. It was no one. No one here but me, he realized. But damn, he'd been so sure, and damn but he thought the single word epitaph damn profoundly relevant. "Goddamn!" he said it aloud when on his other shoulder he felt a light tap like a leaf had fallen.

Then he felt a swirling wind go through his legs as if searching for a hold on his pants-leg but unable to find one.

Then it was gone.

That would have been the last of it, right as the rain began, had it not all lingered so real in his mind. This was a force…an invisible entity.

Some one or some thing or things had embarked on getting under his skin…out to terrify him. It left strange psychic scars– invisible to the naked eye–along his thigh and ankle where it had loop-de-looped as if seeking some weak point, some easy entry to the strata just below his epidermis. Goose bumps had formed up and down his legs. It sure felt damn celestial, damn spirit-like. But I don't believe in ghosts and phantasmagorias, he reminded himself.

"Gotta be some logical answer here," he muttered aloud, holding firm to his faith in his core beliefs and convictions. "Something that the boss has thought up to subliminally egg on the audience, like a bubble machine, maybe, or a mist machine to set the cemetery-like mood. Halloween was coming up soon.

To hell with tomorrow night's crowd. Between the downpour and the creepiness that'd come over him, Cy decided to leave whatever mess he'd not cleaned up for the light of day and some drier weather. "Let tomorrow take care of itself," he said, recalling the old piece of advice from a fourth grade teacher and priest Father Collin Crosby, perhaps the last person Cy had ever trusted. But Father Collin had destroyed that trust by many times over until abusing Cy ended with a cruel death that Cy had devised especially for him. It was the first time he'd ever murdered anyone using paint.

* * *

Aurelia Murphy Hiyakawa's shrink wouldn't hear of it. "No, no, no! You come in before you get on that flight, Rae, before! I'll fit you in. It's no trouble...really, and kiddo, you need all the help you can get. We both know it."

So at the urging of Dr. Lyn Polkabla, Rae had come in, and when she failed to relate anything meaningful about what was troubling her, Dr. Polkabla, grabbed up the idle Gibson accordion–always threateningly at hand–and then play it and play it badly. "To fill the empty silence, Rae, if you're not going to talk!"

She played such an awful caterwauling from this instrument that no one could possibly choose it over spilling the proverbial guts.

As a result, before she'd boarded a plane for Arizona, Aurelia spilled non-stop in an orgy of cleansing that Dr. Polkabla listened to with her feet up in the air, as she always listened intently while sitting back in a fully reclined Lazy Boy recliner, appearing asleep but never so. "Go ahead...make my day," she'd say on pulling the lever to send her ample body and socked feet into the air.

It did feel good to release, especially knowing she was getting on a plane, as Rae was a nervous flyer. Aurelia covered several continuing issues aside from her problems with Nia.

"More issues with the career path you've taken...your work-a-holic alpha femme nature?" asked Dr. Polkabla from somewhere behind her horizontal body. "Go ahead. Launch in at any time." She fingered the idle accordion again, hitting a single note, sounding like a bagpipe cry.

As a result, Aurelia launched into her normal diatribe:

"I never completely shut down, not even in my sleep, not entirely. I am always aware, when wakeful, of the energy around us all, and in particular those who people my energy field–the family of ancestral spirits. Think hyperaware, hyperlink–kids that live with abuse get this way–always consciously aware of everything going on around them, including but not limited to this dimension. There's no way I can do PSI work nude as Gene has suggested, no way I can–"

"You are really going to have to tell me more about Gene some day," Lyn interrupts.

"Ahhh...yeah, some day I'll introduce you. Now where was I? Oh, yeah.... No way I can shut out being too aware of what people are thinking, you see, whether it is flattering or not. I am a reasonably attractive woman, and an attractive nude female is viewed by men as an object, i.e. biological overload kicks in."

"Don't I know it!" Lyn chuckles.

"It freaking overwhelms them and me when their pheromones hit, and it only deflects an entire room away from the task at hand. Certainly, what would be gained in psychic 'hits' is questionable, and even if something were gained by doing my readings in the nude, it would at the same time be a major mistake, a big loss. I just know it."

"Does the experiment need it?" Lyn resets her chair so she can look for Rae's expression.

"I think not. Think I'll just keep with my comfy old terry robe and booties on at the office if it's all the same with everyone."

"Weight and diet issues yet?" asked the doctor in a moment's lull.

"Well...my weight is not optimal for my small stature. I'd still be reasonably pretty with my Asian-Irish features and not skeletal if I lost say another ten to fifteen pounds. I'm athletic but my job keeps me from getting to the gym. What to do? Too much for my height, and muscle is heavy, sagging muscle is even heavier...damn. I need to keep to my seaweed and suet diet, but Enriquiana is such a bloody good cook and her Mexican...God, it can't be refused."

"I know. Those enchiladas you brought me last week...whoa. All right, Rae, let's get serious now. What about your continuing–"

"I know what you're going to say, but I've got it under control. Alcohol is not a problem. No longer an issue, I swear it. Hell, alcohol is a scary area for someone as open as I am; like drugs, it forces the door to the abyss open further."

"Screws with the chemical factory up here," says Lyn,

pointing to her head, "as it depresses the thinking-analyzing part of the brain."

"Oh, I know all that, so I'm being extremely cautious about when, where, and how much I drink as it affects me more than I care to admit. Makes it hard to sort out what energy is coming from where, very confusing so…."

"Sounds like you've given it the serious thought I suggested, but still maybe you should read those flyers I gave you on AA."

"Ehhh, hey, it's not like I'm an alcoholic, Doc. I drink socially, and I get a buzz on from time to time is all. Look, even when I'm not on, people know about what I do…they expect me to be up and on like I'm a cross between David Copperfield or Lucy Liu or some such crap. Everyone wants a freaking special effects show when I'm around. Perform like some trained monkey!"

"Yeah…me too," Lyn laments. "Everyone expects Hollywood. Instant gratification, instant answers."

"Yeah, that too, and everyone expects me to be one-hundred percent on, and they expect to see me completely drained and exhausted afterwards, but it's always the opposite like it is with sex with me. The session only fills me with energy, so much I cannot contain it afterwards, but I give 'em a show of breakdown and trembling, you know, do it to give 'em what they have come to see."

"They've been conditioned by pop media. I know. I see it everywhere myself."

"Everywhere you look, every media says psychic stuff is exhausting–like a David Copperfield performance, which probably is damned exhausting. But using my psychic powers is absolutely invigorating, like a high."

"What about your love life, Rae…any changes there?"

"Jesus, please Doc."

"Well…times up anyway. Save it for next time."

Rae stood immediately, anxious to get away from the doctor, as her last question made her unhappy and anxious. As she stood, she said, "Trust me, there's nothing to tell, now or when I get back from Phoenix, I'm sure."

And so ended the session. On leaving, she heard Dr. Polkabla practicing a horrid rendition of 'What I Did for Love' on her accordion. Tuning up in preparation for her next victim. The receptionist was on the phone, trying to get her temp employer, pleading, "You gotta get me out of here. I'll take anything, yes, anything!"

The last man that Rae Hiyakawa had dated had been a reporter named Montgomery Forsyth, and they'd broken up after less than a month. Then the two-faced jerk had the temerity to write a news story about her, disclosing what she did at the FBI. When she had stormed into his newsroom, demanding to know what kind of amoral bastard he was, he and his editor stood against her on some 'principle' of the 4th Estate. Hogwash. Something to hide behind in their petty desire to embarrass the law enforcement agency in an attempt to set sections of the public against this 'most shameful waste' of American taxpayer dollars. It only backfired, even though it brought down some embarrassment on her at headquarters. The public embraced the notion of tax dollars going to applied psychic sensory investigative techniques. Dateline had picked up the story, and they'd taken a poll. Sixty-nine percent of all Americans believed in psychic powers. She was highlighted as an example of how psychic powers had saved lives. She'd been granted heroine status, fast becoming legend, her colleagues chided. But one misstep–should she make the wrong choices, should she trust too much her own literal interpretation of ethereal conversations between a remote victim and herself–or a remote killer and herself–and failure could unfold. In that visual inner dialogue of image upon image she had with herself–there were no guarantees. Rae knew that she could just as quickly become the stuff of late night comedy. Fodder for Jay Leno's joke machine if she wrongly interpreted the signs. And if a child should die as a result? And if the deviant monster who'd abducted said child were never apprehended, justice denied? The professional consequences could be extremely costly, but even more so the emotional toll; in fact, the asking price to her psyche could be devastating.

By now an FBI courier had dropped off the files on the Phoenix Phantom back at the B&B where she packed for the flight. Said files came along with three airline tickets. While Aurelia packed and dressed for the trip, her mind played tennis with the decisions she'd made in her life. Once out the door and in the cab for the airport, Rae began to relax and ease off herself. She felt badly having lied to Lyn Polkabla about the drinking.

As her cab made its way to Dulles International, this question and the bottom-line answer bounced about in loose cannon fashion inside her skull. But right now something else took precedence. Rae keenly felt the fear of being at the center of this enormous case. And she was acutely aware that it meant she'd be cut off from her safe, cozy pyramid and props. She'd be at remote distance from those back at Quantico and D.C. who worked to unravel her language of images via CRAWL. Perhaps just as important, she'd be without Gene Kiley. Not to mention others who, in their way, supported her without even realizing it. People and places of comfort.

She wouldn't have her bedroom, her home, or the Charles Street Tavern or Joannie the bartender or Lyn the shrink, not there in Phoenix. She wouldn't be near Etta Pace, her frightfully normal best friend, who was about to make the worst mistake of her life by marrying a no good, scurrilous, out-of-work actor who once body-doubled for some long dead star who had ended up an acid OD. This was Neil's fifteen minutes of footlight fame: A stand in actor for a dead guy.

Rae's thoughts flit on and off as if with the passing signs, images, and light filtering into the cab windows. The sun and clouds had conspired to play hide-and-seek all day.

Etta'd gone chemically imbalanced, crazy for the sex, and could not see past her wet bed sheets to the charity of reason. When last Aurelia had taken Etta to task over Neil Cutlip aka Neil Cruise, Neil Kingslover, and Lyle James, Etta became first defensive and then she simply blew her top. Began calling Aurelia names which hurt as they all had an element of truth. Then Etta slapped Rae where they sat in a posh restaurant. To others they must look like a couple in the throes of a breakup. Etta announced, "If you can't accept my happiness, Rae, then step out of my life!" She'd then stormed off.

Now Aurelia was on her way to board a jet plane, doing Etta one better, leaving the state. Doing so without a word to Etta. She leaned back into the worn, ripped fake leather cab seat, closed her eyes, and tried to relax even as her hand found the cell phone.

Rae speed dialed Etta.

No answer at home.

She hit Etta's cell number. She caught Etta at Hillary's Hairnet, her second home. Etta's hair stylist, Ron, answered for Etta.

"Oh, it's you, Rae. I heard about your spat with Etta."

"Put her on, Ron."

"Between you and me, I was wrong about Neil, and you were right."

Ron Martine, Etta's chief enabler in her careless passion and mad dash to the altar, had promised Neil a job cleaning up around the Hairnet if he wanted it. "I am on your side this time, Rae."

"I'll treasure this moment. Now put her on."

"Neil turned out to be a real lowlife."

"He didn't take the job?"

"Didn't want it. Put it down, along with my whole shop, and the whole industry."

"What a surprise. Holding out for bigger and better things, is he?"

Ron laughed into the receiver like a girl on an overnight. "Had something in the works with a possible role on Days of Our Legs," Ron joked and cackled.

Aurelia managed a laugh at this. "Yeah, sure…as if he could audition for a soap from the confines of Etta's apartment."

"He finds the occasional actor's studio gig pinned to a bulletin board at Kroger's. Claims then he 'has work'! The man is like you said, a cunning fellow."

Etta, who'd been beneath a hair dryer when the phone rang, now coolly asked, "Aurelia, dear, sweetheart. I knew you'd call."

"I needed to talk before—"

Etta spoke to Ron, loud enough for Rae to hear. "Told you, she'd call! All is forgiven, love. Like it never happened, Rae."

But it did happen and once again she was not listening. "I called to tell you I'd be out of town. On my way to Phoenix."

"Really? That was sudden. Do you need a traveling companion?"

"This is not a mad shopping spree, Etta. It has to do with my agency work."

"Oh? I see. Then you could be out there for some time."

Rae swallowed hard. "Exactly, and I didn't want us parting so badly, and I wanted to say—"

"That the other day was all your fault?"

She swallowed harder still. "Ahhh…yeah, something like that, and to add my congratulations on your up…upcoming pre-nuptials. I assume your lawyer did draw up a pre-nuptial agreement. After all, you have a bank full of hard-earned mutual funds, stocks, bonds, cash and Neil has zip, *nada d'niero* and—"

Etta hung up, and Aurelia's ear filled with the sound of dead air. "Shit! That went well."

She settled her mind here in the cab, refocusing her energies for the flight. Her thought wandered to how Enriquiana and Nia were getting on. Their flight would soon follow hers.

She then dug into her carry-on for the case file—the building murder book as her cop friends called it. Within the manila file, lay photos of the missing children, all seven of them, the last two with the names of Toby and Julian. Toby appeared emaciated, mal-nourished even, while Julian appeared healthier. Toby was a homeless shelter resident, whereas Julian Redondo had a home and a family. She stared at Julian's keen black marble eyes, shining from out of a photo, his arm draped over the other boy, Toby. The shot looked like a couple of soldiers in a war zone, given the backdrop of demolished crack houses. Like a pair of old men in a way, certainly friends. Not surprising that the two had disappeared in tandem, same night.

Julian's eyes were remarkable. Like a pair of large grapes with shinning seeds at each center. She studied every detail of his innocent and not so innocent features, trying to imagine his life. She studied every detail surrounding the two boys–a playground setting on one side, a brick and rubble yard on the other. The juxtaposition of play area and demolition area intrigued her and recalled to mind the strange images that had been keeping her from sleep for so long now. Even the colors were true. Red and orange brickyard, green and blue playground.

So this is what the images were telling her–foretelling her future. This case. A real place in real time, a place she must go to as surely as she must stand in Julian's bedroom, his classroom, his most secret, special place wherever that might be–be it a tree house or dark drainpipe. Rae was unsure why she was pulled toward Julian and not Toby, but it had to do with the connection, the sense of energy. She feared Toby already lost, gone over.

The cab bumped along now, over speed breakers on the approach to the terminal.

She continued to stare at the backdrop of this photo. The park setting behind Julian and Toby felt familiar, like every big city park she'd ever seen. Green lush trees and brush struggling for light amid the high-rise apartments and squalor of a city's debris.

A third part of her mind nagged that she should call Etta back. Force the issue. Tell Etta what she'd been denied telling her–that Neil was not only once a Nick who dicked another woman out of her life's savings in Seattle, but that said dick had come up on one of her Prime Crime search engines under the general category of asswipes. The type who preyed on vulnerable women. If not the elderly, then the desperately lonely.

"Call her back after I've had wine at fifty-thousand feet," she muttered as she continued to scan Julian's other photos.

But time was up for the moment, as the cab pulled into the departure curb for United at Dulles International. Inside at the terminal gate, she was surprised by Gene Kiley who greeted her with a peck on the cheek. "Didn't think I'd let you go into the field without me, did you? Moment I heard, I was on Raule, but you know, he liked the idea, too."

"Raule's always thinking of me, I know."

"Always got your back, Rae. That's the team, but it's personal with me."

She smiled and grappled with his huge bicep. "I love you, too, Gee." She had taken to calling him Gee long ago.

"I wrangled a seat next to you."

"How'd you manage that on a commercial flight?"

"Showed 'em my badge and cuffs and told 'em you were my prisoner."

"You're bad!" She laughed and he joined her, helping her with her bag.

The elderly grandma-san in the 747 seat beside Rae forced a smile and resettled on the Tracie Peterson novel *Beneath a Harvest Sky* that she was reading.

Ahhh, to be so contentedly beguiled by a graceful pack of lies meant to prove a truth–a novel! Aurelia could not recall the last time she'd enjoyed a book that was not read 'for the job', and the only fiction she'd lately seen was that contract written up by the clown who was supposed to repair her roof. Talk about a pack of lies. Now she'd have to take the man to small claims court but when?

All Rae's reading had become technical in nature, her world a lifelong class in how the mind of a killer was molded, and how such a mechanism for killing worked, and in abstracts written by FBI agents, and in the latest on psychic investigation and research.

The elderly woman beside her climbed deeper into Tracie's magical world of the book where such things as justice prevailed.

Aurelia began going over all the police reports, every single line. As she read the awkward phraseology of the first cops on scene at the discovery of the last victim's body–dead of suffocation but not by the usual means. Suffocation brought on by having had his entire body painted with an oil-based chartreuse lead paint. Previous victims had been found in similar distress. No one had ever heard of such a monstrous method of murder. In reading about it, Aurelia became the reporting officer, going into a mini wakeful trance where she sat. The elderly lady beside her inched toward the window. With Gene Kiley on her other side, Rae felt a sense of protectiveness coming from him. He would field any questions, and run interference with any flight attendant who might happen by with food and drink. He knew enough about her to order wine.

But Gene surprised her by bringing her around with a startling question.

"Rae, why don't you instead take another run at Etta? Rae?" Gene said, taking the autopsy files from her and closing them, indicating the elderly woman on her right who might not appreciate the photos.

"Etta?"

"Go ahead, give her another call." Gene was keenly aware of the situation, having done the background check on Neil Cutlip.

Rae pulled out her cell phone and dialed. "I just want to save her from what can only be a miserable bonding," she said to Gene even as she dialed. "I only want to tell her–" she abruptly cut Gene off. Etta had come online. "Now Etta, do not hang up on me! I'm calling from like forty or fifty thousand feet," she lied as they still sat on the runway. Pause and a beat, and Aurelia launched in. "Either way…whatever you do or fail to do…whatever you decide with Neil, will you at least investigate him under his real name, Brenner, Norman Brenner?"

"What the hell're you talking about?" came Etta's strident reply as large as she was tall.

"No stage names, and in Seattle, his con was his stage, as it is now, Etta. Guys like this prey on people like us."

"What do you mean, people like us?"

"You know, independently wealthy...getting up there in years...slightly to greatly desperate."

"To hell you say! I'm not at all like that."

"And guys like Neil or whatever he is calling himself now, they don't change stripes. Everything about the guy is phony. He has a history of taking women for their money. I have a lot of detective friends and all the resources of the FBI. Etta, it only makes sense! When-in-doubt, check-him-out! And I am, surprisingly enough, a good judge of character, and I tell you, Etta, this guy has none!"

Etta again hung up on Aurelia. "Shit. That went well. At least I planted the seed. Hate being the bearer of bad news to one I love, but she is my best friend."

FBI agent Gene Kiley smiled knowingly and replied, "I could show her documents, if you think she'd stand for it, Rae."

"Not now. Maybe later. And thanks Gee for your help in the background check."

"No problem. Maybe you ought to take such steps with the men you've gotten yourself involved with," he tentatively suggested. "I only mean...I mean in the future, as insurance, so to speak."

"Kind of a predication of life based on actuary tables or something? Kinda like saying, "Psychic, heal thyself, Gene?""

"Sorry, Rae, if I offended you."

"Nooo, not in the least, Gee. Maybe I should do exactly that...but sadly enough, I usually know too much about the man before the first night is up anyway. In a sense, I already have too much information on the guy going in. I read him. His body language, his lip language, his eye, ear, nose and throat language, and sometimes I have an uncanny feeling I can read their middle-aged-crisis minds."

"Can't make for much mystique or much fun, knowing it won't work out the gate."

"Picture a blind date soured the moment he opens his mouth."

"I hear ya. Been dating myself and man alive, it's like a weird roulette wheel. Seems something wrong with every woman I meet. I mean that is...we simply don't click...too many ticks and scars and baggage on either side, I guess."

"You're a good man, Gee. Good and tall enough at what 5'9 and handsome and straight and narrow. Never quite understood that narrow part."

"Five-eight and a half, straight as an arrow," he replied.

"All the same, you shouldn't have a problem finding a woman. How long has it been since your wife passed?"

"Six years now...feels like yesterday."

"You know, Gee, she's all you talk about sometimes, as if it were yesterday. Maybe...just maybe..."

"I know, I sabotage any relationship I might nurture by invoking Rebecca's memory. I know."

The psychic images came as always with God Doubt at hand; as always Doubt like a miasmic cloud metamorphosed into a rising flood of itself, until it became a deluge. After the initial flood was contained, it seeped of its own nature through stone-edged conviction. Even as Rae scripted the unfolding psychic impressions that'd come to her in such sharp resolution. A series of images–made up painted faces, clowns, eyes tearful and filled with one raw emotion: fear. And that fear elated her. A deer with large dead eyes like two black cat's eye marbles. Then she was plunged into these eyes as if shoved into a black cavern.

The darkness felt like a choking blanket stuffed down her throat. But it didn't last beyond a second, too brief to cause her to spasm or cough. Then came a bright brilliant sunlit beach, a colorful ball on white caps, children chasing after it, surfers playing at games on the water. A stone falling overhead, burying her and then *faaa-whump,* the sound of being sealed alive, and she came out of the trance state silently asking what the fuck was that?

Was it some how, some way connected to the case?

Was it the first psychic encounter between abductee and

abductor, between innocent and violent, between torture victim and torturer, between soon-to-be murdered and established murderer? But how was there a beach on an ocean in Phoenix? Doubtful....suspect. It all must be suspect and interpreted, and re-interpreted, figured, ciphered, re-configured.

Could she be picking up signals from the wrong place, the wrong people? Phoenix was surrounded by desert, yet the desert was once an ocean floor, but today it had no oceanfront property, and it had no huge ocean-like lakes. There was Lake Powell, the man-made lake created as part of the water system called the Hoover Dam, not far from the Grand Canyon. This was a body of water with huge waves cascading.

The overall image was that of torture and murder. Something in the cosmic scheme of things screamed and railed against this most horrific of acts, homicide, or any of the *cides* for that matter, as in suicide, matricide, patricide, and infanticide.

Gene Kiley stared at Aurelia where she sat beside him on the plane; he'd been staring at her, monitoring her. Rae's eyes had suddenly glazed over, her body in a troubled repose, her features pinched. Something appeared wrong, and that something was happening to her. Kiley had by now learned to read the signs.

More than anyone on the planet, Gene'd seen her in action, but always with a glass pane protecting her from the world at large. Never in the field. As they'd not worked a case in the field together before. From what Gene understood, her last empathy coach had abruptly quit to write a book about his own psychic experiences and gift. Power to the Sixth, he'd entitled it. Thus far, Mark Diordane had not finished his book, much less sold it to the movies as he'd set out to do.

Kiley had for over a year now admired Rae in her robed lotus pose, beautiful in every aspect, a credit to Buddha, he'd privately joke with Eddy. He secretly more than admired her; he secretly wanted a personal relationship outside the job with Rae, but he had never the opportunity to share his feelings with her.

He instead made himself indispensable to her. Any request she made of him, he immediately saw to it. He wondered if she knew how much advantage she actually took of him, or if she were simply unaware of this aspect of their relationship. She could be that way, so absolutely focused on one thing that she completely overlooked another, far nearer, set of circumstances. Her relationship with her daughter, for instance, so far as he could tell from an outsider's point of view. Perhaps such shortsightedness was a weakness Rae subconsciously didn't want to go near, much less explore. Gene feared it could come back to hurt her some day.

The thought pained him. He certainly never wanted to see her hurt.

"Rae, are you all right? Rae?" he quietly asked.

A passing flight attendant asked after her as well.

"She's fine…just resting," he lied well.

She came out of it. What was that? What just happened, she asked herself.

"What was that? What just happened?" he asked.

"Think I'm getting impressions…don't know…"

"Already? We haven't even landed yet."

"…waves of psychic flotsam…could be Phoenix…or not."

He now held the case files in his hands. He noticed the empty wine glass she'd so tightly gripped in her hand during her 'time away'. Her second drink of the flight. "Likely just responding to what you've read in the files. Just natural." He hefted his weight in his seat and carelessly waved the file, the photo of a dead victim slipping out and leaping into the lap of the elderly woman on Aurelia's right, making Rae gasp. But they both immediately realized the woman had fortunately dozed off.

Aurelia snatched the death photo of the painted child away and slipped it back into the folder Gene held open to receive it. "Never known a serial child killer to paint his victims," she mused. "Sick target we're aiming for, Gee."

Gene nodded appreciatively. "No doubt this bastard is going to kill again and again unless we can corner him and put him away." Gene tucked the file into the space between his arm and the armrest.

"Gotta wonder if he thinks of his victims as...well as canvasses."

"Canvasses? Like as if he's an artist with a palette?"

"Precisely. Works in deliberate intent...his choice of color, size of brush changes according to where on the body he is applying the color. Outlines shapes, features. Layers it on like an oil painting. Works from the first layer out. Verdent green forward to blood-orange to outright red on one, reverses it on another."

"Cops in Phoenix just think he's fucking with us all, the clown faces he paints like leaving a calling card, snubbing his nose at authority, all that."

"Goes deeper...has to do with his psyche. Color is important to him. Color, texture, shape, line, even perspective."

"Perspective?"

"As in depth–edges–like Cezanne kinda. The deep dark green left about the eyes, beneath the brow. The attention to triangular forms and squares for eyes. All very still life."

"End result sure is a still life."

She sighed heavily. "We've got a string of seven bodies, an eighth and a ninth disappearance...all kids of a certain body type, weight, size, age–careful choices made by our mad artist."

Gene raised his shoulders at this. "Most serial killers prey on a type."

"But this is like an attempt to create the perfect mask against the pigment...event the pigment of skin he selects. Now he's gone to white as his base, whereas he'd begun with black, moved to milder brown with the Hispanic victims."

"Rae, you may be onto something."

She thought of the dreams that'd begun to disturb her, dreams of the children in the park so like angels, and the red sea with the satanic beast with its bifurcated tail. Even before she'd been handed the case, she'd been getting images that seemed in some strange way connected to the Phoenix

Phantom.

"Bastard seems to seduce them like a magician in broad daylight to become his victims–street smart kids for the most part," she mused now. "How does he do it?"

"Entice them? Hey kids are easily led by any sorta promise."

"Still...something doesn't sit well."

"What're you driving at, Rac?"

"You know as well as I do, that in this game, there's always doubt, Doubt with a capital D."

Gene smiled wide. "Talking about your god Doubt again, no doubt?"

The god of Doubt and Suspicion....

"Always gotta take 'em into consideration, Gee."

"Think I'll consult a higher power," he suggested, but she'd already gone again, back into a trance state.

Gene felt her agitation and saw the notebook on her knees move, trembling with her anticipation. She'd lifted a pencil, and the pencil soared as if possessed of a demon or an angel. She would do this from time to time, pencil in hand, taking notes from the ether...the nether reaches...the land of nod.

Using pencil on paper, Rae related the scene as closely as possible in her tight, yet conflicted, uncontrolled script–a handwriting not her own but belonging to one of them, one of the family who came to her and asked her to use the gift of her special sight for good and never selfish purpose. Only one in the family had ever threatened her, the dark, brooding one. They came in a group, but normally only one at a time. They came to posit insights for her to follow. They were a markedly Antebellum South family, a commune of ghostly refugees from another time and place, and one had a turbulent, grim nature that might easily destroy Aurelia if ever he unleashed his full powers against her.

She feared telling anyone about the family; feared a revelation would curtail her ability to pursue anything simulating a normal life and destroy what little normalcy she'd been able to create for herself and for Nia. So this she held in abeyance, keeping the details entirely to herself, referring to a single 'guide' on occasion. No one, not Gene, not even Nia knew of this truth.

At times, she had toyed with confiding this to Nia, even to Gene, two people she trusted with her life. But it'd likely only terrify Nia and alienate Gene. Strangely enough, she felt the boy genius, Eddy, alone might accept it as natural and curiously fitting. Somehow, his fascination and knowledge of Quantum Physics plugged into the supernatural quite well.

Aurelia wondered anew as to how much credence Nia or Gene or anyone might give this untold tale. Would Nia, her own daughter, scorn it? Who then might understand it; who on the planet might misunderstand? She cautioned, as she always must, against the source and clarity of the family vision, and the symbolic nature of all things in the vision–including the strange family itself. Not one word of it could be taken at face value, not without verifiable substantiation, yet it felt so authentic, so damnably real.

"There's something I've wanted to tell you for a long time, Aurelia...Rae," said Gene, and for a nanosecond, she thought he was going to tell her he knew her inmost secret–her spectral family. That he'd perhaps seen them, or heard their voices. But Gene continued in a shaky voice. "And now that we've got this chunk of time...well..."

"What is it, Gee?"

"I think...I think...this case is going to be big and the media's going to come at you from all sides, so...and you know I love you, Rea."

She burst out with a smile and touched his hand. "Awww so sweet, Gee. I love you, too." This followed by more pat-pat on the back of his hand. "You're a dear, sweet friend, Gee."

Gene sighed heavily and weighed the wisdom of pushing ahead, when Aurelia changed the subject to her friend Etta. "Speaking of love and how really right Shakespeare was about its making damned fools of us all, I can't seem to get it through Etta's thick head how terribly wrong it would be to marry that lowlife she's banging."

"Thick-headed Etta, heh?" She failed to read the expression on his face, a look of irony mixed with sadness.

The nice little old lady in the window seat looked quite matronly while sleeping, but she hadn't slept soundly, and she awoke amid a jolting turbulence that had turned Aurelia white. Knowing that Rae was a nervous flyer and about to hyperventilate, Gene began telling funny stories about bad dates he'd gone on since becoming a bachelor. The elderly passenger beside them woke in mid-story.

"I tell you, my love life, 'fraid it has been nothing short of an episodic horror novel. Like one of those Evan Kingsbury books!"

"Come now, your life can't possibly be as bad as all that!"

"Truth be known, nothing in a Kingsbury novel could compete with my love life. Maybe it's why I find Evan so comforting."

He produced a copy of Fire & Flesh that he'd brought to reread for the trip. "No, all kidding aside, I could convey to you the worst of the worst blind and computer match dates any man ever encountered on the planet–if I thought you could stomach the tale."

"It couldn't be any worse than…than…" she searched for words… "than the damnable dates I've been on."

"I could match you failure for failure, heartache for heartache," dearie, added the gray-haired passenger beside them. She then chuckled with a memory.

All three next began swapping tales of bad dates, attempting to win the dubious prize. Gene told them of the time a blind date insisted on bringing her cockatoo with her on the date."

"Bull…you've got to be kidding. You are kidding, aren't you?" Aurelia asked, shaking her head.

"The bird was on hand to evaluate the film, she told me.

Said she trusted his ratings above those of Roger Ebert!"

The ladies laughed openly. Gene added, "And I swear the bird was really there to rate me as a date."

"What movie did you see?" asked the old lady.

"*Signs*...Mel Gibson at his worst."

"What did the bird think of it?"

"She and the bird couldn't get past its being Mel. They didn't want to hear the litany of clichés the movie posed, or that Mel only had one expression for fear, a dropped jaw, or the fact the so-called horror film made no sense and had not one frightful event in it. So long as Mel was on screen."

"More to the point," said Aurelia, "what did the bird think of your performance, Gee?"

Gene hesitated. "Frankly, I didn't get much of a chance to perform, but suffice to say, that damned bird had a foul mouth on him, and he had a huge jealous streak...."

"Ah...a rival for her affections...the unkindest cut...ahhh critic of all."

"Pulled no punches?" asked the little lady.

Gene frowned, his beard and mustache twitching. "To say the least. The worst part of the date came after dinner."

"Hold on...did the bird accompany you and–"

"Felicia."

"Felicia to dinner?"

"Felicia insisted on creating a full-blown, home cooked meal for me and the bird. The bird watched over us like a doting father. If the bird became agitated, it'd squawk as if someone were trying to wring its neck–me, I guess–and it became agitated for...for reasons unknown in the universe. But every agitated squawk acted as a mark against me."

"Felicia was keeping score?"

"On a freaking notepad, yeah!"

Aurelia held back a laugh while the little lady beside her released her pent up laughter in a gushing flood, almost losing her bridge. Gene kept talking over the laughter. "If Felix– Felicia had named her male bird Felix–if the bird became docile, my score went up." This brought on more laughter and hawing and ultimately coughing and choking from the grandma san.

"I see." Aurelia could not help but laugh along now. She apologized as she did so.

"Go ahead, laugh. I laughed my ass off, although Felicia didn't understand why. She thought I was retarded. Anyway, end result, she is with bird, I am with Voltan, my Great Dane, who would make a quick and easy meal of Felix. So...you think you can top that one?"

"All right, here goes." Aurelia started in on the tale of the one-eyed man named Snake with whom she'd gone out on a date, thanks to a so-called friend who thought she and Snake, actual name Henry, would have a lot in common.

"Snake...but Snake is really a Henry? That's already scary."

"Henry Hobbes.... Snake was his biker name. I like bikes, I have a Harley in my garage, but that doesn't mean I'm going to fall for a weasel trying to make himself a wolf-hound by dressing in leather and calling himself Snake."

"So what happened on the date?"

"I uhh...I broke his jaw."

"Broke his jaw?" Gene tried to contain his laughter, but was unable to.

"In two places," she added.

"Why did you break his jaw?"

"When I say no, I freakin' mean no."

The gray-haired lady asked, "Did you break his nose?"

"I threw his back out."

"Did you wind up taking him to the emergency room?" asked Gene.

"To get my foot out of his ass, yeah! How did you know?"

The three of them drew looks now as they laughed uproariously.

Rae caught her breath and asked, "Gee, why can't all men be like you?"

"Yeah...well, what can I say? Been making excuses for my gender for the better part of my life."

"Any other man'd be asking me stupid questions by now.

Like, you're a psychic, so why couldn't you've seen it coming? Henry and I settled out of court."

"That was going to be my next question," he said in jest.

"All right, go ahead. Tell me, I should've seen it coming, being a psychic, but how many times does it take for me to learn, I don't do my life. I do the lives of others. Premonitions and foresight into my own personal relationships, nahhh...it just isn't happening."

"Who is any good at foretelling his own relationship? Look at ninety percent of the population? What the bleep do we know anyhow?"

"Given the divorce rate, you mean?" asked the old lady.

"Exactly...exactly."

Not long after, the lady beside Rae was again lulled to sleep. Rae took the opportunity to peek again into the file on the missing Julian Redondo. A strangely prophetic poem lay in Julian's file, a facsimile of the original that read:

Carnivore Man

The blood-red Demon of Demons
Kills angels
While swinging a silver-green sword
And a smoking black hammer,
His tail a spiked venomous blade...
And the Blue Lady of the Bay
Cannot keep death away,
For the red Demon will come
On the arm
Of Bloody Mary.
When he chooses one,
No tears or anger,
Bad language or prayer
Will keep death
In its fearful lair
But it will break out
And it will come

PSI: Blue

At a time
Of full moon rising
Or by day
And by the grace
Of the Blue Lady
Who knows enough
To say
That death is preferable
To life on the street.

By Julian Estaban Redondo

It was signed in a flowing script that denoted pride, according to the handwriting expert whose report helped fill out Julian's profile. She said he was well adjusted, his handwriting showing no peculiarities or disquieting aspects.

"What do you make of the poem, Gee?" She turned the poem over to a doodling scratched on the back. Idle lines depicting errant stars and planets and a homey little cottage on the moon.

"I make of it one lonely boy."

"And the Blue Lady?"

"Imagine it's a fantasy mother who becomes death."

"Hell of an image. Some powerful symbolism in that. And it recalls to mind a recurrent nightmare."

"What nightmare?" he asked. "You've not told me of any nightmares."

"They're likely nothing. You know, for a fifteen-year-old boy, this is damn good writing," she added, clearly not wanting to discuss the disturbing dream of the blue-lit green park of angels and the red demon's ugly coral reef.

"Can't argue that." Gene reached over and closed the file, realizing that the little lady beside Aurelia had awakened again and was staring–slack-jawed–at the autopsy photos.

"Are...are you two medical examiners or something?" asked the lady now.

"FBI, ma'am," Aurelia replied, flashing her badge.

"Oh, how exciting."

"Yes, thank you, ma'am."

"Rosette, my name is Rosette DuSable. Do you think I could get your autographs? For my grandchild, you see?"

"Well...no one's ever asked for my autograph before," said Gene, flattered.

The little lady frowned. "Nor mine, I can assure you."

"What could it hurt?" he asked.

After writing their names on the lady's napkin, they grew silent.

"Oh, please, don't stop in your important work on my account, please," said Rosette. "It won't in the least trouble me. At my age, trust me, I've seen it all."

"I'll bet you have," said Gene.

"The autopsy photos cause you no disturbance?" Aurelia asked.

"Worked as an ER-trauma nurse for thirty five years. I can handle it, dear. Seen it all," she repeated, smirking.

As the plane neared its destination, Gene Kiley, at ten thousand feet over the Arizona desert, pointed out the Grand Canyon in the distance. Rae had told him of her plan to go there with Nia. "It's an absolutely mind-blowing experience. You and Nia will love it. Only wish I could be there to see...that is to share it with the two of you. To see the expression on your faces."

Aurelia, bent on seeing as much of the great chasm as possible, leaned in over the retired nurse she'd come to know as Rosette. Rosette tolerated it well. When the Grand Canyon became a blur, Aurelia settled back into her seat. Rosette now commented on how horrible the dating scene had become for her age group as well. "Just since my Verner died. Oh, I knew it would be hard to replace a man like Verner, but all the same, I had no idea how impossible the odds were until I got back out there, on the market."

Aurelia and Gene exchanged a look and fought back a mild hysteria that only worsened as Rosette began to prattle on, adding, "I've tried everything, even computer dating. You would not believe the scags and scalawags that come out of the woodwork. My granddaughter put me on some computer profile thing, and next thing I know, I am having coffee and donuts with the likes of Lee Harvey Oswald."

"It was that bad, huh?" asked Aurelia.

"I am not easily given to exaggeration."

Gene whispered in Aurelia's ear, "I wish we had a moment alone. Just the two of us. I know it's going to get crazy once we make Phoenix."

"Crazy, yeah, highly likely. What's on your mind, Gee? What's got you so agitated?"

"You haven't a clue, have you?"

"Frankly…no."

"Nia's right about you, you know."

"What's Nia got to do with this?"

"She tells me sometimes you can be ahhh….kinda…well rather thick. I mean…"

"No, that's not Nia's term for it. She says I can be the densest person on the planet if I'm not honed in on her current emotional state, which changes with lightning speed. But, Gee…why're we talking about this? My private life?"

Gene took her hand in his and for a moment became befuddled of speech, lost in the deep pools of her black left eye and right cerulean eye. "I have been trying to tell you for some time now…"

"Tell me what?"

Rosette jabbed her in the ribs. "Isn't it obvious, dearie?"

Aurelia's head felt like it bobbed on a spring between the two of them, searching for whatever the hell it was that was supposed to be obvious when Gene's hand tightened around hers, and she felt an inkling of the emotion and demand he meant to convey. Even so, he was failing miserably.

"Ahhh…no…tell me it ain't so. Gee? Gee?"

"Aurelia, I have so much feeling for you, feelings I feel so ahhh…deeply and ahhh…feelingly."

Shaking her head, she pleaded, "Please, Gee…don't

ahhh...don't take this wrong but ahhh...ye-Gods, I don't know that I can take...I mean, I am flattered, Gene, but ahhh...we can't be thinking such thoughts about one another if–"

"And why not? We make each other laugh. We like each other's company. Nia likes me, and I like Nia."

"You only think you like Nia and me."

"No, it's...more than I can put into words."

"Then don't try."

"It's larger than words can convey, my feelings for you and Nia."

At least he hadn't ever referred to Nia as excess baggage, she thought. But there was something wrong about his sudden revelation of love. She felt uncomfortable at the thought, like being told by a favorite uncle that he wanted to sleep with her. Not that Gene was that much older, but he'd always been like a father in his infinite capacity to make her feel safe both while out of body and immediately after a trance reading.

There'd never been the remotest hint of sexual attraction on either his part or hers in their "warming down" sessions. Their encounters so far as she'd known had always been that of trusted friends. She now racked her brain for any slight moment during which he'd ever unduly touched her or held her over long. She sat here already realizing that his proposal that they become an item had already tainted their long-standing platonic relationship.

"You had to have had some idea how he felt..." muttered Rosette, frowning.

Gee added, "Feels." He was sweating it, uncomfortable with the long silence between them.

Apparently, Rosette also disliked silence, saying, "A woman's supposed to know, and you're not just a woman but an FBI detective."

A medium at that, thought Rae.

Rosette added, "You had to've had some inkling?"

She wanted to shout to the old lady, Stay out of it! Instead she pasted on a fake smile. "I'm sorry, Gene, but I have to talk to you about this in private."

"Sure…sure thing."

"Perhaps maybe sometime after we arrive? Have to sort this out."

"Sure…sure, Rae."

"You understand?"

"Yes…perfectly. Take some getting used to the idea."

She held back the thought she'd never get used to this idea.

"Nia needs a good strong man in her life," whispered the elderly woman at her side, and when Aurelia looked at her, she saw her father instead, a kind of hologram taking up the same space, as the narcoleptic Ms. Rosette was actually asleep again.

She answered in thought only: *I can't fathom this idea, no matter if it is seconded by my spectral father.* Warning bells–alarms screaming: Never go down this path with Gene Kiley. She listed in her head all the reasons why, and all the ways to tell him no. First off, her and Nia's battles would soon wear a sensitive like Gee to a frazzle; he'd be so caught up emotionally in taking both sides, that it would drain him. Besides, her life in general was a melodramatic shambles, and her finances in ruin thanks to the tax shelter bed and breakfast and Tomi Yoshikani. Any sane man would run screaming from a screwed up life with Aurelia Murphy Hiyakawa. Turmoil her constant companion, and that alone ought to dissuade him from ever again broaching the subject. But it wouldn't because there was so much he didn't know.

She mentally said to her father's image beside her: *The worst part of it all is that Gee has ruined a perfectly fine, seamless, unspoiled, faultless textbook working relationship with this sudden bomb.*

"Nonsense," Hiro replied.

But how do I trust him to be there to catch me, to be my safety net, to be mine in the capacity he has always been before proposing these…these damnable ridiculous feelings.

"Since when are feelings to be condemned?"

Damnable ridiculous feelings coming out of some romantic notion of who I am.

"You're being rather hard on the man and yourself."

But, Pappa...this really troubles me. Aurelia outwardly smiled at Gene while concentrating on not screaming. *I like Gene. Hell, I even love the man, but being in love with him, and he me....it's disastrous....*

"Are you all right, dear?" Her father's voice had taken on that of a woman's. It was her mother now in Ms. Rosette's sleeping face.

Yes, mother...just fine, thank you. She turned to Gene and changed the subject on him.

"Ahhh...do you think perhaps I was too hard on Etta, I mean perhaps I went at her too gung-ho, and that maybe a slower paced approach might've been in order? It went so badly with us."

"Etta?" he replied, confused.

"She's still so blind about this guy."

Gene's expression might be read as: *What's that to do with the question at hand?* But he only nodded as if agreeing.

"And there's the case. I have to concentrate on this maniac in ahhh...in Phoenix."

Gene excused himself, saying something about the restroom and working out the kinks in his legs, walking the plane. "Stretch the legs," he repeated, stepping off.

His retreat was a gesture that gave Aurelia some relief.

Rosette, her father, and her mother all remained silent beside her. A twinge of self-loathing and doubt lingered like a nebulous lining around an imprecise cloud; regret at probably having said the wrong thing for the right reason. Or having said the right thing for the wrong reason. In fact, she felt as confused as much as filled with remorse at having hurt Gee, of most assuredly fumbling through, and uttering precisely the wrong words. This mixed concern worried and filled Aurelia's heart and mind. *God, I hope Gene isn't going to ever broach the subject again. And God I hope I didn't hurt him too awfully.*

Etta, she thought. *I'll call Etta again. A good friend is a persistent friend.* She dialed Etta's number back in DC.

Etta wasn't answering. She had caller ID. She knew it was her, and she knew she was calling from the plane. Damned bitch.

Aurelia gave a thought to her immediate future, to stepping off the plane in Phoenix, to facing the challenge awaiting her. The suspense of her rushing headlong toward her prey had begun a slow build, a kind of restrained, measured crescendo within her. Who the hell's got time for romance anyway, she wondered.

Aurelia also found herself at once curiously thinking about why Edwin Arlington Coffin had seemed in such a rush to come ahead of them, to be in Phoenix a few hours sooner. He'd made some remark about setting up the technical aspects of the visit. But this did not jive with his enthusiasm. She recalled his excitement in having "gotten her the gig." Again she wondered about Coffin's motive. Why he had so wanted this trip. Was he just so happy to get away from his controlling parents?

The fasten seat belt sign lit up with a metallic ping. She watched Gene come back toward her with a wide grin. "Fooled you good, there Rae. Gotcha!"

"What?"

"I was just testing you...your circuitry actually. See if I could, you know, get a rise outta you, and I did. You took me so seriously!" He put on a good laugh for extra measure.

She knew what she knew, and he'd not been attempting humor when he'd "proposed" they try themselves on as a couple. This was a lame attempt to take it back and return to ground zero, wipe the slate clean–all quite impossible?

A part of her had already begun gunny-sacking away a bit of anger toward this dear friend and colleague.

"So, did you call Etta again? Saw you on the phone."

"She's not taking my calls."

The captain's voice came over the PA. "Ladies and gentleman, the temperature in Phoenix is a balmy eighty-six with sunshine projected all week. Enjoy your stay and thank you for flying United. We should be at the gate in ten minutes barring any unforeseen delays."

Unforeseen delays, Aurelia thought...unforeseen bombshells like the one Gene Kiley had laid on me?

The amusement park midway had been so heated by the 7 a.m. sun beating down that now the raindrop splattered pavement instantly steamed over, a cloud of it rising over the park. This steam appeared to have a life of its own, a growing, evolving, delicately woven creature. In Cy's state of mind, having been touched by angel or devil the night before, the ghostly circulating steam had eyes. Catlike, narrow eyes. One black, one blue, and they looked out of the empty mist straight at him.

Then a sudden harsh bright light flooded the midway, blinding him and dissipating the steam cloud and the disembodied eyes he'd thought there a moment before–just gone. All of it replaced by the sound of the wrecking ball taking down the Flesh Reaper scaffolding, and the accompaniment of the jackhammers still working to loosen the foundation moorings.

The wrecking ball that smashed into the old boards of the condemned rollercoaster just the other side of the fence suddenly became a rhythmic, incessant, ceaseless *kerrrrrcrack, kerrrrrcrack, kerrrrrcrack. Like a nail being driven through my damned head,* Cy thought.

As chief of grounds maintenance, someone might've told him about this pachyderm monster machine going on three shifts now–twenty-four hours without let up. But no…not these clowns.

Knowing it now, however, Cy felt vindicated at holding onto his beliefs–or rather disbelief in some supernatural element lurking about the fair, as if the souls of those he'd killed had banded together to haunt him here. Yes, sure he had felt eyes on him. Obviously, there had been men behind those lights, men standing in the dark the other side of the mist and smoke, corporeal entities that had been curiously watching him with rank indifference if not a little mirth from afar.

This explained a lot.

However, he continued to wonder how they made him feel touched, how pressure had been clandestinely applied to his body. He so wanted these men, the real custodians and builders and engineers of the park to step forward–to get the joke done with and simply laugh at him, explaining how they had done it, how they had successfully raised the hair on his entire body with some special effects.

But not a one of them so much as smirked or broke into smile; no one stepped forward. And he was left with the steady alternative of the demonic wrecking ball that someone had painted huge, giant eyes on and a happy face.

He realized it for the first time.

The wrecking ball had eyes, one black, one blue, framed in a pair of horn-rimmed glasses instead of a mirror. The wrecking ball crew, for whatever reason, had accomplished a makeover of the ball–and these were the eyes that had been lurking, watching him, encroaching all along. Getting nearer right along with the demolition and the continual *kerrrrcrack*! *Kerrrrcrack* of ripping, tearing lumber. Only the blue eye was not blue; it had only appeared blue in shadow. On closer inspection the eyes were identical.

Still…now so much of the mystery of the last few days of sensing someone or some thing eerily watching him made obvious sense.

Cy breathed easier and with a renewed energy in his step, completed the trash cleanup job he'd left for daylight.

Over the 747's PA, came the captain's commanding voice, telling everyone aboard that in twenty years of flying and trying, that he'd just made the perfect landing. They were on the ground and no one aboard had felt the tires touch ground, as the captain'd made the transition so smoothly. The cabin erupted in response, cheers, hooting, and clapping.

The angels and demons awaiting Rae here seemed dispelled

by a sure reality, her doubts and misgivings gone, replaced by a certainty she could do some good here amid the warmth of mountain-rimmed Phoenix. Still, she felt sure she'd see them all again: the angels, the demons, the self-doubt, and the misgivings.

From where she sat, Rae saw the activity around an FBI car parked near the terminal. An FBI entourage awaited them. "I feel like a head of state," Gene joked.

"A lot of hullabaloo, but what I don't see is any sign of Eddy Coffin. Do you?"

"No...nowhere to be seen."

On departing, they'd been diverted at the gate and routed by a black-suited G-man in dark glasses. This fellow led them to the local ASAC–Assistant Special Agent in Charge–Theopolis Redeoux, a dark-haired, bright-eyed young looking thirty-five who'd recently solved several perplexing cases that'd garnered national attention. Some in the FBI family talked of his one day rising to the top as director. It could happen, Aurelia thought. He's both handsome and quite smart...certainly sharp enough to call on psychic intervention when needed.

Redeoux introduced them to a small army of men and women working on the task force to put an end to the career of this predatory monster. The title of Julian Redondo's poem popped into her mind: Carnivore Man.

"I met your young genius, Coffin, earlier," Redeoux said to her, as he led them to his car. "He is quite the character. Has a little surprise for you." Redeoux's fingers were manicured, his mustache carefully trimmed above an equally cared for goatee, and he wore a three-piece suit that appeared tailor made and warm in this climate, but he seemed immune to perspiration. His manners proved impeccable, and his mannerisms far from parochial, in fact, downright continental. His polished politician's handshake and demeanor certainly marked him for bigger and better things; no doubt he had high aspirations.

Rae halted at his opening her car door for her, saying, "So you say Edwin has a surprise for us?"

"He does, and an amazing one at that, should it actually

work, but I must say, I have my doubts." With an expansive wave of the hand, Redeoux indicated she climb into the interior

"Nothing that Edwin Arlington Coffin might do would surprise me." She slid into the sedan, Gene alongside her. Aside from being her empath, Gee had also been assigned as her FBI bodyguard. She was to go nowhere without Gee, as she was valuable to the FBI.

"This...this gizmo of his is...well...pretty remarkable," Redeoux, said, sticking his head into the rear for a moment. "Coffin's been working on it night and day for a year." Redeoux closed the door on them.

"Whatever it is," confided Gene, "I imagine with Edwin it'll be big."

"Must be what Edwin's been so excited about. His palm-pilot CRAWL, he told me about. Why he had to get here before us."

"Then it's no surprise after all?" Gene asked.

"Eddy can't keep a secret."

When Redeoux climbed in beside his driver, she asked the ASAC, "Has this surprise of Coffin's to do with the investigation?"

"It does, but I am sworn to secrecy. He wants to show you himself, Dr. Hiyakawa."

"Please, no formalities necessary. Call me Rae." She didn't want to burst Redeoux bubble, but it sounded like Edwin was playing it up big.

"And call me Gene," added Kiley. "Exactly where is Coffin now?"

"Not absolutely sure, actually."

"Not sure?" pressed Gene.

"Said he'd meet us here, but I've not seen him in several hours."

Aurelia thought about it for a moment. "Not like Edwin to just disappear unless he has a lab to work in. Perhaps he's using your labs?"

"Edwin's convinced us to give him carte blanche with all our resources, so he may well be, yes."

The sedan pulled from its idle position and started for the hotel, just as Redeoux began telling them about the nice rooms he'd gotten for them.

"If you don't mind, I'd first like to see the area where the last two victims seem to've vanished, this Toby and Julian?"

"Last seen in a forested area off a park, yes."

"A city park? Can we make that detour?"

"Absolutely."

They drove across town to the site where the Hispanic boy, Julian, and his Caucasian friend, Toby, had disappeared in midday as if they'd stepped into another dimension. Or so the talk went. "One minute they was there, and the next they was gone," another youth testified when questioned.

One moment among friends, a crowd even, and the next, gone. It had the feel of a Shirley Jackson story, the feel of a lottery, a sacrifice even. Aurelia and Gene and most trained law enforcement officials took such stories and eyewitness accounts, however, with a huge grain of salt, and if those telling the story were pushed on it, the facts came out skewed differently every time. The element of time itself in such tales was often bent to fit the tale, or to excuse some other small detail left from the telling. No one was more adept at leaving out the element of time, or bending time to his needs than a child witness, and from all accounts, the park that day was filled with children, some of whom knew and "hung" with Julian and Toby.

"Julian was shaping up to be a leader among his crowd," said Redeoux as the car windows flashed the life on the streets here in Phoenix under a blindingly blue and cloudless sky. Billboards and signs and small businesses and strip malls came in and out of the frame of this rolling 'window film'. Behind them followed a small entourage in two vehicles, all the principle people on the Phantom investigation team. These men and women had been working the case for months without consequential result. While they had followed countless leads down innumerable blind alleys, the team had recently begun spiraling into frustration and anger, resulting in divisiveness, leading to a bevy of negative thoughts, until now they'd given into personally attacking one another.

Redeoux, ever the gentlemen, did not go into details, but the ASAC'd reported enough to FBI headquarters to paint a clear picture of lost morale—the sort of thing that erodes cooperation and professionalism.

This had factored into Redeoux's decision to involve the psychic detective most notable for solving the unsolvable—Dr. Aurelia Hiyakawa.

Aurelia had sensed this the moment she and Gene had stepped into this company of field agents while she secretly searched for 'field angels' or a green-blue wash of a park where angels felt comfortable in one another's company. She also sensed tightly bottled up dissatisfaction with Redeoux from his team; and the ASAC was as frustrated as anyone. These were child victims, a cop's worst nightmare.

But the largest emotion on the psychic plain of this team seemed a growing sense of murderous rage against their phantom quarry. While the general population could afford such powerful reaction, an agent or tracker on the scent of his prey could not. Aurelia knew that for a psychic hunter, the confluence of rage and anger at one's target only confused the signs, making it too easy to wrongly read any tracks he may've left in his wake. For proud field agents who felt protective of their territory—*This is my town! No one shits on me in my own town!* She felt some understanding of the problems Theopolis Redeoux faced, and how easily she could get sucked into this emotional imbroglio. Embroiled in emotion was not a state of grace, especially in law enforcement. At the same time, she knew that even more than Redeoux's people, she must remain above the normal human inclinations and reactions people must feel toward this madman.

Regardless of what she knew of the internal dynamic of the strike force here in Phoenix, they did put forth a good front. The team looked and acted the professionals, but she felt no doubt whatsoever that a pervasive fear of defeat in this matter had each in a private hell. These wafting emotions filled the sedan.

The car pulled into a city park named for some obscure fellow who'd helped found Phoenix in its beginnings, but ironically it brought biblical irony to the entire case. The sign read: *Abraham Stroud Field–Phoenix Park District*. The car swept by the public parking area where a few cars congregated, scattered people eating from bag lunches, McDonald's, others suspiciously looking like lovers carrying on affairs, secret liaisons, drug connections, all of it. Redeoux's man pulled onto the ball field and swept across it, kicking up a blood red orange cloud of dust–the color of Aurelia's nightmare.

The other cars followed, adding to the thick red earth cloud. All three vehicles had come to an abrupt stop at a playground filled with sturdy wooden jungle gyms, shoots, ladders, swings, vines. Here stood a colorful, giant labyrinth. A man-made fortress of turrets and tunnels of used tires–all set against a backdrop of a deep emerald and jade forest. Young, homeless children sleeping in the nooks and crannies here scattered like field mice, some shouting, some stumbling, all terrified at the sudden disturbance.

Gene and Aurelia watched the scene in awe and sadness.

"Julian was hanging with the homeless," said Redeoux as he, his driver, and the others leapt from their cars, Redeoux ordering a roundup of the 'mice'. The dark suited agents looked like the Keystone cops as they scattered, giving chase to the frightened children.

Gene remained close at hand when Aurelia climbed from the safety of the unmarked FBI sedan to stand in the midst of a modern-day war zone, a ghetto in Phoenix the other side of the forested periphery of the park. She had come home. For while her Japanese ghetto in LA where she grew up was not so horrid as this Hispanic version in Phoenix, it was close enough to bring back difficult memories. Her parents–all parents in that hell–struggled to make ends meet. She'd watched her father and mother work hard for the money to maintain a meager existence. Yet she had felt blessed, not simply because there were many others in the neighborhood who had less than they, but due to her having wonderful parents, a sense of being loved, and a warm and peaceful home. She knew that many of these children had none of the above. She knew that many had never experienced a peaceful, safe, loving home.

Theopolis Redeoux came around the car to stand with the visitors. "This is the place where the two boys–and not far from here–others vanished without a trace."

Redeoux's driver, who'd earlier introduced himself simply as Fred, added, "One of the kids who disappeared…he was plucked right out of a schoolyard just down a ways. Was playing basketball with his friends after hours."

"Julian himself was, at that time, a 'witness' to the abduction, but none of the boys made any sense. Talked about some supernatural beings at war with one another, nonsense about a blue lady and someone they called Bloody Mary."

"We followed leads, made raids, held over every pervert in Phoenix and the boroughs around Phoenix, all the usual suspects."

"But nothing clicked," added Fred with a grunt.

The noise of men beating the bushes and shouting surrounded them as the search for the mice continued.

Redeoux lit a carved wooden pipe and continued. "Phoenix PD put out the Amber alert, held over, and grilled hundreds of for questioning."

"Nothing clicked," repeated Fred, lighting up a Marlboro, his narrow eyes squinting in the brilliant sun as birds chased one another in the falling red dust cloud among the bushes here. Aurelia took note of how the red dust lightly painted the deep green leaves. The park was an Oasis in a city filled with sand and rock. Fred continued speaking between puffs. "And not a damn thing come of the wild rantings of those kids, not even a smart kid like Julian."

Aurelia began to walk in an ever-widening circle about the playground, instinctively touching objects that Julian may have touched, from swing seats, chains, poles to fence uprights. Redeoux stepped a little ways off and came back to them, cautiously watching the psychic work.

Redeoux now said in her ear, "From what the others told us of Julian's disappearance, the boy was injured playing basketball."

"He'd been checked hard in the face," she replied.

"Yeah...read that in the report, huh?"

"No...no mention of the type of injury beyond a bloody nose."

"We think he got into an altercation with one of the other boys. They said it was accidental, but I came to another conclusion. He was an outsider and this was his initiation."

"Did he pass?"

"He took a beating until this kid Toby Slayter stepped in and ended it. But yeah, he passed.

"But he was run off. He didn't really fit in as hard as he tried but it was no go," she countered.

"You're very good on this surface stuff. I hope you're as good on the big question...."

"The big question?"

"Where the hell is Julian Redondo?"

"And Toby Slayter...and are they still alive?" added Fred.

These men desperately wanted answers.

"Anyway," added Redeoux, biting on his carved pipe, "Julian went off to lick his wounds, from what I gather, ambled off from the others. Toby went after him, his only ally. Once alone, tending to an ankle or a cut on his cheek or a bloody nose or a combination of all three, he went through the forest here, the quickest, shortest route home, Toby following–or so accounts tell us."

Fred jumped in here. "So his basketball buddies said."

"Any sign of a scuffle, a fight in the bushes, dropped items?" asked Gene. "The exact spot where the boys might've encountered an abductor? That's where Aurelia wants to begin."

"Sorry, we swept the whole area, every inch, and we turned up nada, zip," said Redeoux.

Fred added, "PPD got nothing either."

"Fred, want you to round up the kids who last saw Toby and

Slayter walk off that night."

"Those kids've been grilled up and down, sidewise, and through, and besides, they've scattered," countered Fred.

"Just find 'em, Fred." Redeoux punctuated with his pipe.

Fred gnashed his teeth but nodded. "Maybe one or two of 'em will be in the herd we're rounding up."

"Let's try to remember these're kids not goats, Fred."

"You've worked alongside psychics before," she said to Redeoux when Fred stepped away to oversee the 'round up'.

"From Louisiana, Mother read tea leaves."

She smiled at this while Gene frowned.

Redeoux, seeing Gene's reaction, added, "Hey man, I'm part Cajun. Enough said?"

"Quite enough," she replied.

"Perhaps Julian went off, or was sent packing for another reason," said Gene, "other than an injury from a fight."

"Perhaps his friends were covering for him," Aurelia added. "Perhaps he was into something that led to his being more vulnerable than his friends. Perhaps he's not quite the goodie, goodie mamma's boy he's been painted."

"Painted may not be a term you wanna sling around here, especially if you speak to the parents," said Redeoux.

"I didn't mean to sound insensitive."

"I'm sure. Look, do you think he may've been dealing in something out here?"

"I hate having to be automatically suspicious, but there's no skirting the possibility. It needed vocalizing."

"Always difficult to broach with parents, this issue, as every street cop knows," added Gene.

All of them knew that drugs so often led to death in the end. A lot of young people fell victim because they lived a lifestyle that placed them in danger on a daily basis. Still, she could be entirely wrong about this; it was impossible to know just yet. Regardless–even if Julian were trafficking in something he ought not be involved in, no one deserved the kind of torture and death meted by the Phantom.

All previous victims had had closed casket funerals for

good reason, so bruised and damaged were their faces from the series of beatings and burns they'd been subjected to. From all accounts, a cigar had made the burn marks into the flesh. Forensics experts had determined it to be Blackstone cigarillos from the microscopic evidence left in the wounds. So precise was the forensics team on this that they'd narrowed the tobacco down to a single batch shipped and sold on a single day, and from there, it was narrowed to a handful of stores in the Greater Phoenix area that might be breaking the law, selling tobacco to minors. Whoever tortured and killed these boys for kicks, he bought cheap cigars in downtown shops like Smokey Joe's or Smoker Friendly.

But so far, no substantive lead had come from that direction. Some taskforce members were working this angle, threatening to close down every tobacco shop in the city if necessary. As a result sales records were being combed through.

The FBI profilers had him between the ages of twenty-five and forty-five, likely Hispanic, possibly Caucasian and Spanish mixed blood. Possibly conflicted about his parentage; possibly abused as a child. Possibly killed cats and dogs and smaller animals as a child. Possibly enjoyed watching say a scorpion and a tarantula fight to the death in a glass jar when a child. Possibly frequented the many illegal cockfights around the city. Possibly frequented racetracks, truck rallies and wrestling matches. Most likely a less than skilled laborer but perhaps in the building or construction trades. Most likely a blue-collar worker with a history of work-related problems and a person who, while hiding it well, is socially ill adjusted. He'd learned to fake a lot and to blend in. Probable that he lives with a domineering wife or mother, who is likely the only person on the planet he manages to get along with. Only woman who even relates to him on any significant level, although there are problems seething beneath the surface. It's a superficial relationship at best; no depth or commitment on either side. A low-level resentment of the mother...or wife...or both. Not to overlook a deep-seated, long-standing hatred of women in general. Kids as well, and in particular young male Hispanics.

So investigators had to ask why. Why these targeted boys were targets to begin with. Perhaps the profiling team at the BSU at Quantico was right, perhaps the man-turned-fiend had long before filled up a huge psychological gunnysack with his resentments until said bag simply exploded. The end result of some recent trauma in his life as in being fired or seeing his mother die.

A profile was a good start, she believed, but they typically fell short, and they lacked imagination and vision. Items a PSI reader like herself might pluck and prune from the bone yard of a case gone cold often proved the crucial key elements. The BSU people did possess an uncanny sixth sense simply through experience and relying on statistical probabilities, and this often was enough to catch a clumsy killer, but when the lives of children or some other pressing issue were involved, along with a cunning criminal mind, the bosses called on the PSI unit. On people like Aurelia to fill in the significant gaps of a typical profile.

With the street urchins and homeless runaways that'd gone missing, authorities in Phoenix had been slow to respond. Official experience and beliefs had stood the tests so often that logic against it was useless, until a body turned up. In fact, so often police experience set logic aside in a kind of stone trust in 'authorial judgment'.

They wrapped themselves in statistical probability; felt comfort in numbers and the 'sure' knowledge that ninety percent of those kids disappearing had come from other areas of the country to begin with: Chicago, Boston, New York, Kansas City, Omaha, Houston, Dallas, Seattle, not to mention Canada. They were viewed as trespassers, transients, and delinquents, and they came from elsewhere, tarried briefly, and continued on their way. Phoenix authorities gave thanks that most street kids kept going for Vegas, LA, and Hollywood–the runaway's Mecca. "Hollywood is every poor kid's Neverland," went the consensus. "It's where kids vanish," one Phoenix cop had opined.

Hollywood, like Daytona Beach, Florida, shone like a

beacon for these lost children, a Mecca for the runaway. But Phoenix too was a beacon in the long trek toward their sad dream. They came, they squatted, they learned what public services they might avail themselves of, they learned the streets, who ran things, and they lingered or moved on. So many in fact moved on that the disappearance of any number of them did not at first excite the interest of the PPD or the local FBI field office. But when the missing and supposed departed began showing up in Sun-city logo dumpsters and in storm drains and city parks, one floating in a pond where people sailed their remote controlled boats, looking like a large psychedelic doll, a demand to end the horrible series of murders went out. With the disappearance of Julian, a child who was not a runaway or homeless, the outcry became a citywide front page event.

Aurelia felt the atmosphere thick with fear; a sense of a siege had settled in over Phoenix.

"What're you mulling over, Rae? What do you think, Rae?" Gene gently asked her as she walked about the empty basketball court. It was a school day, so the neighborhood playground stood empty, save for the disenfranchised homeless and some busy squirrels chasing one another about in a manner that seemed the epitome of madness, passion, and fun.

"I think I wanna be a squirrel in another life," she replied, pointing. "But I want it now."

"A squirrel, really?"

"Squirrels have more fun than the usual rodent."

She calmly focused her mind and attempted to get any feel whatsoever of Julian. She sat for a time in a swing he may or may not have used. Then she slowly followed a trail leading from the playground and into the nearby wooded area. Gene and the entourage followed like a row of ducks. The chase after the fleeing mice had ended with no result.

She came to a clearing the other side of the trees. The clearing, once pristine, was littered with the leavings of the hopeless–beer cans, a carpet of cigarette butts, discarded wrappers, used hypodermic needles, cardboard boxes turned into 'shelter', and mattresses dragged here from city dumps. In one wooded nook stood a table replete with ashtray, a book, and a lamp, its cord dangling useless here. Beside this surreal still life squatted a ratty, discarded pool chair.

"'Home away from 'ome?" asked Gene.

She lifted the dog-eared paperback book, a worn copy of a novel entitled Whiskey Sour by J.A. Konrath. Some passages had been underlined in dull pencil marks.

"We have a homeless problem that the city council and the mayor say is a transient problem," Redeoux said, shrugging, his tone apologetic. "Or rather a transitory problem."

"Really?" she asked.

"City Hall thrives on a good euphemism. They use a metaphor downtown, that this particular problem is like a river that runs through it–our town–but it will soon dry up and turn its course elsewhere."

"And how long've they been waiting for it to dry up?" She waved his reply off, not expecting an answer.

"Too long, no doubt," interjected Gene.

"This old park's become a favorite meeting place for young people. Lot of exchanges go on here," added Redeoux.

Fred had returned and now stamped out his cigarette butt. "Drugs, sex, you name it. Barter heaven. If you talk to other homeless, they'll lead you here as well."

"We've long been aware of this place, but Julian went off in that direction," began Redeoux, pointing, "according to witnesses."

"But you discount your witnesses? Other teens covering for Julian, thinking they're doing him a favor, you think?" she asked.

"Correct. Precisely what I think."

She closed her eyes, her hands outstretched, taking the measure of what felt like a meeting place, some sort of outdoor, homeless court, the spindly chair a thrown of sorts. "Somehow, he wound up here in this clearing a defendant in some sort of trial," she offered.

"Julian was not one of them; he was not a shelter kid."

Redeoux relit his pipe.

"Yes, but he wanted to belong. I can feel his presence here, and he felt judged."

"Whoa, big stretch," muttered Fred with a skeptic's eye-roll.

She ignored this. "He was drawn here…possibly lured by another kid his own age, this Toby perhaps, someone he thought was a friend, someone who betrayed him…set him up. At least, this is the feeling that is coming through."

"Set up for a beating, you mean? Here in the park?"

"No…worse than that."

"Set up for abduction by Toby, but this Toby's also missing," said Redeoux. "It only makes sense if Toby surfaces or is found in another jurisdiction?"

She nodded. "Sill, I sense someone working for this predatory monster who has Julian now, but I get no sense of Toby's being in danger."

"That's one hell of a leap, Agent Hiyakawa."

"I can only go by my instincts and what my sixth sense tells me."

Redeoux bit his lip. "And it tells you that Julian was into something that led him here in a secretive rendezvous with a third party?"

"Someone rootless, alone, trying to survive, and being used—most likely someone who'd won Julian's confidence."

"There are literally thousands of homeless teens on these streets," said Redeoux. "I suppose one of them could've become an accomplice to murder…."

Gene quickly added, "She means like a pimp, a procurer, right, Rae?"

Aurelia put up a hand to Gene and the others. "Such a third party to this deadly tryst may well be more than a mere procurer."

"Meaning?" asked Redeoux.

"Meaning he or she may've once been victimized by the maniac, an early on victim, but one in whom the Phantom has placed great faith to bait other and more victims. Someone the killer has indoctrinated under pain of torture."

"A form of brainwashing," added Gene.

"You're suggesting that the killer turned out one of his victims, set him free to act as bait for boys like Toby and Julian?" asked Redeoux.

"Or this Toby is the procurer," said Gene.

"Imagine that," said Fred.

"Yes, imagine it. The horror of the tortures this maniac inflicts," replied Redeoux, "is definitely enough to train a young person to do your bidding."

"Somebody in cohorts with the predator," she summed up. "Could be this Toby kid enticed his new friend to become the next victim, and then Toby freaked and left town."

Fred added, "Hopped a freighter for parts unknown."

"No one on the teams even remotely suggested this as a possibility before now," commented Redeoux.

"Makes a certain amount of sense," agreed big Fred.

"It may not be Toby, however," she cautioned, laying the book back onto the table in the woods. "It could be someone else harvesting these victims, which makes Toby not missing but a victim as well."

"We could run a sweep, pick up every homeless kid on the streets say within a fifty mile radius of this location," suggested Redeoux. "It'll take a lot of manpower and man hours, but it may be worth it if it yields an accomplice."

Until now every indication was that the Phantom worked alone. His ability to strike in broad daylight without leaving a trace had been touted as near supernatural, a regular phantom in this horror story he'd wrought. "Perhaps the press and the public have given the SOB more credit than he deserves," suggested Gene, echoing Aurelia's thoughts.

"If he's using a street kid well known to the area, how better to fit in and go unnoticed," added Aurelia.

"Clever," said Redeoux.

"Cowardly," countered Aurelia.

"Let's get on it, men," shouted Redeoux, whose men had gathered round. "Coordinate with PPD's runaways and homeless division. Nobody knows the street kids like they do.

We'll throw out a net, see what gets dragged in."

"A dragnet will just send this person into hiding," she countered.

"What do you suggest?"

"Whoever he is, the procurer's quite aware of what he's doing," said Gene.

"And he's likely filled to his eyeballs with guilt, but his fear right now is greater," she added, pushing an errant lock of hair from her eyes, "perhaps beyond all reason."

"Sure, well, yes," agreed Theopolis, "if this third party does exist, he knows he doesn't want to be painted to death."

She nodded vigorously. "He realizes that all the kids he's procured to stand in for him, have been killed; he's got to be suffering with the idea that Julian will soon be killed as well. But he's also feeling he has no one to turn to, that this predator is omniscient and can grab him off the street at any time and return him to whatever torture rack he peeled him off of. He is even likely feeling in some twisted way that he owes his life–miserable as it is–to the Phantom for having spared him."

A sudden rustle in the bushes alerted them. They'd overlooked one of the mice. "We are not alone," Gene muttered.

Redeoux's men rushed the scraggily dressed young man whose sleep had been disturbed by the sudden small crowd that had stumbled on his wooded home. When they snatched him up, he pulled a long bowie knife, which the agent quickly relieved him of. They led him out of the bushes with handcuffs securing his wrists at his back now. Unclean, unshaven, he looked caveman-like, yet he had the stature and gait of a high schooler. He kept shouting at them some unintelligible mumbo-jumbo about having known they were coming for him as if expecting arrest at any time.

"Could we be so lucky?" asked Aurelia, doubtful this was the person she'd imagined as helping the Phantom procure fresh boys to torture and maim.

"What's he saying?" asked Gene. "What's he babbling about?"

"Zoroaster's minions I know are upon me! Blue Lady come and smite them where they stand. Save me, my sweet Savior, please!" the boy repeated again and again. "Get your Zoroaster hands off me! Your touch is like acid to my skin!"

"It's a chant…just about rhymes too," she said, "it's meant to ward off evil, and in this case, that's us."

The kid appeared old and broken, frail and as thin and hungry looking as a refugee from a Nazi prisoner of war camp. Aurelia got that image clearly as she stared at the incoherent boy. His face grime, his hair a nest of vipers, the kid's body appeared stiff, un-giving, icily hard, and his movements reflected this hard exterior.

"Bastard punk pulled a knife on me, Chief," said an agent named Stewart, one of several who'd subdued the feral teen. Stewart held up the knife in his handkerchief now. "No telling how many crimes he's pulled with this monster."

At a distance, it appeared his dirty blonde head was a brain alive with worms, so wild was his hair. His eyes shone fearful where he stood terrified before Redeoux and his men.

Aurelia quickly went to him. "What's your name, son?"

"Whataya think? I'm going to give you another sword of power to hold over me? My name is sacred. Every name is sacred. I don't have to tell you my name; if I do, you have that much more power over me."

"Then what can I call you?"

He stared into her eyes. "Child of the Blue Lady."

Gene stood close by. She turned to him and Redeoux and they huddled together. "Julian's poem, remember? It mentions a Blue Lady and Zoroaster as well, remember, Gene?"

"Trust me, we've been to the Blue Lady," said Redeoux, "right Fred? How many times?"

"Four, boss…four times."

"And the bar, while bizarre, catering to transsexuals, cross-dressers, and gay folks, appears to have nothing to do with the disappearances. We even staked the place out for a week. We came up nada, zip."

She turned back to the boy, who, even cuffed, bolted.

Redeoux's men dragged him back kicking and shouting, "Damn you Zoroasters! Damn you to hell! Zor-oast-ers are here! Zoroaster's legion of devils!"

Aurelia realized now that this was the unintelligible gibberish the other children were shouting as they'd scattered.

"Can I call you Noah?" she calmly asked him, her eyes never leaving his, probing.

The boy was silenced for a moment, staring at her as if she'd struck him. "Devil people! You are all the Devil's own."

"But Zoroaster was a deity of both good and evil. How do you know we are not from the good Zoroaster?"

"Why'd you call me Noah?"

"I like that name. My daughter's about your age, and her name is Nia. I was going to name her Noah if she were a boy, but...."

"You some sort of a witch lady, aren't you?" he asked, staring into her dark Oriental eye and her blue Irish eye, losing himself for a moment in their unique aura. "What're you lady? A social worker looking to adopt me off to somebody? You get extra bonus if you get so many of us adopted out? Saving up for something special? A trip to the Bahamas?"

Cynicism dripped from the child-man.

"I'm an FBI cop, a psychic from Washington DC, and–"

"I knew you were evil! A cop! A fully glorified cop."

"I'm going to call you Noah, all right?" said Gene.

"Noel...my name is Noel. How's that for a joke?"

"I was pretty close then," said Rae.

"Some psychic," he said with a snicker. "Close. You proud of being close? Close never cuts it in this world, lady. Close'll only get you killed."

Another rustle in the bushes alerted them all, everyone turning to see a second young man coming out of hiding, or what seemed hiding. It was a lost Edwin Arlington Coffin, waving and saying how sorry he was for being late, that he'd just missed them at the airport, and only recently learned they were here because Redeoux had called in and left word of their whereabouts. He'd come up from the other side of the park, something about a cab dropping him there.

Gene held up a hand to Coffin as Aurelia continued speaking with Noel. "I'd like to hear more about Zoroaster and the Blue Lady," she told the boy.

He rubbed his yellow peach fuzz beard.

"How long've you been on the streets?" she asked, her eyes searching past the grime to find his. They were a royal blue.

"Since I was maybe eight, nine."

"How old are you now?"

"Wanting my name...wanting my age...you going to put me in the book?"

"No...I am not keeping book on you, Noel. I just...I am curious about you."

"I think I'm seventeen, but I ain't sure of it."

"Where were you born?"

"You are keeping book!"

"All right...truth of it is, I want to write a book, a book about kids just like you, a book I would like to put you in. A book about what you see every day on the streets. You know any other kids I should talk to?"

"To learn more about Zoroaster and the Blue Lady, you mean?"

"Yes, exactly."

"There're a lotta kids who've seen the Blue Lady more times than me, and lots more who know more about how horrible Zoroaster is."

"I'd like to talk to every one of them."

He stared at her, studying her eyes and finding something special in them. The boy was sizing her up, trying to determine what kind of magic she possessed.

"For the book," she softly said.

"For the book?"

"Exactly."

"So you can tell our story?" asked Noel.

"Yes," she replied, willing to say anything to keep his trust.

"And our faith? You gonna set down our faith?"

"Yes." Whatever that meant.

"All right...all right, then I'll take you to see some of my friends, and you can talk to Aaron." He had warmed to her, was talking about taking her into his confidence.

"Aaron is?"

"Aaron knows the whole history of it all."

"History of your faith, you mean?"

"Yeah, the faith of us."

She smiled warmly at him, her eyes still fixed on Noel's. "But first, how about some hot food, Noel? Maybe a shower and a shave. You okay with that?"

"I could eat."

Redeoux pulled her aside. "Hey, this kid pulled a knife on Riordan and Martinez. He ought to be booked."

"We might get a great deal more out of him and what's happening on the street my way, Theopolis."

He nodded, breathed deeply, and said, "I hope you know what we're doing."

In Aurelia's room at the Phoenix and Dragon Inn, Edwin Arlington Coffin sat at a table across from Rae, proudly displaying his newest ingenious invention, while young Noel was in the shower, having eaten his fill on room service food. Meanwhile, Gene sent out for a new set of clothes for the boy.

Aurelia examined the palm reader that Edwin shared with her; a reader that, according to Edwin, could be used in the field to detail the images she formed in her mind–a remote CRVL that picked up images that could then be sent to DC. It worked so simply; she need only hold the reader in hand while doing her remote viewing. The electrodes she had to attach from the palm reader, however, proved troublesome.

"Works on galvanic response."

"Touch and impulse converted into mental images," she replied to Edwin. "Ingenious, if it works."

"It's working now!" countered Edwin, pointing to the TV screen where he'd inserted a CD taken from the palm reader. On the screen gray ghost images moved in slow motion in a silhouette play that represented some kind of scene, but the fog and static snowstorm created only a whiteout over the images.

"Not exactly high res, is it?" she asked. "Nice try, Edwin, but I think it needs work."

"OK, so bugs needs working out. I'll get it. I will."

"As only you can, I'm sure."

"I want it so you don't have to use a headset, electrodes, all that. It's my dream for you."

"Not to mention it'd be worth a fortune," she countered.

"Maybe that'd make me more attractive to the opposite sex, huh?"

"You just stop that right now, Eddy."

"I mean it. Look at me, the boy wonder nerd. Not exactly

Brad Pitt here."

She placed a hand over his, squeezing. "You're a good looking boy, Eddy."

"The Achilles of nerds, you mean?"

"Oh, Eddy!"

"I'm eighteen now, Aurelia. I'm a man now."

"Sure, I know that." How many years had they worked together?

"Then I would appreciate your not calling me a boy."

"Sure, sure Eddy." She wondered what was troubling him.

"One day, I'm going to get this mini-Crawl wireless right. Just watch me."

"Level with me, Eddy," she said, "the remote is not the only reason you were so excited about getting out of the DC area. What's up?"

"Sorry about being late. It couldn't be helped."

"Working out the final bugs on this baby, huh?" she asked as she handled the thought-imaging palm reader. The unit could not have been more compact. When perfected, she'd be able to carry it in her purse.

Edwin's stuttering answer was, "Ahhh...yeah, that's right...how did you guess?"

"Miniaturization...a wonderful thing." She continued to study the TV screen. Gray globules of Jell-O-like figures making a series of movements, all unrecognizable. Previously, the same forms had appeared as if awash in a sea of grays in the plasma screen on the palm pilot itself. Perhaps one day it might be perfected and the mind image translator program that Edwin had created could be used in the field, but just not today.

"I'm dying to tell you something, Aurelia," he suddenly said in a conspiratorial whisper, as he took the hand held unit and stuffed it in his backpack.

"What is it, Edwin?"

"I've met a woman...a wonderful creature, really."

"Really? In Quantico?"

"No! Here in Phoenix..."

"Really?"

"And…and I think I may be in love."

Oh, great, she thought but merely nodded and said, "I see. Did you two kids meet on the plane coming over?"

"Well…no…we've been corresponding for some time."

"Oh, really?"

"Met on a computer dating service."

Oh God, she thought, red flags going up, but merely nodded and said, "I see."

And suddenly she understood his anxiety in getting to Phoenix so quickly–as early as possible–and his having been late to meet them. It'd had nothing whatever to do with the remote CRVL system, save that Edwin'd used this new device as leverage with the FBI to send him along with Aurelia as part of her team.

Edwin was aflutter with excitement, finally able to share this with the only adult he trusted. While he struggled to produce a series of photos of his first love, she realized the depth of his faith in her, to share this fact and these photos. He splayed out some twenty photos he'd taken of the woman like a deck of cards all across the bed and laughing, he asked, "Isn't Riki beautiful?"

"Yes…quite beautiful." Aurelia stared into a green-eyed blonde's eyes, her hair coiffed in the style of a Marilyn Monroe, her full lips ruby red, make-up her predominant feature. Aurelia wanted to thrash Edwin for being a fool; this woman could not possibly be his intellectual equal, and in fact, she guessed her to be a high school dropout. The suggestive and posed positions in each photo hardly inspired Aurelia to think otherwise, and they also told Aurelia that the young woman appeared twice Edwin's age, but then emotionally, everyone was twice his age.

"Go ahead, Aurelia. Tell me how beautiful she is. She's an exotic dancer. Makes a very fine living at it, too, and supports two children all on her own. I think that takes guts and courage."

"Yeah…very pretty, Edwin, what a woman, and gutsy like you say."

"Hey…you're not just a little jealous, are you?"

She thought about this a moment too long and he jumped on it, adding, "Damn, you are jealous, aren't you?"

How best to answer so as not to hurt his feelings and still withhold any praise of the direction he'd gone in was cause enough for a five-second delay. "No, Eddy, I'm not jealous. I just realized we won't be seeing as much of you on the case as I'd expected."

"That's the beauty part of it. With the remote CRVL, you won't need me around…that is, when I get it working right."

"You want to go easy with this, Edwin. There are a lot of girls out there, and most guys learn too late–after locking in on a commitment–that they're really far more interested in what my Ex calls grazing."

"Damn…you are jealous. Cool."

He was enjoying every one of his new sensations, and from his body language, she read that he and Riki Comfort, as she was called, had long since gone beyond establishing what manner of lovemaking each preferred or the color and texture of the condom. "Ahhh…to be young and in love," she muttered. "Just be careful. Practice safe sex."

"You mean use a condom?"

"I mean don't fall off the bed! Of course I mean a condom, silly but also beware…."

"Be who?"

"Beware, I mean they haven't yet invented a condom for the heart."

"That 'spose to mean something?"

"Just don't want you getting your heart broken, Eddy."

"Aurelia, you've already done that." He gave her a practiced look of hurt, one familiar to her.

She only shook her head. "I'm old enough to be your mother, Eddy."

"Edwin…it's Edwin now at least until I get it changed to Copernicus. As for getting my heart broken, it's mine to break, isn't it? Besides, Rae, isn't it part of the whole game? Getting knocked off your emotions in order to rebuild yourself stronger for the next time? I mean in an emotional sense, to redefine and re-invent one's self according to the dictates of the emotional upheavals and neurological pathways that are the bio-chemical basis for emotions in the first place? Follow?"

"Shakespeare called them 'slings and arrows.'"

"But am I right, or am I mistaken?"

"It means that the scars of your past will determine your future."

"Ahhh…a Buddhist reply?"

"It did not come out of a fortune cookie," she corrected him. "It comes of my own experience."

"Hard won! I know what you really mean: the scars of your past will dictate your future."

As she stared deep into Eddy's eyes, trying to say something that might make him a tad more cautious, Noel emerged from the shower wrapped in a robe too large for him. He looked like Woody Allen in an oversized coat, his glasses no doubt in bad need of upgrading. Gene knocked at the door at the same time. He entered with Noel's new set of clothes.

Noel found the new clothes provided for him worth an encouraging and expansive whistle. To a chorus of some unintelligible tune, Noel dressed in the bathroom.

"What exactly do you hope to get from this clown you picked up out there in the woods?" asked Edwin.

"He's going to act as my go-between, my street person."

"A snitch?"

"No…not a mere snitch. I believe he may lead us to someone on the street who knows a lot more about the Phantom than do the authorities."

He shook his head. Doubtful, he said, "Well…I hope you know what you're doing."

"That it isn't a waste of time, a dead end? Since when have you taken to second guessing me on issues of procedure? This is standard police work to pursue those in the know on the street."

"Based on the notion there is an accomplice, but suppose you're wrong? Suppose there is no accomplice except in your interpretation of the images you got out there in those trees? Suppose you're looking at the forest so hard that you are seeing the wrong trees?"

"Edwin, do you have a better interpretation?"

"Well...from what little you told me of the reading...suppose you're dealing with a schizoid guy...that this predator is a dual personality? Wouldn't that be like an accomplice or have the same feel?"

"An accomplice in the same body? I suppose it is a remote possibility. In fact, I've read of such cases–like the Claw in New York that was written up by Dr. Jessica Coran some years back. But I get a distinct feel to this separate accomplice...younger, smaller, entirely ahhh separate."

"But isn't that the definition of a schizophrenic personality?"

She let out a long breath of air. "Yeah...it is worth tempering my reading with the possibility, I suppose. Still, I have to pursue this avenue."

He nodded. "Of course...of course, you do. It's the 80/20 principle at work." Edwin had turned on cartoons, saying it was for Noel when he'd finish in the bathroom. So the sounds and sights of Sponge Bob filled the room as he spoke to Rae.

"80/20 principle?" she asked.

"An observation of the oft overlooked Italian economist Vilfredo Pareto, 1848-1923 that–"

"Do I really want to hear this?" she interrupted the genius while Gene caught a nap.

"–that in many situations, it's the first 20 percent of the effort that contributes 80 percent of the benefit."

"I see...I think."

He dropped into the lotus position and began a series of practiced Yoga moves. In an effort to impress her the year before, he'd read a stack of books on Yoga and learned it in a matter of hours. It did impress her. He worked his upper body now like a turret as he spoke. "In business terms, for instance, focusing first on the twenty percent of your customers that are most desirable often yields 80 percent of the profit. In effect, Pareto determined that focusing on the events that are the most important–the majors–will allow them to reap the most benefit. The lesson is simple but powerful: The quality of your impact often matters much more than the quantity of your activities. The same principle applies to your career as a psychic detective and for the PSI Unit experiment."

"In other words, if I concentrate on the eighty percent instead of the twenty percent, I could easily find myself back in private practice, reading tea leaves and fired bones?"

"Fired bones?"

"Ancient prophets in Buddha's day and before roasted the bones of their ancestors and read by the cracks created from the heat."

"Did it work?"

"It worked for them...at the time."

"Wow, perhaps Pareto's principle preceded him. What're the odds of that?"

"You mean like Shakespeare's psychoanalysis preceding Freud?"

"Yeah, like that. But imagine the 80/20 principle in a Buddhist Temple circa eons before Christ."

"Then Pareto stumbles on it and dusts the idea off. Maybe 'cause Buddha's teachings are full of common sense."

"You're saying Buddha was full of it?" Edwin joked.

"Yeah, full of it."

They both laughed. In a fluid motion, Rae dropped now into her own lotus position opposite him. She began her own series of exercises. She locked one set of fingers with the other and began pulling while her elbows took flight like a pair of birds. The exercise tightened her features.

Edwin continued his own regimen as he spoke. "You're saying, unlike professional readers like yourself...and maybe professional athletes and maybe actors, the tasks and objectives that are required as a part of business careers are not all glory?"

She nodded and stretched. "More common sense. In fact, the 80 percent of our jobs that offer little chance for differentiation is usually narrowly defined and on the surface quite inflexible."

"Aha!"

"But as with this character Pareto, is it? Success ultimately requires winning the major moments in our careers."

"Right...it is the ability to get beyond merely achieving what others want you to do...to ahhh...break through to deliver unanticipated impact that will give you–and your company or superiors–"

"Or parents," she added for his benefit.

"–yeah, them too. Giving them the most return, creating results that can truly distinguish you."

"I don't know, my young friend. I get the feeling that unlike the 80/20 principle, in business it is usually the last twenty percent of what you accomplish–beyond your predefined objectives–that allows you to truly differentiate yourself. So you've got to be willing to take risks."

"There is another pattern, however, in extraordinary careers. It is the reverse of the 80/20 principle known as the 20/80 principle of performance–keeping the twenty percent that is under your control foremost in your and your boss's mind–and it is the successful application of this principle that allows you to play and win the majors in your career."

"Tell me then, Edwin, what in the hell are we talking about?"

"The Pareto principle, of course."

"And it's exact opposite, and either works?"

"I have found that it is in one's attitude and how one applies such principles that will determine success or failure."

"And how do you determine success in the end? How do you define it?"

"Success is success."

"Success is getting what you want from an experience?"

"Exactly."

"But there can be unintended results of getting what you want."

Edwin gave her a perplexed look. "I've heard of such things happening...to others."

"For example, you succeed with the remote CRAWL, you

can't foresee the ripple effect it may cause in the use of psychic detection in law enforcement, and the gaming industry, or the psychological problems some people will develop in a careless use of this technology. It could be a dangerous electronic Ouija board in the wrong hands, see?"

"Not so for me, because I have anticipated every conceivable use and misuse of the device," he countered.

"All right...I give up on this conversation, Edwin."

"You do that a lot, Aurelia. What fun is playing chess against one's self?"

"At least you always win."

"Yeah...always."

"Gets boring, always winning?" she asked.

"I like a challenge."

"You think Riki plays chess?"

"I don't know...maybe. Didn't ask. We were kinda busy, you see."

"Spare me the details."

"Knew you'd be hurt."

That's what he wanted, for her to confess her hurt and her jealousy, but all she felt was concern. "Sex can only take a relationship so far, Edwin."

"Yeah but it's a damn fine way to keep boredom at bay."

"Ahhh...the devil that torments us all."

Noel re-emerged looking as if someone had absconded off with his body, someone entirely different in every aspect until he opened his mouth. "Any more 'round here to eat?"

Theopolis Redeoux and his men had been taken aback by Aurelia's unorthodox approach in cleaning up the street kid and following Noel's lead. For the time being, they were sitting it out. No doubt in a Deli someplace having a meal and cracking jokes at her expense, she surmised.

Meanwhile, Aurelia, Edwin, and Gene had left the hotel, following Noel, pinning their hopes on his lead. But as they hailed a cab, Edwin decided to opt out since Gene had chosen to accompany her and the street kid. Edwin's begging off, citing his need to get back to the lab to tinker with his mini-Crawl, was not wasted on Rae, who knew where he was going and why. Her eyes bore into him as he made his excuses, so that he knew that she knew precisely his plans, and that he was not fooling her, but then she realized he read only green envy and jealousy into her stare. How wrong could a kid be? She knew he was jeopardizing his career in the bargain, but she also knew he wasn't listening to her, and that all she might say was skewed inside his head.

She could not switch roles to become a demanding parent here. Edwin had escaped the immediate grasp of his tyrannical parents, and she'd be damned if she was going to take their place in any way, shape, or form. Perhaps nature taking its course was the *right* course here; perhaps Ricki Comfort might well be the perfect instructor for Edwin.

Going their separate ways, Edwin had split from Rae and Gene who'd taken a cab with Noel in hand to an older section of the city. She promised herself that she would not worry about Eddy.

With dusk approaching and an Arizona sunset that caught one's breath, Noel led them directly to an enclave of homeless children who by day lived beneath a viaduct, and by night sought out the parks and sometimes the homeless shelters. These children stood within sight of the infamous Phoenix Sun Basketball Stadium–an oasis of light in the dark–past a strip of fast food chains, sports bars, restaurants, tourist traps, and nightclubs. The final nightclub and strip joint displayed a garish green neon sign that read: **Pulp Friction**. The homeless children did not at first recognize the new and improved Noel, and they held judgment on the strangers he'd brought to them.

Gene remained at Rae's elbow, a bit tense, as they stepped below the viaduct, hidden from view and in deep shadow–a stark contrast to the still blue light of the Arizona sky.

Below this viaduct, the judge and jury looked Gene and Aurelia up and down, some making jokes, some making threats, one lifting Aurelia's skirt with a cane that was an obvious scepter. This was their leader. King Hector he proclaimed himself; he stood taller and broader than the others. He let her skirt fall.

One shorter and dirtier boy calling himself Tio seemed fearless. "See that green sign over there?" he asked after introductions.

"Yes," replied Aurelia. "It's a little hard to miss."

"Angels love colored light, especially green neon."

She soon learned from Tio and the others who piped in that "after nightfall in Phoenix the angels come out."

"In mass."

"To-to make war on the red armies."

"Red armies?" Rae asked.

"Armies of the devil Zoroaster," said Noel, "Who else?"

Tio tempered the others like a storyteller correcting his audience. "But sometimes the angels just come out to play.

Hector parted the younger children, some boys, some girls. "Angels alight on the top of the CitiBank building," he began, adding, "always haloed in either a green, pink, or golden glow, and sometimes all three."

"They eat light," said Tio.

"Eat light?" she asked.

"So they can fly," eight-year-old Marty piped in.

"The angels use the CitiBank building for their headquarters," explained Noel as if they were discussing traffic or the weather.

"You see, there's a whole great lotta killing going on in Phoenix just like Miami, LA, Chicago, you name it," added Hector. "Lotta kids getting' killed all over. Angels don't like that."

An eleven-year-old girl named Ameliana pushed the others aside, and apologized for their stupidity. Then she solemnly added, "The angels study their battle maps all day long in that skyscraper before they dare go out and kill demons. Tio or Noel ought to've told you that first."

"I see." Aurelia had never heard of this new urban mythology; apparently every street kid in Phoenix knew it in and out.

Hector now said, "You want to fight, want to learn how to live, you got to learn the secret stories. Else, you don't stand a chance."

Tio added, "Yeah, else you disappear."

"Gotta be on your toes at all times," added Marty.

"You mean....or else you disappear like these kids the cops are finding dead?" Rae asked.

"Sure...how else you explain such things?" asked Ameliana.

Noel said, "It's the demons like Zoroaster and his minions against the angels. Simple as that."

Aurelia and Gene listened to the strange tales as they unfolded. An older boy who had remained silent, sullen, wary suddenly piped up with, "Christmas night the year 2001, God ran away from Heaven."

"God ran away?" she asked, realizing the significance of this to the runaways. Their god was a runaway, too.

"To escape a really bad demon attack," replied Noel, "tell 'em Hector, Peter. Pete knows the whole story. Hector, too, Hell, he taught all'n us."

Peter was the sullen one whose eyes had never left Gene and Rae. He quietly said, "A regular celestial shock and awe offensive is what it was. The demons smashed God's palace of beautiful blue-moon marble to dust and ashes."

"TV news, CNN, MSNBC, Fox & Friends, all of 'em, including the New York and LA Times, they all kept it secret," added Noel. "Tell 'em, Peter. Tell 'em!"

"Only the homeless children in shelters across the country are awake and alert to the holy war," said Peter.

"Awakened?" asked Gene.

"Alerted how?" asked Rae.

"By our dead relatives," Peter now said, stepping close to Rae and placing himself close enough to feel her body heat. "No one knows why God has never reappeared, leaving us–and his poor unhappy angels–to defend his earthly estate against assaults from Hell."

"Damned demons found doors to our world," added

Manuel, an eight-year-old hugging his older brother's arm. The older brother, Miguel, who seemed to take his lead from Peter, nodded now in solemn agreement."

Aurelia felt stunned at these revelations, that children so young were coping not only with the street but with a war between Heaven and Hell, and they found themselves on the battlefield. In fact, the object of contention. They not only faced the horrors of the real world, but for some bizarre reason, they'd created a mythological world of gods and demons at war over their heads. She supposed it a coping mechanism to both understand and defeat the terror commonly called reality.

"How…when…I mean," she tried to formulate her question so it would not sound condescending, but King Hector read her mind and replied instantly to her hemming and hawing.

"The demonics's gateways to and from Hell are everywhere." He pointed to an abandoned refrigerator, a broken mirror leaning against a Dumpster, a discarded toilet amid the ruins of a crack house turned to ruins. They can make a portal of a discarded Pepsi-Cola bottle if they want. They got huge powers."

"And Ghost Town," added Tio, Miguel and others shouting agreement. "Yeah, don't forget Ghost Town, Hector."

"Ghost Town?" asked Gene, who had been absorbed, intent on every word.

"County Cemetery," explained Peter. They can come outta graves."

"And Humvees with black windows," added Tio. "They like anything black or red. The Angels like green mostly."

"The demons feed on darkness and dark human feelings, you know," continued Peter. "Emotions like jealousy, hate, fear, or negative anything…like when you can't stand yourself even…or your own kind… but you can't get away from who you are, can you?"

"So a lotta people commit suicide 'cause of this, and its score another one for the demons," said Noel.

"You can change, you can build on things, get an education," Aurelia countered, but this only brought a scowl to both Hector's and Peter's faces, and their dual expressions signaled that the others were to clam up and say no more."

Noel, picking up on this as well, said in Aurelia's ear, "I think that's all this bunch is going to give up today. We should go now."

There was no uncertainty when the group began one by one to turn their backs on the strangers, a ritual for disengaging and possibly setting members adrift like excommuniants.

Noel said in Rae's ear, "Come on, maybe you can meet with Danielle's coven."

"Danielle's coven?"

"They stay close to the Salvation Army's emergency shelter. Come on."

Noel led the way.

Gene whispered, "Do you believe this? Amazing. But how is it relevant to our case?"

"I'm not sure, but I have a feeling it is somehow connected, somehow relevant."

They soon found Danielle's camp–its epicenter an abandoned garage off a drainpipe large enough to drive a Mack truck through–part of a reservoir system that took the runoff in the event of a flood during what the locals called the monsoon season. Danielle herself looked like a youthful truck driver, an Eileen Wournos weariness to her features, but she could not be much older than King Hector. She too held a large stick, cleaned of its bark and varnished as a scepter, but Danny as the others called her, barked at people in the language of truckers.

Once she decided that Aurelia could be trusted not only to keep their secrets but to spread the word of the war between Heaven and Hell going on in Phoenix and across America, Danielle warmed to her topic. "One demon is feared even by Satan himself," she began.

Aurelia said, "Oh, really?"

"Yeah, in LA shelters where I come from and on the streets, and now even here, children know her by her English name and her Spanish name: Bloody Mary and La Llorana."

"The Crying Woman," said Aurelia, knowing a little Spanish.

This impressed the homeless children gathered about Danielle, as many were Hispanic.

"The woman weeps blood," one child added.

"Blood," echoed another, "and sometimes black oil tears."

Red and black again, Rae thought.

"From ghoulish empty sockets."

"And she feeds on a child's terror."

"It's why you can't be scared, and why you can't be a child."

Why you can't be a child? Aurelia rolled over the comment in her mind, thinking how sad.

The chorus of them talked over one another now. But

Danielle silenced them all with her upraised scepter. "When a child is killed accidentally in gang crossfire or is murdered, La Llorana sings, dances, cheers."

"And if a child goes missing?" asked Gene.

"She is feeding on the kid," Noel blurted out.

Danielle added, "If you wake up at night and see La Llorna, and you hear her song, you have to go with her, 'cause....'cause it's like being hypnotized."

"Turned into a zombie," added a ten-year-old black girl.

"That's right," continued this one's sister. "Bloody Mary's clothes'll be blowing back, even in a room where there's no wind."

"Hell," replied an older boy who looked stunted, "if you see her, you know she's marked you for a kill."

"What about the angel lady I heard about?" asked Aurelia. "Tell me something about her."

They all fell silent, looking for Danielle for guidance. "She is our chief ally. She is beautiful, so beautiful it hurts your eyes to look into the light surrounding her, but even that is a good hurt."

"What else can you tell me about this Blue Lady, is it?"

The youngest girl blurted out, "We don't got no other name for her."

Danielle glared at the girl even as she added, "The light around her is blue like water. You touch it, it ripples like...like one of those new TV screens in Wal-Mart."

"Plasma screen," supplied Gene.

"Yeah, that." After a moment, Danielle added, "She has white skin, white as a cloud, and she lives in the ocean. But... but she can travel through time and space in an eye blink, so she can astral project to here from any time and any place. But...still...even though she's got magical powers, she is handcuffed."

"Handcuffed?" asked Rae.

"And...and she has a limp...scars from the war...the victim of a spell, maybe two spells."

"The demons did it to her," piped in the kids again.

"They captured her and tortured her."

"Underneath her white robes, she's bleeding worse than..."

"...worse than Bloody Mary herself."

These homeless children had again exploded with the need to share this cautionary tale."

"Ultimately, our Blue Lady only has power if you know her secret name," corrected Danielle. "She's kinda like my mom. She has a lot of aliases. But the one with the power...nobody knows that one."

"Can you tell me the other aliases?" A moment ago Danielle had said that the Blue Lady had no other names, but now this.

"One is Alia, one is Elisyan. That's all we know."

Aurelia pursued this and learned from Danielle that her mother had gone through three rehabs for crack addiction. Danielle was part Spanish, part black.

"So what is the Blue Lady's secret name?"

"That's for you to find out. It is useless if someone just tells it. You have to find out all on your own. But anyone who learns it is turned into an angel for the war, so you disappear either way, only this is a nice place to disappear to, 'cause you end up an angel and not a devil filled with hate." Danielle leaned on her scepter.

Noel added, "It's like when the Indians go off alone to find their spirit guide, their mani...Manitou."

Gene cautiously asked, "Then if, say for instance, that you and your friends are on a street corner when a car comes shooting bullets, and only one of you knows her true name and yells out her true name, that only you will survive?

"No man. You don't get it," said Danielle. "You see her and she whispers her real heavenly name, then it means you gotta go with her. You're dead, yeah, but you got eternal life as one of hers and that's heaven, man, and it makes you superhuman so you can fight the evil."

"Got it."

"It's a spell that takes your soul up and it's very loving."

"She can stop bullets if she wants to," added a small, wide-eyed black boy.

"Can make you invisible to any harm, she can," said another. "But that's not normal."

"That's rare," added Danielle. "He means it like never happens but when it does, it's 'cause the angels need you here."

"Even if bullets are tearing through your skin?" pressed Gene.

"The Blue Lady makes them fall on the ground. She can talk to us, even without her name. She says for us to hold on."

"There'll come a day," said another.

"Hold on, hold on," the others began chanting.'"

A blond six-year-old with a bruise above his eye, swollen huge as a ruby egg and laced with black stitches, nodded vigorously at this. "I've seen her," he murmured.

A rustle of whispered 'me too's' rippled through the small circle of initiates.

Aurelia silently realized, *they instinctively know to curry favor with Danielle, and to remain under her considerable protection, they need only agree with everything she says.*

"And where is Zoroaster in all this?" Aurelia asked.

Danielle glared at Noel. "Damn you, Noel! How much of your guts did you spill to these outsiders?"

"I just want to understand," pleaded Aurelia, "to see the connections, the patterns. How is Zoroaster related to the Blue Lady, for instance?"

"They are interconnected by mutual hatred and war."

"What is Zoroaster to La Llorana?"

"They are lovers. Evil, twisted lovers, addicted to a high that comes of seeing us suffer."

According to the Phoenix County Homeless Trust, some 2000 homeless children currently found themselves bounced between the county's many shelters and welfare agencies and the streets. Aurelia felt the empty hopelessness wanting to overwhelm her as she stepped away from Danielle and said a tearful goodbye to Noel, who steadfastly refused any further suggestion of help from authorities. This was heartbreaking for Aurelia all the more knowing his reaction was a performance for Danielle and the others, so that he might continue to belong with his street family. He ranted loudly as Gene and Aurelia found a cab. The last words they heard out of Noel disheartened her further. He cautioned his fellow homeless by saying, "They might seem nice, shower you with presents like they did me, but they could still be working for Zoroaster."

Danielle further cautioned the others against Aurelia and Gene, adding, "And once you go into the system, they have your picture and your information, and it goes into his and La Llorana's files, and once you're in their files, it's only a matter of time before you disappear."

Myth and fear of authority had gotten all twisted and balled up for these children, and as far as establishing any sort of lasting bond of friendship with any of them, as Gene said, "Forget about it. Impossible. For people on the street, and especially children on the street, nothing is permanent– especially bonds."

Aurelia knew from experience and reading police reports that a common rule among homeless parents was that everything a child owned must fit into a small bag for fast packing. But during brief stays in shelters, children would meet and tell each other stories that became urban myths, and these myths while terrifying and paranoia-laden, had likely also kept them alert to danger. This by embracing their fears and paranoia. Actually, there could be no calculating the lives these myths may've saved, aside from simply getting a kid through the harshest of nights.

She knew from her own heritage as the daughter of both a Celtic believer and a Japanese Buddhist that folktales are usually an inheritance from family or homeland, and that the religions of others was considered cultural folklore by non-believers. But what of children enduring a continual, grueling, dangerous journey? No parent or adult in a uniform could possibly steel such a child against the outcast's fate–the endless slurs and snubs, the threats, the fear. In the cab, moving away from King Hector and Queen Danielle, Rae said, "What these children do is snatch bits and pieces of ghost stories,

Halloween fables, TV news, and candy-coated children's games like Chutes and Ladders, combine them with Bible stories, and like determined little birds building a nest from scraps, they weave their own myths."

Gene quietly agreed, as he had been disturbed to his core. "The secret stories are carefully guarded knowledge kept in the group. All very tribal."

"Never shared with parents for fear of being ridiculed–or spanked for blasphemy. But their accounts of an exiled God who cannot or will not respond to human pleas as his angels wage war with Hell must be–to shelter children–a plausible explanation for having no safe place, no safe home."

The taxi bumped along streets in need of repair, the landscape of urban distress just the other side of the darkened glass. Gene reasoned, "These stories engage their spirits by engaging them in an epic clash of cosmic proportion."

Rae nodded. "Has the dual purpose of engaging them in something larger than themselves, and in making their lives meaningful."

"The–the purpose of any religion," Gene Kiley finished. "An astute shrink could do a lot with these kids."

"An astute folklorist could do even more. I see traces of old legends in all new invention. For example, Yemana, a Santeria ocean goddess, resembles the Blue Lady; there is a similar wandering lady in Celtic folklore. In all cases, she is compassionate and robed in blue with pale skin. And in the Eighties, folklorists noted references to an evil Bloody Mary– or La Llorana emerging among Hispanic–"

"You knew about all this all along?"

"I know very little of their unwritten oral bible. But I know that children of Mexican migrant workers first named this La Llorana. She started here in the Southwest."

"Mexican lore. It figures."

"She is known now among the homeless children of all races all over."

"Every group has to have their ghost tales, demons and fairy godmothers, I suppose."

"Mother used to tell me Celtic tales of revenants, vampiric zombies digging their bloodless bodies from graves, returning souls, visitors from the land of the dead sent to console or warn, harm or help."

"Sounds like you were pleasantly tucked in each night."

"I begged to know, are you kidding. Trust me, all the various revenants and creatures of the dark arrived in America centuries ago with the first Native American, who likely had an Asian father and mother. Then the Puritans arrived on the East Coast with their belief in the Invisible World of Satan all around us, fueling the paranoia, and feeding the bloody roots of witchcraft hysteria in their culture."

Gene stared for a moment, as always astounded at how much Rae kept in her head. "Still what Danielle and Noel and these kids are shoveling, well, it's outrageous bullshit, not religion, not any more than the worst cult that has Jesus arriving on the second coming in a freaking flying saucer."

"Well…while you may disagree with their version of reality, you have to remember our reality is an absolute 360 degrees from theirs, no less than our reality is to a Puritan minister in 1692. Look, these kids are born into pain and addiction, and they suffer experience rather than enjoy life. People not of our world, we can't conceive of what has shaped their minds."

"Guess you're right on that score."

"I didn't see bullshit, but a social order holding these kids together predicated on their beliefs, and I felt a deep-seated fear like a wound in the soul."

"So they make myths."

"Bizarre myths to our ears, but they also have a validity, and they resonate with the myths of African tribes, Asian tribes, Afghanistan tribes, hell…all the tribes."

"It's the certainty and detail that gets to me."

"What about the Phantom, Gene? What do you think he thinks of the shelter children's 'religion'?"

"You assuming he knows about it?"

"If so, how does he figure into this war of angels? Is he a

real life Zoroaster?"

"How do we know there is a connection, Rae? What instinct are you drawing on? You see something in your reading you kept to yourself?"

"No, just an old fashioned cop's hunch, this time. Nothing PSI about it, nothing extraordinary…just a gut feeling."

Aurelia looked across the dinner table at her daughter, Nia, who'd arrived in Phoenix earlier in the company of Enriquiana. The empathic psychic mother mentally compared her daughter's sheltered life to that of the homeless children of the Phoenix streets, unable to do otherwise. Hollywood's Dracula would have called them the children of the night, and he would've routinely fed on them. Perhaps that was exactly what the Phoenix Phantom thought of the homeless child population at his feet

Aurelia studied the fine, graceful lines of her daughter's countenance, so angelic, so lovely, so perfect in its Oriental refinement. Like one of those Japanese dolls sans the bamboo bonnet. Nia would never don a bamboo bonnet, or wear traditional Japanese dress, never exchange her Levi's for a silken kimono, not even when they'd had the masquerade party at the country club. For one so young and so American, Nia carried herself with a haughty self-respect and an arrogance born of confidence and knowing who she was and what strengths she possessed and how intelligent she was and how sure of her future she was–and yet she could be such a little witch at times.

Rae had given Nia all the advantages that a caring mother could possibly provide. Part of Aurelia wanted to march her down to the Phoenix shelters and introduce Nia to kids like Noel, Hector, Peter, Danielle, and the rest. Just telling Nia about their hopeless plight would not do; getting it second hand would be ineffectual. How could she share their pathos and their folklore with Nia? How could she inform her daughter without her daughter's taking some offense, taking it wrongly?

"Is everything all right, mom?" Nia asked now, but then she

undercut the tone of concern in her voice with her next utterance. "Or should I ask is *anything* all right, mom?"

Nia had for so long been protected and had lived–while not in luxury–always in comfort and had never spent a night either cold or hungry. No child should have to witness the excesses of parents in emotional turmoil as Nia had, but kids without parents, or with only one parent, *and she on cocaine*, did not compare. Nia had never once spent a night alone, nor a single night with hunger and cold and discomfort gnawing at her insides. Nor had she ever had to create mythological underpinnings out of fear and need and self-preservation, both physical and mental.

Aurelia wanted to do something for the children of the street. She knew that her donation to the local shelters a sad drop in the bucket, and now a sense of guilt rose as she sat here in the hotel in comfort, eating a sumptuous meal in the warm glow of a fire, a candle-lit table, Gershwin music live from the piano man.

"Most of us live lives of movie stars and take it for granted," she quietly told Nia.

"Whoa, reality check, where's that coming from? Am I supposed to thank you for yanking me from the biggest-most-important-est soccer tournament of my life to the middle of a freaking desert! Is that what you wanna hear?"

"Frankly, I'd like to hear any word, a single word from the daughter I used to know, the one without all the anger. Just one soft word."

Nia dropped her gaze but said nothing, stabbing at her salad.

Aurelia began telling her of her day, how she had met the homeless children and about their mythology, giving it a stab. After listening for a time, Nia said, "Sounds so...so sad...so strange but also so sad and...awful."

"It is sad and awful."

"Wow...bummer big time."

They sat in silence, each with a lost appetite.

"How was your flight?" Nia asked politely, trying to change the subject.

Aurelia dared not go into detail about the flight. "Smooth…it went smoothly." She launched into how the pilot had made his perfect landing.

Nia frowned at this. "We really don't have a lot to say to one another, Mother. It was a foolish notion to drag me along with you when all your time's going to be spent on a case."

Aurelia felt a surge of frustration rising. "When the case is over, you'll have me all to yourself."

Nia flashed a look that ended in rolled eyes. "Sure…sure. I get the leftovers as usual."

"Nia, that's not fair."

"Fair? I'm going up to bed."

"Wait. We could do the shops in the hotel plaza. Like old times."

"You mean when Dad was with us?"

"Nia, your father's no longer living with us isn't entirely my fault."

"I suppose it's all Pappa's then?"

"I didn't say that."

"You just said it wasn't your fault, and you keep saying it wasn't my fault, so—"

"It takes two to make a wedding, Nia, honey, and it takes two to make a divorce."

"But not before the two of you made a baby."

"You're no longer a child, Nia."

"Whoa up there! Since when? Flash bulletin coming through! News to the world."

"Keep your voice down."

"You can be such a hypocrite, Mom. You still treat me like an infant, until it suits your purpose not to, and then I'm…I'm…"

"Spit it out."

"…I am supposed to act grown up whenever you need me to?"

"Something like that. Yes. Seems reasonable to me."

"I'm tired, and I'm going to bed. Jet lag."

"Goodnight then, and Nia," she grabbed up her daughter's

hand. "I do love you, and I'm going to make time for you, and we are going to go see the Grand Canyon no matter what...together."

"Sure, Mom...sure." She pushed from the booth and to her feet and was gone in a huff, her heels tapping out an angry tune in her wake.

Such a beautiful child, and yet so full of anger. She knew it was teen angst and entirely misguided, but knowing so did not lessen the pain of its being directed at her mother.

Her cell phone rang. Agent Theopolis Redeoux. "Have you decided to get back on course with the case?" His tone spoke reams of pent up exasperation. She imagined him biting through his pipe.

"Do you know anyone at a local university who knows anything about mythology and folklore?"

Redeoux coughed and cleared his throat at the other end. "Well...the University of Phoenix campus is likely full of geniuses on the matter, but what is it you hope to gain by–"

"Theopolis, you arranged to fly me out here to give my special PSI powers exercise right?"

"Yes but thus far–"

"To help locate Toby Slayter and Julian Redondo, and to catch a child predator, right. A BTK type killer right?"

"That's correct. It was my idea. I'd read about your previous successes in the bulletins."

"Then you must trust my instincts. A great deal of psychic power is reading others, recognizing signs, translating body language, and listening closely...with an ear to the ground as they say."

"I am trying to maintain my trust in you, Dr. Hiyakawa."

"Good, then if you will continue to have faith in your own instincts about me, will you please arrange for us to see the university's foremost authority on folklore and mythology there?"

"At this hour?"

"A child's life–two lives–are at stake, and maybe more on the horizon. Every moment we delay is crucial. He could be disposing of another body as we speak."

Redeoux abruptly agreed. "Right...of course. We'll wake someone up."

They met at the Caribou Coffee house on the green at the University of Arizona at Phoenix campus, a place so well manicured and pleasant it could pass for a Hollywood back lot for a remake of Disney's Pollyanna. Professor Elliot Alandale stood six-foot two with a neatly trimmed beard and mustache below a pair of near invisible Silhouette glasses, a full head of disheveled black hair with a few strands of gray streaking through. He wore a pair of blue jeans, an Apple Computer logo T-shirt, Docker shoes, and a tweed sports coat over all despite the near eighty-degree Arizona heat. He looked every bit the Southwestern professor in his leather boots this evening.

After introductions, Aurelia told him of her day spent with the children of the street, and their strange modern-day mythological constructs.

Once finished relating what Danielle, Noel, Peter, Hector, and the others had imparted, Aurelia watched closely for his response. Alandale's eyes had narrowed, and his face pinched as she had related the religion of Phoenix's homeless children.

Alandale's hands opened and closed. If she were interrogating him, his body language would say he felt uncomfortable.

"What is it, Dr. Alandale?" she asked.

He stared at her as if she could see straight through him and into this heart. "I find this so...so strangely coincidental."

"How so?" asked Redeoux who had accompanied her along with Gene.

"Well...you see, a group of us at the university are studying these very phenomena right now. We've compiled a lot of statistics on these very children. I happen to know Danielle and Noel, for instance. Not as familiar with Hector or Peter, but I am sure one or more of my research assistants is."

"That is a coincidence indeed," said Redeoux in a tone that said he didn't believe in coincidence.

Alandale acknowledged Redeoux's skepticism with a quick glint in the eye but merely continued. "These created street religions are striking examples of what we term polygenesis."

"Poly-genesis as in Genesis?" she asked.

"Precisely. The folklorist's term for the simultaneous appearance of vivid, similar tales in far-flung locales."

Aurelia bit her lower lip and asked, "You mean...are you referring, sir, to the similar themes running through all these homeless shelter stories?"

"Try identical themes, and yes, you're correct. The same over-arching themes. Each linking the myths of thirty-five homeless children in county facilities alone; facilities operated by the Salvation Army—as well as those of forty-nine other children in Salvation Army emergency shelters in Oakland, Miami, New Orleans, and Chicago."

Even Redeoux sat silent, impressed.

"These children range in age from six to sixteen, seventeen, and when by our field teams, what stories, if any, they believe about Heaven and God—it's always the same. God has been deposed, his thrown taken over by the forces of evil—Satan's soldiers—Zoroasters."

"So you are chronicling the folklore?"

"For a book?" asked Gene.

"Look, most of these kids don't write or don't know how to write, so they're asked to draw pictures for their stories with crayons and markers. Their parlance and pictures from here to Miami is the same. Children use the biblical term "spirit" for revenants, for instance, never "ghost." Why? Because ghost is, in their vernacular, a scaredy-cat baby word for such as Casper cartoons, so not real to them."

"Not like spirits?" asked Gene.

"Spirits are real and dangerous."

"I see," replied Aurelia, digesting all of this.

"In their lexicon, they always use "demon" to denote wicked spirits." Alandale took a long moment to sip his coffee and to allow these facts to sink in. An irritatingly happy John Denver sang Sunshine on My Shoulder in the background.

Aurelia said, "Their folklore appears to cast them as comrades-in-arms, regardless of ethnicity."

Alandale stared long into her one blue, one black eye. "You are quick, Agent Hiyakawa. The fact you made them feel comfortable enough so quickly to share their secret stories with you. That is in itself remarkable. It took us months to get near them."

"Could be you and your people broke the ice with them. Made it easy for us."

"Some of our research team could not get anything from them. I'd have to constantly reshuffle the deck."

"I want the names of your team and where each can be found," Redeoux told Alandale.

"Sure...sure if it helps. I'll have my assistant fax 'em over tomorrow first thing."

"That'd be great, Professor."

Alandale downed his coffee in a final gulp. He took in a deep breath. "For these kids the secret stories do more than explain the mystifying universe; they impose meaning in this chaotic world in the telling and retelling."

"Story has power, always has," she mused. "And this gives purpose to their lives."

"You've got it. As you've learned, these stories are told and cherished by white, black, Ukrainian, Polish, and Latin children, for the homeless youngsters see themselves as allies, spiritual comrades of the outgunned, yet valiant angels."

"Not too terribly different from African-American folklore through the horrors of slavery.

"Folktales are the only work of beauty a displaced people can keep," he explained. "And their power can transcend class and race lines because they address visceral questions."

I love the way he talks, she thought.

"What kind of questions?" asked Gene as Van Morrison replaced John Denver.

"Why side with good when evil is clearly winning?" said

Alandale, shrugging, his fingers idly beating a rhythm to Van Morrison on his upturned empty cup. "And if I am killed, how then can I make my life resonate beyond the grave?"

"You make it sound like a sense of mission," countered Redeoux. "It's ridiculous. These kids know what's what. They know they're making up shit as they go."

"This shit, as you call it, keeps them anchored, Agent Redeoux. You're likely familiar with Cajun beliefs, given your name. A belief system and a culture is necessary to well-being. It provides a sense of mission."

"I agree with Professor Alandale," said Aurelia. "Their beliefs may explain why some children in crisis–and perhaps the adults they become–are brave, decent, and imaginative, while others more privileged–" she flashed on Nia's face–"can be "callous, mean-spirited, and mediocre."

Aurelia only now realized that Alandale and Redeoux, each from such disparate worlds, the professor and the seasoned FBI detective, stared across at one another like two pit bulls, and between them, Gene was looking more and more the referee. "I grew up in inner-city Chicago, Agent Redeoux," challenged Alandale, "and let me tell you, there was very little sign of God on the landscape there. I wish I'd had half what these kids had in the way of a spiritual leaning or anchor."

Aurelia added, "The homeless child lives in a world where violence and death are commonplace, where it's highly advantageous to grovel before the powerful and shun the weak, and where adult rescuers are no place to be found."

Redeoux gave her a look like he'd been betrayed, but said nothing.

"Ahhh, the ability to grasp onto ideals larger than oneself..." began Alandale. "To exert influence for good–*a sense of mission*–you see."

Redeoux only frowned and waved him off.

"This sense is nurtured in these eerie, beautiful, shelter folktales as sure as they were in *Beowulf* to bolster men to go out and slay dragons," continued Alandale, shaking his head. "I could go on."

"Please don't," replied Redeoux, his hand still up in the air. "I'm sorry, Professor, but regardless of any good intentions you two have for the homeless, this all begins to sound twisted Christianity after a point. And that amounts to bullshit as far as I'm concerned."

Elliot Alandale dismissed this and spoke directly to Aurelia. "In any group that generates its own legends–whether in a corporate office, a police department–" he gave a jibe-nod to Redeoux–"an agency like the FBI, or a remote Amazonian village–the most articulate member becomes the semi-official teller of the tales. The same thing happens in homeless shelters."

Silence except for Van Morrison reigned at the near empty coffee shop. Alandale said to Rae, "Again, you've done remarkably well to gain even a temporary hold on these kids."

Redeoux threw down a twenty to cover the coffee and left.

Gene, staring after the FBI Special Agent in Charge, decided to have a talk with him, alone, so he got up and left Rae with Alandale.

Aurelia asked, "Is this true even in a transient population like in a shelter?"

"The most verbally skilled children–such as Noel and Danielle–and this Hector and Peter you describe–they impart the secret stories to new arrivals."

"Ensuring that their truths survive…"

"Yes, regardless of their own fate; they see it as a duty. It's felt deeply by these children, including one ten-year-old Phoenix girl who, after confiding and illustrating secret stories, created a self-portrait for us at the university."

"Really?"

"A gray charcoal drawn gravestone meticulously and carefully inscribed with her name and the year 2010."

"So this is what I was told by the children at the shelters–the secret stories lay down the rules of spiritual behavior?"

"Yes, spirits appear just as they looked when alive, even wearing favorite clothes, but they are surrounded by faint, colored light. When newly dead, while the spirit's lips move, no sound is heard."

She nodded as he spoke, recognizing the words of the children in his words. She added now, "The spirits must learn to speak across the chasm between the living and the dead."

"And for shelter children, spirits have a unique function: providing war dispatches from the fighting angels. Like demons, once spirits have seen your face, they can always find you. So beware...be careful, vigilant at all times."

"That's precisely what the children told me over and over."

"There is something more...something far more disturbing coming out of our research." Alandale absently knocked over the empty Caribou-logo coffee cup and it slid beneath the table.

"And what is that?"

"Well...simply put, the children may have trusted you, Agent Hiyakawa up to a point where they draw the line on first meetings." He leaned in closer as if they were in a conspiracy. "Bottom line... in their theocracy, and this is quite strange, Bloody Mary and the mother of Christ, Mary, are in essence one and the same."

"What are you saying?"

"Mary laid down with Satan to beget another child–Satan's child who will carry on his evil."

"The street kids believe this?"

"Worse–Mary killed her son, Christ, and she abandoned God on his throne. She in fact betrayed Heaven itself, showing and leading the way for Satan's minions to overthrow God's throne."

"I didn't hear any of this from the children."

"This is their secret of secrets. Since, they don't believe anyone'll believe them, they hold this much back. I can show you our documentation if you wish?" He began rummaging through a brown valise he'd carried in with him. "I have it all right here."

"That's such a perversion of Christianity. Glad Redeoux stepped out."

He slapped down the pages of a manuscript for a book he'd continued work on throughout his research. "What this means

166

to the average homeless child out there," he said, pointing out the window, "is that the forces traditionally in Heaven, all the powers of God's throne overhead, is now under Satan. That we are in the midst of an apocalyptic war, and our angels are not only on the run and bedraggled but losing and losing badly."

"And why? Why are they losing?"

"Largely because they are abandoned. Abandoned by an embittered God that has seen his son killed by his mother who has slept with Satan."

"Sounds like Hamlet. Sounds like enough to put God off his throne, but it also rings unbelievable."

"Unbelievable? Not so to someone facing death on the streets and a daily battle to survive and at the same time remain good and pure."

Shaken, she took the pages offered her. "Dr. Alandale, I thank you for coming out so late to meet with me and discuss this so freely, and good luck with your research and your book. I'd say at this point, it is sorely needed."

"Not at all. I am pleased someone is showing an interest not only in our research at the university but in the shelter children. You do get attached."

Rae stood. "Can I call on you again, should I have further questions about all this?"

He got to his feet. "You may indeed. Any time, Agent. How long will you be in Phoenix?"

She knew instantly that he was interested in her. "As long as the child predator remains at large."

"Ahhh...as long as it takes to corner him?"

"Yes."

"And how exactly does the mythology of the street children fit into your investigation?"

"I am not entirely sure just yet, but I always trust my first instinct about matters."

"And matters of the heart?"

"Well...I tend to be wrong in that area quite a lot. Psychic investigation is easy compared to mysteries of the heart."

"Perhaps we could remedy that."

"Perhaps…another time."

They parted with a lingering shake of the hand. She was as attracted to him as he was to her, but she held herself in check. She had far too much on her plate to get involved with this scrumptious, good-hearted, good-looking professor.

Aurelia watched a nine-year-old girl repeatedly mouth the word *help* where she stood at the entryway to a large brick caldron, fire rising behind her where the doors began to close. A sign read Salvation Army Northwest Shelter. Somehow she already knew that the small frail black girl and her mother had been here for a month, and that they had become homeless after the father was arrested for drug dealing, and mother couldn't pay her rent on her fast-food restaurant income.

"There's a river runs through the city," said the black child. "One side is called Godawful Town, which is where the demons took over." She drew pictures as she spoke, pictures in crayon of homes, kittens, children in a playground reminiscent of the visions of angels in a park Aurelia had been seeing in dreams. "The other side the demons call Godpeace Village. Everyone there's rich and they live on the beach, and they wears diamonds in they hair even when they's swimming."

This is a dream, Aurelia reminded herself. A compensatory dream, one that compensates for all that I saw and heard today.

The little girl's mother explains, "My Sara here believe Satan hates big cities, account-a-his being humiliated once in New York City while searching for more gateways for his demons to enter the world and the war."

The child picked it up here. "He needed evil thoughts and nasty emotions to open more doors. Satan's trip began good for him, and he moved easy 'mong all the high rise buildings and homes of Manhattan and such places as Brooklyn and Brookline, even though his skin was red as fire, and layered with gold and silver scales like a snake."

"Nobody knew it was Satan? No one noticed?" Aurelia's dream self asked.

The little black girl said her name, Sara Victoria Meghan

Walters. She added, "Satan wears brand name clothes and fits right in. Tommy Hilfiger, Nike, Old Navy, you name it. Who's going to know?"

"Smokes cigars, drinks brandy, and he found a big hole right here in Phoenix where an asteroid once hit out on the desert. The bad spirits come walking in off the desert like zombies." The mother shook her head knowingly. "My daughter told me so."

"He gives away Porsches and Jaguars to people to make them his," added Sara Victoria. "But the angels will catch him some day and destroy him."

"He's afraid of holy water." The mother sprinkled some from a vial.

Sara added, "Holy water makes his skin dissolve and turn to steam, and this weakens him."

Aurelia saw a large figure in the distance, a strange steam coming off him. The figure appeared flanked on two sides. On one side, a woman, on the other a child.

Then she awoke with a start and a knock at her hotel door. She quickly responded, throwing on a terry cloth robe, and placing an eye against the peephole. Magnified on the other side stood Gene Kiley, his features a mask of concern. "Damn it," she muttered, pulling open the door. "Gene, it's three in the morning." Even so, she was secretly pleased to have been awakened from the disturbing dream.

"Don't you think I know this?" he replied, stepping inside.

She closed the door and regarded him, reading his body language. An obvious agitation there.

"Look, Aurelia, I can't stop these feelings for you. I can't stop the what ifs."

"The what ifs?"

"What if we got together? What if we became a couple? What could it hurt? In fact, it could solidify what we already have, which is not a real relationship at all."

"But...but...but damn man...no, the last thing you want to do is get involved in my screwed up life. I would not wish myself on a–"

"But I do."

"You've no idea what you're saying."

"But I do."

"You're repeating yourself, Gee."

"Sorry, but I can't help it."

"I've already got enough problems; adding you to the list'll just screw with my head, and if you knew how screwed up I am, you'd run like hell from any such notions as–"

"You're a psychic, so why didn't you see this coming?"

"I've told you, it's no good on a personal level. If it were so, I'd be at the race track or playing the Lottery!"

"My own foresight tells me we have an excellent chance at a good outcome, Rae."

Her immediate reaction was an image of a broken heart. White feathers, red roses, and a broken heart. But she said, "There is a famous Japanese philosopher named Yohda Ken–"

"Yohda? Like in Star Wars Yohda?"

"Not quite. Yohda Kenko who once said...hmmm..." she paused to get the words exactly right. "'A man's heart is like the flower seed, but unlike a seed, the heart needs no wind to be scattered abroad–or something like–"

"An old Japanese proverb? That's how you respond to anyone who gets too close, Rae? And...and it's gibberish, meaningless."

"Means your asking for trouble! The heart is fleeting and changeful, and what a man wants today is not what he wants tomorrow. The same goes for a lotta women, Gee! Is that blunt enough for you?" She turned her back on him and stared out the balcony and into the black and tan night of Phoenix, the town making her think of an old black and white noir film.

He came to stand behind her, tentatively placing a hand on her shoulders. "Still stinging over your divorce, aren't you?"

She pulled away, opened the balcony door, and stepped outside into a warm breeze even as she said, "Well...yes. Isn't everyone?"

He pursued, stepping outside with her. "So you won't even consider the possibility that we might be good for one another?"

"I'll give it some further thought, Gee, dear sweet Gee, but don't hold out hope."

"I can change. Whatever it is about me that does not fit your–"

"No, Gene, please. I wouldn't change a thing about you. You are a dear, sweet friend. Just ahhh....it's me. I've not been very good for anyone. Not right since my husband, and it...it would only end up hurting you...destroying what we have in the bargain...and so hurting us both...and so why bother?"

"Then you only see a bad end to a romantic relationship between us before it begins?"

She failed to answer, but it was true.

"That's sad...really."

She had no answer for this except to reply, "You are far more astute and psychic than you give yourself credit for, Gee."

"Another thing we have in common."

"Can you imagine the horror of two psychics in love? It would be as mercurial a marriage as any Hollywood match up."

"Is that the reason Nia and you are having problems?"

"Whatya mean?"

"She's psychic too, after all, isn't she? I mean, being your daughter, wouldn't she have to be?"

"No, not at all..." she said, a birdlike flutter of confusion swiping past her eyes. "Why do you say that? She has never once spoken of being the least bit psychic, and she has never shown any signs in that direction."

"You don't want her to be psychic, is that it? Of course, you want to save her from the pain of it, but you can't, Mother Hiyakawa. No one can."

She turned to face him. "Who'd wish this on her own child? The kind of life I lead? What peace is there in what we do, Gee?" She stepped back inside and grabbed up a notepad with writing on it. She held the pad to his eyes to display a painful, over-large child's handwriting that blared out a handful of words: *I want to die now, please.*

He breathed deeply, taking the notepad in his hands, staring at the unfamiliar script. Tight, withholding, fearful script. At the same time, Gene asked, "This isn't Nia's writing is it?"

"No."

"Are you like channeling this Yohda Kenko guy? Huh? Channeling?"

"No…'fraid this is a direct communiqué from Julian–if not from one of the dead spirits of one of the other boys the Phantom abducted and tortured to death."

"When did you write this?"

"Sometime in my sleep. I can't say precisely. I found it on my bedside table when you woke me."

"And you think it's Julian, and that he's pleading for someone to put him out of his misery?"

"That's how I read it, yes."

"Any images come through with it?"

"None I can recall. I was dreaming of the street children and their Blue Lady, and Bloody Mary."

"Maybe all that street stuff is getting in the way. Have you considered that?"

"I consider everything. You know that. But my instincts tell me that there's something somewhere somehow connecting the street stories with this child predator."

"And if you are wrong?"

This stopped her cold. Her greatest fear. Being wrong and someone's life in the balance, gone because she came up wanting. She stepped back out onto the balcony and watched the traffic below. "Then they can kick my half Japanese, half Irish ass off the case."

"What kinda 'half-assed' approach is that, Rae?"

This made her laugh, and she hugged him. "Gee, our relationship, as is…it is so right, so perfect. Let's don't screw with it, please! I beg you."

He hugged her back and nodded. "All right…okay…if you're sure, but I can't promise you anything."

"And I won't promise you anything." She hugged him again, and over his shoulder, she saw Nia, where she stood at the balcony alongside them. She prayed Nia hadn't been there long, and now her daughter silently slipped back into her room under Aurelia's stare. *God, what must she be thinking,* Rae wondered.

Cy went about the work of putting the hook through the neck at the base of the spine to hold Toby Slayter's now glowing, clown-like body and face upright and dangling in the fun house. Countless people would see Cy's artwork, his 'sculpture' made from the raw material of the homeless brat before his body would begin to decay. For a time, the early desiccation odors actually added to the experience and creepiness of the creep show here, but it was not soon after that these odors became so bad that even Cy could not take them anymore. It rather amazed him that not even the three layers of paint on the body could hold back these odors. At which time, he'd have to replace Toby as he'd done the others before him, this time with Julian–still chained to his radiator and losing weight on a bread and water diet.

Cy stood back and examined his masterwork.

"This one's a good, Cy...very good," said Clem Hicks, a roustabout who did odd jobs about the carnival as well, acting as Cy's helper at times. Hicks had slipped up on Cy, giving him a start.

He offered Cy a drink from his bottle of Dickel whiskey. Cy turned down the offer so often he thought Hicks ought to have gotten the message by now, but he always asked. Said it was politeness to ask a fellow before he drank.

"You wanna help, then get over to Jake's kiosk and set his motorized gizmo to work. Seems his ducks don't move today."

"Sure...sure, but I heard you working late last night, so I figured you might need a hand here this morning."

"No, all is fine here, Hicks."

Hicks disappeared. If he kept creeping around, he would wind up a large clown here in the darkness. Damn fool.

Alone again with his creation, Cy wondered why some

people found clowns scary; made little sense to him. He'd known a lot of clowns over the years, kicking around from carnival to circus and back and forth across the states, finally settling down here, but he had never met a clown who would harm a kid. In fact, most were down and outs sad drunks and hard working stiffs.

He had never met a one who was frightening either in or out of costume. People didn't know what was truly terrifying, most never experienced a real scare, not like Toby and others before him had. Now getting painted to death…that was scary.

He also liked the aspect of hanging the results of his peculiar 'art' for anyone passing through the funhouse to see and admire, and get a fright from if it brought up a fright. Cy had at one time three dangling here, each with a different psychedelic color that shone brightly in the black interior. He was down to one now. Julian would make two if he got the job done soon enough, and Mary or another who procured for him would likely soon bring him a third. He liked rotating the artwork in threes if he could. Three was a nice revolving number, and he had gotten used to three at a time and there was no going back.

He had a lot of calls today from this, that, and the other people at various venues here at the carnival who needed something patched, fixed, or remedied. He was a jack-of-all-trades for the carnival, a real Mr. Fixit indeed, with a tool for all occasions. All he ever wanted to be, however, was an artists, a real artists with a style all his own and a medium he made his own. He had painted every mural at the carnival, including the hideous faces of giant monsters looking out over the midway from the funhouse. But he longed for more, for a wider audience and for a larger venue. His secret dream was to one day have a real showing at a real gallery somewhere.

On his days off, he'd wander downtown Phoenix and speak to gallery owners and show them his portfolio–photos of his murals and 'sculptures' of the boys which he called collectively *The Boys Life*. So far he'd gotten a lot of hemming, hawing, and curiosity, but nothing substantive, nothing like an okay or a commitment.

"Thanks...we'll take time to review your portfolio. You see, it's not any one person's decision. The gallery board has to review all such suggestions, and you have to fill out these forms. Fill them out and bring them back with three representative pieces–either the original or a photograph."

"Wouldn't they shit to see the original of one of the boys," he had mused. And if he showed up with an entire wall mural?"

He had not got it together. Maybe one day.

For now he had to get onto the next job here at the carnival, a plumbing problem in the public restroom. Damn fool people kept throwing any and everything down the toilets; a never-ending story.

Aurelia requested again to see the area in Jefferson Park from where Julian disappeared. Theopolis Redeoux escorted her there with what he called her entourage, Gene Kiley, Coffin, and his high-tech toy. Once in the park, she went into trance state, and now she watched in her mind's eye images related to the abduction–a vague figure in a dark cloud reaching out to a child, mouthing promises. There ran a gazelle-like animal past the image, followed by a strange jellyfish creature that grew larger and larger until it blotted out everything else. Then nothing.

"I want to visit Julian's home, see his room, touch his things," she told Redeoux now.

"It'll be arranged."

"Thanks Theopolis. I know this can't be easy on the parents."

"That's been rough, yeah."

"Rough on you in having to deal with the family, I'm sure."

"That's the truth, but not for the reasons you think...."

Birds flit about the trees around them, singing mating songs. The morning sun glistened on the dew.

"Oh?" she studied his narrowed eyes, a hurt in them. "What is it?"

"Ahhh...the kid's parents. They're not exactly the perfect

parental pair…imagine if you will, Ted Bundy and Lizzie Borden in holy matrimony."

"I see."

"The Osbourne's look like Boy Scout leader and lodge mother beside these two losers. I wanted to push the guy's face in."

"I suspected Julian came from a dysfunctional family. The reason he may've been hanging with kids like Noel and this missing Toby. At least Noel has a family…of sorts."

"Yeah, funny huh? I'll pave the way for you, Dr. Hiya…ahhh Aurelia."

"Whatever it takes, I need to handle some of his things. It could make a difference."

"Then let's have at it."

Gene asked if she were all right.

"None of the images I saw were particularly frightening or emotionally challenging, not like my dream of the other night. I'm fine, Gee, but thanks for asking."

Gene and Edwin exchanged a confused look.

"What is it?" she asked.

"What I saw on replay on the palm monitor, now that was… frightening," replied Edwin. "Wouldn't you say so, Gene?"

"Whoa, what'd you see?" she asked.

"Take a look." Edwin replayed the CRVL CD. Aurelia watched in disbelief as a red, scaly demonic-looking woman in rags, blood dripping from her, lifted a hand out to a small child. The cadaverous figure had large empty eye sockets and shining deep flame rose in each socket of the featureless old hag's face. "Bloody Mary," she muttered.

"Who?" asked Edwin.

Gene put a hand up to Edwin. "Aurelia, could your subconscious have created this image? Given all that we heard yesterday on the subject?"

"Perhaps."

"What'd I miss?" asked Edwin.

"Gene'll fill you in on the way to Julian's home. Guess your palm CRVL is doing its job…picking up on all my conscious and subconscious imagery."

"I'll get the images sent off immediately to Quantico. Still have to work out that instant access thing."

"No matter...very impressive."

"Thanks, Rae."

"I'm beginning to suspect that this street mythology stuff is getting in the way of fine-tuning our search for Julian," suggested Gene.

"Perhaps...perhaps not."

"Aurelia...I've never seen you in such a state of confusion," Gene finally said, his eyes firmly fixed on hers.

"I'm going to the kid's home for a session of telekinesis. Either of you coming?" she asked them.

Edwin was talking to himself: "Could this be a major scientific discovery, a separate subliminal...a second subconscious, deeper, further removed from consciousness than we'd ever imagined?" He stared at the palm screen images as he spoke. "Inside our brains nonetheless. A kind of third realm of the mind that not even our subconscious is aware of – like a three-dimensional chess game?"

"You mean like the Egyptian's third eye?" asked Gene.

"Good luck figuring it out, gentlemen." Aurelia pulled herself from the image on the screen and stepped off, going for Redeoux's unmarked car and leaning against it.

When Gene and Edwin joined her at the car, Edwin said, "Damn sure would love to throw conventional wisdom on its ear. I gotta be on top of this. You guys go ahead without me. Here, take the palm reader with you, 'case you need it."

With that Gene and Rae left with Agent Redeoux, going for Julian's home.

But when Redeoux got on the phone to Julian's mother, she insisted they not come right away. She wanted their lawyer present, and she said she wanted to tidy up around the house first.

Rae pulled the phone from Redeoux and asked Mrs. Redondo to touch nothing in her son's room, which she wanted to see it as it was when Redondo had gone missing.

"All right," agreed the gravely-voiced woman, "but I still want our lawyer present. Do you know they suspect us?"

"Standard procedure, ma'am, to check out the family first."

"I've heard all that. Not without the lawyer, no more!"

"When can you have your lawyer present?"

"I'll call you back."

Hours passed at headquarters where Gene and Rae met the entire team working on the vanishings. They were treated to every sort of theory as they even met with members of the Phoenix PD, and the Arizona State Police. An amber alert had been put out nationwide and John Walsh's Most Wanted team had put it up on the MWA website, displaying Julian's photo and what he'd been wearing when he disappeared.

Evening had come on and no call back from the mother. Angry, Redeoux again contacted her. The boy's mother said that her lawyer had "Quit us just like that! Left high and dry, and we can't find no one we can work with."

"Mrs. Redondo, we're coming ahead with a search warrant I obtained while waiting for your call that never came," Theopolis said as politely as he could manage. "So lawyer or not, we are on our way."

They made the trip to the boy's home, an apartment in the nearby city projects miles from Abraham Stroud City Park, where Julian had taken to hanging out, and from where he'd vanished. Why was Julian frequenting this park so far from home, she wondered. It must have to do with meeting and befriending the homeless Toby, Noel, and others. Perhaps Julian became enamored of their strange mythology, but even more likely, given what Theopolis Redeoux had to say about Julian's family, perhaps he'd adopted the street family in retaliation. Or rather for an emotional survival.

And if Julian had a connection to the homeless? What did it portend? What connections were made, and which if any had to do with his abduction?

The drive from the city park to Julian's home took them through a landscape of bricks, like the bone yard of bricks in her vision, past falling down bungalows and adobe-styled single homes and two-flats, each looking the clone of the other after awhile, miniature Alamos. Small fortresses set against the world. Inside families eked out a living.

Soon they pulled into a weed-infested driveway cracked from years of neglect, bushes overgrown, lawn littered with broken down appliances, standing water in discarded tires, a breeding ground for mosquitoes. In fact, it looked as if an entire vehicle had been dismantled on the lawn. Near a shed at the rear, rusted and looking like a dead deer, lay a scavenged Harley motorcycle. Ahead of them, in the driveway, sat a late model Oldsmobile in fair condition, appearing in running order. A light inside the otherwise darkened home displayed a large-screen TV, giving the dingy home a blue white glow.

As they climbed from the Redeoux's unmarked FBI vehicle and started up the broken walk to the crumbling stairs, Rae felt as if the small bungalow with its arched windows and flat roof glared at them. Foolish yet it felt so.

Theopolis rang the bell and greeted the mother, who stood behind the screen door like a guardian to this little domain, a cigarette dangling from her lips, ashes drifting to the screen and to her feet. She spoke with the cigarette bobbing in her mouth. "Redeoux...you could've waited, but no, you come with reinforcements, heh?"

"Yes, you might say so, Mrs. Redondo. I'd like this to be your choice, so I will ask again, may we come in for a look at Julian's room?"

She stood her ground, a smoker's hacking preceding her next words. "Since your last visit, all the neighbors are thinking we did something to Julian! How awful is that? To have all your neighbors thinking you killed your kid and put it out that he's been abducted by a creep who, up till now, has only gotten hold of homeless kids?"

"We sympathize with your situation, Mrs. Redondo," said Rae, her eyes going to the lady's eyes, imploring.

"I keep telling you people to just send me the taxpayer's money you're wasting on looking for Julian. The kid is in LA or–"

"Gert! Who the hell's at the door?" shouted the man of the house even as he came to investigate. "Oh, it's you, Agent."

"I've brought Agents Hiyakawa and Kiley along with me, along with a warrant." He held up the paper. "If it's all the same with you, Mr. and Mrs. Redondo."

"Whataya 'spect to find in Julian's room?" he asked.

"Nothin' in there," she agreed. "Hell, I've done searched high and low for drugs."

The father put in, "I know that scat's been piping something, but he's clever as a fox."

"Get's that from you, Juan."

"Just let 'em on through, Gert, so they can get in and be gone," said the father. "I'm missing Fear Factor."

She frowned behind her cigarette but opened the door to them, stepping aside. "Just a waste of everybody's time," she muttered as hubby nestled back onto the couch where his pork rinds, dip, and beer sat waiting.

Aurelia and Gene followed Theopolis down the narrow hallway to a back room with a stolen Phoenix city stop sign hanging on a nail. Inside the small space of Julian's room, Aurelia put a hand on Redeoux, stopping him from turning on the light switch. "Leave it as is for a moment, and both of you, out."

"Ahhh....well, okay, if you like," replied Redeoux.

Gene squeezed her hand. "Be careful in here, Rae."

Aurelia saw a large broad-fingered hand reaching out to her through the semi-darkened room, creased and sculpted by an eerie light from an orange-glow-sodium vapor street lamp practically in the back yard. In another instant, she recognized the huge dark hand for what it was–Julian's baseball mitt hanging by the drawstring. She lifted it off its hook and slipped it on her hand in the dark.

Outside the door, she heard Julian's mother, agitated and talking to Redeoux and Gene, asking, "But what's that strange-looking Jap doing in my boy's room alone in the dark!"

Gene and Redeoux worked hard to quell the woman's

concerns. A muffled shout from the husband came through as well, something about another beer.

Aurelia concentrated on the feel and smell of the well-worn glove. Julian loved sports. He'd dreamed of winning a scholarship in baseball, and of becoming a professional in one or the other of his favorite sports. For him, getting a decent life, being paid for what you loved, this was his greatest goal in life.

Suddenly Aurelia felt as if her hand were trapped inside the big mitt. She felt red-hot stakes going through each hand, as if being crucified, and it made her want to scream in response.

Using her free hand, she instead turned on the light and studied her free hand where it burned.

Nothing.

She'd half expected some sort of blood or stigmata.

She again studied her burning hand.

Nothing.

No sign of a sting, no reddening, nothing.

Finally, the fiery burning subsided.

She lifted the mitt and shook it and examined it for any sign of a spider or insect or scorpion. No doubt Phoenix was rife with scorpions. But this was no physical attack but rather a mental one–a spectral sting, an ethereal bite or the byte of a psychic message?

Was Julian alive and sending out psychic pleas? Was his psychic energy focused on the one place where he felt safe–the confines of his bedroom where a lock had been placed on the inside, so he could cut off the world, including his parents? Could he be focusing on this room...on the mitt he left dangling on the wall, his bed, pillows, private things? Things below and above his bed; things on his walls...things kept hidden from parents. These all defined the victim before he'd become a victim. They gave him a sense of who he was. And all that lay here in the tight little space of a single room.

Aurelia imagined how many times he'd escaped this room in search of something more. She imagined how now he must long for this scorned place. It might be the only thing keeping him alive and fighting, the memory of home, but for how long?

How long before Julian Redondo would give in to the torture and simply give up his life out of a desire to end his suffering?

She wondered if in that moment, when the child victim completely gave in to his own desire to be let out of this world, if this was the time the predator chose to end the torture and the life he held within his grasp. Was Julian conveying this, or was this her notion. She could not be sure.

On the other side of the door, the others were getting restless, and mom was threatening to come through.

Aurelia lifted a photo of Julian with his dog, a bull terrier. As if awakening a dragon beneath the bed, Rae heard the dog in the photo growling a low but building snarl. Then she realized it was not in her head or coming off the photo at all. The snarling came from a corner dog bed inside the room. The dog'd been asleep, nestled atop some of Julian's discarded clothes. If Julian'd run away, he'd have taken his dog with him, she reasoned. The love for the dog came through in spades in the photo.

Aurelia exchanged the photo with a notebook that turned out to be a journal that Julian had been keeping. The growling grew back of her. The journal dated back a month, a lifetime for a young person. He had filled it with the mundane steps of his every day, the trivia of existence, from wiping his nose to brushing his teeth, to going to the corner store for a can of tuna, a jar of mayonnaise, and smokes for mom. It was no doubt a forced writing assignment the boy's teacher at nearby Kingsbury Junior High insisted upon–keep a daily journal.

She started at the sudden banging on the door, when a slip of paper floated from the diary and onto the floor. It was a drawing. Below the rough sketch of an ugly woman who looked like a homeless and wretched old lady he had written words that read: I know her secret name.

"It's Bloody Mary," she said aloud to Gene and Redeoux as they came though the door, no longer able to keep mom at bay.

Gene took the charcoal drawing she extended. With Redeoux on his shoulder, Gene studied the crude drawing of a raggedy old woman as mom soothed the growling dog.

"Easy Buttons, easy," Julian's mom whispered to the dog, her cigarette smoke choking the pooch and burning its eyes even as she hugged it, crushing it to her sagging breasts.

Redeoux said of the depiction, "This could be any homeless old crone on the street."

"Exactly." Gene continued to study every line of the rendering. He turned the drawing in various directions. "Someone we all see but don't see...someone we look through instead of at. By the way, Julian's got a raw talent for drawing."

"Yes, all of us adults might not see her, but the homeless children certainly do. And Julian claims here to know the old woman's secrets."

"Meaning the homeless kids filled him in on their secrets," added Gene.

Redeoux looked harder and longer at the drawing. "Perhaps...but..."

"But what?"

"There's more to Julian's disappearance, I sense...much more."

"Agreed." She cracked open the boy's scrapbook. There were sketches and photos of children all throughout the book, photos that Julian himself had taken with a twenty-dollar camera that sat on his bureau top. A work in progress again for school, she imagined, but perhaps even more for Julian himself. There were photos of Noel, Danielle, Hector, Peter, Toby, and others of the street families.

In Julian's pencil drawings, he proved a fine artist for one so young. He had a gift for catching the essence of a person in the eyes and around the mouth, even the nostrils which seemed to flare with life and to breathe on the flat surface of the paper.

Aurelia glanced over the writings and settled on an entry that chilled her to the bone. This entry, dated several days before his disappearance, read: *I saw Bloody Mary tonight. She eats snakes alive, and she eats kids who don't know her secret name.*

"I need a drink, Gee. Let's get outta here."

"You know alcohol dulls the psychic sense, Rae. You don't

really want to go there."

"The hell I don't. Dulled senses sound awfully good about now."

At the door, Julian's father stood just gazing in at them, curious, and shaking his head. "All this trouble over that no good kid. Told his mother, and told the first cops come through here, and now I'm telling you two," he addressed Gene and Aurelia, "the boy just run off."

"How can you be sure?" asked Gene.

"He was always threatening to do it, and now he's done done it. And that's all there is to it. Hateful ungrateful is all he ever was."

Aurelia nodded thoughtfully. "He seemed to have friends among the runaways. Seemed to hang with the street crowd near the shelter."

"He admired on 'em is what he did. He and I didn't always get along, sometimes we'd come near to blows, and he'd always tell his mom that either she gets rid of me, or he gets rid of himself, meaning he'd go live as a runaway, a homeless. You see, I ain't his real father. I don't care what Gert put on the birth certificate. He couldn't be no kid of mine, the pansy."

"I would've never guessed."

The father went on. "Swore he was going to leave for LA and Hollywood altogether and see some of the world. I told him it was all the same shit this world."

"I'm sure you were an inspiration to him, Mr. Redondo."

"That's right."

The mother, a thin, frail woman who looked like a refugee out of Mexico if not Bangladesh–something exotic and pretty in her features long lost to smoke, booze, occasional pot and the worry lines–joined them, still holding onto Julian's dog. She stood now at her man's side in a pathetic show of family ties. Aurelia recognized healed over bruises about the temple and eyes.

"Whataya doing with Julian's things?" she asked, dog squirming in her grasp, her voice slurred, the effects of whatever she'd been smoking all morning. "I mean when he gets home, he's gonna go straight for that book he draws in, and that baseball glove you're holding."

Aurelia had unconsciously held onto the glove and found it indeed in her hands. So she stepped close to the mother and placed her hand around the woman's wrist and stared into he eyes. In a moment, she had convinced the grieving mother to allow her to keep hold of the boy's sketchpad and notes, along with the glove.

"Sure...sure, I guess, but he's gonna want 'em back."

On their way out and down to the car, Gene said, "You handled that well, Rae. I wanted to strangle those two."

"The little good it'd do."

She summed up, "Julian was in effect homeless."

"Right." Redeoux lit his pipe and stared at the stars overhead. "His own mother's not emotionally here for him, not even now, with him gone missing for days."

"Who called him in missing?"

"An aunt named Agatha Layton."

"We've got to talk to Danielle again at her coven near the Salvation Army shelter."

"What do you hope to get from Danielle?" Theopolis wanted to know.

"They knew Julian. He hung with them. They knew him, and they have a greater fix on what happened to him than do the PPD or the FBI. Come on."

Danielle opened up to Aurelia, telling her a story about herself and her mother. "One night last year, we made a bed out of a refrigerator box, newspapers, and plastic grocery bags in a Kansas City park where junkies gather. It was my turn to stand guard against the "screamers.""

"Screamers?" Aurelia asked, making all of Danielle's followers laugh.

"Packs of roaming addicts–screamers," explained Noel.

"Anyhow, while mama slept, I guarded her. That's when all of a sudden Charlie was standing there, dressed in his army uniform."

"And Charlie is?"

"My dead brother."

Gene groaned. "Sorry."

Died in Iraq after the war was 'spose to be over."

"I'm so sorry, Danielle." Rae reached out a hand to her, but she pulled away.

Danielle then gulped and teared up, but she kept on with her story. "'The Devil got loose from under the red sea of lost souls!' is what Charlie was saying out of his dead mouth. Then he said, 'The rich people didn't stop him!' And then he added, 'The angels need soldiers.'"

"Red sea of Hades?" Rae flashed on her bad dream about a satanic coral reef. "So he was warning you, your brother?"

"That's what I'm telling you."

"Do you know where this red sea is located?"

They all laughed. "In Hell," said Noel.

"Danny," said Rae, "where is your mother now?"

"County hospital...sick...up here." She pointed to her head.

A chubby boy piped in, his name Chico. "My dead cousin told me that as soon as holy water touches the Devil's skin, it turns red...and...and it causes his invisible horns to sprout from his head. The dry arroyo fills with a river of blood; spirit screams and bones of children the Devil's done murdered float on the blood-orange water."

"And just when the angels think they've convinced Good Streets–people like us–that they are in as much danger as Bad Streets," explained Danielle, "Satan vanishes through a secret gateway beneath the dry river bed, or the river, or a lake, a pond, or any way he can find to go below the surface, you see."

"I see," said Aurelia.

"Now he's coming your way," Danielle warned. "You'll need to learn how to fight him."

"What do I do?"

"Pray to the Blue Lady?"

"I will...I will."

Gene noticed that the boy named Chico carried a math and spelling workbook around with him, and asked the boy about it.

"I can't go to school," said Chico.

"But you carry school books," Gene replied.

"Thanks to Julian. He got them for me."

Noel added in shaky voice, "He ought to've grown up... so he could be a teacher."

"Perhaps he will, if we can find him," Gene said.

Chico dropped his wide-eyed gaze in a gesture of sadness.

"Study hard," Julian told us all," said another of the children.

"Stay strong and smart so's you count on yourself, no one else, is what he said," added Danielle. "And we taught him, too...to never stop watching out, to not let his guard down and how to pray to the Blue Lady, but I guess he let his guard down."

"And Toby?"

"He should've known better. He was 'spose to be smart, street smart."

"Watch out for Bloody Mary," said Chico.

"I told Julian what I am telling you now, Aurelia Hiyakawa." Danielle's voice had become ominous. "Bloody Mary is coming with Satan. And she's seen your face. She's picked you out for a no good end."

Gene placed a hand on Aurelia's shoulder at this warning. "What about the Phantom, the one the cops and the press are after, the child killer?" Aurelia asked Danielle point blank. "How does he figure into this war of angels and with Bloody Mary?"

"How do you know that the Phantom is a he?" she asked in return.

"I've assumed that much from statistical probability."

"You think Satan cares about your statistical probability? I think Bloody Mary is the Phantom. Or at least, she is directing his movements."

"Why do you think so?"

"Nothing goes on here on the streets without her hand on it."

"And she works for whom?"

"Satan...Satan of course."

"And the Blue Lady?"

"God, she works for God."

"And where is God and the Angel Warriors and the Blue Lady? Where can I see them?"

"Hiding out."

"Hiding out where?"

"Hiding out in plain sight. In hospitals, banks, schools. Julian was an angel, and for all I know, you could be one of them–a warrior angel."

"That's sweet of you to say."

"It's not sweet. It's instinct–pure, simple instinct." Danielle then looked her hard in the eye and added, "Look...I have nothing to give you beyond the facts of life on the street, but soon maybe...maybe I'll know something. I have my eyes open and my ears to the ground. If you guys are willing to pay...."

"We're budgeted to pay for information that leads to this killer, sure."

"All right, then you're going to hear from me again...soon."

"If you've got any specific information, Danielle, anything at all..."

"I'll get back to you on that. Promise."

They parted with a complicated, street handshake, which Rae bombed at, but it made all the children laugh, and their laughter felt like a golden, melodic rain on her ear.

Same time, Quantico, Virginia FBI Headquarters

Miranda Palmer Waldron used an electronic pointer to mark the area on the huge overhead visual of Aurelia Murphy Hiyakawa's mental images sent via satellite from a CRVL station hastily assembled at the Phoenix field offices to FBI headquarters in Quantico. Thanks be to Edwin Coffin. She was told these images were instantaneously harnessed via Coffin's new handheld CRAWL unit, gathered while Rae Hiyakawa worked her magic on site. Miranda thought it beyond amazing.

She conveyed this to her assembled team.

Around a conference table, a team of interpreters discussed each image, and what it might portend, and how it might point to a killer. Every conceivable angle. Every conceivable path. Every conceivable interpretation.

The team examined each image from all sides, top and bottom, over and under, through and through. All ideas aired. The essential images narrowed, those non-essential discarded. Even the most mundane references came to light here; even the most remote, the most hair-brained, the most over the edge came into play. Results of this think-tank could mean life and death.

The PSI interpretive team at Quantico was made up of an array of professionals in parapsychology, psychotherapy, forensic psychiatry, profiling, criminology, sociology, history, literature, folklore, archeology, and the humanities–experts from university professors to psychics, including a woman who called herself a symbologist, an expert on symbolism. No longer were psychic investigators working alone. This unit worked as machine under the umbrella of the Psychic Sensory Investigation Unit. Many of its members overlapped with other FBI units.

Dr. Waldron, who'd come to respect Aurelia Hiyakawa as both a human being and an extraordinarily gifted psychic, made it her job to bring all the disparate images filtered through Aurelia into the best focus. Like an orchestra director, she oversaw the dissection of Aurelia's psychic visions. Not only was Miranda Waldron routinely joined by the brightest in every field, she had the green light and resources to haul in any expert in any field not accounted for should she feel the need.

It was the job of the team then to make some coherent pattern and sense of the images. They were not always successful, but they could be dead on at times.

The ultimate goal, when egos were set aside, was the right interpretation of the images; to convert image to clue. And for Dr. Waldron, as for Aurelia herself, the interpretation that saved lives was everything. Also like Rae, Waldron's life seemed sacrificed on this altar every bit as much as the psychic. Due to this connection, the two women had become closely attached and the best of friends. Aurelia knew that Miranda could always rein her in, and that for Miranda, no one person, no one ego–not even Aurelia's–was as important as saving a life.

"Come on people. What does all this mean? Stylized park, garden... rocks, water trickling through under a dark moon–a river runs through it. Are we content with the clichéd notion of a Garden of Eden here, peace, love, truth, beauty with these angels caressing one another?" Waldron coaxed. By phone from Phoenix, Rae had admitted to having had these images bombarding her nightly for several days now.

Waldron continued orchestrating the symphony in this search for underlying meaning and ultimate truth. "Or...or is there something else going on here? Something below the surface...just out of sight...just inching and slouching over the horizon of this image? Does the damned image have any bearing on anything–anything–you have ever seen, felt, smelt, touched, tasted, or sensed ever before?"

She was met with silence.

She felt like cursing.

Instead, she continued to cheerlead the team. "Does it have a correlation with something you can reference? Help me out here, people, because for me, all I see is a g'damn Grandma Moses print here."

"Yes, primitive rendition but with an otherworldly quality, a surreal feeling to it," replied Dr. Cable Gaston, an expert on psychoanalysis and dream interpretation.

"I find it interesting that the trees lining the periphery are so entirely stiff and stylized, rigid as though unreal...as though artificial," added Dr. Singe Olynx, a professor of sociology, whose feminine whiskey voice filled the room.

"Bone hard, a phallic symbol," said Dr. Walter Roberts.

"Everything is phallic with you, Walter," replied a colleague beside him, making them all laugh except for Dr. Singe Olynx. She said, "It speaks of separation. Bondage even in nature.

Isolation in nature, as if to say ultimately all living things, while inter-connected, are disconnected and stand alone and separate and must face life's horrors alone."

"'You gotta walk that lonesome valley...'" sang out the rebel of the group, the parapsychologist and psychic Dr. Lee Madden, a former marine, his stature imposing even while seated. His long mane of yellow corn silk hair tied in a ponytail, Lee looked the part of linebacker, huge and hulking, but his size and overgrown eyebrows and overhanging brow masked a keen mind. "'You gotta walk it for yourself, nobody else can walk it for you....'"

"Enough already with the Johnny Cash imitation," said Waldron.

Lee replied, "And so on, and so on. This is still cut rate clichéd nonsense–Singe's interpretation."

"Name calling is not necessary," cautioned Waldron.

Lee ignored this. "Aurelia's visions are not about archetypes–never are! They are about individual events and situations."

"But those individuals she is honing in on, they most likely do think in terms of typical archetypes, so we can hardly throw out the clichéd or the mundane," countered Dr. Willetta Heising, a Ph.D. in literature with seventeen books on literary and biblical imagery and symbolism to her credit. "Regardless of how unique Aurelia's and perhaps your thoughts may be, Dr. Madden, most people, Americans perhaps more than any other nationality, think in terms of archetypal structures and metaphors."

"Oh please, give the public some credit for brains," countered Lee.

"The norm is a fourth grade reading level, Lee!" countered Singe. "Our lives are permeated with and shaped by our clichés and our familiar metaphors, right down to how we think about our pork chop dinner, our children, our local team, our country, our flag, our bloody wars...you name it. Hell, read George Carlin!"

"Ahhh...the conscious of a nation...the American George

Bernard Shaw," replied Madden, nodding. "I take your meaning, Doctor."

Miranda Waldron once again was reminded that she had her hands full with this group.

"Are you saying we are controlled by our symbols?" asked Dr. Maria Sendak, an historian.

"Linguists agree, language is thought, thought is language, and our language is riddled with archetypal symbols–shapes we automatically plug into as say in the face of death, burial, weddings, graduations, you name it."

"Plug ins?" asked Madden, grinning, nodding, agreeing. "I like that." Madden and Dr. Heising began making eyes again.

"From the fish to the dove to the olive branch and beyond," Sendak added.

"So what do the trees represent archetypally speaking, if not dicks like Walter says?" asked Lee Waldron, always interested in shocking everyone. "And for that matter the angels caressing among the greenery, one or two hugging the trees?"

"Eden of course. Trees routinely mean life…the staff of life, the tree of life."

Miranda raised her shoulders. "But these trees are dead, people, despite their greenness, despite their stilted leaves. And while angels generally depict goodness, light, beauty…well the same can be said of the angels depicted in this imagery–stiff fakes."

"Interesting interpretation," replied Madden. "If you will notice the angels are rather cardboard cutouts. How much of this might not be Aurelia's mind sifting, maneuvering around, massaging the actual images she is getting? I've asked this question before, but no one seems to want to deal with it."

"For fear of its implications," added Walter.

"Everyone's so anxious to believe in Edwin Coffin's genius that we dare not question the validity of the images or the software or the hardware involved?" Dr. Heising joined this little rebellion, nodding appreciatively, blinking. "Does the psychic distort the image even as she receives and sends?"

Everyone fell silent a moment, all their hard work of

studying the images made gigantic on the screen over their heads having been called into question. Shouting broke out on both sides of the issue.

But Miranda Waldron shouted them down. Finally, with everyone again silent, she calmly said, "Aurelia has no conscious knowledge of doing anything of the kind. I think we have to assume we are seeing what she is seeing." No one readily countered Miranda Waldron or attacked this notion.

"This place...I can't quite place it...but there is something strangely familiar about this park," said the symbolist, Dr. Naomi Shulatte.

"I'd like you all to pursue any possibilities that may come to mind," Miranda now said. "It could be extremely important to the case."

A second series of beamed images ran alongside Aurelia's mentally-created images–police reports on all the murdered children and on the missing Julian Redondo and Toby Slayter in particular.

"Can we move along to the other major image she has sent us, the red orange thing with the monster?" asked Dr. Sendak.

"All right, we'll report what little we have made of the angel park image back to Aurelia in the field."

They began in earnest on the far more fluid, alive image, riddled with what are routinely negative images, Satan straddling his captured souls amid that strange, alluring coral reef.

"Satan straddling a bloody coral reef," said Singe. "Certainly something new."

"Perhaps...perhaps not," said the historian. "I seem to recall seeing a painting once quite similar to this. But I don't know where or when I saw it. Perhaps an illustration of a horror story in Horror Garage or Cemetery Dance." Sendak explained that his secret guilt passion was horror literature, and that these magazines were devoted to horror writers like John Weagley, John Everson, Martin Mundt, Edward Lee, Joe Konrath, Brian Yount, Chesya Burke, Geoffrey Caine, and Evan Kingsbury. "I'll look through some back issues."

"That fits in with what Aurelia is telling us about the direction she's taken with respect to the killer," said Miranda Waldron. "She believes that while he is surrounded by people on a large scale, and lives a normal life, he is completely isolated in his head, so he leads a second life."

The room fell silent when Chief Raule Apreostini stepped in. After a glance at the red-orange glow of the Hades Sea and the straddling Satan figure, he launched in on his concerns. "We've got to crack these images, to decipher their meaning as soon as possible."

"What sort of timeframe are we talking, Chief Apreostini?" asked Dr. Waldron.

"Historically, he kills within a week's window, leaving the painted body to be found by authorities. That means Slayter and Redondo have at tops twenty four hours–at least one of them has unless he decides to do them both at once."

"Twenty four hours?" repeated several of the assembled, as each exchanged either a look with Waldron, Raule Apreostini, or the image on the screen.

"That means we are in lock down, people. We can't have another child in Phoenix turn up in a dumpster or drain pipe painted like a fucking clown."

Nodding to the chief, Miranda Waldron said to her team, "So I suggest we get seriously moving on this."

Same day, Phoenix, Arizona

Back at the hotel, Aurelia stared at the barstools lining the bar at the Lucky Horseshoe Watering Hole. Every single barstool was an authentic western saddle, and so to sit at the bar, one must straddle the saddle. She scanned the room. She could take a booth but already some bozo was lifting his glass to her. She much preferred a stool at the bar when alone in such places as a barstool simply offered easier, more efficient means of escape from barroom bores.

"I know...the saddles–right?" asked the bartender, a young blonde woman. "Told 'em it was a sucky idea especially for ladies in business suits. But if you like a challenge."

The bartender looked no older than Nia. "Always up for a challenge and a Jack whiskey sour with an orange slice and cherry." Aurelia climbed aboard. Soon, she was confiding in the stranger who she was, why she was in Phoenix, how her feet were killing her.

The young bartender was no Joannie as she only half-listened. Listening was a dying art form, Aurelia believed. Still she launched in, speaking extemporaneously about troubling issues, and the bartender, curious, asked, "What's-at feel like, being psychic and seeing into the heads of like a Ted Bundy or a John Wayne Gacey and shit?"

It was an open invitation to lay it on the poor girl. Aurelia thought for a mere millisecond and replied calmly, "Strangely enough, it is not like the movies or TV shows like *Medium*, trust me."

And so it went:

"My reaction to the horror I not only see but feel, as if living it, when investigating a crime via remote PSI, psychic sensory investigation does not leave me a basket case. After such a session, I do need quiet time and warm hugs to begin to emotionally detach from the intensity of what I've been immersed in, what I have tasted, touched, felt, smelled, seen, and sometimes heard. But in a strange way, the experience reinvigorates me, since I've made peace with it, you see... makes me want to work even harder to locate a killer and end his career."

"Fascinating stuff. Make a hell of a movie," interrupts the bartender.

Still, if the victim feels terror or panic, so then do I, and the terror and panic is not some abstract emotion belonging to someone else. It is mine. I own it...until I regain some detachment from these emotions and can again realize they are controllable. Until I get back to the ability to sense that this is I...me...myself...and this is not I or even me or myself, not really, but someone else that I must pull myself from. This regaining of oneself is neither spontaneous nor simple. Especially not with the extreme degree of something no one has a name for, that 'at-one-ment' I have with the victim. Takes time to first discern and then to recognize the sensation, then identify its source–this is the detachment I'm so poorly explaining.

"No...no, not at all. Go on," replies the bartender as she makes another whiskey sour for Aurelia.

It's why I cling to Gee–ahhh Gene Kiley–my spotter as we call them. Why I cling for a long, long hug as his energy in a hug is far stronger than the victim's. It is the reason I might be in tears too. Tears of horror, not weakness as we know that strong emotions and reactions make most women tear up, and that anger is a decoy for that. Anger is nonproductive as are tears, but so far as I know, last I looked, I'm just human. That body-to-body hug from Gee helps me to center and gather together–within my, by now, scattered energies.

"Wow...this Gee guy sounds hot. Is he?"

Gee's hug, his touch, it is not in the least sexual; it can't be to be effective. A spotter and his psychic have to maintain a special level of trust. Sex would only screw with that. I'd be on guard the whole time, worried, and I couldn't be helped by Gee–

"Wow…what a helluva life you must lead."

Gee, he slapped me with a tough relationship choice on the plane coming down here, brings up some troubling issues. He freakin' made a pass…well, not a pass but maybe worse, a…a proposal we become an item.

"No! What a bastard."

Well, no, he's really a great guy and would be a terrific catch, but I gotta trust him to catch me, and personal stuff gets hairy. We all know that, and Gee just has to know in the pit of his heart that if we're to maintain the relationship we have, that this stuff has to stop. I went back to my earlier diary entry regarding Gee's hug, and I must make him see it as I do, make it make sense to him, else all of this talk can only further deteriorate our working relationship. Shit, why'd this have to happen? Doesn't make sense. How to screw up a perfect platonic relationship. We can be very, very good friends, the closest, even able to flirt and tease and be physically affectionate with one another–touchy feely maybe–but…but…

"But never fuck buddies."

Crass as you put it, yes! You do cut to the bone. Underneath, it's got to be a platonic relationship–else how do I feel safe with him for the unique sort of partnership we are in? And since he crossed the line just talking about US in capital letters, hasn't he already ruined what we had?

"Men can always find a way to screw up a good friendship. It's like genetically coded they do so." The young bartender wiped down the bar in what must be nervous energy and habit.

Aurelia found her cell phone and called Nia's cell number, and she quickly learned that Nia and Enriquiana had had a wonderful day of *shopping-Nia's-heart-out* along Phoenix's own version of Rodeo Drive in downtown Phoenix, where only upscale shops were found. Aurelia spoke to a happy, civil Nia from the Horseshoe saddle, a soft buzz on, finally feeling some relief from the day, winding down from its every taxing moment, of which there'd been many.

While she sat alone on her saddle, secretly pleased to have some time to herself, she stared at the saddle beside her where Julian Redondo's sketchbook lay, his baseball mitt hanging from the saddle horn. Theopolis had dropped Gene and Aurelia off at the door, saying he had to see to some things back at headquarters. Gene had gone to find the pool in order to get in some laps, he'd said. She'd replied that she meant to get in some laps, too–at the bar. Gene, ever the watchful protector had warned her off too much alcohol. "Remember, Rae, it dulls your psychic sensibilities. It gets in the way."

"Right at the moment, Gee, that's exactly what I need, to dull my senses–all six of them, if you don't mind. Besides, my Irish genes require a certain amount of booze, and I'm a pint low."

That was when he chose to leave, the only one at Quantico who knew of her increasing habit. "What in hell do they expect," she asked under her breath, "Superwoman, Wonder Woman, freaking Zena the Warrior Princess?"

The young bartender gave her a curious look on hearing this.

The noisy, too bright, too impersonal Horseshoe Lounge was no good. For one, Joannie was missing…not here to confide in, to simply talk to. Replaced instead by a blonde young lady with a painted on smile that Revlon could be proud of–a bartender who still had to review her playbook when asked to make a Zombie or a White Russian, and young enough to be Aurelia's daughter. Certainly not old enough to give advice, or to understand the adult gunnysack of angst faced by the typical person Aurelia's age–a tapeworm of related problems any right-thinking person would stop life cold in its tracks in order to address.

The young bartender was making a lot of Margaritas for the other patrons, as whenever anyone asked for anything other than a Margarita, the bartender–calling herself Tawny–grabbed for her bartender's bible. Who could fuck up a Margarita?

Aurelia had turned in her saddle. She now sat with a view to the main lobby where she expected Nia and Enriquiana to appear any time. She thought of going up to her room to wait there. She thought of how a shower would feel. She thought of how hungry she was fast becoming, just as Tawny placed a bowl of pretzels in front of her. Then she thought of the weight gain the salted pretzels meant. Then she thought of how long it'd been since she'd had a real workout in a real gym, the one where she continued to pay dues but seldom saw any results because she was never there.

She gnawed on the pretzels for a while and quietly, even demurely sipped at her drink while some guy looking like the aging hotel dick eyeballed her, lifted his glass, and saluted. Tawny noticed everything. She noted the jerk at the end of the bar, and she noticed the sketchbook beside Aurelia.

"I'm kinda studying art. Mind if I thumb through your pad?"

"It's not mine, actually...belongs to...to a friend, a kid named Julian."

Hadn't the girl enough customers to keep busy? Apparently not. The two of them were soon studying Julian's pencil and charcoal drawings together.

"Nice technique. Your friend's got...well, he's got a deft hand...real potential," Tawny said.

"Are you some kind of genius with this stuff?" Aurelia glanced more deeply at Tawny. The wire thin girl, no breasts to speak of, her hair done up in that strange do that made a person look as if she'd walked away from a lightning strike and somehow survived, gave Aurelia the sense that she knew art.

"I'm going to teach art some day. Working on my degree in art-Ed at the university. Job here is just to make ends meet."

"Oh...well then, you do know something about art. That's a good thing. Going in to teaching, passing along knowledge, stomping out ignorance daily."

"Oh, I don't intend to be one of those career teachers, you know, the really truly dedicated ones like Mr. Chips or Mr. Opus or Miss Jean Brody or Helen Keller's teacher, what was her name? Oh yeah! Ann Sullivan or any of those types."

"Hey, you could be a great teacher if you put your heart into it," Aurelia encouraged Tawny.

"Naaah, not me. I just want a steady paycheck, so I can live halfway decent while I go on casting calls. What I really wanna be is Hillary Swank or Julia Roberts, see, an actress of the first order. But teaching art, I figure that pays the rent. Level headed of me, my mom says."

"Yes...I'd have to agree with your mom."

"I'm writing a screenplay too."

"Really?"

"Well...I have sixteen pages done, but I've got writer's block right now, so..."

"What's it about?" Aurelia felt a sense of *déjà vu* as she had had this conversation with the bellhop, the doorman, the desk clerk. Everyone in Phoenix had a film script in the works it seemed.

"It's a twist on Women are from Venus, Men are from Mars kinda but no aliens. In the year 2525 every girl child is being drowned because of laws enacted by men, laws to allow men complete rule over the world without any kind of controls over male behavior, see? No controls for a species with no controls anyway, see? What happens is the men begin to revert."

"Revert?"

"Back, they go like planet of the apes ape-shit, all hairy-backed, walking on their knuckles, the whole cave dweller degeneration, kind of like the opposite of evolution called de-evolution."

"And I take it that it's up to some Charlie's Angels types, the women remaining, to ahhh...."

"To unite and kill Bill, so to speak...kill off all the men."

Aurelia realized in an instant that Tawny did not particularly like men.

"Who's this Julian who did the art?" Tawny switched subjects. "Your kid? The one you were talking to on the phone?"

"No, not my kid. More like nobody's kid."

Tawny noticed the bulge in Aurelia's armpit, catching a glimpse of the metal, a Smith and Wesson .38, her service issue. "You some kind of cop?"

"That's right."

"God...I could never be a cop...ever. What you people see. I mean, I sympathize. I read a lot of cop stories from my favorite writers, you know Joe Haldeman, Joe Walker, Joe Konrath...all the Joe writers who don't pull any punches, you know. God if their stories won't keep you out of law enforcement as a career move, then nothing will. But I would love to play a cop on like a TV show or in a movie like Marge what's her name or the one on Law and Order."

Aurelia saw Nia and Enriquiana enter through the revolving doors at the lobby entrance. "Sorry, Tawny, but I gotta go."

Tawny handed her the sketchbook. "Whoever this kid is, his art seems to me a cry for help. I mean it's a raw plea."

"That's quite insightful, Tawny. Perhaps you'll make a better teacher than you know."

"Yeah but I never want to abandon my dream and just be a teacher. Anyone can teach."

"You think so? How many of your teachers throughout your schooling had an effect on you, a real effect?"

"Well...Miss Page...yeah...her."

"And?"

"Ahhh...I get your point."

Hopefully right between the eyes, Aurelia thought but only waved and said, "I'll see you around the hotel, Tawny."

Aurelia had noticed that Nia had gone directly to the concierge desk, and Enriquiana, her hands full with shopping bags, stood off to one side looking uneasy, tired, and fretful.

Aurelia slipped up alongside her daughter just in time to hear the much older and handsome Latin concierge suggest the name of several local spots for nightlife. "Forget about it, Nia. You're not going clubbing in a city where you know no one," she informed her daughter.

Nia wheeled to see her mother, her mouth falling, but she recovered enough to say, "Please, Mother, don't embarrass me."

"I'll try hard not to." She then grabbed the stunned sixteen-year-old and hugged her tightly to her. "I've missed you!"

"Duh…we've been shopping for hours, haven't we, Enri?" she asked the housemaid. "You shoulda found time to join us."

Aurelia kissed Enriquiana. "Thank you for bringing her home, and accompanying her today."

"Oh God, I am going to die here!" Nia gnashed her teeth, one eye on the handsome Ruben who pretended business and deafness at his desk.

Aurelia guided them toward the elevators for their rooms. Nia's voice carried all round the lobby. "Since you were no place to be found this morning, Mother, Ruben over there was kind enough to tell me and Enriquiana where the best shopping was."

"Yes, I see you've been a busy little bee! Help Enriquiana with the bags."

"I'm so hungry, so tired…."

"And when you get upstairs, do not–I repeat–do not take off a single tag. Not until I see how it looks on you."

"You are so controlling, Mother!"

"Me? Controlling?"

The three of them rampaged through the lobby as the adults tried to keep up with Nia's angry step. "It's hot here and all my clothes are for Virginia," she complained. "I don't have one Southwestern outfit, and I look like a hick…have since getting off the plane."

They stood at the bank of elevators now, awaiting one to open. "It looks to me like you have plenty of clothes now!" Aurelia fired back, pointing at the bags.

"Well yeah, now I do," replied Nia, reaching for the bags she'd left in Enriquiana's arms.

Once safely on the elevator, Aurelia asked, "Where did you get the money for such purchases?"

"Borrowed it."

"Borrowed it? From whom?"

"I am sorry, Miss Hiyakawa," said Enriquiana.

Aurelia's eyes fired sparks at the woman.

"Don't blame Enri! We had fun, didn't we, Enri? I made her

take me, and I bugged her until she floated me a loan."

"How many times do I have to tell you, Nia, a credit card is not money. You don't borrow plastic!"

"Look, I didn't want to come on this stupid trip to begin with, but here I am, come all this way to follow you out here, and what do I find? You're not anywhere to be found, Mother, so we went shopping! Big crime!"

"How do you intend to pay Enriquiana back?"

"I've got a job all lined up with the local pimp, Ma!"

"You spoiled insolent little–" Aurelia's hand hovered overhead, about to slap, but she stopped herself.

The elevator doors opened on a honeymoon couple getting aboard, all smiles. Nia charged off the elevator, and Aurelia and Enriquiana followed. Mother, daughter, and maid rushed for their separate rooms–separate corners–both Aurelia and Nia stinging and feeling hurt by the exchange.

When Aurelia closed the door behind her and leaned against it, she began to cry. "Damn it, and I so wanted us to do something together tonight. I handled that so well."

The other side of the door, as Nia fumbled with the electronic key to get into her room, Aurelia heard Nia's raised voice. "I told you...see? She hates me, and she's making me miss soccer too!" she was saying to Enriquiana. "A plot to keep me under surveillance like I'm some kind of criminal or something."

"No, no, no," protested Enriquiana.

Nia raised her voice, wanting her mother to hear. "If she could, she'd strap a camera on your head, Enri, to watch my every move! What kinda life is 'zat?"

"No...no, she don't hate. Your mama, she loves you, Nia. I know this."

"Maybe...maybe not. Who knows? Hey, did you see how Ruben was looking me over?"

Wiping tears of frustration away, Aurelia made a decision. She sat alongside the telephone and called for Ruben, the young and handsome concierge to come to her room, telling him to bring all the information he had on the city and environs, emphasizing that he "bedazzle her daughter with his knowledge of Phoenix's various wonders and must-see destinations." She also promised to buy discount tickets for any Disneyland styled theme park or rollercoaster ride or mine shack or ghost town, and any number of shows and other attractions if he would hustle. "By the way, Ruben. Tell me, how long've you been a concierge with the hotel?"

"This is just my third week, but it's only a day-job, but I've held it since starting at the institute."

"Institute?"

"Arizona Institute of Architecture. I'm working toward being an architect some day."

Never judge a book by its cover, she thought and said, "That is so…so ambitions and marvelous. I'm so glad to hear it. Now do find all you need and come up as quickly as you can."

She hung up on his "Yes ma'am."

She then dialed Nia and asked her to come to her room. "We've got to talk, Nia, and besides, I have a surprise for you."

Nia softened after a moment's hesitation. "A surprise? Really? What kind of surprise?"

"Just get over here. I'll leave the door unlocked. Watch reruns till I get out of the shower. I won't be long, and if someone comes to the door, let him in."

"Who's coming to the door?"

"That's the surprise."

"Oh really?"

"And Nia, please don't dally."

"Ok, mom, and hey, I'm sorry about earlier."

"Did you have a good time in Saks and Neiman Marcus?"

"Are you kidding? We had lunch at Kevin Costner's new restaurant, the one he's opened in Phoenix to make up for the one his ex ripped off in Pasadena, California!"

"Oh, I didn't know the actor lived around here."

"He doesn't. It's a new chain."

"So you didn't see Kevin?" she joked with Nia.

"Naaah, they say he's not there till at least two or three in the morning if he's in town at all," she stretched the sarcasm out.

Aurelia hung up laughing. She stripped off her clothing and rushed for the spray of a hot shower.

She considered the concierge a handsome, well-groomed young man with a job–a rare breed. Not one of Nia's boyfriends at home had a job or cared to have one. So perhaps Ruben might not be a bad development. Perhaps Nia would find more in sunny Phoenix than she'd bargained for. Aurelia, showering, thought she could use young Ruben to advantage, to help keep Nia out of trouble.

She now lathered her body and washed her hair to the thought of Nia settling down one day with a rich architect, doctor, or movie mogul. Some poor *schlep* who could afford Nia's lavish taste and also make her happy in all the ways a woman should be made happy. She wanted so much for Nia.

One day, Nia would understand and appreciate this.

Think of it, she told herself. The boy is studying architecture and holding down an honest job. She could do far worse matchmaking for Nia.

When she stepped out of the shower and toweled off, she allowed her mind a brief respite to worry over the worrisome day, the toll the case was taking on her, and the problem of Nia. Instead, she luxuriated in the lovely white robe furnished by the hotel, and blow-dried her hair.

She heard Nia's voice when the blow dryer kicked off. She was arguing with someone in the other room, her voice raised. "Oh, shit," she moaned and quickly tied her robe and rushed through the door, her hair still wet, skin glistening. Nia was at the door, refusing to let the young concierge pass the threshold, trying to make him understand her by repeatedly saying the same thing over in a kind of mantra getting louder as it went: "This is my mother's room! You fool! My mother's room! You've come to the wrong room!"

Ruben kept holding up brochures and complaining, "But your mother sent for me!"

"Nia, welcome Ruben in!" Aurelia stood behind her, a hand

on Nia's shoulder.

Nia wheeled and stared into her mother's eyes. "This is your surprise?" Nia asked, now at a gasping frustration level. She pulled the door wide and disappeared into the room, plopping into a chair near the window and staring out at the pool. The TV blared a torturous MTV hit–the latest Aerosmith thing.

Aurelia turned off the set and asked Ruben to sit down. "I want you to tell us about the best places to eat, the best places to see, things to do, all that your beautiful city in the desert has to offer two girls on the town." Aurelia brushed her hair as she talked. Nia continued a pretense of boredom.

Ruben began laying out brochures and talking about the attractions, sounding like a circus barker. He had his spiel down pat. Aurelia caught the occasional glances between Nia and Ruben. Perhaps this just might work, and Ruben would show Nia around Phoenix, and perhaps she could trust Ruben with Nia. Perhaps it might culminate in Nia thanking Aurelia and thinking her MacMommie. At the very least, it must affect some change in Nia's attitude. And Aurelia knew that attitude was everything.

Aurelia awoke to a ringing phone, and her clock read 3:00 a.m. She feared the worst. Toby Slayter's or Julian Redondo's mangled, tortured body must surely have been discovered in a city pond, drainpipe, or dumpster. She and the PSI unit and all authorities had failed another boy.

But the stuttering voice on the other end was not Theopolis Redeoux or Gene, but…

Edwin Arlington Coffin, his voice slurred. He laughed and said in a drunken stupor, "Congratulate me, I'm a man!"

"Edwin?"

"I can-can-cannot tell you how…how very excited being here in…where are we?" He laughed uncontrollably. "She's the one, Rae, the woman of my dreams."

"This woman you met online, you mean?"

"Sex is her middle name."

"So I gather."

"She knows male anatomy."

"Edwin, are you all right. Are you safe?"

"Safe, all right? That's for children. I'm a man. Today I am a man."

"Glad to hear it, but Edwin, you have to know this woman you've had your first drunken fling with, she is likely entirely wrong for you, Edwin." Aurelia rubbed sleep from her eyes.

"Agreed, Rae. She's entirely wrong for me...on the one hand, but absolutely per-per-perfect for me on the other."

God, how can I warn Eddy off this course he's taken? On the one hand, I feel like cheering him on, but on the other, I fear for him. Her thoughts raced even as she cradled words in mind she wanted to speak aloud to him. It reminded her of Etta Pace's situation back in Virginia. How does one tiptoe through the minefield of a loved one's love life and live to befriend them another day?

Finally, she said, "I'm on your side, Eddy, you know that, any time you can successfully break with your parents and show some courage in doing so, but don't confuse courage and stupidity, okay, Eddy? Edwin?"

After a silence that distinctly shouted fuck you, Edwin hung up on her.

Meanwhile, unable to sleep thanks to Edwin's wake up call that had brought her out of a sound peace, Aurelia sat up in bed, pulled all the disparate files and Julian Redondo's art sketches to her lap, and began again working the case. What else is a psychic investigator with insomnia going to do, she silently asked herself, call an all-night masseuse, order up a hunk, or watch late-late TV? Her mind wandered to the college prof, Alandale, thinking he'd be so perfect for her, intelligent, hardworking, but not too Calvinistic, handsome, a light for life in his eyes, an energy and enthusiasm for his work. "Yeah, but a masseuse doesn't ask for you to turn over your entire freaking life to him, now does he?" she asked aloud of the empty room.

The silence of the room, the ringing in her ears, her aloneness conspired to move her hand to the remote, and she turned on the 24 Hour-Phoenix News channel just to have some background scatter as she worked. At the same time, she dove back into the paperwork and paraphernalia she'd accumulated on the case.

Aurelia studied each file, each location where a body had been found, searching for any thin thread of a pattern. Killers left traces, trace elements, fibers, hair, and habits. What the forensics people told her was that dog hair was found on every child, but it was not the same dog hair on every child's clothes, but rather an assortment of breeds. Police had concluded each child had access to a dog, and that this had nothing to do with their abductions. Julian, too, had a dog. Kids and dogs simply went together.

"But our killer would know this, too." She glanced through a slit left in the drapes to see Phoenix's city lights. "Who would have access to a number of dogs at any one time, dogs used in the enticement of kids into this creep's lair?"

A dog walker, a dog handler, dog groomer, a vet, a person who worked for a vet, someone who kept a dog stable–one of those doggy hotels replete with a doggy park? Someplace with a cute name like The Barking Lot back in Virginia? The Bark Stops Here? Doggie Heaven?

How damn tired am I, she asked herself. She pushed all the files to one side and got up from her lotus position on the mattress, pillows flying, and dug out the Phoenix Yellow Pages, and bypassing M for Masseuse, she dug around for Pet Stores, Pet Supplies, Pet Boarding. Under these headings, she searched for cross-references to dog liveries, dog pounds, doggie hotels, her eyes skimming past a pet cemetery section.

Could the killer be intimately involved with animals, caring deeply for animals and yet capable of binding, terrifying, maiming, and killing young boys? It seemed a contradiction, and yet all of the information collected over fifty plus years of FBI intelligence on serial killers, and how they think, reminded her that contradictions made up a large part of sociopathic behavior. Not to mention a sociopath's daily appearance, if not sociopathic thinking.

Research findings said that the same pathological urge to harm small animals was a prelude to harming small children, and if so, The Phoenix Phantom could well have weaseled his way into working in close proximity to both animals and children–to be near the source of his greatest gratification. This she reasoned as sound.

If so, what facility or facilities in the greater Phoenix area would allow a killer to move among people while freely working with helpless, likely caged and leashed animals, and have interaction with homeless children and the public, allowing for a strange, eerie double life?

She continued scanning the huge resource in her lap now. Then it struck her. Who would care to know about such as the homeless shelter children? Who would want to create a program of hope for them? Who would know that pets help save children from every day fears and horrors, traumas and exigencies of life on the street, that homeless children in particular are helped by the unconditional love of a pet? Kids without a daily routine, life without a bed and a roof and four walls and a lock on the door could be softened by a pet.

Who indeed would be interested to know all this? The revelation coming in at her felt so horrible, so distasteful that she wanted to scream out its impossibility even as it formed in her mind. Dr. Elliot Alandale, or someone in his research team...they'd be uniquely positioned to know about such things and use them against a kid. If there were a program in place to put homeless children in physical touch with orphaned puppies, impounded, facing extinction, who would know?

She made a quick call to Julian's mother, waking her, asking how Julian had gotten the dog and was it from a pound.

The woman hung up on her.

Pets. Did the others all have pets? She dug through the files only to find them sorely lacking this detail. This could well be a dead end or a direct path to the killer. Surely, Dr. Alandale knew nothing of the murder of innocents. Surely, if there were a single thread linking him to the horrendous crimes, it must be that someone in his organization, one of his many field operatives who went out among the children and interviewed them, learning their morbid religion and using it against them along with the enticement of a pet through a county 'save a pet' program.

What kid wouldn't be enticed to help an animal facing euthanasia?

Sure it was a wild, anxiety-ridden bird this notion, one that fluttered insanely and flew in chaos inside Aurelia's brain, and perhaps ought to remain there, but too late. She already sat astride the back of this 'fowl' idea that had invaded her mind. The idea that Dr. Elliot Alandale not only concocted such a program, but that he did so to create the perfect cover for his secret desire to torture, maim, and kill the very children he proposed studying, learning from, and helping–the tribe of the homeless street children of Phoenix.

Rae grabbed a protocol done on one of the victims and stared down at the cold type on one line that read: *Suspect hair– male, approximate age mid-to-late thirties, Caucasian, likely sandy brown in appearance.* It fit Alandale. Another line read: *Nail clipping found in folds of victim's pants-leg also from Caucasian male approx. age thirty to fifty.* Again it pointed to Alandale. But none of this was in the least conclusive. Entirely circumstantial, and she of all people knew this. Still, the god-awful gnawing at the pit of her stomach and around the edges of her soul about Alandale and his program continued inexorably to erode away sane notions and to taunt her psyche. So often good things were done in the name of humanity, religion, love, brotherly concern, fatherly passion, a mother's love, for god and country, and so often it proved a complete lie, a fabrication, a distortion, an illusion. It was one of life's tragic comedies, and largely due to her experience and training–she must pay close heed to her instincts and suspicions.

Elliot Alandale, tall, strong, handsome, bronze-skinned, had in a matter of minutes become a suspect. One reason she truly hated this life path she'd chosen.

She cursed under her breath. She did not want it to be true, but even more, she had not wanted to have such notions in her head about this man in the first place. She wanted him to be Albert Schweitzer and Mother Theresa all rolled into one caring, concerned, driven human being with a passion to help others, not a twisted, demented desire to see, hear, feel, taste, and smell the suffering and agony of others–others who in this case were innocent and helpless children like Julian Redondo and Toby Slayter.

She must determine if a connection could be made between Alandale's home and the children, and if he kept a dog kennel or a dog run somewhere out on the desert. Must investigate him quietly and carefully until a warrant to open up his life entirely could be gotten from a federal judge.

"And suppose I'm way off base?" she said aloud. "End of any chance at intimacy with the man, for sure."

Just then the TV news turned to the biggest crime story Phoenix had ever known, the missing Julian Redondo and

Toby Slayter, and the five previously murdered homeless kids.

The anchor asked a reporter standing before a sign outside Phoenix's Police Plaza downtown, "John, are the police any further along in this awful case than say six weeks ago when these killings began?"

The reporter immediately replied, "Darren, local police and FBI are no closer now than from day one, and they are revealing nothing about the investigation. So tight-lipped are they, in fact, we feel they've got nothing whatsoever to report, because they are facing a killer who's left absolutely nothing for them to work with."

"Yes," agreed Anchorman Darren, "this Phantom Predator of Phoenix has that seeming quality of a vampire, some kind of super human ability to simply go as undetected as…as well the wind."

"Amazing, John. But what can you tell us about a persistent rumor that the FBI has called in a sort of ghost-sniffing psychic just to offset the nature of this fiend?"

"Again, we hear rumors but officials are keeping stiff-lipped on this, too, although there may be some truth to it."

The camera came back to the anchorman who'd somehow smiled through all of this. "One item that is hardly rumor is that the mayor and the governor are up in arms about the whole matter, and they're screaming for an end to it. After a message, we'll be right back with the coverage promised on the Native American Indian arts and crafts fair down at the civic center running through the weekend."

Rae switched off the TV. Somehow, it'd become five in the morning. She rang for room service. A breakfast of coffee and a roll. Gaining her composure, Rae again rifled through the medical examiner protocols for patterns, but this time she was searching for patterns to discredit her fearful suspicions.

I suspect him, but I don't want to. Still, she asked repeatedly of herself, "How do you not suspect someone once you suspect that someone. How do you kill suspicion when suspicion is an emotional state of mind that is as impenetrable and defiant as the hide of a buffalo?"

A few hours later

"Yes, exactly right, Theopolis, at each and every location, yes, Theopolis," Aurelia told the still sleepy FBI field chief over the phone. "I want to visit them all, and do my thing at each place where the killer left his victims."

"You mean go into trance at each location?"

"I do."

"I have to hand it to you. You're a glutton for punishment."

"I am."

"You know how the press is hounding us? It'll get out, you know, and then–"

"Screw the press. I don't care what the press says or does. They don't crack cases. Look, remote psychic work is one thing, and it is helped out by...by my receiving as well as sending psychic impulses, and I'm getting nothing from Julian any longer."

"What does that mean in real terms?"

"Means he is either unconscious or near death, or God forbid.... Look, what I am telling you, Redeoux is that the closer in proximity to the target I can get, the stronger and more powerful the images. Should any one of these discovery sites yield anything, it might simply be that we are physically closer to the Phantom's lair."

"Yeah but...hey, you're talking about dead kids...gone...six foot under now. What possible–"

"Kids who died a traumatic, violent, and sudden death often are left in a limbo. They sometimes send out messages– confusing and vexing and conflicting images, yes but images nonetheless."

He sighed his end-of-the-rope sigh into the phone. "All right."

"Look, Theopolis, it may lead to nothing, but it may give us a lead."

"And we damn sure need a lead."

"I'll pick you up. You wake up Kiley and Coffin."

She hung up and rang Gee's room, telling him of their plan

for the day. She then tried to get in touch with Edwin but he was not answering his cell. She then telephoned Enriquiana, and after this, she rang Nia.

"You'll have to fend for yourself again today, so you and Enriquiana ought to get Ruben to help you find some suitable, nice places to visit."

Nia only groaned into the phone.

"Like that Museum of the West thing he was talking about, or that desert amusement park thing they call Rimfire Phoenix, or something."

Nia, still half asleep when Aurelia had called, replied with an exhaust of her breath into the mouthpiece and a "Yeah, ma, right!" Then she hung up, going back to sleep.

Aurelia knew she'd disappointed her daughter in the past and would do so again in the future, but after last night, sharing about the homeless, she'd hoped to see a change in Nia. Having to go to work and leave Nia on her own today, this really hurt.

She put it out of her mind and quickly dressed for her day of detecting.

The car ride over to the last murder location took them into proximity of the university campus and Alandale's office, and this disheartened Aurelia, but she kept suspicion of the good professor to herself, even when Gene asked if there were something taxing on her mind. She laughed lightly and repeated the understatement, adding, "In my life, Gene, there is always something taxing."

They took up the back seat of Theopolis's unmarked vehicle, Gene filling his lungs with her morning perfume. Redeoux had directed Fred to the location. Both local FBI men remained silent, thoughtful until they started talking about the upcoming Sunday football action. Now they chattered away like two magpies.

Shortly, they all stood before an isolated, desolate area where a housing development dumpsite awaited dump trucks. Mute, silent witness, it was an arid, desolate patch of desert where all the discarded building supplies from empty pales and paint and tar buckets, roof shingles, rusted rat-trap-like twisted fixtures, useless siding, broken slabs of wall board, cable, wire, hoses, odd cuts of two by fours, ruined insulation sections all slept in a cemetery of waste.

Closer to the footsteps of the killer here, Aurelia sensed what little was left behind by the cold body tossed unceremoniously amid this rubble, painted in successive coats with a shocking color. She sought out ethereal stamps, marks left by the dead…to mark his passing here.

"I'm getting nothing," she finally told the others after circling the exact spot where the body was found.

In the car going toward the next dumpsite, she said, "I got a sense of something wrong with the boy's heart back there. Like a stab to the heart."

"No one knows about that," said Theopolis. "We even convinced the coroner to keep it off the record."

"Keep what off the record?"

"Asked the ME to keep the detail out of his final protocol until we apprehend this guy. You know, as a control against all the idiots coming out of the woodwork to confess to the crimes."

"Understood. But what detail?"

"The killer puts a knife into their hearts as a final insult to the corpse, or maybe he doesn't believe they're dead, so it's a final shot to be sure," explained Redeoux. "So how did you know?"

"I felt it from the leavings here, but I'm afraid it's about all that Lionel left for me to feel."

"Are you…all right? You look a bit faint."

"Doing this field work…it's kind of a double-edged sword. What I see, I feel."

"That's gotta be tough."

"There's a price to pay. Sure they…they'll let me see, but they pull no punches. This was a child."

The others realized that Aurelia was holding her hands across her heart. Gene put an arm around her, where they sat in the rear.

It was a long day. The scene repeated four more times, but in each instance at another location. The killer's pattern was never a body left in the same place twice–a drainpipe, a lonely train viaduct on the outskirts of the city, an abandoned long-defunct freight car sitting on an equally weed-infested, overgrown unused stretch of idle track.

The next location they stopped at was the drainpipe. Not six miles from the university in an alleyway behind a row of adobe brick homes wherein resided a community of immigrant farm workers. Aurelia tried her level best to get more images that might add to the growing mosaic of events and to the face of this killer, but she found fewer and fewer. While all the other boys after Lionel had also been stabbed through the heart with a huge knife as a final kill stroke by this vicious monster, so far only Lionel had 'spoken' to her.

Late in the day, they arrived at the last dumpsite. This one stood the furthest from downtown areas and the university. When they climbed from the car, Gene stared at the desolate scene out on the desert, sagebrush waving in the wind, alive, proliferating among the rocks and sand.

"Whoever this bastard is, he sure knows the terrain," said the driver.

"He's scouted out and used every nook and cranny, that's for damn sure," Theopolis agreed, having to shout over a desert wind that threatened everyone's eyes with stinging sand. A magnificently painted sky commingled with a rock-strewn expanse of rolling foothills rainbowed in shadow; clouds joined the symphony of light and dark, dancing in slow motion–clouds smeared carelessly and curiously with hews of purple, orange, and pink contrasting perfectly the painted sky here at sunset. Arizona beauty and peace stood in complete disparity here as well, thanks to what they knew of this place. What man had done here.

They looked across at a deserted clapboard filling station with creaky, near falling down structures. Holes large enough to throw a cat through. The body of Jimmy 'Gopher' Salinas had been dumped here, the body left inside where the killer had kicked in a useless padlocked door to gain entry, and Aurelia saw this in a flash. The psychic leavings here were powerful as if the desert and the location itself supported and sustained them.

Aurelia rushed ahead of the men and stepped up onto the broken, rotting steps and through the doorway that swung in the breeze. As she stepped through the portal, she felt a presence like a warm wind whoosh through her and circle the interior in one fluid motion.

"Jimmy," she muttered below her breath.

She stepped to the area where she felt the body had lain, still alive until the plunging final knife stab. But this feeling directly contradicted what the ME's report had said of Jimmy. His body had had no reaction to the stabbing; he'd been dead before he was stabbed through the heart. But he'd somehow frightened his killer. Perhaps a muscle spasm or an escape of gases. Tests proved him dead before the stab to the heart, but what had prompted this first victim to be killed twice over?

Once the coroner's people had gotten the layers of paint off the body, they'd discovered bite marks–two sets of bite marks! Perhaps the painter was not the same as the man who'd disposed of the body?

She surmised that Jimmy's soul had been here and had remained here, and that on some level, he knew of the stabbing and so felt it. She had a flashing image of Jimmy, many open wounds, many of them taunting stab wounds, but all such wounds had been deep enough to bleed out. He lay before her nude except for the paint, his wide eyes open and imploring her to help him, to save him, even now…even after all this time.

Gene held the others in check at the doorway.

Aurelia reached down and closed the boy's ethereal eyes by placing her hand over them, and she quietly asked, "Who did this to you, Jimmy? Who? Tell me…give me a sign."

Jimmy's form faded but his features changed; they changed into the features of Dr. Elliot Alandale.

The sight chilled her to the core.

Then Jimmy was gone, and she held onto empty air. "It's

over for you, Jimmy," she said to the roof overhead, shouting it to the rafters. "You've been found, and your body has been taken from here. Time for you to go. God is still on his throne. Go toward those calling you."

"Who's she talking to?" asked Theopolis of Gene, but Gene went to Rae.

"You saw him full on, didn't you?" he asked, his calming hand on her shoulder.

"Yeah...I saw the kid," she replied. Still she resisted implicating Dr. Alandale until she had more to go on. Given the fragile and complicated nature of the mind, she realized that it could well've been her who had morphed Jimmy's fine features into becoming Elliot Alandale, and not Jimmy's doing at all. She had possibly posited the notion into the scene from her own subconscious and her growing suspicions. But she could hardly accuse Alandale of these heinous crimes without more to go on than what was in her head. There was a time when law enforcement might do just that, but not today.

They filed out and climbed back into the car and drove away from the sad scene. Redeoux finally broke the silence. "So...what'd we accomplish today, Dr. Hiyakawa?" Theopolis's voice was tinged by fatigue and frustration.

Aurelia considered her words carefully. "On every surface and wall of that last location, the victim's last thoughts resided, but he left as soon as I reached out."

Redeoux crooked his neck to have a stare at her.

"And the boy's last thoughts went with him. Sorry."

"Well...I suppose, in a sense, it's for the best," said Gene.

"What's for the best?" asked Theopolis.

"I mean," explained Gene, "if the boy's spirit's lingered here all this time, even after his body's been laid to rest, well this may mean he knows Aurelia is on the case, looking for his killer, and that he can rest in peace."

Theopolis gave Gene a doubtful look.

Aurelia said, "Thank you for understanding, Theopolis." She breathed deeply and closed her eyes and leaned into Gee here in the back seat. A sense of escalating fear rose in her.

Doubt was king. Still for Theopolis and the other agent, she added, "It was worth the try, I believe."

Gene asked quietly, "Took an emotional toll on you, I know."

Aurelia, her eyes still closed, said in a tone as soft as an angelic whisper, "Now I fear only one fate inevitable for Toby Slayter, the shelter boy, and for young Julian."

"Why do you say that?" asked Gene.

"This is what the signs are screaming."

"Have you noticed how the first victim, Jimmy, was put way out here," mused Theopolis, "and gradually but surely, the killer took less and less concern in hiding the remains, each closer and closer in from Phoenix, until the last one was in the area of the university?"

"You think the Phantom has some connection to the university, Chief?" asked Fred.

"Could be...could be. BTK was a g'damn security guard at the university in Wichita, Kansas, right?"

Aurelia felt that Redeoux was having thoughts about Alandale and his seemingly wonderful work with the homeless children.

Same time, FBI Headquarters, Quantico, Virginia

With each new psychic reading, the Quantico headquarters DC team headed up by Miranda Palmer Waldron received more reports and information coming in from the Phoenix field office, from Theopolis Redeoux, and from Aurelia. They set out to fulfill their duties in "interpreting" Aurelia's images. But the team had become destructively argumentative: short with one another's ideas, scattered in their focus, fragmented in their thinking, cliques forming, sides being taken. For Miranda Waldron, it felt like a Mensa version of a Survivor episode.

More and more cross with one another and at odds on the meanings of images and symbols, they sat among discarded food containers, plastic tableware, and overturned coffee cups. All of them had gone without sleep, and all of them had had to telephone home to tell loved ones they'd not be seen for some time.

Miranda didn't have anyone waiting dinner for her save Tromby–short for Trombone–as she otherwise lived alone. No children to pick up after school, no mother to visit in a sick home, and no father to cook for, but there was Tromby, her silken black and tan, fat Maine raccoon feline, and he'd need feeding. Even she–the one the others called Dr. Iron Ass, had had to make arrangements.

Miranda took all the disparate ideas, philosophies, notions, wild hair ruminations, and knee-jerk reactions to Aurelia's readings, and like an orchestra leader, attempted to harmonize them one with another, to read between the metaphorical and the symbolic, the idyllic and the honest images and emotions Rae daily forwarded the group via Coffin's device.

In the past, this process had never taken so long as in the Phoenix case; consequently, a good deal of disappointment had come along with the lingering session. Like a hung jury, nerves had gone from frayed to un-raveled. Miranda learned, right or wrong, that everyone had held the expectation that with Aurelia in the field, outside of that metal pyramid of hers that her psychic power would only increase tenfold, being in closer proximity to the events she was reading. But it appeared, as Gene Kiley had predicted when he'd privately spoken to Dr. Waldron, that distance had no effect in a psychic reading, and that Aurelia was just as close to the killer in Phoenix while in her chamber, safe inside Quantico. After all, she'd been nearly a thousand miles from Florida where the abducted heiress to the Maurice Van Holder fortune had been held and found. Gene had been against using Rae in the field, calling it the first step toward killing the golden goose.

"In astral projection terms, there're no inches, no feet, no miles, no distance," Gene had explained. "Only one time and one space."

Still common sense had everyone believing otherwise, until now. Apparently, Aurelia was no closer to the killer today than when she'd been here in Quantico, as her visions of parks and angels and coral fire and demons had begun before she left. Perhaps her going out into the field was not only risky, but also worthless and exorbitant. Certainly, the bean counters would be screaming.

So here they sat wringing their collective hands, waiting with baited breath for the next clue in the enormous puzzle that played out before them in a darkened room on a huge plasma screen. Each expert and genius watched the latest images sent from Aurelia.

Another major disappointment for Miranda Waldron had been learning that Edwin Arlington Coffin's newfangled mental imaging palm-reader had bugs and gremlins in the works. Which of the images coming through could be trusted? With this breakdown in plans, Waldron had had to have a CRVL device installed at the Phoenix field office labs. All of this had taken time to sort out, followed by greater costs, and then more time.

Again Waldron looked around the room. Everyone had reached the end of his or her private rope or very near it. Nerves stood out like naked wires–frayed and stinging. She'd had to tiptoe about, take care with each word, choose her every sentence with caution to appease and bring together the diverse egos in the room.

It seemed a hopeless mish-mush of useless and disconnected information that, so far, her exhausted team had managed. Her disappointment showed, and theirs in turn became apparent. Some things were beyond hiding. But to their credit, no one had stormed out, no one had quit…and that in an arena wherein they knew up front this was an option.

Miranda again wondered why she loved it, this damnably exciting terribly taxing exhilarating mind-blowing job. A job she could not share with family or friends, a job she could not describe even if it weren't against her contractual agreement.

Rae Hiyakawa had E-mailed all of her findings on the street children and their strange mix of Santera, Christianity, and doomsday mythology, and she had reported all that she'd learned not only from the children about a wandering Bloody

Mary or La Llorana, the Blue Lady, and Satan. Adding to this most interesting accumulation of street culture, Rae reported on an interesting research study being done on the homeless children's shelter religion, and interpretations she'd learned of from a Dr. Elliot Alandale at the University of Phoenix.

Miranda did love her work; so many interesting twists and turns, so many interesting people and fascinating minds to deal with. But it was the type of career that offered next to no time for a man, and while Rae stalked a killer, Miranda vicariously stalked this monster as well, albeit from a safe distance. She certainly did not wish ever to be in the same city with such a fiend, or sitting across a table in a jail cell interrogating such a fiend. She wanted to end the careers of such monsters, but at a distance that did not turn her hair white.

She certainly admired Rae for having the gumption and the chutzpah–and what was Japanese for chutzpah?–to take on such a task as this within so close a proximity to such a deviant mind as that which derived satisfaction and possible sexual lust from the torture of young boys, from slow-torture, slowly asphyxiating their flesh below coats of paint.

Dr. Waldron again tried to reach her neighbor, Mrs. Boone, on her cell to ask the elderly dear if she would once again mind feeding Tromby and letting him out for his evening solo stroll. In mid-plea to Mrs. Boone, Miranda thought, even that Tomcat leads a more exciting social life than I do.

Once off the phone, I'll have to face the team again, work up my energies to cheerlead them on. Part of her just wanted so badly to go find Tromby instead, and to hold him close and be awash in his unconditional love.

Aurelia's cell phone rang. In the backseat of the FBI sedan, she answered the call. Nia sputtered on the other end, sounding tearful, complaining about Ruben, the concierge.

"What is it, Nia? What about Ruben?"

"He…he hasn't answered my call all day."

Aurelia frowned at this. Aurelia listened to her daughter's pain and disappointment even as she was struck with a wounding sense of failure in the case, as she feared one day soon to be staring into Toby's and Julian's dead eyes.

"You'll just have to call him again, Nia," she suggested.

"Ohhhh nooo! Not on your life. If he doesn't call me, do you think for one moment that I'm going to call him?"

Aurelia realized that Nia's pain and hurt was just as real and powerful as any child her age whose concerns were normal. She worked to remain calm and not to snap, for her mind was on a creeping image of herself standing over Julian's corpse, gasping at the layered and caked paint covering his body.

In her ear, young Nia droned on with every complaint she could throw at Aurelia about how she hated Phoenix.

"I hate it here. Hate the weather. Hate the people. Hate the hotel."

Another 3AM in Phoenix

Theopolis Redeoux becomes her surprise savior on white charger when he sees her falling apart. He whisks her from a gruesome double murder discovery. Both the Slayter boy and Redondo. Theopolis uses his Morgan steed to knock Gee down and out of this strange world. In a dream, a Morgan horse can be albino and a drip like Redeoux can be a hero. Somewhere back of her subconscious, she realizes she'd been spending too much time with both Gene and Theopolis.

He takes her to a posh restaurant, a favorite of his, where they dismount Monty, his lovely horse. Theopolis points out that had her interpretations been followed, and had people like himself spent more time following her lead instead of fighting her, then perhaps they might've together saved Julian—as the boy may have been found in time. She denies this possibility. Tells him that she had seen the boy dead even before she got off the plane in Phoenix—a lie to assuage Theo's pain, and immediately now she recognizes how ridiculous this all is, how wrong, and how silly and disjointed a dream it is, and one not particularly soothing. Not in the least. Still, she relaxes now and allows the dream to move to its inexorable ending like a disjointed novel or imperfect, flawed opera.

"SEER who SEES in capitals," she tells Theopolis like a drama queen.

"What does that mean when you see something in capitals?" the dream Redeoux asks now.

"It means unchangeable, fated."

He argues this. She curses him and gets up to leave, but he grabs hold and she beats his chest as he imparts the fact that he and his men had acted on her last reading and interpretation while the FBI argued and debated the images. "We raided a place the killer recently vacated. He was there only hours before."

She lets out tears. He holds her as she lets out the accumulated pain and grief of having literally lived through the suffering of the children. When they touch, it is magical but it feels wrong, as she has had not one sexual feeling toward Redeoux, but then she looks up into his eyes, and as he is kissing her, but she realizes it is not Redeoux but Dr. Elliot Alandale!

Transported like angels they float from their standing position to the ceiling in Marc Chagall fashion, he floating above her, twisting and turning to kiss her despite the pain it must cause to contort himself in this way. It's a dream all right, she reassures herself. Then their dream forms float downward and like two leaves they waft in a warm coiling wind that gently places them onto a large, soft bed. In bed together against her better judgment.

Suddenly, the warm glow of attraction is gone, and with the magical attraction cooled, she leaps from bed and races from him, angry with herself for letting her guard down. "You don't–you really, really don't–want to get involved with me and my life, Elliot. I can tell you now that it simply couldn't work, even if you have had nothing whatever to do with the deaths of those children. I know anything that might blossom between us…that it would only come to a bad end. Hell I've already tainted it, just by suspecting you of horrors unspeakable."

Dr. Elliot Alandale does not like losing. He continues to challenge her. "Is that how you do it? Keep men at bay by frightening hell out of them? Telling them that you can see the end before it's arrived?" He shouts this as she slips on her shoes and is floating angel-like through a portal into a blue light over a green landscape of a hallway that is some kind of trap, a labyrinth without exit.

Behind her, like a howling wind, through the labyrinth Alandale's shout is one continuous question of her: "Ever hear of the self-fulfilling prophecy, lady?"

She turns on him. "I invented it! I got that boy killed. I'm going home to DC. Taking Nia and going home."

"You can't go!" he held up a phone as if it were a badge.

"Try and stop me!"

"They've sent the dogs out; they're looking for us both."

She takes tentative steps toward the phone. "Another one gone?"

"Without a trace unless you can find your way through that!" Alandale's eyes had widened, staring at the tunnels behind her. She turns to see that the blue and green maze has become flame red, the heat searing her skin and the hair on her eyebrows and eyelashes moments before she's engulfed.

The terror of it woke her, and she bolted upright in bed.

PREDATOR STILL AT LARGE blared the newspaper headline left outside Aurelia's room this morning. She lifted the less than hefty Phoenix Sun News, and she scanned a story that told the public that the PPD, the FBI, and now the FBI's secret weapon, one Dr. Aurelia 'Rae' Murphy Hiyakawa had all failed to get any closer to solving the case of the Phoenix Phantom than on day-one of opening the investigation. The reporter's name was Don Gwinn, and Gwinn's writing style, so far as she could see, stank to high heaven of purple prose. "Must come with the sagebrush," she muttered as she scanned the front-page story.

Gwinn told a story of how the FBI had called in a psychic—technically, he was already incorrect. She worked as an FBI agent, not an outside contractor. Then he referred to her as a fortune-teller, which was also technically incorrect. Then he gave an opinion on psychic investigation, summing it up as a sideshow in an investigation without leads and without a future, a sideshow that created more myth and nonsense, Gwinn wrote, than anything of substance or use.

She silently put a curse on this unknown reporter. While it may not have any effect on him, the act of it made her feel a twinge better. But she knew that to some degree the fool was right.

They had not made any headway in the case, not any real substantial headway at least. But Aurelia knew she must guard like mad against feelings of failure, or summing herself up as a failure. This could lead to a mild depression, which could lead to a greater depression, which could then could spiral out of control. Aurelia knew she must guard against feelings of anxiety, panic attack, and depression, for such emotions could buckle her from knee to neck and put her on her back if she were to give in to such a personal tsunami. And like an AA member, one who had had close encounters of the manic kind, she wanted never to go back down that path ever again. That path her ex had sent her down as surely as if he planned to gaslight her.

"Never again," she vowed. Never would she turn over her life and her personal power to a man. Never again would she allow a man to hurt her as Tomi Yoshikani had.

The phone rang and she went for it, but realized as her hand hovered that it was her cell phone in her purse. She grabbed it up and saw that it was a call from Etta Pace. Etta tearfully filled her in on a startling discovery she'd made, that her no account intended was having affairs with five other women he'd been corresponding with on the computer–using her computer in fact! "He told me...I thought...he was doing his income tax with TurboTax!" she wailed. "But it was all a lie, a cover-up for his late night chat room fantasies. The bastard!"

Rae agreed, "The bastard!"

"I know....kick me in the ass," continued Etta. "You tried to tell me he was no good, and you were so damn right! Do you always have to be so fucking right, Rae?"

"It's going to be all right, Etta...Etta, sweetheart."

Aurelia heard the clattering of objects being hurled, glass breaking, and Etta storming about her place. Etta demonstrated a devastated heart by cursing and throwing things, as in the popular country song 'She Took It Like a Man'–a good sign for Etta.

"And to think I lost your friendship over this...this piece of human waste!"

"Don't be foolish, Etta. You haven't lost my friendship in the least!"

"Your respect then!"

"Etta, love makes fools of us all."

"All of us are fools to let love in in the first damn place!"

"Get it out. Let it all out, honey. When I get back, we'll do some serious shopping and partying together."

More tears in the phone.

"You'll see," Rae encouraged. "Everything's going to be all right. That is if you're sure he's gone for good and out of your system."

"Completely flushed! If there'd been a gun handy, you'd be talking to a fugitive right now."

Aurelia laughed lightly.

"There's really nothing funny about this!" Etta took on a tone with an edge now.

"Are you sure about that? I'd have loved to see old Neil's face when you threw him out."

A moment of silence suddenly turned into an explosion of laughter, first from Etta then from Aurelia. The sound of it reminded them how deeply they felt toward one another, and it recalled their good times. "How long're you going to be away? Can you hurry back? You are sorely missed, Rae."

Rae blinked and told her how the case had seemed to grind to a halt, and finished with, "I can't promise anything. I can't even promise Nia anything, although I dragged her out here with me,"

"She's in Phoenix with you?"

"With Enriquiana, so's we could maybe have some quality time together, see the Canyon maybe, Sedona perhaps."

"Oh dear…Nia's really with you?"

"No, I lied. I kenneled her. Yes, what do you think?"

"It just sounds…well, I know how Nia and you've been getting on lately, so…"

"Let's not go there now, Etta."

They talked a bit longer before each said good night. Etta ended with, "It's a real dear friend who will take a friend's call at three in the morning, Rae. Thank you."

"I'll collect on it someday and do the same to you, Etta, now good night."

Aurelia breathed a sigh that released months of a long pent up relief over Etta's circumstances. Things had worked out for the best after all. All the effort, all the investigating, all the ranting had next to no effect, and Aurelia feared she'd wasted far more energy on this than she had time and emotional energy for. She could've as well sat back, done nothing, and let life and nature take its course–had she been able to predict as much!

"Some fortune-teller, Mr. Gwinn."

The following morning at breakfast with Nia and Enriquiana, Aurelia's cell phone rang, silencing their talk about going out to see the nearby Navajo trading post out on the desert, or perhaps going up to see Sedona even. Maps and brochures littered the table, lying atop half-empty coffee cups and breakfast leavings. Aurelia looked at her lit up phone and said, "I gotta take this."

Nia's face fell, and Enriquiana's smile faded.

On the other end was a cold-voiced Theopolis Redeoux. "We've got another painted body, Dr. Hiyakawa. I've ordered no one touch the body until you arrive, not even the ME, who is standing nearby and angry as hell. I've sent a car for you. Please meet it outside and hurry."

"Julian? Julian?" she asked.

"Don't think so."

"Toby?"

"It appears so."

"Damn…my God, no. He never…never had a chance. We didn't even get close."

The others at the table and nearby tables reacted to Aurelia's open tears. "That poor boy," she added.

"Hurry over, Doc," said Theopolis.

"I'm sorry, mom, but I knew something like this was going to happen. I just knew it," began Nia.

Aurelia put up a hand to her while searching for a napkin to wipe away tears.

"You get too close to these people...like those homeless kids you told me about...and what do you expect? You're going to get hurt and hurt badly one day if–"

"That's enough, Nia," she chastised. "No more." Aurelia had clicked off her phone, and now she got control, instantaneously changing her demeanor. She snatched at the maps and brochures, until Enriquiana took charge.

"Go...do your work, Ms. Hiyakawa. We will be all right."

"Soon as this case is closed, Nia," she assured her daughter, "we...we're going to do all these things together, I promise you."

Nia sullenly nodded. "Sure, mom."

"This is my job, Nia."

"I know that but–"

"You have to understand that."

"All right, I've heard it all before."

"It's what I do."

"Your arena, where you shine...I know all that."

"I have this within me, this...this ability, and I have to do the best I can with it, Nia! Gotta find the best damn use for it that I can, and you, young lady, you're just going to have to understand and stop judging your mother."

"You think you can control things, mom. How nice for you. It must feel good. Wish I could feel that way just once," replied Nia, getting up and marching off.

"Stay with her Enriquiana, please."

"*Si*, Doctor, of course."

"She thinks I feel some control over things. How wrong can that child be?" she asked while watching Nia's backside disappear through the café doors and down the corridor. She looked into Enriquiana's calm eyes and said, "Just once I'd like to change an outcome or win with that child."

"Yes, but you two...she is you, and you are her. You are so much alike."

"Why don't I have a millimeter of control in my own

immediate corporeal world? Damn the gods for it."

"The...the gods?" asked Enriquiana.

"Ancestors, gods of my father and my mother."

"Oh...no, Doctor, no," Enriquiana had thrown up her hands over her ears. "No want to hear, no *comprende*...no talk like that, Dr. Hiyakawa."

Aurelia rushed for the lobby and out the door, leaving Enriquiana to her hysterics. "My God, a boy is dead and Nia is worried about my feelings, and Enriquiana is worried about God striking me down for blasphemy." At least Nia was thinking about her mother's feelings and not her own this time.

But what did Enriquiana mean when she said the two of them, mother and daughter were so much alike. Since when? But then Gee had said the same. But Rae didn't see it, and she kept thinking, since when?

The best that could be said of the body was that no knife had been plunged into the heart. Immediately, the differences in how this young person died compared to the others was obvious. No paint, only the paint of a fire.

Nearby onlookers shouted obscenities at the authorities for not doing enough. Aurelia had long since telephoned Gene Kiley, who'd been absent from his room and likely in the pool or out on a morning jog. She left a message to join her here at Sunset and Keeler, and here she stood without him in a back alleyway littered with discarded furnishings, bedsprings, and boards from a nearby house being gutted and renovated. The body had been laid inside a discarded oak wood bureau drawer made over into a makeshift coffin in search of a lid.

Aurelia no longer knew where Edwin Coffin had disappeared, and she still hadn't been able to reach him via his cell. She chose to go ahead without either Edwin or Gee, and so she now kneeled over the charred remains of the young boy that she had failed. The fiend had completely fired the body, igniting it with a pungent accelerant, most likely kerosene from the smell of it. The body had been charbroiled and blackened, all skin and blood bubbled away, the extremities buckled and twisted, the bones cracked from the flames the body had lain in. She prayed the boy dead before the fiend had torched him. Why do this to Toby Slayter's body? None of the others were set aflame.

Aurelia next clasped her hands about herself, and she rocked under the torment of this horrid moment, under the finality of death.

"That's not Toby or Julian," said a voice in her ear.

She looked over her shoulder to see Noel had gotten past the tape, and behind him stood Hector and Peter and behind them an array of other street children lined up and staring. "What? Then who is it, Noel?"

For the first time, Aurelia stared into the blackened, creosote painted face and she saw it first in the eyes, the recognition that this was young, dirty-faced, sad Danielle...or rather Danielle's battered and bloodied body. Someone had killed the teen, someone who did not want Danielle easily identified.

"I recall her street tattoos," said Redeoux with a little hard swallow, a frown, and a shrug as he pointed to the skull and cross bones that had been badly gouged out of her skin along her left bicep. Aurelia, too, recalled the tattoo and now she saw another one of an angel along the girl's naked inner thigh. She had been stripped of her ratty homeless clothing, and quite possibly sexually molested from the look of things. Rae felt an instant guilt that she had not seen this coming, so intent had she been on learning about Julian and about the street religion of these children.

Theopolis had allowed Noel and the others to come to this side of the police line to ID their Danny.

Gene now also stood in her face. He'd come bounding toward her from the police barrier just behind Noel.

"It's not Toby or Julian, Gee! Do you hear me? It's Danielle."

"The–the young woman we spoke to the other day?"

"Yes, leader of the street angels."

My God...we were just talking to her yesterday." Gene

stood shaking, moved to his core.

"Coincidence?" asked Theopolis, his grim look, his creased forehead saying, "It's gotta be, but I don't believe it."

Gene was also having a hard time fathoming just how this could be. He repeated the single word question– "Coincidence?"–as he stared at the carnage of the body amid the ashes.

"I don't dare guess if it is coincidence or happenstance," Aurelia replied, wrapping her arms about herself, suddenly feeling a chill in the warm Arizona air. "Given that she lived on the street and all the victims've been street children except for Julian, it might simply be...but then...then this means that Julian and Toby are possibly still alive."

"Quite possibly." Gene stood planted, not wanting to go nearer the body, fearful of his own reaction, she sensed.

"So who killed Danielle and why?" she asked, continuing the Socratic dialogue.

"A random act of violence, perhaps a disagreement over turf? Certainly does not fit the Phantom's modus operandi, or is it a house cleaning job since our guy likes boys, not girls?" asked Theopolis.

"She'd promised to bring us some information," said Rae. "The Phantom cleaning up a loose end and making it appear the work of someone else, maybe?" Aurelia paced, gathered her thoughts, heared her father's voice in her ear saying, "Steel yourself, Rae. I brought you up Zen. Don't let yourself down. You are Hiyakawa."

"Easy for you to say," she replied. "Right now, I feel more Murphy than Zen."

"What's that, Rae?" Gene looked confused.

"Nothing...just talking to myself."

Gene looked pale. "We were just talking to a living, breathing, dreaming, feeling, sentient young girl with hopes, with a belief system–however warped–and now she's a hollowed out conch shell tossed in a garbage heap. God, Rae, I hate this bastard."

"No less than I, Gee, but hatred can easily overwhelm me

and just block my work. I gotta take my father's advice. Hold firm to my Zen."

"You're father? So that's who you've been seeing."

"Ahhh, no Gee, I'm referring to my upbringing, what Father taught me about–"

"Rae, it's me. I know you've been seeing someone; I've known it for a long, long time. I just didn't know who...until now. It's okay."

"*Shhhhh*...damn it, Gene, no one needs to know I really do see ghosts."

"Plural?"

"My mother visits from time to time, and at times like this, I sometimes see the deceased or some aspect lingering like the afterglow of a flash camera. But Gene, this stays with us."

"Understood. Did you see anything of Danielle's spirit?"

She pointed to a nearby phone pole. "She's up there, looking down over the scene, but curious about feeling no electric current going through her body."

"Electric current?"

"She's perched on the wire with birds on either side of her."

"Is she, you know, stuck on this plane?"

"She thinks she is needed in the war."

"The War of Angels?"

"The one she told us about."

"She's lingering here, so she can fight back?"

"Now she has the power, yes."

Theopolis came to them. "Do you want to do a reading over the body before the ME and his people grid the scene?"

"No...she's left me with a sense of betrayal...that she was betrayed somehow, and that is all she has except for her clinging to her creation myths. Something we all wrestle with, apparently even in death–otherworld and underworld myths–to answer questions of heaven and hell, life and death, burial and resurrection, what the dash between the dates on our headstones will say about our time spent here."

"Wow...your father taught you well."

"My father had his gifts. Everyone sought his advice. He

proved wise most of the time, but he underestimated me. Perhaps as all parents do."

"As perhaps you do with Nia?"

"Gene, you have no idea how spoiled Nia is. She's become a huge brat, and sad to say a quite selfish one at that."

"She's wrestling with demons you don't even–"

"Yeah...demons like her mother and T-Mobile."

Again Theopolis interrupted them. "The ME's asking that all of us get clear of here so he can work. He's a crotchety SOB, and he thinks anyone within a ten mile radius of the crime scene could conceivably contaminate it."

"Who is he working for? FBI or Phoenix?"

"Neither. Technically, he is the county coroner. We draw on him because he is the most convenient."

"Why don't you call in Dr. Jessica Coran from Quantico? No one has had more success with serial killers than Coran, and besides, the BSU is already working on this case."

"I've shot my budget already this year. No way I can afford to bring in anyone else from headquarters and still please the bean counters. We're stuck with Dr. Ira P. Ataloss, I'm afraid."

"At a loss?" She laughed lightly. "Is that what the locals call Dr. Daedlaus?"

"For good reason. A truly good forensics man is as hard to come by as a good lay, you might say." Redeoux gave her a look that intended to convey that he thought himself a good lay.

"All right, anyone need a drink?" she asked.

They made for the car to leave when Noel shouted at her from the barricade. "Please! Help me! I know Bloody Mary got Danielle, and I know I'm next! You've got to hide me! Hide me!"

Hector pushed Noel hard to the pavement. "To hell with that! I saw her. She's coming for me, man! Yous got to hide me, bitch! Else I am dead like Danielle."

The youngest of them, Peter, his face streaked with tears, shouted out now. "Don't let Bloody Mary get us!"

Hector shouted, "It's La Llorana! She's killing us one by one until there are no more children left in the world, so all humankind will die off!"

Aurelia rushed to them, assuring them that nothing would happen to them, but even as she said it, she knew she could not promise anything of the kind. She turned to Theopolis. "There must be somewhere to place these children, some kind of witness protection program for kids in this terrible condition? We know they are being targeted and stalked as a group. Theo, we have to do something and do it now."

"We can get family services involved, make them wards of the state, but there's nothing we can do as feds, no. Other than calling on these agencies, and when these...these tykes see a family service clipboard in anyone's hands, they run for the bricks."

"Will you do as we say?" she asked Noel and the others. Some eleven children had followed the flashing police lights here out of curiosity, and all of them had been followers of the dead angelic Danielle, or close to her in some capacity. Learning it was their leader who'd been brutally murdered, they hadn't time to grieve when fear had gripped them. Overhead a flashing neon green billboard sign with a Black Panther logo read:

Arizona Panther Gin....Cheaper Than a Shrink...NO LIE.
Trust Arizona's only home brewed GIN since 1948

Sitting on the sign, swinging his legs, as if giving his sanction to the Panther label, Hiro Hiyakawa, wrapped an arm around Danielle's shoulder as he spoke in her ethereal ear, an ear that was no more there than was Aurelia's father. Still, Danielle appeared fascinated with Hiro's every word, caught up in rapt attention. Yes, Danielle had found her way home.

Aurelia sensed that the girl only sought peace now. She had had enough of warring angels and demons, and she cared not to share her horrible experience with the living.

For now, in this world, Aurelia looked like a Mother Goose or a Pied Piper as the children filed in behind her, all going toward a row of patient squad cars, their colored lights flashing crazily against the dancing leaves in a growing wind. It seemed an ill wind portending worse to come.

Theopolis made a call that would bring out social services. They'd make arrangements with the street kids who wanted help. Things calmed. Rae aimlessly found herself leaning against a Phoenix cruiser.

She felt convinced that Julian and Toby remained alive. Trapped. Held hostage. A pair of prisoners. Caged. In a limbo somewhere between a Twilight Zone-like cerulean blue and green angel's park and the screaming red coral sea. At least these two remained alive in Rae's mind so long as their bodies were not discovered in some ash heap like Danielle's, they still had a chance.

Rae felt this in her bones. In the core of her being. Alive and still in pain and suffering emotional turmoil. But alive. Just where and how to locate them before they, too, wound up in a city dumpster or in a river or lake, floating face down while fish picked at their flesh. Aurelia could not say how she knew it, but she sensed Julian in particular strongly, a sign of life. It was not just maddening, it was increasingly maddening, as the sense of him weakened with each passing hour, as it was surely linked to his physical waning. Still she felt nothing.

Once social service people came in and Rae saw that the children were being taken care of, she and Gene returned to Redeoux's sedan, parked amid an array of police cruisers.

"Relax. Take it easy. Calm now. Find your center." All the prompts that Gene kept repeating where she leaned into the sedan, but none of it gained hold or purchase. She remained as far from detecting this killer as when she'd arrived.

Theopolis joined them at the car.

"Theo, we've got to locate this woman the children call Bloody Mary."

"Everyone in Phoenix knows Bloody Mary. She's a mental. She goes around exposing her breasts, and she shouts at you while her breasts are sagging straight down as if nailed to boards, and she is screeching something about Satan being afoot, and Satan sucking on her and turning her into his sex slave queen. But she's insane, a lunatic."

A uniformed cop, overhearing, said, "She routinely hangs out on Division at Trent, not far from the park where the kids keep disappearing. That's where you'd normally find her, but she's being arraigned tonight for assault on an officer. She's a full-blown lunatic all right."

"Assault on an officer?"

"Yeah, me to be exact. Kowalski. He flashed his nameplate at his breast pocket: Louis Kowalski."

"I've got to talk to this woman. Can you guide us to her, officer?" Aurelia asked.

"Sure if I can clear it with my sergeant. Take me off this shit detail. Take me a couple minutes, then you can follow me."

All the frightened children were carted off, the last site Aurelia saw that of Noel looking grimly and sternly back at her as if his predictions about Aurelia turning him over to the authorities had come true. Maybe the kid was psychic.

Gene and Aurelia climbed into the squad car behind Officer Lou Kowalski while the huge Pole cleared things with his superior. Theo followed as they pulled from the murder scene, going in search of Bloody Mary.

"They also call her La Llorana on the street," Aurelia said to Kowalski.

"Yeah, heard that name for her, too. To be politically correct, she's a Latino mix. To be accurate, she's what we call around Phoenix a mex, but a Tex Mess, some call her, since she's such a g'damn mess. PPD has had the loon in for questioning, but she practices a wily kind of lunacy that can avoid anything resembling a straight answer. Frankly, I think you're wasting your time."

"Oh, why is that?"

"For one, I think this maniac Phantom killer we got running around here killing street urchins is one of them typical 'street cleaner killer' types. The kind who goes after prostitutes but this one likes young boys, but he kinda you know justifies abduction and killing by convincing himself he's like doing a public good."

"A public good?" Rae asked.

"Like a community service kinda thing, you know…cleaning scum off the streets. I read up on all kinds of serial killers. I keep up. Read the police gazette, you know."

Agent Redeoux is of the belief that this woman knows nothing, and will be just another dead end, and you seem to agree?" Aurelia shifted in the seat behind Kowalski where she and Gene sat in the 'cage' behind the grid where the arrested and cuffed usually sat.

"The man is right, I think. Bloody Mary, she knows nothing, and I don't see her murdering or abetting in a murder."

"She's terrified these children. They believe her the wife of Satan. I want to talk to her, Officer. I want to question her."

Kowalski grunted. "I'll arrange it."

"Tonight…now. We go to her. We confront her."

After cruising for a bit in silence, Kowalski asked, "You really think she's procuring these children for murder?"

Gene leapt in. "What's in it for her?"

"Why does anyone procure for a killer?" replied Rae. "Favors. Fear? A vested interest?"

"All manner of reasons, I guess," Kowalski thoughtfully said, his eyes searching hers where he saw them framed in the rearview from behind the cage grid of the cruiser.

"Pretty sure about now they'll be taking Bloody Mary down to the courtroom," Kowalski told them. Pulling into the Phoenix City courthouse parking lot and quickly slipping into a squad car zone, Officer Kowalski told them that Judge David Alba–always presiding over night court–disallowed any guns in his courtroom. "In fact," he continued, "the man is so obsessively against guns in his courtroom that he won't even allow his bailiff a firearm–his own damn bailiff. Think Bloody Mary's real name is Grace, but sometimes she goes by Mierta or Theresa Santiago."

As they climbed from the rear of the squad car, Kowalski offered to hold onto their weapons until they returned, popping his trunk. "I can put 'em in my evidence lock box in the trunk or under the seat up front if you like. Save you hassle going in."

They took him up on his offer, turning over their Smith and Wesson police specials to Kowalski.

"You're sure this Bloody Mary is here now?" Aurelia asked.

"I am. If I wanted it to go hard for the poor old wretched thing, I'd just show up. Judge Alba hears my side of the story, he's gonna throw everything in his arsenal at her. She don't have no control of herself; hell, they put her outta the asylum with a bottle full of pills and expect her to know enough to keep up with pills. She doesn't even know where her g'damn pills are much less–ahhh, you get the picture."

Rae thought Lou Kowalski one of the good guys and told him so. Gene gave him a perfunctory nod, and as they entered the building, he said, "Not sure Officer Kowalski is doing the homeless old crone any good by not showing up and making the complaint. Heart may be in the right place, howev–"

"Agreed. Road to hell's paved with good intention," replied

Gene.

"We oughta know, hey Gee? On their way in, she informed him that Etta Pace had finally come to her senses and had kicked her con-artist lover out.

Inside they were subjected to a metal detector search, despite flashing their FBI identification. "Alba's orders," commented one uniformed guard, shrugging. The other guard looked comatose.

They soon found Judge Alba's quarters and met the swarthy small-statured Native American judge. He agreeably had Bloody Mary taken to a separate room saying he would not allow the woman in his chambers. "Despite the delousing and bathing given her, there remains an odor I will not allow to infect my chambers."

Aurelia gulped at this and peeped out to see the tall, stoop-shouldered, scraggly-haired, wild-eyed, feral looking woman who could easily pass for a longshoreman grunting and cursing under her breath in animal-fashion, her gaze taking in everything while in a pretense of blindness. Aurelia realized here was a woman who lived by instinct alone, and Bloody Mary, under the harsh courtroom lights, was as out of place as any fish tossed ashore or any bird with a hole in its wing.

She felt a wave of empathy and sadness wash over her for the woman.

The judge had gone out to the courtroom, and keeping a safe distance from Mary, asked his bailiff to escort her to room number 1148.

Her handcuff chains rattled like ship's rigging as she stomped, heavy footedly from the room, head slumped forward like some new species of captive animal with a strange curve to its spine, a species yet to be given a name.

"I'm getting nothing but bad vibes here, Rae," said Gene in her ear as she watched Mary disappear through the door.

"It may well be a dead end, but we won't know that until we talk to her, now will we?"

"I got an instinct about her."

"I know she's addled in the head."

"So," he replied, how can we trust a word she tells us?"

"I won't know until I talk to her. You can wait outside if you wish." She had found the hallway, Gene trailing after. They located 1148.

"Not so sure now about good ol' Officer Kowalski's motives," Gene whispered.

She stopped cold and looked at his eyes. "Meaning?"

"You smell the wake of this old crone? Kowalski probably is still trying to work that stench out of his nostrils. He probably simply didn't want to go near her again."

"Well…he did have to wrestle cuffs on her pre-delousing and bathing, and he was bitten by her."

A light laugh accompanied the two of them into 1148. Once inside, and with the bailiff stepping out, Aurelia sat across the table from Bloody Mary. She introduced first Gene, who remained standing and imposing nearby, and then she introduced herself.

"I need my meds," the woman replied. "Did yous two bring me my meds?"

"Sorry…we're not medical people, Mierta."

"You know my secret name! How?"

"Magic."

"Ahhh…you know, I got a magic blanket, you know, one I can spread out on command and ask it to fly. A flying carpet. Give it to you for some meds. You want my magic blanket?"

"Ms. Santiago…."

She reacted to her maiden name as if hit by an arrow.

Rae continued, saying, "We've come to ask questions." Aurelia held a handkerchief over her nose. The odor exuding off the woman was preternaturally powerful. Something akin to a fetid overripe melon mixed with the odors of a horribly active gastro-intestinal problem that economically let out small increments of bowel odors, odors as of the inner linings of the large and small intestine, all in measured doses. Bloody Mary seemed a walking candidate for spontaneous human combustion if there were such a thing.

"Finally, somebody wants me for something," she

pathetically replied.

Gene stalwartly held his own against the assault on his senses from this homeless wretch. The judge had been right. Even cleaned up, her skin appeared dusky and covered with a gray patina. She appeared Spanish or Black or a mix of both, but it was impossible to say with any certainty. Her accent sounded Mexican.

"Let's make a deal." A mantra for her. "Let's make a deal. Anything you want." Obviously, this was her usual method of relating, through some sort of barter.

Twenty minutes and they learned nothing from her. She kept wanting to talk about an amusement park and a ride she'd once taken, presumably as a child, deep into the bowels of a haunted castle. Her eyes were alight with the tale. But her words rang out a cryptic bell of annoyance for the FBI people."

Finally, unable to take her voice–like a nail through the head–or her stench–like a spike of sewage through each nostril–Gene pleaded that Aurelia come away.

She'd gotten no confirmations, no assurances, no vibes, no connectedness here between Mary and the homeless children, and she'd gotten none between Mary and the Phantom either. If this homeless woman knew anything, she had likely forgotten it. She seemed possessed of a short-term memory problem to say the least. In any case, Aurelia got so little from her in a psychic sense, nothing beyond mayhem in that mind, that she decided against touching or holding the woman's hand, feeling it likely a waste, and fearing the same as Kowalski, Judge Alba, Gene, and now she herself. A primal fear that madness somehow might be transmittable through touch, a breath, perspiration through a handshake. It made no sense, and yet it was there, a persistent fear of this madwoman.

The phrase 'there but for the grace of God go I' took on more layers of subconscious meaning in the presence of someone like Bloody Mary. Aurelia could see a once pretty face, a once slim and well proportioned body in Mary, and she imagined her once a child, a lovely child named Grace in a kindergarten setting, in early grade photos, nothing in her appearance or demeanor ever denoting what she'd eventually become. No one set out in life to become this.

"My real name is full of grace, for I am Grace," she muttered to Aurelia as the two FBI agents slipped out the door, deciding they'd get nothing substantial from Bloody Mary. Out in the hallway, they heard her shouting inside 1148, "My fucking real name is Grace! You know 'cause I have a friend who digs earthworms in the cemetery! She ties 'em tail to head, head to tail and makes jewelry outta worms. Living jewelry! Says its eatable jewelry, and the idea will sweep the nation, make her a rich crazoid bitch, which will make her eccentric instead of mad. But she damn well ate 'em all! Now that's sick! Her name is Grace! She had an accident."

The woman was confusing her own splinter personalities with one another. She was also battling the DT's.

The accident with Grace. The phrase just popped into Rae's head. An accident of some sort had brought Grace to become Bloody Mary.

Suppose Bloody Mary was once a graceful person named Grace, a child named Grace, and how fitting that she, like the Mother of God–according to the street children had fallen so far from Grace....

Aurelia concentrated on all of this, mulling it over as she and Gene made their way to the elevator; gave it continued serious thought all the way past the checkpoint and out the courthouse doors and to the squad car where the affable Kowalski stood waving them on.

"Thanks for waiting so long on us, Officer," said Rae.

"Wise man, Kowalski," said Gene, "not going near that woman."

"Something connecting her to all this, to the children, to the killings, to the killer," Rae firmly said. "I just know it. I just can't put a finger on it, but it's inside her. Locked away inside that lunatic brain, inside one of her personalities."

"I got no sense of that whatsoever," Gene replied as they climbed back into the rear of the car. "All I got was a morass of meaningless gibberish going on at all times."

"Kowalski," began Aurelia, "is there an amusement park anywhere near here, anywhere that Bloody Mary might wander into?"

"Ahhh…well, there's the old Tombstone Riverview park just outside of town, an old west gunfight–reenactments, that sort of thing. They even got their own mine shaft and miner's cemetery."

"I'm not talking about a museum. An amusement park. One close enough that Bloody Mary or Grace or whatever her name is could be sleeping there."

"How about my gun?" asked Gene. "We damn left 'em in the trunk."

"Nah, I decided against all that trouble," replied Kowalski. "Got them up front on the seat with me. Never left my sight." Kowalski opened a small window in the grate separating them and cheerfully passed each .38 Special back to them.

"God, I could use a cup of coffee," said Gene.

"Got a thermos up front." Now Kowalski pressed a thermos through the retractable grate door in the cage.

Cage, Aurelia thought, flashing on the single word as if it were a buoy in a sea of confusing images, and next she saw the Satan sea of her visions and wondered what it had to do with cages, and seeing all the imprisoned souls, she recalled how caged her sense of the victim had remained throughout. Caged…encased…encased in paint.

Gene was thanking Kowalski profusely while pouring the hot liquid into the thermos cap. He offered it to Rae, who declined, and next he gulped down caffeine. "Maybe this'll help me keep my eyes open."

"Not getting enough Z's huh?" asked Kowalski.

"Got that right. What with the case and all."

"Gotta be rough on you both, I suspect."

"That it is…so true."

Aurelia gave a thought to her own fatigue, a wave of it washing over her where she sat. It'd be nice to close her eyes and just give into it. With all that had gone on, she'd gotten precious little sleep.

"Concierge at the hotel showed us a brochure on an amusement park in the area, one with a Ferris wheel, the works," began Rae. "Can you swing by this amusement park, Officer Kowalski?

"Sure thing, and call me Lou."

"How far is it to this place, Lou?" asked Gene, his voice thickening.

"Oh, not far really. Fifteen, twenty at the most."

"You're a good man, Lou, to chauffeur us about like this."

"Are you all right, Gee?" she asked, seeing his eyes roll.

"Feeling much further…ahhh better, yeah, I mean best-er? I mean how much further." Gene sounded incoherent now, repeating himself.

She realized that Gene had gulped down two cups of the coffee, and now he held out a cup to her. Kowalski answered Gene's last question over his shoulder as he drove. "It's as far as the home of Jigoku."

The Japanese word for this mythological god of Hades instantly alerted Aurelia. Where would Officer Louis Kowalski have picked this up, and what exactly was his meaning?

"What? What do you know about Jigoku?" she asked, wondering what a Polish cop in Phoenix knew of the Japanese Buddhist equivalent of Satan? At the same time, in a little corner of her brain, she realized how politically incorrect her questioning of this fact was. Anyone could find out anything he wanted about Japanese culture and religion and myth on the web these days."

Gene, looking groggy and unable to focus all of a sudden, asked, "What the hell is a Jigo-ku? Rae? And why are you spinning around?"

Kowalski was saying at the same time in a calm, chilling voice, "Emma O, from the Sanskrit for Yama–Lord of Jigoku, Lord of Hades who judges souls and places each in a certain hell appropriate to one's crimes–hardly different from our Christian beliefs, really–Dante Allegeri, Divine Comedy, the nine rungs of Hell."

She knew the belief in Emma O or Jigoku well. "The eight

rungs of hell. A popular subject for Japanese scrolls and some dark artwork."

"And that would make you Jizo, the savior of souls condemned by me!" he shouted as Gene passed out entirely alongside Aurelia, and she for the first time looked at the identification on the dash for Kowalski. There was some resemblance, but God alone knew where the real Kowalski lay and if he were dead or alive.

The man at the wheel, whoever he was, hit a control button and the back door locks, like a pair of gunshots, simultaneously bolted. She drew her Smith & Wesson and aimed it at the killer's head, shouting, "You pull over right now or I put a bullet through your fucking head! Now!"

He sped up.

"Now!" The weapon shook in her hands. She'd never used it on a real target.

"The gun is disabled," he quietly said.

She instinctively grabbed for Gene's gun.

"Your partner's gun is useless as well. You left me alone with your weapons. Some FBI you two turned out to be. FBI 101–never relinquish your weapon under any circumstances."

"What the hell've you done to Gee?"

"You were supposed to drink the coffee, too. A strong sedative."

"This is more than a sedative. He's foaming at the mouth. You've poisoned him!"

"All right, so I lied."

"Damn you, what did you put in that coffee?"

"Just a touch of arsenic with the sedative."

"Bastard! And just where the hell're you taking us?"

"You said you wanted to go to the amusement park, something that bitch Grace told you about! My park. Now you'll see it up close and personal."

She tried kicking out at the window, but it was no use. Spent, she held onto Gene, rocking him, pleading with him to hang on.

The killer mimicked her pleas, laughingly repeating, "Gee,

hang on, Gee, hang on. Hang on for what? For death! Let the poor bastard go!"

Aurelia felt like a fool to be so trapped, so caged by the killer.

"You were getting under my skin," he said from the front. "I mean really creepily under my skin...literally. I could feel you getting closer and closer till you were around the corner."

"You can bet I've been on you!" she shouted.

"Saw your eyes–black and blue eyes. And here they are." He stared at her eyes in the rearview, just as in his vision. She glared back.

"Knew you were coming, so I took the offensive; started scouting for you. Ran up on that bitch, Danielle, spying on me. She'd followed old Grace to the park until finally, she located me about the same time I snared her."

She began dialing her cell phone, and he saw this in the small rectangle of the rearview. "Give me the phone, Dr. Hiyakawa or else–"

"Fuck you!"

She'd speed dialed Theopolis's number.

Suddenly, the killer had a gun pointed at Gene's head. "Both phones! Now! Toss 'em up here! Now!"

She kept her phone line open, gathered up Gene's cell, and tossed both hard through the grate opening, sending them to the floorboard below the dash. It worked. She had an open line.

"When we get to the Prairie Sea Amusement Park, are you going to kill us both there?" she shouted her question. "Won't it be crowded? Is that where you've got the boys, Toby and Julian? Are they sill alive?" She kept him talking, distracting him from pursuing the open phone line. She prayed someone the other end had enough sense to know what he was listening to.

Cy sped for Cy's lair beneath Cy's amusement park.

Aurelia had not simply stepped into a well-set trap, but she was trapped with a dying Gene on her hands. The Phantom had her precisely where he wanted her. She could not help but think of Nia, and the vision of her daughter holding her as she lay dying. She also could not help but flash on Danielle's fired body. She could not put anything past this predatory animal that had her at his mercy.

Aurelia's head had begun to spin in a frantic for Gene, and thoughts of life tomorrow without him on the planet rushed in, vying for her attention. She called out over the noise of the passing life on the street, pleading with her captor. "We've gotta get the arsenic out of his system before it kills him!" But she was drowned out by traffic, the hum of the motor, and the ongoing police band radio that had, until now, been mere background chatter. She helplessly prayed that Theopolis on the open line might hear her shout for needed medical assistance.

"I laced it with enough barbiturates he won't feel a thing," the Phantom assured her. "Now shut up!"

"Look at him, damn you! He's in pain and he's dying!"

She feared it may already be too late to help Gene, and her tears for him freely flowed.

Another squad car pulled alongside them, a Phoenix officer firing at their tires, missing as nothing blew, and the killer didn't lose control of the wheel. Instead, the Phantom eased his window down and fired off several rounds of his own, hitting the driver, sending the squad car into a tailspin that ended with a crash into a standing construction dumpster in front of a home being gutted and refurbished.

"How the fuck did they know!" Cy lamented, confused. "Must be they've decided Kowalski's gone missing too long."

"Bullshit," Rae challenged. "We've been closing in on you for days!" she shouted. "You may's well give it up!"

"That's bull, a lie! If that's true, what is my name? If you're so close to catching me, what is my fucking name?" he demanded, talking to the mirror-framed eyes.

He's superstitious as hell, she thought. "PSI powers'll get you."

"Cy?" he nervously said.

"Simon says," she replied. "You like Simon Says?"

"Fuck!"

Cy was short for Simon. In her mind she played out names that might be relevant. Obviously, she'd hit a nerve quite by accident when she said PSI–pronounced cy–" and her knowing his name unnerved him. "Simon the Satan of the Sea."

"How could you possibly know of my ocean?"

"I see things. Your preoccupation with heaven and hell, angels and demons. You paint them!" Then she said aloud, "You're Simon Says, right? Cy with a C-Y, right!"

Although she could see little of him in the rearview mirror, she did catch his frozen expression. She had hit on his name. The man in the driver's seat, as in her visions. It was him, the shadowy Satan who straddled the helpless children in the red coral cauldron.

"You're the one Julian wrote about, Carnivore Man, aren't you? Carnival Man!"

The man's eyes shone profoundly moving, profoundly sad, profoundly guilty. In that moment, she understood him, understood how much pain and suffering he'd himself endured, and how much it all meant to him as he'd been so conditioned to it that only in inflicting suffering could he feel any 'normality' or calm or human emotion whatsoever. It was why she'd been unable to read him, unable to decipher anything of him, despite their proximity; it explained why he made a perfectly calm and believable Officer Lou Kowalski. He was driven by his hatred and need, and she hated him for both.

"How the fuck did you get that?" Simon 'Cy' the Phantom, muttered into the rearview mirror, acutely aware of the eyes on him, her eyes framed within the same small rectangle that held his own from where she sat. Somehow he knew their eyes shared the same space in time here in a strange way, so like his nightmare fear of the eyes that'd haunted him now for over a year, for longer than she had any way of possibly knowing his identity. Perhaps they were the eyes of God upon him after all...after all this time, after all he'd done...God had had His infinite eye on one Simon after all...perhaps since birth, but he'd never believed. He'd caught that Danielle girl lurking around, and he'd thought it her eyes all that time. Now he knew better.

"It's not too late, Simon, to give yourself up, and if you turn over Julian and Toby to us, sparing their lives...well, that would go a long way toward finding mercy on your soul from a Federal judge, not to mention in the eyes of God."

She's reading my mind, he thought.

The man she now called Simon teetered on the brink of the right decision for only a moment, when he suddenly grasped the rearview mirror and forced it in another direction, off her eyes. When he did so, he saw what Aurelia had been watching from out her one eye out the back window. He saw the array of power mustered against him. He saw the snaking parade of police cars that'd emerged from out of the darkness of the otherwise unknowing, unfeeling city.

"They come near me, and I take the two of you out with me," he told Aurelia.

Her phone rang at the same time that the cruiser's radio crackled into life with the voice of Theopolis Redeoux. "We know you have hostages in the car. Stop the vehicle, release them unharmed, and step slowly away from the vehicle, hands on head, sir, or you will be shot dead, sir. We have sharpshooters with a red laser at your head as we speak."

A high-speed chase ensued, sending Aurelia to the floorboard alongside Gene's unconscious body. Gene no longer coughed, no longer seemed capable of breathing. She feared doubly for him now. Crouched and hiding, she saw that her father did the same the other side of Gene. "Look what a mess you've gotten me into now!" he muttered. "Some damn psychic."

Aurelia's cell phone kept ringing incessantly. She wondered who it might possibly be. Her mind racing with the possibilities at lightning speed: Nia with complaints about the heat or an ill-fitting tank top? Enriquiana to report that Nia had fallen into bad company and was throwing a wild party in her room? Etta to say she'd patched things up with Neil and the wedding was on again? Joannie about Rae's bar tab? Dr. Polkabla about canceling an appointment perhaps? Or her plumber, roofer, or electrician back at the B&B, calling to refuse any additional work until the check cleared? Or perhaps a dream call from Dr. Alandale about a date he'd been contemplating?

Finally, she thought about those tickets she'd purchased from Ruben at the hotel for a party of two to ride the Grand Canyon railroad and the reservation at the Canyon Inn in the gorge to which they were to hike, mother and daughter, in a bonding with nature and one another.

She was about to die in debt to her eyeballs. In financial woes, yes, but even worse an emotional debt she owed Nia. She blamed herself for Nia's current bad taste in clothes as well as the child's poor manners and horrible attitude toward others. How would Nia turn out if Aurelia lost her last chance to be a real mother to her? How could Nia know that her last thoughts were of her?

The car took a wild turn, tires screeching, but only two tires screamed and burned, as the other two must be airborne.

The window pressed against her face, Aurelia saw the green-blue park and the angels kissing in a huge mural at the amusement park all along one wall. No sign of Satan and his coral reef, but here, staring back at her, was the mural of her life altering dream, a dream that had brought her this far, a dream that might yet get her killed.

Gene breathing now dangerously shallow. She felt for a pulse. Faint but he remained alive. "Hold on, Gee," she whispered in his ear. "Hold on."

"You conniving bitch," Simon shouted at her. "Your phone led them to us! It was running the whole time!"

She inched her eye over the back seat to see that he held the phone in his hand and was extending it through the cage to her. "Answer it!"

"Answer it?" she chorused.

"Yes, and tell them to back off, out of sight or else."

"Or else what?"

"Else you get a bullet through your pretty little brain, and the bullet will come from your own gun!"

She got on the line as the car threw her across Gene's inert body. He had gone unconscious....slipping into coma.

Rae shakily answered the phone.

Her situation was desperate; she had never known such terror, but she fought to remain calm as she answered her ringing cell phone.

On the other end she heard: "Rae, it's me, Miranda...calling from Quantico. It's a great day. Listen to this Dr. Hiyakawa–" at FBI headquarters, Miranda Waldron held up the phone and Rae's support team at the PSI/BSU cooperative task force cheered as Miranda said, "We are happy to report that we have a fix on those visions of yours."

"Your time could not suck more!" shouted Rae.

"They are artworks. Museum art!"

"Artworks?"

"Paintings to be exact, two distinct, separate not well known artists who rendered their nightmares in symbolic imagery."

She thought of the serendipity of this, how it fit in with the painting she'd seen as they'd entered the fairgrounds here in Phoenix. She recalled the angels in caress in the stylized park, and Satan straddling condemned souls below the hotbed of coral. And now, finally, Dr. Miranda Waldron summarized the task-force findings–artworks, paintings.

"Miranda, I'm pressed for time." Again Aurelia was tossed like a bobbing cork about the back of the squad car. Her phone went flying, and it scampered below the seat.

She could hear Miranda's high-pitched voice even as she searched with outstretched fingers for the errant phone. She located the phone and caught the tail end of the calm Dr. Waldron's explanation: "Symbolic of our Judeo-Christian iconoclastic ruts. The artist was torn between depicting stylistically the very symbols of religion he despised, and yet he must for the patron depict the symbols of faith when in fact the artist himself is devoid of faith."

"Miranda shut up, will you? I need help here."

"But it's all true. Your vision is an actual painting by a guy named William Degouve de Nuncques." She even spelled the name out for Aurelia, adding that he was French. The painting is entitled the Angels of Night, 1894. Oil on canvas 48 by 60 centimeters."

"And I am about sixty centimeters from death here."

"That's why I've always admired you, Rae, your sense of humor in the face of all this. In any case, the artist is rendering a poetic evocation of childhood dreams...hence the nocturnal vision in which angels kiss in a ghostly supernatural park...."

"Miranda!"

"It hangs in a Russian museum–the original, of course."

"A Russian museum? Miranda it's of no immediate help! I'm in the middle of a hostage crisis here at the moment, and I am the one in crisis!"

It was as if Miranda had gone deaf, so excited was she at the team's discovery. "We also found the exact duplicate image of the watery red coral Hades you depicted in your psychic visions."

"And you're burning to tell me about it, right?"

"Jean Delville–Satan's Treasures, 1895. Oil on canvas. 258 by 268 centimeters. A huge canvas. Brussels museum."

"Thank you, Miranda. Now–"

"Deville–also French–" believed in a divine fluid incarnation and dangerous telepathic forces of invultuation–"

"What I need right now–"

"–as in voodoo dolls and masks, burning wax images over a toasty fire or stabbing wax images, all in a state of ecstasy. DeVille depicts luxurious bodies that lie sleeping among the seaweed and coral as Satan with a dancer's agility bestrides and takes possession of them. Exactly your vision, Rae."

"Yeah, Miranda, great...but–"

"Dr. Naomi Shulatte came up with all of this on her own. Showed me a depiction of both in a book she's found entitled simply *Symbolism*. If you get hold of it, check out page ninety five."

"Are you quite done?"

"Ahhh...yes. Rae are you in some kind of trouble?"

Aurelia hung up on Agent Waldron.

Her phone immediately rang again. She answered. It was her ex bitching about some furnishings he still wanted in his possession. She hung up on him.

Then it rang again. This time Etta was on the line, saying she was again fighting with Neil.

She hung up on Etta. "A little busy here!"

Edwin called with some question about how the female vagina was stimulated. "I don't believe this!" She hung up again. "No, I do fucking believe this!"

Certain that she was going to die, that the vision of herself bleeding in her daughter's arms was now minutes away, and with Simon rather busy at the wheel, Aurelia speed dialed Nia's cell phone, praying it was paid up and that Nia was not on it. She got a ringing, the sweetest sound to ever enter her ear. Pick up....pick up, Nia.

"Hello...hello?"

"Nia, it's me. I love you, Nia...so much, you will never know."

"Ma? What is this? What's wrong? Are you...." Nia's voice trailed off, breaking up.

"I just wanted you to know that I love you."

No answer.

"Can you hear me? I said, I love you, baby."

"Get it said. Say your goodbye's right!" warned Cy.

"Baby, do you hear me?"

Nia came back on the phone. "You're cutting out every time Enriquiana and I go to the top, but when we're on our way down, you come in, Ma."

"Sweetheart, what're you talking about top, down?"

"We're on the giant Ferris wheel at the amusement park, Ma and it's...going...'gin...'" she faded out.

"Fuck!" Nia was here! At the very park that Bloody Mary spoke of. The park where so many young boys and Danielle were killed! The park where this madman made his lair, where this madman now pulled up and ran along the outer circle back of all the kiosks, running for some hole at some dead end back lot.

Cy worked for the park, likely in maintenance for the place, as he knew every inch. The place had the feel of back-lot to a film studio, a place of gayety on one side of the facades, a dull, sad reality this side. Funland–at least on the surface and along the Midway with its valley of kiosks decorated with dangling stuffed animals and toys and balloons and streamers. Prairie Sea Park, a place at the top of Ruben the Concierge's list of attractions for Nia to see, and Aurelia imagined seeing the wild gesticulations of a young woman on the Ferris wheel where she sat alongside Ruben right now–Nia! Here in close proximity to her mother's last moments of life

The killer had found her easily enough; he'd gone on the offensive after seeing Aurelia's photo in the latest news account. The FBI's not so secret weapon. She recalled how cameras had flashed about them when she had insisted on seeing the various dumpsites and when Danielle's charred body was discovered. She felt a wave of fear now that Cy was precisely what the street children said he was, Satan and as such he had the powers of a god, the powers of the fallen angel to see into the hearts of men.

Somewhere in the back of her mind, Nia stood shaking and shouting Aurelia's name, and the image of Nia holding onto her mother's battered, bloody body crept over her, blotting out all other thought.

Julian's abductor stared again into her soul through the now magic rearview mirror, trying to decipher the grim look on Rae's face.

Simon's stolen police car tore past barriers now that she'd thought impassable, and onto the dark side of the amusement park grounds in the shadow of a large scaffolding–a wooden rollercoaster that went within feet of the Ferris wheel, but the coaster was half destroyed. Silent monster cranes, looking like dinosaurs stood about, and Rae noticed the wrecking ball dangling like some giant fist.

Simon knew the terrain well, and now the stolen squad car sailed along the rear alleyways of the carnival. Rae watched helplessly as they whizzed by dumpsters, crates, discarded work materials, and back lot doors–the less than colorful backside of the carnival.

Lou Kowalski's impersonator sped the car into a garage he opened by remote and they were plunged into darkness when the door rattled down and hit with a thud behind them. Using a flashlight and pointing the way with his gun, the killer ordered her ahead of him.

"Leave him!" he shouted when she held onto Gene.

She hesitated and he struck her across the face with the gun barrel, which cut a swath across her cheek, blood rising. "Now!"

She knew how to kill a man twenty ways with her bare hands; she held a black belt in Jujitsu. If she got one chance, she knew she must take it. Gene somehow found the strength to grab hold of her skirt and hold on, muttering, "I'll p-p-pro-tect you Rae," when his grip on her evaporated. He lay back again on the seat, again going out of consciousness.

"I want you to meet Julian," Cy said.

"Then he's alive?"

"Little bastard's got a plan. He's the one sent for you, isn't he? With that supernatural shit?"

"I was reading you, not Julian!" she lied, unsure what to say but thinking any way that threw him off guard was good.

"Julian needs to hear that and to know Carnivore Man is going to paint you now, Dr. Hiyakawa! That you are mine!"

"And you've gotta rub it in his face because he's not cooperating with you, right? Hasn't cried out enough. Hasn't excited you enough!"

"He's alive just long enough to see you're here!"

For how long, she wondered. For that matter, how long did Gene have, or Toby, or she herself.

He guided her at gunpoint from the maintenance garage that snaked along the rear of the haunted house to a set of stairs leading to a door marked **Staff Only** in bold red.

"Wait, if you think I'm going into some bloody hole with you, then you're crazy!" she suddenly shouted, struggling against his hold.

He reached out to push her, but Aurelia grabbed his arm and simultaneously brought the ball of her hand up and into his chin, missing the killing opportunity to jam his jaw bone up into his brain by a hair's breath, her hand slipping away and breaking his nose instead as he twisted away. She toppled him down the stairwell, the gun landing somewhere below him.

He scrambled to his feet, his shirt painted with blood streaming down his face. Looking like the madman he was, he ducked through the door just as her deadly heel hit the door instead of his head.

She grabbed up the 9mm. Glock he'd held on her and gave chase. She fired at his fleeting shadow, missing. She had opened the door on a maze, one tunnel taking her into the haunted house, the other going down into the bowels of a network of passages below ground. The underbelly of the amusement park.

He had gone for the haunted house.

She inched forward, going for the passage below, care in each step.

She realized only now how much she'd perspired. How much she trembled. How much fear had balled up in her stomach.

"She came to an underground room with broken carousel horses and junk piles of unused materials. His workshop. More painted signs and a stack of paintings, all of poor quality. The broken merry-go-round ponies eyed her curiously as something new here.

She did not recall any headless horses in her visions of this place, but she did flash on her daughter holding her while she was hurt and bleeding and perhaps dying.

She wondered where in this horrible place Julian awaited, and if he were alive or dead. "Where is the lair beneath the lair?" she asked herself and then saw the portal of a trap door lowering ahead of her. Another level yet below. How deep a hole did she want to climb into?

Suddenly over a PA system the man who'd masqueraded so successfully as Officer Kowalski said, "I sent for you, Doctor. I wanted an end to it. You didn't find me; I found you, and-and in the bargain, I found my own soul, because I sent for an angel to put an end to the predator in me. I have the advantage here. You kill me, I'm fine with that; I kill you, I'm fine with that."

"You knew I was coming for you, didn't you!" she shouted in return. "Sweating it out the entire time. Hope you suffered."

She saw movement to her right, drew a bead on the movement, and held firm. He darted from behind wooden doors stacked one atop another, their rusty hinges tearing at Lou Kowalski's uniform. She followed and entered yet another room, and there he stood laughing hyena-fashion, but now she saw some thirty odd clones of Cy. He stood to her right, to her left, to her center, above, below, in, out, down, over–in every direction here in the hall of mirrors.

She picked out the one from whom the laughter seemed to originate, and she fired, shattering glass to his laughter. His voice seemed to come from all sides. She'd entered his maze, on his turf. She shattered a second mirror and another to no avail. He remained standing, his reflection now in shards atop the floor of mirrored glass tile.

Then he was gone, disappeared.

She gave pursuit, unsure which direction he'd taken as each reflection had gone out another door.

She stepped through and into hell–a room devoted to Hades, the mural in the round had her in Satan's ocean, on Satan's reef, the same blood-red reef as in her vision.

She thought how proud Gene'd be of her, seeing the physical signs of Aurelia's symbolic journey falling into place. All her predictions coming true. A park. It had all begun with a park that night in her bed when she dreamed of angels kissing. An old carousel of sea animals filled the room, explaining some of her more bizarre images in the early stages of the case. But where was Toby Slayter and Julian Redondo? And could she get to them before Simon who might yet kill them out of spite?

She wandered cautiously about the labyrinth of darkness, the out of use, ready for demolition 'Fun House of Horrors'. She followed a glow-in-the-dark path marked with beastie footprints through a maze of old tricks and sound effects when she bumped into a dangling dummy painted in brilliant orange.

It turned slowly in the blackness to face her, and she recognized the dead features even below the clown face: Toby Slayter's bone structure, the wide forehead, the high cheeks, the shape of the mouth. Toby Slayter covered in glow paint.

Because Enriquiana was terrified of roller coasters, she and Nia sat atop the Ferris wheel instead, and Nia had been bored up to the moment of her mother's strange phone call that felt like a final good-bye. Here they sat, trapped, unable to do anything to help her mother, knowing that her mother was in serious trouble, while she was stuck in the air like a floating balloon.

Still, Nia had her Nokia.

She frantically tried getting the signal back to at least make a phone connection with Aurelia. But this failed. She tried the police at 911, but this too failed. She became angry and cursed the phone and their ever having left the DC area. Then she realized that her cell phone was dying. Then she realized that it had been dead since her mother's static-ridden call.

As the Ferris wheel brought them down and up again in a flurry of wind that snaked around their bare heads, Nia felt a wave of horror flush through her. She simply knew her mother was in grave danger. So much for her plan to ditch Enriquiana and to rendezvous with Ruben, whose Latin good looks proved she could melt here in Arizona. Hell Ruben could even melt Enriquiana's patented cold glare.

They'd actually been enjoying themselves when Nia had answered her mother's call. As she'd looked out over the park and the Midway below, Nia had spied a police squad car with the large number 48 atop it. The image immediately struck Nia like an arrow through the heart. For how long now had her mind been telling her to beware the number 48?

The police car moved at a high rate of speed–its lights wildly spinning. The cruiser careened past back alleyways of the park. A police helicopter with a spotlight searched for the errant squad car even as Nia watched it go in and out of view, until it suddenly disappeared as if by magic. She felt so limited by her vantage point on the big wheel, and yet if she'd not been here at this moment, she'd not have seen a thing.

"*Ai Dios mio!*" Enriquiana was shouting repeatedly as the chopper hovered above the wheel they were on, its Cyclops eye searching yet for any sign of the now invisible car. The light settled on one back-lot building, and the ground troops moved in, focusing on this single building.

Pointing, Nia cried out, "Enri, my mother's in there! I know she's in danger!"

Enriquiana continued praying, but she stopped to grab Nia in her arms as she did so, interrupting her hail Marys to take this action. "Your mama will be safe…she will be all right…she is strong and so smart, you know."

Then Nia saw a large figure moving away from the structure, but in deep shadow. In fact, she was unsure she saw this large man in shadow or not. Just outside the campfire circle of the Cyclops eye of light provided by the chopper–which light only made the outer circle blacker and denser.

"I feel her close, and I feel she is in terrible danger, Enri! We've got to get off this damn machine! Now!"

Enriquiana must squint to see what Nia pointed at, and she saw the hefty figure in shadow moving as if wounded, staggering on foot away from the light, lurking about a closed off construction area. This was at the older section of the park where over a wall, where idle machinery from a wrecking crew sat alongside an old roller coaster being ripped down beside a haunted house slated to come down beside it. All this at the end of the Midway. Now Nia and Enriquiana watched the other police cars surround the park and a S.W.A.T. team was being deployed, converging on the same area. Sharpshooters busily located a position from which to fire.

"Mother Mary help us in our time of need! Keep Nia's mama safe!"

"We've got to get off this damn Ferris wheel," Nia shouted. She had twice now shouted to the operator to let them off but to no avail.

As they again passed the Ferris wheel operator, a lanky, bored-to-tears smoker who saw none of what had transpired save the chopper, Nia threw her cell phone and hit her target on the back of the head. An instant curse exploded from him, and he shook his fist at them as they whizzed by.

Just at this moment, Ruben, who'd grown tired of the chaperoned date and had wandered off to buy cotton candy and make a few phone calls, stood with his mouth hanging open, witnessing Nia's spoiled brat routine. He retrieved her phone for her and said to the operator, "Something is wrong man! Get that thing to a stop!"

As she was sent back up into space, Nia's screamed words faded. "Get me off this fucking gerbil ride! It's an e–mer–gen–cy! Life…death…and every…thing…like thaaaaat!"

Inside her head, Nia saw her mother spattered with blood, her features contorted in pain as Nia held her in her arms.

It was a horrid nightmare Nia'd had many times now for months. The awful dream had created a fear and tension in her that erupted in ways she could not control, as in anger toward her mother and with herself over their newfound inability to communicate. She was partially angry because her 'psychic' mom couldn't draw a clue as to the terror Nia lived with, and why? Because she had her mother's blue sense gene, the one that caused her to have what she'd termed in her head as the shared curse. She shared her mother with the world of law enforcement, but she also secretly shared her mother with monsters and terror; she shared her visions of children in a garden being plucked like ripe fruit to fulfill the needs of a satanic devil who made them suffer in a sea of fire and coral. But the worst sight was that of seeing herself holding her dying mother in her arms.

How many times and in how many ways had she told her mother to find another line of work? In how many torrents of rage had she 'spoken' of it, and yet the psychic mom read nothing clearly from her daughter.

"Get me down off this damn wheel!" she again shouted when suddenly the wheel shuddered and slowed and groaned, and she and Enriquiana were being brought down.

Ruben had tossed the two cotton candies, and he'd slipped a twenty into the attendant's hand to do as Nia pleaded. Even before the lorry carrying them came to a full stop, Nia, who'd pushed the safety bar overhead, leapt onto the wooden platform, falling from the momentum, scratching and bloodying her knees, but climbing to her feet and rushing past a confused Ruben, shouting, "It's my mom! She's in trouble!"

Nia raced for the last location where she'd seen the car marked 48, where she assumed her mother to be. The number 48 had for months now haunted Nia. Everywhere she looked it came up. On her plane ticket, on jerseys on TV sports, on doors, on ambulances going by, and now this.

Enriquiana grabbed Ruben and shouted, "Get the cops! Get the cops!"

The young concierge who'd had designs on Nia stood frozen in place until Enriquiana open handed him in the back of the head and shouted into his face, "Go! Now! Have them follow us! This way!" She pointed and then raced after Nia who'd disappeared through the crowd ahead of her.

Ruben saw that the wheelman remained exactly in place, turning to his machine levers to help the remaining riders disembark from the Ferris wheel.

Ruben asked, "Isn't there some kind of alarm that you can set off?"

"Hey, man, I mind my own business. I go setting off an alarm, it's my ass if this all turns out nonsense."

Ruben rushed off toward the flashing lights of the nearest police car, his hands held high. "All this to get laid, man," he told himself. "It just ain't worth it."

Still if he could pull off this heroic thing and help Nia save her mother, she'd have to be real, real grateful.

Even as she fires again inside the noisy haunted house where Mazzy Star wails out Ghost Highway in an ear-shattering, nerve-racking fashion, Aurelia is thinking, My God, Nia is here and in harm's way, and I bought her tickets! What kind of mother am I?

Rae fires again when he suddenly shows himself once more in all the remaining mirrors.

The whole scene felt like something out of a hundred haunted house movies she'd seen. Again he was gone when suddenly she felt the blow. He had let a huge sandbag release from overhead, and it hit her in the shoulder like a charging rhinoceros, sending her skidding across the glass floor. But she held tight to the gun, as her training had taught her, and when she saw him coming down at her with the fire ax, she rolled and the ax sent shards of glass exploding into her body. She felt the blood trickling and tickling along her arms, chest, legs, and face. Glass shards had embedded in her hair and skin in random fashion. Rae had no idea the extent of her wounds but hadn't time to think about them or the sudden blood loss.

Focusing and holding the gun had become a sudden mountain to move. Her eyes had gone blind with blood pouring into them from forehead wounds, and her hold on the gun may as well be a hold on a bell weighing a ton as she fired at a target a mere two feet away and missed.

The ax came at her again. She knew she'd never see the outside world again and would die with Mazzy Star blaring in her ear; knew she'd never see Nia again, not in this life, never hold her, rock her, tell her all would be okay, not ever again, when she heard an angelic voice. Nia's voice shouting for her mother.

The ax held in midair over Cy's head, and Aurelia saw his

now huge, looming form had straddled her like the satanic creature in the painting on the mural revealed in the next room—the sea of fire and coral.

The big creature agilely turned on Nia, stepping away from Rae, going for her baby.

Nia screamed as the ax was raised over her.

At the same instant, Aurelia forced herself to steady the weapon still in her hand, to hold on and fire although only half conscious from blood loss.

She fired again but the recoil proved stronger than her hand, the bullet going astray. She heard Cy's maniacal laughter as the ax he used went into a preliminary spiral as he handled the thing as a demon might a deadly stinger-tail or other limb, when at the same moment a strange sound–*baparrumpf-kerrrrcrack*! *Vaparrumpf-keycrack*!

A huge black fist came tearing through the wall, and the wrecking ball smashed into Cy, and picked him up and sent him through one of the remaining glass walls until his body was slammed into the coral sea where the depicted Satan now stood vigil over Cy's inert body. Cy's body had slid down the mural in his own spilt blood, coming to rest below the demon's legs, at Satan's feet.

Mazzy Star was replaced with I'm Deranged.

Nia rushed to her mother, grabbing her up in her lap and holding on, rocking her, pleading with Aurelia not to die. Her mother was bathed in blood from a hundred shattered mirror shards. Nia, crying, began to remove glass from her mother's hair and pieces embedded in her face.

"Don't die, mama, please don't die! You can't leave me! I need you…so so so much!" she wailed.

Aurelia saw the entire scene from overhead, her astral essence looking on, a natural offshoot in a traumatized person. Removed from the body, she felt no pain.

S.W.A.T people poured in behind the wrecking ball that some genius had decided might be a good way to break into the locked, condemned haunted house slated for demolition.

One of the officers tried to pull Nia away from Aurelia, but

Nia fought to remain. "This is my mother! Get medical help, now! I'm not leaving her!"

Theopolis Redeoux with Dr. Elliot Alandale on his arm rushed in, and Redeoux ordered the others to leave Nia, awash in Aurelia's blood, at her mother's side.

They radioed for medical help, while some of the uniformed cops milling about stood down, pulling off equipment and studying the dead Phantom's fractured body.

"Puny prick now, isn't he."

"Dirty creep."

"Lousy child predator."

"Pedophiles ought be rounded up and put in ovens."

"Sent back to hell."

"This guy was no pedophile," said Redeoux for all to hear. "He just got his rocks off torturing children. He had no concern for them, no love for them, except as objects to make suffer."

With the wrecking ball still swaying nearby, the floodgates to black humor were opened when Fred said, "In the end, he had a ball."

Laughter filled the "Fun House of Horrors" as Aurelia's coma deepened.

"Might say he's been *balled* but good," added another cop.

"Better to have balled and lost than never to have balled at all." This one kicked out viciously at the dead man.

Nia felt her mother's body shudder in her arms.

Aurelia felt herself drawn back into her body through a silver-lined cord, a kind of astral umbilical cord through which her spirit traveled, clinging to life. She had far too much unfinished business.

She somehow found the will to move her vocal cords, "Nia...Nia...Gee...got to help Gee."

"Gee...she's saying Gee! Gene Kiley. She's worried about Gene."

"Medics have him," said Alandale, reaching out for Aurelia's other hand and holding it firmly.

"Yeah...yeah," added Redeoux. "Gene's being worked on."

"Ju...Julian?" she asked through a haze.

"Julian is alive, and we have him. He's in a bad way, but we think he's going to be all right..." Theopolis added.

Alandale added, "With therapy...if we can get him the right help."

"I...f-found To-Toby. He's gone..."

"'Fraid so."

Aurelia feared if she passed out again, she'd never recover. This thought came as paramedics stormed in, shouting for everyone to move away from her. She heard a cadre of voices, but then she wafted out again, her final thought: The blood loss must be bad.

"Is she going to die?" pleaded Nia. "You can't let her die! You've got to stop the bleeding and make her live!"

Alandale and Redeoux managed to move Nia off. She threw herself into Ruben's chest and allowed her tears full vent as Ruben awkwardly comforted her.

"Why'd you lie about Kiley?" asked Redeoux of Alandale.

"She needs all the strength she can muster. She doesn't need bad news."

"Bad news?" asked Nia between sobs. "What? What's happened to Gene?"

"Ahhh...we didn't want to upset your mother with the news that we...we didn't get to Gene in time," confessed Theopolis. "He...he expired. But some how the man showed superhuman strength."

"How so?" Nia asked.

"Died of arsenic poisoning, which we learned of thanks to your mom's fast thinking.... We had the medics on hand to help him, but."

"Your mom's fast thinking, keeping her phone line open," said Fred, "is how we knew of Agent Kiley's having poisoned."

"Gene somehow managed to climb into the cab of that crane," added Theopolis, "to send that wrecking ball through at precisely the right moment."

"Yeah...musta been psychic," Nia thoughtfully replied, tears for her mother joining with those for Gene. Nia's color drained and she lunged at Redeoux, pummeling him with clenched fists and crying out, "What is it with you people! You use my mom and people like Gee, and you can't keep them safe? Damn you, damn all of you, damn your FBI to hell."

Redeoux grabbed onto Nia and held her, but she pulled away and threw herself into a shaking, sobbing Enriquiana, who held her and cried with her.

The paramedics had cut up small strips of a new adhesive mesh bandage like those used on battlefields nowadays. They frantically worked on Aurelia's larger wounds, taking a triage field approach to the wounds, determining which were life threatening, and which could wait.

Nia went to the paramedics, pleading that they save her mother.

The female paramedic spoke calmly to Nia. "This new bandage is a life-saver. Developed from space exploration for battlefield conditions. If anything will stop her bleeding out, this is it."

The other paramedic added, "Sorry about your friend in the crane. We suspect arsenic from what we've been told, but an autopsy will have to tell."

"Shut up about autopsies around the kid," muttered the other medic, giving his partner a punch.

The music had continued to blare around them and Redeoux pleaded, "What the fuck is this music?"

The song had flipped. No one seemed to know. Someone said it wasn't Marilyn Manson but a Manson rip off.

"It's CroniX Aggression," said Ruben. "They're in town, and I got tickets for the concert."

"Shut the shit off, O'Malley!"

"We haven't found the box."

"When you do shoot it!"

Suddenly the music was killed, and everyone's ears began working back toward normal. "We've got her stable enough to transport. We've got a medic chopper setting down in the parking lot outside right now. Will rush her to Presbyterian for the best care in Phoenix which means Tucson, about a two hour drive overland."

"Please, I have to stay with her. She can take energy from me." Nia's eyes had enlarged to take in every aspect of the lady medic's features.

"All right but just you."

"Is she...will she live?"

"She's a fighter, and she's stabilized. That's the best I can do."

"Thank you...thank you."

"The boy goes with us too," the other medic said to Redeoux and Alandale, indicating Julian wrapped in a blanket, paint smears over his features. He'd been chained to the merry-go-round.

"We'll meet you at the hospital with, Nia," Theopolis said, "and I would in a heartbeat take her place if I could. Right now, she's going to need your love and blood. And every member of my team will be lining up at the blood bank." He pointed to the mural painted of Satan straddling his victims. "I am told that Cy–Simon Blakthorn–painted that mural, and the one of angels outside."

"Your mother ended this predator's filthy career of torture and murder," added Alandale. "Thanks to her, the Phantom can never again harm another child."

Nia shook the handsome man's hand, unsure who he was. Alandale added, "We'll see to it she gets the best possible care, right, Agent Redeoux?"

"Absolutely. Whatever it takes, we want her back."

"You can't have her back!" countered Nia. "This is the last straw. She'll never work another case, never. I won't let her!"

The paramedics carefully placed Rae on a stretcher and wheeled her out to the waiting medi-chopper. They boarded, Nia holding onto her mother's hand with her right, and holding onto the traumatized Julian on a second stretcher with her left. Julian was not completely painted over, his facial features still unmasked by paint, but his eyes had rolled back in their sockets and his lids remained open, zombie-like. Both patients were put on IV drips even as the helicopter lifted away.

Enriquiana waved them off, tearful, with the handsome Dr. Alandale's arm draped about her, talking kindly into her ear while Agent Redeoux went about shouting orders to his men.

It was over…finally.

Mother would regain her strength. She'd be fine. Her scars would heal. And mom would be as beautiful and as loving and as caring as ever. Poor Julian Redondo would be given every bit of professional help the FBI could muster to return him to a normal life…and one day, he would smile again, play again, draw, and paint and live again. One day, given time, he'd spend an entire twenty four hours having not one thought about Carnivore Man.

Nia believed these things with all her heart.

The chopper rose higher and arched, and it went near diagonal rather close to the ground. In fact, she could read road signs as the helicopter raced for Tucson, following I-10, and as coincidence would have it, she looked out just at the moment Exit 48 came into view. She prayed it meant nothing ominous.

Could it mean her mother would be dead in 48 minutes, 48 hours? "Why so far?" she asked the medics.

"Redeoux's orders. We wanted to take her to Tempe," the medic shouted back over the noise of the wind and rotors.

"Why?"

"Said something about a theory out of HQ in DC from the BSU and the PSI if I got all those acronyms right that the killer and torturer has to be two people and not one."

"Two? Two people? And Redeoux wants her out of harm's way.

"We'll be there in three," the medic looked at her watch, "twenty four minutes, give or take."

Paranoid now, Nia's mind did the math. Two times 24 equaled 48.

"Teeth marks," Redeoux said simply. "Took 'em all this time, but our coroner here in Phoenix, well suffice to say, he isn't so swift" Redeoux had escorted Nia from her mother's room where Rae remained in a guarded stable condition. Nia had agreed to a truce in the way of a hot chocolate break in the doctor's lounge. They now sat in a chaise lounge in a semi-darkened, pleasant room where soft music played, Nat King Cole at the moment, gently belting out the words unforgettable in every way....

Redeoux continued, saying, "Dr. Miranda Waldron back in DC had the bright idea of pleading with Dr. Jessica Coran to fit the case into her stack of back-logged cases, and Coran amazingly enough found two separate, distinct teeth markings on each of the victims."

"Just from the photos!"

"Coran corroborated what our coroner had hinted at early on. Dr. Coran then ordered that Phoenix exhume one of the bodies and our coroner is now double-checking his own facts to be absolutely certain of Coran's findings, but I suspect it'll only verify her findings."

"Then that means this old hag you had arrested, this one they call Bloody Mary, was not only procuring victims for this bastard Cy Simons, but also having a hand in torturing them?"

"That's what it is shaping up to be, although this woman, Grace Havelin her real name, has no history of this level of violent behavior, a new mystery within a mystery. We've got several shrinks working on the woman to determine what she is capable of, but so far nothing you could call conclusive."

"And her dental impressions?"

"They don't in the least match the second pair of teeth. You're good, Nia. Ever think of becoming law enforcement?"

"No, never. So what about the teeth marks? Who do they belong to?"

"Right now, I'm afraid they are as useless as a fingerprint without a match. My instincts tell me they belong to another of the men working at the amusement park, a crony of Cy's, but so far it is a no go."

Nia thought of the creep running the Ferris wheel, and she voiced her suspicion.

"Background checks on every employee are being done as we speak. We even called in a handwriting analysis expert, the best in the business, and she will tell us at a glance who is a killer among them. We're also gathering dental impressions from those we can convince along with DNA samples. Trust me, the Prairie Sea amusement people are going through hell right now. But so far, no one has hopped a freighter out of town."

"And if Julian ever comes out of shock?"

"He's certain to know something, yes."

They sat a moment in silence, when Theopolis added, "The other possibility is when your mother gets better, that she might put something together for us, say if we had her do a walk through of the old haunted house–before they demolish it."

"You're not going to put my mother through that, sir, not if I have a say-so."

"It may be the only way we can get a fix on this accomplice."

"She's been through enough!"

He offered her more cocoa.

Nia shook with anger, stood and said, "I'm going back upstairs, be with mom when she wakes."

"They said it'd be hours."

"Then I'll wait hours." She stormed off, still angry at Redeoux for letting this happen to her mother and for the loss of Gene Kiley.

Darkness over Tucson appeared complete, a beautiful sunset gone forever. At Tucson's Presbyterian Medical Complex, a figure in a dark hooded jacket slipped into a closet marked Medical Personnel Only. In a moment, he emerged with a mask over his face, a surgeon's cap and gown, a stethoscope dangling at his neck. He went to the nurse's station and acting as if he owned the hospital, he located and rifled through the patient charts, showing a particular interest in two of these, both of which he dropped back into hanging files.

One nurse who had her heart set on marrying a doctor stood across the room studying him, unsure of him except that he looked good-looking as well as a medical man earning big bucks. Debra Carter thought she knew every doctor and intern on staff, but she couldn't place this one. And it bothered her that he really did not study the charts as a doctor might but rather cursorily moved from one to the other. The second one was left askew in its hanging file as the doctor moved now down the corridor, his step quick as if he knew precisely where he wanted to be.

It was as if he had simply wanted to know room numbers.

Nurse Carter stepped to the charts and dug out the one he'd last scanned. It was room 8765, Dr. Aurelia Hiyakawa's room, a woman brought in near death, but who had stabilized. She was on IV and resting comfortably now, trying to regain strength and color. The other room he seemed interested in was the boy brought in as the last victim of the Phantom. The boy's drunken alcoholic parents could not be bothered to come visit and sit up with him. Sad case.

But who was this strange doctor? And what was his interest in these two patients?

Right then the elevator pinged and off stepped Ms. Hiyakawa's daughter and the handsome FBI agent who'd taken her for a break in the doctor's lounge. Carter, whose uniform tag red DEB, rushed to them. "The doctor's looking in on your mother right now. Perhaps you should hurry so you can talk to him."

"Dr. who? Which one?" she asked.

"Ahhh...honestly, I never saw him before, but he was looking over her chart, along with Julian Redondo's."

Theopolis bolted for Aurelia's bedside, leaving the two women to follow. He snatched out his gun as he went. He rounded the entryway and there stood the phantom doctor with a knife that had sliced through the IV tube, and he held the tube poised in his mouth. He meant to blow air into her veins and kill Aurelia with air bubbles. One blow into the tube, and she could go into shock and die.

Redeoux fired instantly, without thought, sending the man in surgical garb and mask through a curtain and dead on the floor.

The single gunshot painted the curtain and floor red, and the sound of it reverberated throughout the hospital and people came running, and the single .38 bullet had ripped through the killer's heart.

Aurelia had come out of her sleep, the tube in her arm cut and dangling like some parasitic worm squirming about with her movement. "What the hell's happened here?" she asked.

Nia rushed to her mother, and they hugged as Theopolis stepped to the body. His fingers hovered over the mask, half expecting to see the madman was none other than the boy genius Edwin Coffin. Coffin, who had made a show of returning to DC to work on the palm reader in his lab. In the dark room, the corpse looked as if it could pass for the kid that Redeoux theorized had built up some jealous rage toward Aurelia, and who had somehow connected with Cy long before the show he had put on here in Phoenix.

Aurelia slipped from her hospital bed to the protestations of her daughter and Nurse Carter, but she had to see who it was Redeoux had killed, who it was who'd attempted to kill her.

"Take off the mask, Theo," she said.

Redeoux knelt over the body and snatched away the surgical mask. "Damn," he muttered. "Unbelievable."

"My God." Aurelia stared down at Dr. Elliot Alandale. "I should've followed my instincts, trusted in my subconscious. What about Julian. Did he get to him? Is he all right?"

"The Redondo boy is fine," said Nurse Carter. "This man...he came straight for you. Was about to kill you with one breath of air before Agent Redeoux fired."

"You scared hell out of him, Rae," said Theopolis. "He couldn't take the chance you or Julian would finger him."

"There were two sets of teeth marks on the victims, Mother," added Nia. "There were two killers all along, not one."

"Damn me...damn it...I never had an inkling in all the visions, not an inkling. A procurer, yes–"

"Bloody Mary pimped for Simon, and apparently for Alandale as well." Theopolis, gaining his feet, added, "Mary

Grace is in custody as we speak, and now come to think of it, Alandale showed an inordinate interest in the case, citing his concern for the street children as his reason. When I got your distress call, Rae, Alandale was beside me, asking how the investigation was going."

"Jimmy tried to tell me."

"Who's Jimmy, mom?"

"One of the Phantom's victims. His first. But I never saw two killers. A procurer and a killer, yes, but not two psychopaths who found each other."

"Don't beat yourself up over it. You did great," said Redeoux. "You read the same ME's protocols as the rest of us. Anything said about two separate bite marks was cursory at best, speculation. The ME did not even bother to farm it out to a forensic orthodontist."

At the door to her room now stood Noel as if he'd come in Alandale's company. He looked shaken to the core. He shouted out, "I didn't wanna do it! They made me do it! The devils and Bloody Mary, the three of them! They made me get the boys to go there! To the park!"

"What're you saying, Noel?" asked Theopolis.

"Noel..." began Aurelia as Nia's eyes grew wide. Aurelia and Nia simultaneously extended a hand. Both felt the boy's palpable fear. Even Redeoux sensed that Noel was about to bolt. Rae finally said, "Noel, we need you to testify against Bloody Mary and put her away, behind bars, for good!"

But Noel did bolt.

Theopolis raced down the hospital corridor after him.

Noel then appeared again, sticking his head into Rae's room to say a heart-wrenching, "I'm sorry, Dr. Hiyakawa about lying and Julian and Toby and Danielle, and all the others."

He bolted again as quickly as he'd appeared, sprite-like. In police parlance, the kid was hinky...unhinged. He'd make an unreliable witness, but worse so far as Rae felt were the layers of physical and psychological horrors this boy had been put through by Alandale, Cy, and Bloody Mary Grace. Worse yet, the mental anguish remained, eating away at the boy like a parasite on a feeding frenzy inside his head.

All along, Noel had tried to tell them; all along, he'd had the answers. From the beginning, he cried out Zoroaster.

Well now they knew–Alandale was Zoroaster. Cy was his demon. Cy had painted Satan straddling his captors, and he had modeled Satan on Alandale's physique and stature. An intelligent university professor. What better way for a 'demonic' to go undetected?

Aurelia thought back to the time when Noel was in her shower and in her hotel room, changing into his new clothes; he likely had feared it all a trick to get him back in bonds on that damnable merry-go-round where others had died. Noel had been selected for, or rather, gave into Alandale's master plan. Noel'd been turned to their twisted ends…turned into the Judas. How horribly confused must his mind be at this moment tormenting him…with Danielle murdered alongside Toby Slayter, and Julian scarred for life and in hospital.

Rae sent out a psychic plea to young Noel telling him she'd forgiven him. Telling Noel that she did not hate him or blame him, and that he should come back. She prayed it would work, but she had little hope of it.

What child his age would not, given a choice, trade his life for another and another? Where the old woman procured for Cy, Noel procured for Alandale. The horrid adults in this tale of terror were become preternatural and supernatural monsters in Noel's eyes–the stuff of Cy's murals–the monsters of the Midway, the monsters of the shelter child's religion.

Noel, no doubt, had been convinced that Cy and Alandale were capable of knowing his every move and his every thought. This meant that Noel was yet another victim of the troika of evil in this heinous tragedy.

Theopolis returned from his futile attempt to overtake Noel, saying, "Fast as a field mouse, and he'll be just as burrowed in before dawn, I'm sure. We'll find him, eventually."

"I want to go be with Julian," Rae replied. "Help…help me up out of this bed and down to his room." To Theopolis, she said, "Pull that wheelchair over."

"Sure Mom," said Nia. "We'll both go."

"He's gonna need our help, as much as we can provide. I've been hearing whispered remarks of how his parents haven't come to visit, after all that's happened to him."

"We'll get him the best help money can buy," Redeoux promised.

"I want my...my friend...Dr. Lyn Polkabla of Quantico, Virginia flown out here at our expense and for her to oversee his treatment."

"Whatever you say, it's in the works."

"What about that other boy, Mom? Noel?" asked Nia. Rae felt heartened that her daughter had been touched by Noel's plight.

"We can only hope and pray for Noel. Apparently, he's decided to run from us, from his foster home hopes, from the authorities. He fears every adult now and that's certainly understandable."

Aurelia and Nia, arm in arm, left for Julian's room. "Mama, tell me why a man wants to torture a boy to death?"

"That would take a book to explain, sweetheart. Maybe on our way to the Grand Canyon, I'll have time."

"We're really going?"

"You bet we are."

Epilogue

They found Officer Louis Kowalski's body stuffed in a drainpipe in his BVD's. When Professor Alandale's home was opened to scrutiny, authorities discovered all manner of pedophilia materials, and among his tapes, several that displayed the brutal last hours of boys like Toby Slayter. They also discovered a dog run in the rear; he kept six animals in various stages of starvation. All lures, it was surmised, to get boys into his home. He'd been led to Cy's place by Bloody Mary while ostensibly doing his research on the shelter children, all a perfect cover for taking advantage of kids.

Dr. Alandale had worked the streets, worked Grace, worked the children, going among them like an angel when in fact he'd become their worst devil. As for Noel, no one had any inkling of where he might now be; the prevailing wisdom had him running off to Hollywood, California to start up a new life on the street there.

And so all the loose ends of the case were coming to light, each thread finding a tie-in thanks in large measure to the efforts of Theopolis Redeoux, who perhaps now could count on that transfer to his hometown of New Orleans. Julian Redondo survived his crushing wounds, and both Nia and Aurelia regularly visited the boy in hospital. Aurelia arranged to have Julian's baseball glove, his sketchpad, and a box of other incidental belongings brought to his room, and young Julian began to show an interest in something other than the ethereal world he had retreated into. Photos of his room and his dog had helped somewhat. Then his mother and father showed after their two-week long drunken state of unconsciousness, sober and speaking of getting help for themselves.

Too late, as Aurelia and Theopolis had already set in motion a series of events, which would culminate in Julian's finding a new home with foster parents through the Phoenix Family Services.

Meanwhile, the healthy Aurelia healed quickly as was her habit, her cuts and bruises doing well. The worst lacerations slept below bandages that, according to Nia, gave her mother the appearance of a swashbuckling pirate who'd painfully and seriously lost the duel over the plank.

Edwin Arlington Coffin had surfaced. Rumor had it that he'd gone back to his obsession to perfect the palm reader CRAWL, a man so completely sated by his sexual adventures that he now subscribed to one of Aurelia's bumper-sticker epitaphs: Success is getting what you want, but happiness is wanting what you get. Edwin sobered up immediately when Aurelia asked him from her hospital bed if he would oversee the horrendous problem of getting Gene Kiley's body back home to his family.

Aurelia had sent a grateful Enriquiana home to see to opening the bed and breakfast, as new guests would soon be arriving. Thereafter, she and Nia rented a comfortable sedan, purchased two bags of junk food for the trip, and bought a handful of maps to guide them on their way to the Grand Canyon via Sedona.

Two girlfriends bonding–Thelma and Louise style–at least it felt like girlfriends, and it was indeed bonding.

They had pulled off the tarmac and cut across a plain leading to the edge of the Grand Canyon, still mimicking Thelma and Louise. They now stood up on the white leather seats of the Stealth convertible and looked out over the canyon at dusk, the changing light and dark of moving clouds passing over the canyon changed its nature and appearance from moment to moment.

"It's so damn beautiful," said Nia.

"Like a religious experience, so shut up and enjoy. Take it all in."

The car radio played Nat King Cole's *Fly Me to the Moon.*

They sank into a serene and profound silence, just the three of them, Aurelia, Nia, and Nat. All to themselves, sitting at the edge of the Grand Canyon, staring into the new depths carved by new and changing clouds and shadow and light dancing along ancient rock formations, their minds bathed in the absolute wonder; wonder that had wrapped them in it, wonder that held them in rapt attention when a cell phone rang.

In unison, they said, "Damn."

Both grabbed for their phones.

As each was about to check to see who might be calling on whom, here in the waning sunset, now to Nat's *September Song*, mother and daughter froze in mid pickup. They eyed one another, each studying the other closely now when all of a sudden, Aurelia threw her cell phone into the gorge of the Grand Canyon.

The canyon swallowed up the phone in a silent, profound instant. Nia laughed as she hurled her phone in after Rae's.

As both their phones had the same tone, Nia asked, "Whose phone was ringing anyway?"

"I'm not sure."

"What does your sixth sense tell you?"

"That it doesn't matter."

"Agreed. Let's keep the world out for awhile." Nia smiled wide, raised her arms to the canyon, and felt the wind whip about her. She made like a butterfly.

"I'm so glad you're here and in the moment, baby." Aurelia touched her daughter's cheek, and they hugged to *Your Nobody til Somebody Loves You.*"

"Right now, you and I, mom...us...together...now that matters."

After a moment's tight hug, Aurelia said, "Let's get to our room at the Canyon Lodge and stay until we're sick and tired of the beauty of this place, and until we get to know one another a great deal better."

"You got it, Mom, but I do have another soccer game day after tomorrow back at school, not to mention...."

"I know, baby."

"Gee's gonna be missed. Such a sweet, sweet caring man."

"I know baby. Hurts so much that I couldn't save him."

They held onto one another again. "I think he loved us, Mom."

"He did. If it's any consolation, I know he's watching over us still."

"You mean like grandpa and grandma?" asked Nia.

This made Rae freeze, and she studied Nia's expression. "Wait a minute, Nia. Are you saying you've seen your grandparents' ahhh…spirits?"

"I've been seeing them for years, Mom."

"Aurelia laughed and hugged Nia to her. This came as both a shock and a revelation. "Then…what Gee said…. It's true?"

"What'd Gene say?"

"Said you and I are…that we are more alike than I knew. Said you were struggling with your own problems because of it…because you share not only my genes but my psychic gene."

"I didn't ever want it. Hated it for so long," she replied, tears coming freely now. "Mother, it's so frightening at times."

Aurelia held her close. "I know…I know baby. Somehow we…people like us, we're just wired differently. For whatever reason, but it doesn't make us freaks, and it doesn't mean we have to let it control our lives."

"But that's just exactly….I mean, you're devoting your life to it; you're a celebrity at the FBI because of it."

"Over your shoulder, Nia, there, look down there at the rim of the canyon and tell me what do you see?"

Nia sniffed back tears and turned to look in the direction Aurelia had pointed out. "What?"

"Do you see what I see?"

It took a moment before Nia saw them, standing near the rim, an old couple, the man with white hair and Asian features, the woman with red hair, Caucasian features.

Nia gasped and held her breath.

Aurelia smiled and cried at once.

The ethereal light playing around the elderly couple at the rim had them both turn and smile at mother and daughter.

"I thought we were alone," said Nia.

"We are alone, yes, but never completely. Your grandfather, Hiro Hiyakawa, and your grandmother, Loretta Murphy, are always near us, and we are always near them, Nia. Look harder."

In the sunset, it was hard to make out their features. Perhaps it was her Hiro and Loretta. Like a complex hologram made of the light and shadow here on the canyon rim. There were no other cars nearby. How did the elderly couple get here? For a moment, the couple appeared corporeal, and Nia believed them anyone but her grandparents. But then the couple disappeared as if they had flown out over the rim and into thin air.

At last, Aurelia understood why she'd been guided here…

End

Robert W. Walker has gleaned his writing and marketing techniques from selling over forty novels to major publishers in New York City. In addition, he is the acclaimed author of the Instinct and Edge Series of forensic and suspense novels and has taught writing in all its permutations for over 25 years. Robert, a master at crafting and selling commercial and literary fiction, has helped numerous writers get their work published including Pat Mullan who is now sitting squarely on a nominations list of this year's best thriller writers with famous authors such as David Morrell and Dean R. Koontz. Robert is a graduate of Northwestern University and holds a Masters degree in English Education. Visit Robert a www.roberwwalker.com and at www.echelonpress.com.